TOTTENHAM
OUTRAGE

M. H. Baylis

First published in Great Britain in 2014 by Old Street Publishing Ltd
Yowlestone House, Tiverton, Devon EX16 8LN
www.oldstreetpublishing.co.uk

ISBN 978-1-908699-67-1

Typeset by JaM

Printed and bound in Great Britain.

To my beautiful wife, Emma

Chapter One

Terror, Rex knew, could strike at any moment. Not just any moment, in fact, but at the very moment of highest road-confidence and car-handling aplomb. He could blithely conquer the dozen tangled exits of the Great Cambridge roundabout, or the roaring spaces of the flyover – and then, suddenly, while trying to shift from 4th to 5th gear, glimpse one of those makeshift, flower-and-photograph shrines tied by the grieving to the grey metal barriers at the sides of the road, and think: *No. I cannot be here. Doing this.*

Sometimes there wasn't even a trigger. He might just be idling in the traffic down Green Lanes, behind some van dropping off wads of *pide* bread and buckets of olives at one of the borough's three hundred Turkish restaurants, when a snapshot of himself at the wheel would suddenly rise before his mind's eye, and amidst the cold sweat and the thudding heart, it would be as if he'd never learnt to drive. Now, or before, in the old life.

If you were acquainted with the bulky, suited man at the wheel of the rust-coloured car passing slowly down the Lanes, you might understand a little of his dilemma. You would know that there was more to the predicament of this man of 41, about to take a belated driving test, than met the eye. If you didn't know Rex Tracey, on the other hand, you might see only a faintly familiar-looking man, rather gaunt in the face, a little tubby round the middle, with a

1

hangover and an understandable longing on this bright, blustery March Monday to be anywhere other than in a traffic jam crawling through the heart of Haringey.

Traffic jams were the worst. The longer he was still, the more time he had to ponder what the hell he was doing, and the greater the chance of that simultaneously cold and hot flush passing up and down his body, leaving in its wake the desire to crack open the door and flee. Out of the car, out of the borough. Perhaps out of the country.

The van in front moved forward. Rex started up – and stalled. Horns sounded behind him. He swore. Terry placed a calming, priestly hand on the dashboard.

'Fuck 'em. Take your time. Everyone stalls. They won't mark you down for it.'

He couldn't run, of course, he knew that. He'd been caught in one of fate's pincer movements, a little man swept up in big events. Like the simultaneous expansion and contraction of the borough he lived in, worked in and worshipped. There seemed to be more people arriving, certainly there were more flats being built. Yet more and more of the old bakers and grocers on the Lanes were closing down, with new signs appearing in their place, making dangerous promises like Cash4Gold and PayB4PayDay.

Meanwhile the local newspaper for which Rex worked, the *Wood Green Gazette*, had uneasily morphed into an online news site called News North London, whose territory expanded every day, while its dwindling staff were required to put in six days' work for four days' money.

A further development was that Rex's boss, a formidable yet elegant New Yorker named Susan Auerglass, had strongly intimated that his extended news beat could no longer be covered on buses. He'd been able to ignore her until the photographer, his colleague Terry, had started moonlighting as a driving instructor to cope with the new mortgage he'd taken out shortly before the pay cuts.

Hence: Rex, a man with every reason never to get behind the wheel of a car again, behind the wheel of a car again. New laws said he had to re-take his test if he hadn't driven for a decade, which was exactly how long he hadn't driven for. So here he was, with Terry, in Terry's 1982 Vauxhall Chevette, taking one final lesson before tomorrow's test. They often combined these lessons with assignments, and today reporter and photographer were heading south to Finsbury Park to interview a local author.

The ancient thoroughfare they were on stitched a path from the high plains of Hertfordshire down to the stews of Islington, taking in a dozen ethnic enclaves in between. Green Lanes ought to have been, perhaps was, a symbol of the new, fast-moving, global society. But nothing, neither goods nor people, ever moved along it without a great struggle.

'I swear they were digging the hole on the other side when I went by here first thing,' Terry grumbled, as a bottleneck around some sewer-related digging finally eased.

'What were you doing down here first thing?'

'What's this bloke written, anyhow?' Terry asked, ignoring Rex's query, as they passed under the railway bridge, with its greetings in seven languages. 'Book about Finsbury Park is it?'

'Something about the Outrage,' Rex said tightly. He wasn't comfortable talking while he was driving. 'He insisted on meeting in the caff in the park.'

It was true. The man had insisted to the point of rudeness, in fact, seemingly unaware how lucky he was to get a free mention in the media for his self-published local history book. Rex was not looking forward to the interview.

After turning right onto Endymion Road, he reversed towards what had looked at first a very generous gap, but which seemed to have shrunk radically now that he was attempting to park in it. It didn't help that the car behind contained a trim, elderly, bearded man, sitting in the driving seat and passing judgement on Rex's parking skills with an assortment of rolling-eye and shaking-head gestures. Terry countered with a soft mantra of encouragement, but his pupil's nerves grew increasingly frayed as he rued not just his failure to park today, but the inevitable failures of the morrow, which would take place under the gaze of an examiner, wielding a clipboard. With a sickening crunch Rex reversed into the bumper of the bearded man's car. The man shot out of his vehicle as if he'd been jabbed with a spear.

'I'll sort it,' Terry said, unbuckling his seat belt and reaching across to the wheel. 'You get out and calm the old git down.'

The 'old git' was in his mid sixties, neatly turned out in a navy blazer and pressed grey trousers. It was an unfamiliar look in these parts.

'Insurance details,' he snapped. He held out a hand, and when Rex didn't immediately put paperwork into it, he clicked his fingers.

'Perhaps we'd better assess the damage first?' Rex said.

Nothing had occurred to the man's front bumper other than a slight scuff, but after some time spent on one bended, knife-creased polyester knee, scratching and sniffing and apparently tasting the damage site, the man felt otherwise. He stood up.

'I'm assuming you do have insurance?' he rasped charmlessly.

'My friend has full cover,' Rex said, gesturing toward Terry, seated in the now perfectly parked car. 'He's teaching me to drive.'

The man snorted, and was clearly about to offer some sardonic comment when the tough, wiry frame of Terry emerged from the car, and stopped him in his tracks. He froze. 'You,' he said quietly.

'Aye,' replied Terry, inclining his long, buzz-cut Viking skull. 'Me.'

'You two know each other?' Rex asked.

'This is the bloke who lives next door,' Terry said bitterly.

Rex, and everyone in the office of News North London, had heard a great deal about the bloke who lived next door to Terry. About the dispute over the bins, and over the slamming of the shared front door, and how the tempers of both men had flared up within a day of Terry moving into the property eight months ago, and not receded since. They also knew about the man's typewriter, and his habit of operating it, loudly, in the room adjoining Terry's bedroom, between midnight and six am, and about the man's habit of communicating his dissatisfaction with his neighbour's transgressions via a stream of neatly-written Post-it notes.

After scrimping for years, and then dangerously over-extending himself to purchase a little Edwardian half-house in a street behind Turnpike Lane tube station, Terry had, as the editor Susan put it, landed himself a turkey.

'Well since you're here, I might as well tell you I'm not happy with the colour of that section of glass you replaced in the front door.'

Rex saw the Geordie's fingers curl and uncurl, his bony chest rise and fall. He was displaying remarkable self-control, Rex thought.

'Actually, could we just swap insurance details and talk about the other business later?' Terry said. 'I'm supposed to be photographing some local writer bloke in the caff, and I'm late.'

The man gave a thin smile. 'If you went to "the caff" now you'd find your "local writer bloke" wasn't there either. Because he's standing on Endymion Road talking to the clowns who just crashed into his car!'

It was not a great start, and the three men made their way in silence to the park. There had been a time when the mere mention of Finsbury Park conjured visions of discarded needles and gang rapes. Yet, thanks to an injection of Lottery money and the council's somewhat Blitzkrieg-like approach, that was all in the past. They'd put in lighting, bulldozed the reeking catacombs of sin that had once passed for lavatories, dredged the Boating Pond (finding, in the process, a human finger), and tamed the hedges.

Today, a bright morning after a long, stone-grey winter, the area around the café was buzzing with kids and parents enjoying themselves with the vigour of the newly-freed. Even though the air was cool, and the park had a chewed-up look after the ice-melt, it felt pleasantly warm in the new, octagon-shaped café, sitting in the sun that came through the huge windows. The man – a retired history lecturer named Dr George Kovacs – was about to publish a book about the Tottenham Outrage, an infamous, politically motivated wages-snatch that had taken place in the area back in 1909. The book wasn't actually out yet, due to what Dr Kovacs called 'stupid and inexcusable mistakes by the printers'. This meant that Rex hadn't been able to read any of it, which, irrationally, made Dr Kovacs even more irritated.

'So what new light is your book going to shed on the story, Dr Kovacs?' Rex asked, doggedly sticking to the questions he'd prepared.

Kovacs had large, sad, spaniel eyes with prominent bags beneath them. He rolled them fractiously. 'I'm not going to provide you with a synopsis of my book,' he replied, in a prickly, precise manner that reminded Rex of Prussian officers in war films. His accent had a trace of Merseyside in it. 'If you or your readers wish to know what's in it, then you and they will shortly be able to purchase a copy from one of the three outlets I have already mentioned but will now mention again: the Big Green Bookshop, Muswell Hill Books or the Bruce Castle Museum Shop.'

Rex started to speak but Kovacs interrupted him.

'Suffice it to say, Mr Tracey, I have interesting new information, which throws light on the Anarchist terror group to which the robbers were connected. And on what happened to the money they stole from Schnurrman's Rubber Factory.'

'I thought both of the robbers were killed as they tried to escape,' Rex said, glancing up at Terry as he made his way back from the toilet.

'A comment which merely demonstrates your ignorance of the subject. One, Josef Lapidus, shot and killed himself at the end of the chase. Another, Paul Helfeld, was shot by the pursuing police and died two weeks later from his injuries. Neither was found in possession of the money stolen from the rubber works.'

'And you think you know what became of it?'

'Historians assess evidence and draw conclusions.'

'I see. So what evidence makes you conclude that people might be interested in a robbery that happened here in 1909?'

'It was the first hint of the Tottenham we live in now. Global, multicultural, connected. Latvian anarchists committing crimes in London to fund acts of terror in Russia. Robbing a factory so dependent on a casual, ever-shifting immigrant workforce that the bosses weren't even aware Helfeld and Lapidus had been on the payroll under false names. A rubber factory, I should add, that processed latex from our colonies in Singapore and India into bicycle-tyres for use on the cobbles of Tottenham.' Kovacs paused. 'I have no idea whether that interests "people", Mr Tracey. I imagine most "people" would rather read a footballer's biography. My book is not written for them. It is written for the sake of history.'

'Good luck with the sales,' Rex replied, brightly.

The bickering might have continued but for a sudden outbreak of shouting from the playground outside. They looked round. A tall, bearded youth in a combat jacket stood over a family of Hasidim picnicking at one of the wooden tables by the climbing frame. The youth said something, roughly, but not as aggressively as his first outburst, then laughed. Lobbing something into the bushes, he walked over to join his mates: a clutch of Asian lads dressed in a combination of long, Islamic-looking shirts and sportswear.

'I just seen that lot out on the boating lake, giving it all this,' Terry commented as he reached the table, snapping his thumb and fingers together to imitate a yapping mouth. 'They don't listen, do they – dressing up like that?'

'Can we get on?' Dr Kovacs groused. 'I had an unexpectedly long walk this morning, followed by a traffic accident at your hands. I'd quite like to get home as soon as I can.'

Rex suggested they go outside to take some photographs. It was getting warmer, and they positioned themselves under a sycamore tree next to the main playground. Kovacs glowered into the lens as Terry snapped away and Rex took the opportunity to study the boys who'd allegedly been making trouble on the boating lake. They'd now gone into the café, where they'd swiftly become mired in some sort of dispute with the Polish girls behind the counter.

It was a classic Haringey tableau, he thought: kids at play, a United Nations force of knackered mums, gnarled old men with worry beads – and a small number of under-occupied young men spoiling it for everyone else.

He looked back at Dr Kovacs, squinting into Terry's lens. The man was an anomaly. The blazer and the trousers had a grim sheen on them; old but not great when they'd been new, either. On his feet, though, was a pair of soft, dove-grey boots that might well have been made for him. His watch was an old-looking Rolex – again something quietly announcing wealth. A man who cared about the details, perhaps, but not about the bigger picture. Did that make a good historian?

Suddenly a scream pierced the scene, then seemed to drain it of life. It wasn't the usual playground shriek, from a child going too high on the swings or being dragged reluctantly home. This was an adult scream. A woman's scream.

Everyone stared towards the farthest of the wooden picnic tables. A slim blonde woman – her fashionable sheepskin boots and her high ponytail announcing which side of the park she lived on – held an identical-looking little girl by the hand. The girl gazed tearfully up at her mother, who in turn stared down at the table, muttering something over and over to herself.

Slumped inertly around the picnic table was a family: a mother, a father, a girl, a boy and an infant. Their heads rested on the slatted wooden surface, among assorted tupperware and bowls and cups. They might have all suddenly fallen asleep. But they were not asleep. The groups of people who fearfully approached the table knew it, as did all the people who had remained rooted to the spot with sudden dread. With a gust of spring wind, a black felt skullcap rolled from the table onto the sandy soil, picking up a shred of damp, pink blossom on the way. A child's chubby arm dangled loosely in space.

'They look like them freaky ones up in Gateshead,' Terry whispered. 'Orthodox.'

'Not Orthodox,' Dr Kovacs said quietly. 'Hasidim. Hasidic Jews. From the Dukovchiner sect.'

'How can you tell?' Rex asked, staring in horror at the way the older boy's blond ear-curls had spread out like seaweed across the table.

'The woman. Most Hasidic women wear wigs. But not Dukovchiner. They keep their own hair.' Kovacs' voice appeared to choke up. Rex glanced up and was surprised to see how pale the man had gone. Their eyes met.

'I have to go now. I'm sorry,' Kovacs said suddenly. He hurried off towards the main gates, turning just once to look back at the picnic tables.

'Has anyone called the police?' Rex asked, realising as he spoke that a dozen people, including Terry, were doing exactly that. Meanwhile, the blonde mother who'd discovered the bodies was pointing a finger at the Muslim boys who'd emerged from the café. She began to advance on them threateningly, her little girl, for the moment, forgotten.

'What did you do to them?' she shouted, patches of red forming on her cheeks. 'I saw you. I saw you spray something at them!'

Immediately, without answering, the boys scattered, two charging through the sandpit with their shirt-tails flying, one running out of sight behind the café building, and the big army-jacketed one – the one Rex had down as a sort of ringleader – bowling right past him along the path. Sirens began to wail in the distance. A

child sobbed and an old, ship-sized Turkish granny recited 'Horrible thing, horrible thing', like an elegy.

* * *

I pray with them sometimes. I don't know what E and T would
say to that. I like that they don't know – something of mine after
all those years we three spent shivering together, knowing each fart
and scratch and dawn-rising cock and nightmare of our fellows.

On their Sabbath, Widow Cutter and her daughter pray in their
house. Remind me of Old Believers a little. Some I once hauled tim-
ber with in Yakutsk called themselves 'priestless ones'. Widow and
daughter won't have any truck with the smooth, fat-faced, frock-wear-
ing extortionists, either, and I admire them for that. Admire the way
they kneel, on the hard boards, in front of the bare wall. Don't even
have a cross. So I kneel with them, a little way behind, out of respect.
Don't really *pray*, of course. Haven't *prayed* since I was a boy, with
Grandfather beside me. Stopped saying prayers when a soldier on a
horse ran the old man through like a shashlik.

No, what I do is just look at the daughter. Leah. The soft, cop-
pery hair on her long, slender neck. The grubby undervest and
petticoat I can glimpse through the holes in her Sunday frock. It
has been so long. So cold. And there is no warm like that warm.

Then I grow hard, and it feels wrong, in this bare, quiet, freezing
room, with these solemn women and their made-up God. So I
recite my own prayer. I remind myself who I am.

I am George Smith, a gas fitter. I was born in Goff's Oak, county
of Hertfordshire, year of Our Lord 1869, joined Her Majesty's
Navy at 14, sailing under the Union flag, and a few more besides,
for 25 years. Now I reside at 11 Scotland Green, lodge with a Mrs
Vashti Cutter and her unwed daughter Leah. I have a wife and six
children, back in Goff's Oak, send them a four-shilling postal order
every Saturday evening. Here are the dockets to prove it.

No, I'm not a hero. I'm just an ordinary subject of the King, doing what comes naturally when he witnesses an outrage on the streets of this fine borough. Honest. Ordinary. Upright. Upright as I can be with a spine like a corkscrew.

* * *

Rex and Terry had been the first media representatives on the scene, but by the time they'd made it back up Green Lanes to the offices of News North London, Sky and the BBC already had an army of tanned and blow-dried anchor-folk doing live broadcasts all over the borough. Sky had gone for the panic-inducing ticker-tape legend, 'Jewish Family In Suspected Muslim Poison Plot', while 'Terror In London Park', was the more restrained message at the bottom of the BBC screen.

Susan had both channels on in the office, and was flitting back and forth from her own inner sanctum to Rex and Terry's desks as they updated copy and uploaded fresh images to the website. They were busy and focussed, yet a faint sense of futility hung over the whole enterprise. They'd stayed at the scene as long as they were allowed, taking pictures, interviewing bystanders, waiting to give their own statements to the police. There was no doubt they had the best insight into what had gone on at the park. What difference did that make, though, when everyone would just click the little icons on their phones and their tablets, and get live footage from the big players? News North London's budget didn't stretch to an 'app'. Even if it did, the chances were that few would download it.

Yet everyone in the room cared. From the Whittaker Twins in their little ad sales corner, to the vast, unshakeable Brenda on Reception, everyone cared about their jobs, about the end product, and most of all about the sprawling, teeming, unloved area they lived and worked in. It was just that no one was sure anymore, in this new, pixelated screen-filtered world, whether caring was enough.

At the bottom of the TV screens, to occupy viewers during the inevitable dead time and pointless waffle of rolling news broadcasts, there were texts, tweets and emails from the general public. On her way past, Susan stopped and peered at them, emitting a slight grunt of approval.

'Outrage,' she said, tapping the screen with her pen. 'This guy uses the word outrage. We should get that in. New Outrage At Tottenham.'

'People will think it's about Spurs sacking their manager,' Terry said.

'Plus Finsbury Park isn't Tottenham,' Rex added. 'And you know what'll happen if we get the parish boundaries mixed up.'

Just about the only thing that could really goad the local populace into tweeting, texting, emailing or phoning in its views was a geographical error. Confuse Wood Green and Tottenham, Crouch End and Hornsey – mistake any ancient parish for the one immediately to the north or south of it – and you'd be on the end of a public onslaught. Melting pot this borough surely was, but it had its own peculiar code: you might be stateless, or hail from a global region continually changing hands and borders, but once you got to Haringey, you made damn sure you knew which part was which. Maybe that was why the gangbanger kids kept stabbing each other over postcodes.

On the TV screen, the BBC reporter, a Tamil woman, stood outside the recently-opened mosque on Brownswood Road, where, earlier that morning, the boys had, it was alleged, attended a talk by an inflammatory preacher. As she spoke to the camera helicopters hovered overhead, stoking up the pulse rate. It wasn't hard to imagine the scene unfolding inside the building behind her, as well as in the cafés and the halal butchers of the surrounding area. It would involve jackboots and Tasers, and a distinct lack of niceties. And quite possibly it would turn more young men into the sort of young men who were being hunted.

The reporter repeated the descriptions of the missing men, then cut to an interview with the man who hired out the boats on the boating lake. Irish-looking, with a boozer's nose, he seemed depressingly proud to have played a part in the whole affair, or at least to be on the telly talking about it. The Asian boys had hired out a rowing boat from him, he said, the same boat the as-yet-unnamed Jewish family had been on shortly before. The boys had rowed theirs over to a little island in the middle, where people weren't supposed to go because it was for nesting ducks and geese, and he'd shouted at them. They'd obeyed him and rowed away, returning the boat earlier than necessary. He'd seen them walk over to the table where the Jewish family was eating, but that was all he'd seen. He'd had to go and answer his phone.

Brenda approached Rex with a cup of tea. She placed it at the very edge of his desk, and remained standing at a distance, observing him fixedly.

'You look very pale,' she announced.

Brenda, receptionist, sub-editor, mother of five and matriarch to the entire News North London staff, often accused Rex of looking pale. Or feverish, or thin, or bloated, or needing to have his bad foot looked at by another, better doctor. Today, though, her concern was tinged with something else. Something manifested by the way she avoided coming too close to his desk.

'Brenda, I am not radioactive,' Rex said, reaching across the desk for his mug.

She wasn't the only one to have had the idea. At the teeming crime scene, while technicians in chemical attack suits moved with balletic precision, and a unit of soldiers tented the centre of the park under yards of opaque plastic, Rex and Terry had been measured with a Geiger counter. Later, in a Portakabin that had suddenly appeared on the athletics track, a chatty, snub-nosed young doctor had taken blood, saliva and skin swabs. No one knew what, if anything, had been sprayed at the picnicking family, or even whether it was related to their deaths. No one, understandably, was taking any chances. A laminated card now in Rex's pocket told him what to do if he suddenly experienced any palpitations, blackouts or shooting pains. The trouble was, Rex experienced most of those symptoms in the course of an average morning.

'It's great copy guys, thank you,' said Susan, elegantly sipping green tea from a silver flask-top as she came out from her lair. She was attired in layers of light-coloured shirts and waistcoats and scarves, giving her the look of a priestess. 'So where now?'

'The mosques, get some local reactions?'

The boss shook her head, a dark ringlet coming loose from the central bun, and pointing to one of the screens on the wall. At that very moment, the fat bloke from Sky News was standing outside a different mosque, the larger and far longer-established one at Finsbury Park, talking to a group of silver-bearded elders in astrakhan hats and waistcoats.

'Everyone's doing that. Get over to Stamford Hill. Find out what they're saying there. Community in shock, that kind of jazz.'

'We don't know they came from Stamford Hill,' Terry said.

'A Hasidic family, in Finsbury Park. Where do you think they came from, Terry? Chelsea? They'll be Lubavitch or Satmar,' she went on, mentioning the two main groups of Hasidic Jews in the area. 'And they'll have come straight down Seven Sisters Road.'

'Aye, in a clapped-out Volvo,' Terry added, with a hollow chuckle. Nobody laughed back.

'They weren't,' Rex said, suddenly remembering what Dr Kovacs had said, just before hurrying away from the scene. 'They belonged to a different group. Dukavitch or...'

'Dukovchiner?'

'Yes,' he said, surprised, turning towards Brenda. 'How did you know?'

'Because that silly child Ellie couldn't spell the word,' Brenda said. 'And I spent a month correcting it every time she wrote it.

Rex won't remember,' she added, to Susan. 'He was off in Thailand with that doctor girl.'

Last year Rex had taken a four-month sabbatical, after being stabbed. He'd spent much of it in Cambodia, in fruitless pursuit of a woman, and in his absence the Dukovchiner sect had apparently made the headlines. Susan leaned over Rex's keyboard, calling up the relevant issues from the archive for him to see.

'Micah Walther,' she read out loud, as an image of a gap-toothed, ringleted teenage boy filled the screen. The paper was dated September 2013. 'Fourteen years old. His family were Dukovchiner.'

'All the same, aren't they?' Terry said. 'Black hats and beards and Volvos.'

'They have different groups, though,' Rex said. 'They all started in different towns in Eastern Europe and… I don't know, some of them like Israel and some of them hate it. That sort of thing.' He looked towards Susan for confirmation, but she merely shrugged.

'Kids again,' Brenda said sorrowfully to herself as she looked at Rex's screen. 'Always kids.'

'What happened to him?' Rex asked.

Susan shrugged. 'CCTV on the railway station showed him heading towards the study-house to meet his father. He never got there.'

'And they're still looking for him?'

'Someone is, I hope. We did a lot on it at the time, but… teenage frummer boys with skullcaps don't get quite the same public response as blonde toddlers.'

Susan could sound hard. But Rex knew there was an intensely decent human being underneath. One who'd given him a job when all his other doorways had closed. One who cared about this grimy, fascinating patchwork-quilt of a borough as much as he did. 'Read the archive,' she went on. 'Ellie couldn't find out much about the community, but I'm not sure how hard she really tried…'

The mention of Ellie Mehta, formerly the paper's Junior Reporter, had soured the air. She'd left after insisting on a pay rise just as everyone else was taking a cut, and then abruptly gone to work for far less money on the *Daily Telegraph*. Although Ellie was alive and well, living just down the road in a fashionably horrid part of Hackney and making daily appearances in a major newspaper, she'd become a sort of mythical pariah figure in the office. The regular malfunctioning of the printer was blamed on Ellie Mehta, as was any new computer glitch, and the recent disappearance of a Canon EOS 1DX camera.

'Anyway,' Susan said. 'Let's meet at six. We'll refresh at eight tonight, okay, people?'

'This was supposed to be my afternoon off,' Terry grumbled, as the boss sailed back into her office. He wiped his forehead. 'Is anyone else boiling hot?'

'It has got a lot warmer outside,' Susan said.

'In March,' Brenda said. 'Climate change.'

The working day had changed in this new, digital age. In addition to meeting the traditional once-a-week deadline for the old *Wood Green Gazette* – which still existed, as a free ad sheet with a bit of news and comment slapped on the front – they had to update the website every evening, shifting the placement of stories, adding new material in response to the day's events. A good hour's work followed that, too, responding to tweets and posts, ensuring all the links were working and the old material correctly archived. Technology was supposed to make everything easier, but Rex found himself working harder than he'd ever done before. If he were honest, he didn't always mind. It stopped him brooding about what had happened in Cambodia. And before. It meant less time for drinking, too.

Not that he felt much healthier for it. In fact, now that Terry had mentioned it, he did feel hot. Outside, the sun was now shining in a cloudless sky, and down on the High Street below shoppers were strolling about in T-shirts. Rex wasn't reassured, though. He took the card out of his jacket pocket and read it. It didn't mention fever.

He glanced across and saw that Terry was looking at his own card. They grinned at one another, partly from embarrassment, partly from something else.

'Why don't we go out and take a few pictures, then you can get off home?' Rex suggested. 'I'm sure you're aching to get back to your lovely neighbour.'

'Did I tell you what the scabby bastard said to me last week?' Terry said, sniffing loudly as he started assembling various bits of camera kit in a canvas bag. 'Instead of sitting up in your bedroom typing all night, right next to the end of my sodding bed, why don't you just go downstairs and do it in your living room? And you know what he says?'

'Why don't you go sleep in your bathroom?' Rex said.

The story had already acquired legendary status. As had Terry's response, which he'd written on a Post-it and stuck in the shared hallway. Meeting the notorious neighbour in the flesh had done nothing to diminish his image – quite the opposite. Except for that final moment in the park, when his prickly manner had evaporated. It hadn't just been sadness or shock on Dr Kovacs' face. Rex was sure he'd seen something else. Something closer to fear.

The lower part of Green Lanes had been screened off behind tall metal barriers, forcing Rex and Terry to pick their way southwards through Tottenham. They were less than a mile away from a suspected terrorist murder in a much-frequented park and yet, at least from his seat in Terry's Vauxhall, Rex could see no sign that the local population knew, or cared.

Things were different once they headed down the broad Edwardian slopes of Stamford Hill into what had been, since the early 20th century, the heartland of the Hasidic Jewish community. The shops were all open as usual: Minsk Housecoats selling the distinctively Hasidic range of long Puffa coats and modest, navy-striped knitwear; Richler Fish with its windows of carp and herring. Plenty of customers were passing in and out: homburg-hatted men in what must have been, for the day, impossibly heavy overcoats; women with bobbed, dark-brown wigs and pushchairs; and kids, dozens, hundreds of kids, everywhere. But outside every Jewish business, as well as several of the vast, beetling villas used as prayer-houses and schools, were the *shomrim*.

The *shomrim* were one aspect of the community that did occasionally make the news. Dressed in distinctive fluorescent orange tabards with Hebrew lettering on the back, they acted as a subscriber police force for the community. Occasionally, they were accused of racism when they challenged and chased black and Turkish youths who often hadn't done anything wrong. More rarely, a *shomer* became a media celebrity when he interrupted a mugging or rescued a baby. Amidst the rollercoaster of controversy and congratulation, few people recognised the day-to-day business in which the *shomrim* were engaged, for little or no money: patrolling school crossings and guarding buildings.

'Last time I seen them all out like this was during the riots,' Terry croaked. He'd coughed and wheezed the whole way there. 'This has got to be something to do with the park, hasn't it?'

'Let's ask them,' Rex said. 'Can we park up somewhere?'

'Why don't you have a go? You're the one who needs the practice,' Terry said. Rex ignored him. He shifted about in his seat. He'd gone from feeling hot in the office to shivering in the car. Now he felt as if his hair hurt. What was wrong with them him??

They stationed the car down a side street, next to a small business whose bright, egg-yolk-coloured sign said: 'Solly Scissorvitz Haircuts: classic, fashion and ritual'. As always before a long walking session, Rex swallowed a couple of painkillers to numb his left foot. Ever since a car accident a decade ago he'd had arthritis in it, and he walked with a limp, which grew more pronounced as the day wore on.

Terry commenced taking snaps with a practised discretion which Rex had never ceased to admire, holding his camera at chest height, and appearing to be examining something on its top control panel whilst actually photographing passers-by. Periodically, to establish his innocence, he took long, wide shots of roofs and sky and street signs. It was a vital subterfuge in this borough, where people's reasons for being camera-shy ranged from the cultural to the criminal.

Rex looked around for people to talk to. He soon recognised a face amid the lines of guarding *shomrim*. Outside the Beis Rochel Satmar Girls' High School stood a short, almost tiny, dark-featured man, legs wide, arms folded, a fedora cocked back high on his head. You might have thought the man slightly comical, if you hadn't heard of Mordecai Hershkovits.

Hershkovits, whose small ear-curls and modish hat announced him as a scion of the forward-looking, politically active Lubavitch sect, ran classes for the local kids. Not Hebrew classes, but workshops in the deadly art of *krav maga*. This was a martial art developed by the Israeli Army, in which, it was said, disciples could learn six ways of paralysing an opponent with only their thumbs. True or not, Hershkovits's offer to teach it to the Stamford Hill boys, and even the girls, had divided the religious Jewish community, and a considerable chunk of those outside it. At the height of the debate, he'd rather spoiled his case – or perhaps strengthened it – by using *krav maga* on a pair of Bulgarian scaffolders who'd refused to move their truck from the entrance to a Clapton synagogue. Both had spent time in hospital.

Mordecai Hershkovits looked now as defiant as he had on the day he'd received a two-year suspended sentence and 300 hours' Community Service. Rex had interviewed him then, on an icy morning a few years ago, and found himself liking the man. He wondered if Hershkovits would remember him.

'Ah, same blue suit,' the little man said, as Rex approached. 'When are you going to get a new one?'

'This is a new one,' Rex said. 'I had it made.'

'Who by? A plumber? What do you want?' Hershkovits demanded, in a way that might have seemed unfriendly if you didn't know better.

'I wondered what people are saying about the Dukovchiner family.'

Hershkovits wiped sweat from his brow. 'They are not "the Dukovchiner family". It's not their surname,' he said in the same brisk, argumentative tone. 'You want to print that, go ahead and print it, but you'll be printing dreck.'

'I know. I mean – I don't know what they were called, but I know Dukovchiner wasn't their name. That's the name of where their original rabbi came from, right? Like the Lubavitcher follow someone from, er… Lubavitch?'

'It's Lyubavichi. And Rebbe. You say Rebbe for a Hasidic leader. Yes. Okay, so you've looked at Wikipedia, good.' He paused to nod to a pair of book-clutching, black-hatted men passing by, so serenely detached from the worldly buzz around them that they seemed almost to float above the ground. 'What else did your website tell you?'

'Erm… that Hasidism is a mystical sect formed in Poland in the 17th century, since when it's split into hundreds of different groups, some focussed on a strict revival of Jewish law, others more on direct communion with God. But all of them expecting the imminent return of the Messiah.'

'You said that without taking a breath.'

'I'm good at memorising,' Rex said. 'I was an altar boy.'

Hershkovits smiled faintly. 'The family name was Bettelheim. Yaakov and Chaya Bettelheim. Three children. Eytan, boy of thirteen. Simcha, girl of ten. I don't know what the baby was called, but it was small. Not even a year old.' He whistled sadly through his two, slightly prominent front teeth. 'Their families will be… I don't know. Destroyed.'

'They have relatives around here?'

'Not many, I think. She came from somewhere… I don't know, maybe Brooklyn. Yaakov's family are in Manchester. He moved down here because he divorced, I think.'

Although he'd struggled to grasp the unfamiliar names and words in the man's rapid recital, Rex was pleased. This was useful. Unprintable, of course, before the police had told the relatives. But helpful for his own enquiries. He glanced around for Terry, to ask him to take a photo of Mordecai and saw that he was leaning against a lamppost. He looked exhausted. Rex realised he was starting to feel pretty weird himelf, but he pressed on with the interview.

'Only three kids, twelve years between the first and the last. Isn't that quite an unusual family, by Hasidic standards?'

'Not by Dukovchiner standards.'

'So are they not really part of the community? I mean, as much as the Lubavitch or the Satmar?'

'They're Jews, so they're part. But...' Hershkovits frowned, as if caught by a twinge of toothache. 'Different in a way that if I was to describe them to you so you would understand we would need to start with the forests in Poland in the eighteenth century, and I'm not going to do that because I'm busy here looking after my people this afternoon, okay?'

The line reminded Rex of Moses in the Cecil B. DeMille film: 'Let my people go.' You had to admire any man who could talk about 'my people' outside of a Hollywood epic and carry it off. 'So what do your people make of what happened?'

'We want those Muslim boys caught and punished.'

'If those Muslim boys did anything.'

'Sure,' Hershkovits replied, curtly. 'So with messages on the TV and the radio every hour, why don't they come forward, if they did nothing?' He responded to a crackling call on his walkie-talkie, before adding with a vague wave: 'By all means quote me, but if you want to talk to Dukovchiner people I'm no use, okay? Try vegetables.'

He left Rex pondering this strange utterance for some time before realising that there was a dimly-lit food shop called 'Vegetables', more or less in the direction Hershkovits had waved. Its name

– or perhaps another, catchier one – was also written in Hebrew letters, along with a telephone number starting '01', suggesting that telephone calls from the general public were not of crucial importance.

Terry shook his head when Rex mentioned the vegetable shop. 'Feeling too rough, mate,' he said, wiping sweat from his forehead across his scalp. 'I'm going home for a kip. You don't look too good yourself.'

'As long as I don't experience palpitations, blackouts or shooting pains, I reckon I'll stick at it,' Rex said.

Terry forced a smile. 'See you in the nearest A&E.' As he shouldered the heavy bag, his expression changed. 'Rex. You don't honestly think…'

'What? We've been poisoned? Come off it. Look. They've got our numbers, and they said if anyone started feeling ill, we'd all be called in. Has anyone called?'

'Maybe everyone else carked it before they could dial the helpline.'

'Maybe we've got both colds coming on, the weather's suddenly turned ridiculously sodding hot, and your imagination's working overtime.'

'Aye. Mebbe. I'll email the snaps in.'

Rex watched him go, suddenly worried. Terry seemed an unlikely hypochondriac. And he did feel slightly dodgy himself. Then again he nearly always did, more so lately than ever before. But it had nothing to do with mysterious sprays, everything to do with the arthritis in his foot and the stream of Polish lager and painkillers he took on board every day to numb it. He headed over the busy road to the shop.

Outside 'Vegetables' was a brand-new van: a jazzy, modern version of the old, corrugated silver Citroen vehicles you'd sometimes see rusting in the grounds of French farmhouses. Rex wondered if it belonged to the business, which was a shabby place, with grimy windows and a single, fluorescent tube casting a bluish light over the interior.

Inside, it was cool and dank, and a welcome change from the freak Mediterranean weather outside. A huge, yellow-haired man arranged potatoes and carrots and some twisted root vegetables on a series of tables, while a slender woman stared into space behind an ancient till. Rex was greeted by a smell of male sweat, mixed with brewer's yeast and a top note of soil. The man stared, open-mouthed, as Rex went in, but the woman seemed not to notice.

'Nice van,' Rex said to the man. 'Is it yours?'

After a pause, the man jabbed a thumb in the direction of the woman. 'Hers,' he said hoarsely.

Rex smiled vaguely towards the woman, whose face didn't move. He tried again. 'How much are the red potatoes?' he asked, alighting upon the first item he saw. He'd remembered the advice of his first boss, who'd been much given to aphorisms and *bons mots*: *the shopkeeper who can't sell you anything, won't tell you anything*.

Rex had addressed the question to the large man, but he just continued staring, wiping a hand on his dirty white shirt and silently mouthing words to himself.

'One pound, one pound,' said the woman suddenly, as if waking from a trance. She had straight brown hair, a weary tone, and her accent was that of someone who'd spent her life in this part of London.

'I'll take two pounds, please.'

'Yitz.' At her command, the big man noisily weighed out the required amount, a single tuber at a time, muttering to himself and puffing. The woman returned to her trance, twisting a lapel of her work-coat over and over, while Rex looked around the shop. Its pale green, tiled walls reminded him uncomfortably of a hospital, and were entirely without adornment, save for an ink drawing of a young boy with the same long, tumbling ear-curls that the man wore. There were a few other provisions for sale, besides vegetables: candles in little tin holders, a pile of something or other in neat little brown cones, and some cans covered in Hebrew writing. It was another century in there.

'Your son?' Rex asked amiably, pointing at the picture as the potatoes were poured from the weighing-scale dish into a carrier bag. The man shook his head. The woman asked him for two pounds, which Rex counted out and held out to her. The silence grew increasingly tense. She refused the money. He didn't understand.

'You don't want the money?'

'I don't want to touch you,' she said.

He felt himself blush. 'Sorry.' He put the money on the counter. 'I'd read somewhere that you had rules like that, but…'

She held up a finger. She had a long face with wide nostrils – sombre, somehow, but attractive. 'I've got dirty hands.'

Was she teasing him? He wasn't sure. The shop was so dark and her manner so unfamiliar.

'Can I ask you something?' he said. 'I notice there's no *shomer* outside your shop. But they're everywhere else today.'

The man and the woman exchanged short sentences in Yiddish. 'We don't pay *shomrim*,' the man said at last, very slowly, brushing some soil from his baggy black trousers. 'So they don't stand outside.' He spoke in a more obviously Yiddish way than the woman, with a guttural *r* and a luxurious *s*.

'When you say "we", do you mean just this shop, or all the other Dukovchiner shops?'

The woman tutted. 'There aren't any other Dukovchiner shops.'

'You know Dukovchiner?' asked the man suspiciously.

'I heard about the Bettelheim family,' Rex said. 'Did you know them?'

The woman coughed.

'Police?' the man asked.

'A journalist. My name's Rex Tracey. From News North London.' The woman put a hand up to the collar of her high-buttoned blouse. He smiled at her and asked again. 'Did you know them?'

'Yes,' replied the man, adjusting his carrots. The woman – his wife, Rex assumed – admonished him, but he ignored her. 'I used to work with Yaakov. Quiet man. The wife I don't know. From Peru.'

'Peru?' Rex echoed.

'Yitzie! She was from Sydney,' the woman interjected, in a weary way, like a mother tired of a child's nonsense.

The bear-like man shrugged. He even seemed to do that slowly, with great effort. 'Some place crazy. She was crazy.'

'She wasn't.'

'She comes in looking like a zombie drug-person!' Yitzie suddenly roared at his wife, growing red at the neck. 'Remember? When the little girl ran in the road and she just stood here, staring at the beans?' The big man paused, out of breath, sucking back the bubbles of saliva that had formed on his lip during his speech. He slowly tapped the side of his head. 'Crazy.'

'She has problems,' the woman said to Rex. 'Poor health. Three young children to care for. A husband she barely knew before she married him, and her family's all in Australia! Anyone would stare at beans, don't you think?'

Rex sensed that she was taking him a short way into her confidence. He smiled. She gave the faintest of smiles back. Yitzie, meanwhile, just sighed – out of words, it seemed, for the moment. He shuffled over and locked the shop door, pulling down a dirty, pale-green blind. As Rex watched the big man lumbering across the shop, he realised there was more to the vegetable offering than spuds and carrots. On another table were long, speckled red runner beans; elsewhere, a stack of crooked, hairy, yam-like items. He was about to ask what they were when Yitzie spoke again.

'Who is alone here, Rescha?'

Rescha made a disgusted noise. Sensing a further chink in the armour, Rex addressed her directly. 'Did you know Chaya?'

'Yes,' she said, in a thick voice. Rex could see tears forming in the woman's eyes, because of the dead family, perhaps, or because of the set-to with her husband. 'I liked her,' Rescha went on briskly, seeming to put her emotions to one side. 'But she didn't come in much.'

'You didn't worship together? Sing in the choir?' He felt himself blushing again. Did they have choirs in synagogues?

'I don't go much,' she said.

'She prefers to listen to the radio than to God,' said Yitzie.

'Nothing to do with the Narpal then?' Rescha shot back.

'How would you describe the Bettelheims? As a family, I mean?' Rex asked. He wasn't sure if his informants were really arguing or if it was just a routine they did together. He certainly didn't know what a Narpal was.

'Like everybody,' Yitzie said.

'Which is...?'

'Quiet. Religious. Daddy works, studies, prays. Mummy cooks.'

'Because that's all a woman does,' said Rescha. She mimed someone idly stirring a pot. Rex couldn't help smiling. This time she didn't return it.

'So they weren't the kind of people to make enemies?'

'You see them now because... because some kind of dreadful accident happened to them,' Rescha said quietly. 'But ordinarily, they are the kind of family you wouldn't even see. Nobody saw. Nobody ever saw them.'

'That's what you think it was? An accident?'

She was silent for a while. 'It's all I can imagine,' she said. 'This isn't like England... here. People here don't do the awful things to each other that you write about in your newspaper. People are good.'

Rex sensed he'd antagonised her. 'You said that he – Mr Bettelheim – prayed. Is there a synagogue he went to?'

'It moves,' Yitzie said enigmatically.

Before Rex could ask more, someone knocked on the shop door.

'Shop closed!' Yitzie barked.

The knocking resumed, hard enough to shake the door and make the blind shoot up. A pretty face peered for an instant through the mucky glass, then darted away. Yitzie shrugged, pulled the blind down again, and took up a broom. He began to sweep the shop floor, humming tunelessly.

Rescha put the money in the till, handed Rex his potatoes, and moved to open the door. Before she got there, the telephone rang in a back room, and she went off to answer it. Yitzie looked as astonished as Rex felt: perhaps the phone really did only ring once every decade or so in that shop. At any rate, this didn't sound like a social chat. Rescha could be heard giving a series of stark, one-word answers, before hanging up and heading deeper into the building's interior. Yitzie carried on sweeping, leaving Rex to see himself out, potatoes in hand.

Further down the hill, 'Mega Glatt Meat Mart' had about as much in common with 'Vegetables' as Reuters did with News North London. It was a dazzling, chilled hall, with prices on digital displays, and staff in white coats and matching plastic trilbies. No one wanted to speak to him, though, until he asked what 'glatt' meant. At that point, a ruddy-faced butcher, who wouldn't – minus the ear-locks – have looked out of place selling sausages in the Lincolnshire market-town Rex grew up in, gave him a detailed lecture about the kosher slaughtering process, and the extra-rigorous demands of the Hasidic meat clientele.

'So did the Bettelheims come in here?' Rex dared to ask, as the man wrapped up six beef frankfurters for him.

'They stopped eating meat,' the butcher said. 'They all did. All the Dukovchiner. About a year ago. Something to do with their Rebbe.'

'They seemed to do a lot of things that put them outside the rest of the community,' Rex said. 'Did that make them unpopular?'

The butcher shrugged. 'We don't understand what happened. The Dukovchiner are very quiet, peaceful people. But bad things keep happening. First the boy, Micah Walther. Then this...' He paused. 'Maybe it's what happens when you don't have a leader.'

Before Rex could ask why their Rebbe didn't count as a real leader, an old, fork-bearded man rasped, 'A Bratslaver can say this?' Everyone except Rex laughed. 'He follows the Rabbi of Bratslav,' the old man wheezed, pointing to the butcher. 'Who died in 1810. They still can't find anyone else for the job!'

There was a gale of further laughter but it quickly died away. It was as if the entire shopful of people had simultaneously remembered what had happened in the park. The old man tutted softly. Rex felt it too, an overwhelming sadness. He hadn't been able to get certain shards of the scene out of his mind. The baby's hand, hanging in space, chubby and still mottled. That petal of pink blossom on the discarded skullcap.

As in 'Vegetables', he got the sudden impression it was time to leave. He wanted to know more – wanted to understand why the man had said the Dukovchiners' vegetarianism was to do with the Rebbe, then seemed to say they didn't have a Rebbe. He was starting to sense how complex the picture really was. Stamford Hill wasn't one community, but dozens: some on jovial terms, others distinctly cool towards one another; some in step with 21st-century London, others in Neverland. Somewhere on this spectrum were the Dukovchiner – vegetarian, eschewing the local security service, quiet, reclusive. Who were they? And would answering that question help explain the strange, quiet death of a whole family of them, in the midst of a crowded Haringey park?

He scanned the street. In spite of the warmth, everyone still had their coats on. It seemed to be a world of coats: double-breasted crombies and thin gaberdines for the men, padded anoraks for the women, cagoules for the girls. *By their coats shall ye know them.* He tried a few more shops: Solly Scissorvitz, in spite of its jaunty name, was a melancholy, fungal-smelling unit where no one would venture beyond monosyllables. In the baker's, on the other hand, they were garrulous, but only on the subject of the new parking restrictions. It was frustrating, especially because the streets were full of women – always the best source both of opinion and hard fact, especially on a subject like the death of a young family. But he knew none of these pious women would welcome being approached in the street by a strange, limping gentile in a crumpled suit. He needed an 'in'. An introduction. But who would give it to him? He scanned the streets for Mordecai Hershkovits, but he was nowhere to be seen.

It was late afternoon now, the day's sudden warmth turning almost muggy. An odd, scratching sensation had started to make itself known at the back of Rex's throat. Was it what the leaflet termed a 'shooting pain'? He didn't think so. He jumped on a bus, heading south towards the edgier, trendier Stoke Newington, and found a pub in which to sip a brandy while he formulated his thoughts. The brandy turned seamlessly into a pint, then a number of others.

It was just after nine and dark by the time he emerged, shivery and more than a little drunk. He'd managed to email in his copy using the pub's free Wi-Fi, but there were still things to be done in the office. Buses travelling westwards, back to Wood Green, had to be caught from the top of the hill. He trudged back up the slope, sucking on some mints to ease his sore throat. He wondered how Terry was feeling.

The women and their pushchairs had all departed the hill and gone inside, as had most of the children and the bearded, hatted men. The orange-vested shomrim guards kept up a reduced presence, but the pavements were crowded with Hasidic girls in long, navy skirts, heading home from what must have been a very long school day. He wondered if they were even remotely like other teenage girls. Then he wondered what other teenage girls were like. He didn't know now, any more than he'd ever known.

By the time he reached the top of the hill, the clock on the big Catholic church said nine-fifteen. He paused at the summit, more than usually breathless, then spotted a very different type of girl. Dark-haired, smartly dressed, in her late twenties, she was swearing at a black-cab driver outside the now-shuttered fishmongers.

'You can't pick and choose!' she shouted. 'If you stop and your sign's on, you have to take the fare.' The cab drove off and she stepped into the road, shouting and gesturing after it.

Rex stopped. 'Hello, Ellie.'

His former assistant stared at him, flushed. 'Fucking fat bastard!' she said. 'Asks me where I want to go then says he's fucking going home!'

Rex glanced around. 'You might want to tone down the language a bit.'

'No, I don't,' Ellie said, stepping back onto the kerb. She looked thinner, cooler, Rex thought, in her black shirt and trousers. She probably didn't bother with food these days. 'I hate this bloody place.'

'I saw you earlier on, banging on the door of "Vegetables". I was inside.'

'What is it with those people?' she asked, tossing her hair back. It still smelt of lemons, he couldn't help noticing. 'They've either got their blinds down or they stare out at you like you're from Mars…' She paused and looked at him. She touched her hair again, smiled. 'How did you get on? Hey – have you got a favourite pub round here? Silly question. Where haven't you got a favourite pub? Shall we have a quick one?'

He was a sucker for a pretty face, and Ellie Mehta, half-Indian, half-Home-Counties-rose had one of the prettiest he'd ever worked alongside. He also rarely refused an invitation to a drink, even after he'd had several. But he still wasn't thick.

'I didn't get anywhere either, Ellie.'

The smile vanished. 'I'm not after your crappy leads, Rex. I couldn't give a shit. I just thought you might, you know, want someone to talk to.'

'About what?' he asked.

'Jesus. Shit. FUCK. You haven't heard, have you?' The voice expressed sympathy, but she looked almost pleased.

'Heard what, Ellie?'

Ellie had grown up with three brothers, Rex recalled. Which partly explained why she was so very annoying. And also why she felt the need to play a round of 'who can piss the highest' with every man who came along.

'Heard what, Ellie?'

'About Terry.'

Rex's heart thudded. 'Where is he?'

'He was arrested this afternoon. For murdering his next-door neighbour.'

Chapter Two

Terry Younger was formally charged with the murder of Dr George Kovacs at 7:31 am on the morning of Tuesday the 2nd of March. He was now in a holding cell, awaiting transfer to court to enter a plea. He left no one in any doubt what that plea was going to be.

'I'm not fucking guilty!' he rasped, hammering on the wall. 'Not. Fucking. Guilty.'

Amid the chorus of curses from the adjacent cells, many of which no doubt contained people who were very guilty, Rex put a calming hand on Terry's shoulder. A lot of favours had been called in to get five minutes in the cell with him. He didn't want to waste them.

Terry sat back on the black plastic mattress, head in hands, the sudden rush of energy gone. A hard-living Geordie lad, fond of his brown ale and his fags, Terry always looked pretty rough. Now, rheumy-eyed and clammy in his strange blue paper suit, under the punishing strip light of the cell, he'd have passed for a cadaver. Rex wasn't sure he looked any better himself. He hadn't looked in any mirrors lately.

It seemed that Ellie's contact, a Mauritian PCSO who'd been hopelessly in love with her for years, had been telling the truth. Terry had been picked up by a police response team, answering a 999 report of a disturbance from a female caller who'd said she lived in the road. The caller hadn't seen anything unusual around the front of the house, but when the police arrived Terry was inside the downstairs kitchen of his neighbour's dwelling – the neighbour bleeding profusely from a stomach wound, Terry standing over him with a vegetable knife.

On his way to the North Middlesex hospital, Dr Kovacs had died.

Terry had said nothing to the attending officers, except that the knife in his hand was his own, and that he felt fucking terrible.

'I meant fucking terrible because of this bloody shivering, sweating thing I've had since yesterday. Not that I'd done anything to him!'

'Has a doctor seen you?'

Terry nodded. 'I told them about that spray thing at the park. They just gave me Lemsip. They said no one else had reported feeling ill.'

'So you were at home, having a hot bath, listening to your iPod,' Rex prompted, trying to piece together what had happened since he'd parted company with Terry the day before. 'And you thought you heard a noise.'

Terry cleared his throat. 'Aye. I thought it was in the kitchen, so I just hopped out and poked my head round the door, like.'

It wasn't hard for Rex to picture the layout of Terry's new home, not only because he'd been round a few times, but because Terry had been discussing every byway of its purchase and renovation for months. The kitchen and the bathroom were downstairs, the living room and bedrooms at the top: a traditional set-up for Haringey's half-houses, which were basically double-fronted terraces split in two down the hallway.

'I saw I'd left the kitchen window open – I mean it was stupidly hot, wasn't it – but there was nothing going on, so I shut the window and went back to the bath. But I'd managed to pull the plug out when I was getting out, and all the water was gone, and by that point I was shivering like a fucking rabbit. So I got dressed, and I made a cup of tea, and I drank it.'

'And that's when you heard the front door slam and the glass breaking?'

'Same coloured glass I'd looked all over London for and then spent half a day fitting before the old git complains it's not the right colour.'

Rex remembered yesterday's conversation with Kovacs at the park. It seemed a decade ago, in a simpler, happier time when their only concerns were things like parking, and local authors with shitty manners.

'So I got me socks and shoes on, and went out into the hall, and I see all the glass has fallen out, and then I see his door's open, over the hallway. And I just –'

He clenched his fingers. The effort to suppress his feelings brought on a spasm of coughing. 'I thought – you bastard. You went on and on at me for slamming the door and breaking a tiny bit of the fucking glass, and now you've gone and done it yesself. So I went in. I didn't charge in, like… I wasn't up to charging anywhere. I called out. But there was no answer. He had his jazz music on as usual, but I never minded that, really…' Terry shook himself. 'Then I went in and I saw him. On his floor. Blood everywhere. His eyes were open and he was breathing a bit, but he didn't seem to know I was there.'

'Thing is, Tel…' Rex paused for a moment to blow his nose. 'If that'd been me, I'd have dialled 999 straight away.'

'And what if you'd looked down and seen it was your fucking vegetable knife he'd been stabbed with?'

'You're certain it was yours?'

'It's a proper ugly thing my sister sent from Cyprus, with an olive branch handle and a kind of… outline of the island carved into it. I thought I'd lost it in the move.'

'So you picked it up?'

I didn't think! Okay? I felt like shit, I'd seen a dead family in the park, then the next-door neighbour's lying on the floor with his stomach open... I just saw it, and I picked it up. I was weak as a kitten, man. I told them, there's no way I could have stabbed someone!'

'And it was just your luck that a response team had finished attending a domestic on Carlingford Road, and were thirty seconds away when the neighbour called 999.'

Terry sighed deeply. His breath, like the whole cell, smelled tinny and foul.

Rex swallowed painfully, feeling a pricking in the glands under his jaw. 'Well, Terry, a decent brief like Bernadette Devlin will have all that knocked into a falafel wrap in no time. They've got fuck all except circumstantial.'

Terry stared at him with grey eyes, forlorn as a Tyne drizzle. 'Yeah. Fuck all. Except I'd reported him to the Council Noise people last week, because of his fucking typing all night, and when they refused to come out, I sort of, lost it a bit on the phone and said something.' He hung his head. 'I said if someone didn't sort things out I was going to end up stabbing the bastard.'

With an effort, Rex stayed upbeat. 'Okay. An angry outburst in the middle of the night. I'm sure the Council Noise Team hear a lot worse.'

'Turns out he'd reported me, too.'

'Kovacs? To the Council?'

Terry shook his long, shorn head. 'Day after that, I went to Get-It-In for some fags, and he was in there, giving them a load of shit about the expiry date on the milk. You know – he's always got some argy-bargy going on in there, or else the fucking newsagents.'

Rex nodded. It fitted easily with his impression of the man.

'So when he's gone out, like, I said to the shop guy, you want to sell him some really out-of-date milk and poison the old git. But he was still there. Probably getting a free read of the papers.

And he went and reported me to the police for making threats. Said he'd show them a Post-it note I'd written to him, telling him to 'drop dead'. I was on the list for a little visit from the Old Bill, apparently.' He gave a bitter laugh. 'Then they came anyway.'

The door opened. Rex was faintly relieved to see the slight form of D.S. Brenard standing there. He was a good copper: intelligent, honest, thorough. But the best copper in the world could hardly deny the fact that Terry looked guilty as hell.

'Good luck,' Rex said, patting Terry on the upper arm. Neither was the hugging sort. 'Fingers crossed for bail. Ring me if you can.'

Terry stood up and straightened his shoulders, determined to look tougher than he felt. It was a wise strategy, especially if he ended up on the remand wing in Pentonville.

'Rex, I didn't do it,' he said in a low voice. 'I need your help.'

'You've got it.' There was nothing else Rex could say. When Terry had left, he turned to D.S. Brenard. 'You know Dr Kovacs was with both of us earlier on in the day at the park?'

'Terry told me,' the Welsh detective replied. 'We're looking at all the angles.'

'The angle to look at, I'd have thought, is why Kovacs left the scene so suddenly after the family was found dead. I'm wondering if he saw something. And maybe someone else saw that he saw.'

'Like I said, Rex,' Brenard replied, a slight edge to his voice. 'We're looking.'

'Seems a bit odd, though, doesn't it, that the witness to one lot of murders is murdered himself a few hours later?'

Brenard rubbed his head. He was going grey, Rex noticed. '*If* Dr Kovacs witnessed anything. And *if* the person who was found holding the murder weapon and had repeatedly threatened to stab or otherwise kill Dr Kovacs didn't actually murder him.'

Behind them in the cell, Terry embarked on another painful-sounding coughing jag.

'Well in any case, he needs medical attention,' Rex said. 'We've both felt ill since we were at the park.'

'You've probably got what my missus and three of the kids have got,' said Brenard, in his lilting Valleys accent. 'Either that, or you're both allergic to Shalimar.'

'To what?'

'Shalimar. It's a ladies' perfume, and it's what lab tests have just confirmed was sprayed at the Bettelheim family. Ordinary perfume. Smelly, but completely harmless.'

* * *

Rex met Susan in the Jerk Shack, a café stall in the basement of Shopping City. All the major coffee chains could be found in the Wood Green area, but people who liked drinking coffee, rather than three-quid mugs of hot milk, got theirs from the Shack.

They sat over a pair of steaming cups on high stools, while Rex filled her in on his chat with Terry, and they worked out how to handle things from a news perspective.

'My instinct is to fill the whole front page with the word "INNOCENT", but we can't.'

'Why not?' Rex asked. He knew the answer, though.

'Because we have to be seen to be clear-headed and impartial. We can't let anyone assume that we're only supporting Terry because he's one of us.'

'What about: "I'M INNOCENT"?'

Susan nodded. 'I'm innocent. A photo of Terry. Whatever facts we can legally get away with. And an appeal for information. It's the best we can do.'

They sipped their coffees in silence for a while as the espresso machine hissed.

'I always thought, if anyone at the paper was going to end up in big trouble, it would be you. But you're actually okay, aren't you?'

Rex smiled. From anyone else, it could have been rude. From this slim, dark, elegant New Yorker-in-exile whom he'd known for twenty years, it was almost a compliment. He'd had his big trouble, and come through it. Not least because of Susan. And Terry.

He felt okay in another way that morning. Since D.S. Brenard had told him about the perfume, most of his more worrying symptoms had mysteriously disappeared. Now he felt as if he was getting a cold – a nasty cold, but even so, just a cold. He wondered if Terry was experiencing the same sense of relief. He doubted it.

The music changed, and people winced. The Jerk Shack was run by twin sisters, whose only discernible difference was in musical taste. One liked old reggae and ska numbers. The other, whenever she got the chance, switched them off in favour of urban, shouty stuff.

'I'm inclined to agree with you,' Susan said, crumbling a bit off her pastry but not eating it. 'Like, there could be a link. Maybe Kovacs did see something. Or recognised someone in the park. It's worth exploring. But there's one problem.'

'What?'

'It sounds like there were dozens of people who'd have liked to put a knife in Dr Kovacs. Maybe you should talk to Lawrence.'

'Lawrence? Why?'

'He might know if Kovacs stepped on any toes or ruffled any feathers while researching his book.'

Lawrence Berne wrote News North London's 'Laureate of the Ladders' column, which offered amusing ditties on subjects of local concern, like closing libraries and mounting levels of dog-shit. He also covered Arts and Local History, and had, as Rex now recalled, been quite annoyed that someone was bringing out another book on the Tottenham Outrage. A few years back Lawrence had been in talks with a Radio 4 person about doing a centenary documentary about it. He still regarded it as his own personal territory.

Even so, wasn't his boss's new angle a bit far-fetched? Surely local historians only murdered each other in TV crime dramas?

'I'll tell you one thing,' Susan said, zipping up her handbag. 'Even if the guy's book never comes out, the Tottenham Outrage is going to stay in the news.'

She was right. It might have happened over a century ago, but the doomed robbery offered perennial good value for local newspapers. The terrorists' wages snatch had given way to a lengthy chase across the Tottenham and Walthamstow marshes, featuring a hijacked tram, a stolen milk-cart, the slaying of a teenage boy and a policeman – not to mention the firing of some 300 bullets.

In the aftermath a number of ordinary citizens had been commended for bravery, and, this still got a mention whenever a Tottenham resident committed any notably selfless act. The Outrage also got name-checked whenever policemen were shot, and whenever recent immigrants were being blamed for crime – two rather more frequent occurrences. Rex had read a couple of passably interesting pamphlets on the original event over the years. He might even have attempted Kovacs' book, if it had actually been available. And the man hadn't been such a twat.

'I gotta run,' Susan said, stepping down from her barstool as if there were a definite, correct way to do this, and she'd learnt it. 'Seeing the bank manager. The stuff on Stamford Hill was A1. Lots of reader comments underneath. And on the forums. Getting Terry off the hook is important, but don't let the other stuff go cold, okay? We've still got a paper to bring out. Kind of. Oh...' She pulled out a phone – or a silver ovoid incorporating that function along with many others – and waved her fingers over some central part of it. 'Nearly forgot. Sylheti Stores. You know it?'

'The cash-and-carry on Turnpike Lane... Yeah, I know the guy who owns it.'

'Mr Rahman. He left a message this morning. He's been getting funny packages. Something like that. Can you look in? He asked for you.'

Rex felt a stab of alarm, remembering an unpleasant interlude the year before, when anonymous gifts of raw liver and handcuffs and wheelchairs kept arriving at his door. But that was all over, and the sender – his wife's nephew, it had turned out – was safely back in Paris. The tragedy that had provoked the boy's cryptic campaign, though, was far from over. It never would be. Rex realised he hadn't seen his wife for over a week. Maybe longer.

But now his presence was required in a large aromatic shed on the end of Turnpike Lane. He set off down the High Street, past a spanking new set of wooden benches outside the Council Housing Office. These had been of little benefit to the locality, except to give the street-drinkers somewhere to sit that was better than the crappy narrow red shelves attached to the bus-stops. One of the regulars, a man known locally as 'Bird', was on a bench now, necking a deadly 10% brew called Navigator.

It was another oddly warm day, but that made no difference to the scrawny, elderly black man. He wore a thick sheepskin coat in all weathers and spent his days shouting abuse, chiefly at the various offices and officers of Haringey Council. Years ago Susan had tried and failed to find out what the man's beef was with the Council. Today, Bird's refrain was 'Evict me, Turkish bitches!' along with something less distinct about 'budgets'. Or maybe that word was *bitches*.

Rex hurried past, head down, keen to avoid eye contact. He wondered briefly why they'd come up with the name 'Navigator' for a drink that could only make you feel as if you were lost in a storm.

Under normal circumstances a trip to Sylheti Stores was a treat, a form of low-cost tourism. The place was a narrow but deep pre-fab, like an aircraft hangar, with a covered porch piled with exotic vegetables. But the real treasures lay inside: row upon row of spices and snacks, betel nut and henna and drums of ghee, in a riot of oranges and greens, with a different scent every ten paces, and nasal Dravidian show-tunes rattling from the loudspeakers.

Today, though, there was no chance to enjoy it. The owner, a dapper old gentleman with a soft, wavy beard, marched Rex down the aisles, straight to the back of the shop.

'You've had some funny stuff in the mail, is that right?' Rex asked.

'Can't talk here,' muttered the man, opening a door to a store-room at the back. Rex paused. It was pitch-black in there. The man urged him in. He obeyed instinctively, only to find the door shut, then locked behind him. Panic rose, fell and rose again as the darkness was displaced by light from a single bulb.

The first thing he saw was a video camera on a tripod. It stood facing an Islamic flag, tacked on to a tower of rice sacks.

Then he saw the four young, bearded men. The largest of them, tall, hefty and hawk-featured, was dressed in a combat jacket and keffiyeh. They were the boys from the park.

Rex glanced back in alarm to the video camera, the Islamic flag… He'd seen this before. On TV. It was an all too familiar set piece – and one that only ever ended messily. What the hell were they planning?

'Relax,' said the big man.

'Easier said than done,' Rex said.

The big lad handed him a DVD in a see-through case. 'My name's Anwar Hafeez. We want you to release this on your website. It's important.'

He set down a folding chair, inviting his guest to sit. Rex began to take in more of his surroundings. Cutting through the aroma of spices was a powerful tang of body odour. Around the room, amongst the oil-drums of ghee and the man-size sacks of gram flour, were rolled-up sleeping bags and blankets.

'You've been sleeping in here?'

'His mum's uncle owns the place,' said Anwar, nodding towards an acne-scarred boy with a straggly beard. 'But he wants us out. That's why we're trying to get this sorted.'

'Sorted?' Rex echoed. It seemed an odd term for a terror cell to be using. He glanced at the DVD in his hands.

'This was never meant to happen!' said the spotty lad bitterly. 'It's fucked-up, man.'

'What wasn't meant to happen? The Bettelheim family dying?'

'We weren't nothing to do with that!' said Anwar. He sounded like an aggrieved schoolboy. 'I just... I lost my temper with them a bit. Because of the way they was looking at me.'

'We'd been at a meeting,' the other young man broke in. 'A *khutbah* off a geezer who'd been in Syria. A talk. I filmed it for our brothers who couldn't be there. Then we went on the boats at the park – none of us had college in the afternoon. And that Jewish lady left, like, some perfume in the boat.'

'So I goes up and says, is this yours?' Anwar continued. 'And she just flinches, like, and backs away. And they're all just sitting there, staring at me. I'd just had enough of it. We'd been getting evils from all those *kuffar* in the park ever since we got there. So I sprayed it at them and I chucked it in the bush. That's all I did, man. It was just perfume...' A helpless terror appeared in Anwar's eyes. 'We need your help, man.'

'So your mum's uncle's message about strange packages – that was just to get me here?'

There were nods all round. Rex looked at them. They all spoke like black boys. Not sprayed – *sprrehd*. Not chucked – *chokk*. Jaminglish, it was sometimes called: a hybrid of Caribbean and Cockney that all the kids did round here, wherever their parents or grandparents had come from. They spoke like that because they belonged here – not doing *jihad* duty in Syria or Somalia.

One of the boys who hadn't spoken was openly snivelling. There was a biochemistry textbook on the floor at his feet. The cops and the spooks and the more panicky sections of the press would have a field day with that book, though it was quite clear to Rex now that these were just college boys who'd had a bit of fire put in their bellies by a lunchtime sermon. The streets of Tottenham and Wood Green were full of them: setting up trestle tables, dishing out badly-worded pamphlets and getting into verbals with passing Christians. They were the new Mods and Rockers, he often thought – and in most cases no more likely to bring society to its knees. He wiped sweat from his forehead and cleared his throat.

'What's your connection to Dr Kovacs?'

'Who?' Anwar looked at his co-conspirators, who seemed equally puzzled.

'Old bloke, short beard, nasty blazer. Ended up dead shortly after witnessing your little display at the park.'

'Brother, I swear, we didn't notice no one 'part from that Jew family and that white bitch with the ponytail.'

Rex looked at them. They seemed to be telling the truth.

'I can do three things. I can write about this on our website. I can put you in touch with the best solicitor in town. Who will not, I guarantee, let you down. And I can ring a policeman who – I promise – isn't an agent of the Zionist *Kuffar* CIA conspiracy, and get him down here.' Anwar made to object but Rex interrupted. 'One thing I'm not going to do is put your film on the web.' Rex waggled the object at them. It rattled in its cheap plastic case. 'If you want people not to think you're terrorists, don't release a bloody video message like you're the Voice of Al-Qa'eda in Haringey!'

'I told you it was stupid,' muttered Anwar.

'Shut up,' said his lieutenant. 'It's all right for you. My dad's going to kill me.'

Rex homed in on the ringleader. 'Can I also suggest that if you choose to dress up like a Chechen warlord, then you accept that people are going to look at you a bit funny from time to time?'

* * *

Mr Park his name is but the old lady calls him Mr Parkses. So she says, *Leah, set Mr Parkseses gloves by the stove to let them warm.* I know what he wants to warm. Pink face like a boy, with wet lips and shifty little eyes. I catch him looking at Leah sometimes and when he knows I caught him a flush goes up his neck and his cheeks, like a young girl. Good position, clerk at the bank they say, so he can lord it over me, with my rough boots and my bent back. *Your accent has a touch of the Scotch in it, Mr Smith, surely?* Surely not, sir. Bit east of that, you sow's teat. *So what work do you do?* he asks me grandly one Saturday over the tea. *Ho, bombs and dynamite, Mr Parkses. Terror, by the individual and by the masses.* What I should have said.

Missus Cutter's got him lined up for a suitor for Leah. So she has him to tea on Saturdays. Feeds him up. 'Mr Parkses might take a little more jam.' And when she sees me putting butter on my bread she says, 'Mr Parkses, help Mr Smith finish up that butter will you?' meaning I'm to hold off and he's to latch his little wet mouth to the nipple in my place when I'm the one as pays rent. I roll my eyes at Leah and she half-smiles I think. May be wrong, mind. Got it badly wrong about a girl before.

Missus Cutter has taken to leaving the two of them alone in the kitchen. Going out to fuss around her hens so he can press his case. Or press something. I'd have hung about today, sat there at the table and polished my boots and got right in the fucking middle of the pair of them, but I'd got to meet E and T downstairs at the bookshop.

You say the word for birch-tree – *bereza* – to the damp old Litvaker behind the desk and he lets you down to the basement. There's a mimeograph down there, and books. Ought to be an all right little hidey-hole but across the yard at the back there's a Schochet, and when the slaughterer's not singeing feathers, he's letting the blood and fat into the drains, and it sits there and it stinks. Better now in winter, at least. In winter it only smells of the Litvaker upstairs.

Elephant and Torch were – believe this – taking it in turns to read out loud from Bakunin. Like a pair of yeshiva-boys at their Talmud. Torch was reading when I came in, and he doesn't stop, neither of them look up even, so I have to sit down and listen. He reads like the stupidest boy in my village chedar class, Torch does, all slow, stumbling on every third word, as he bites his knuckle and blinks. Elephant just sits there, that pair of big caterpillars on his forehead all knotted up in his effort to look pious and serious and clever. Why did Velkis stick me with them? Revenge? Penalty? Test?

I said 'Amen' at the end, because that's how they read it. Not like it's meant to be understood, like it's magic words, like the old grannies say their Hebrew tongue-twisters over the heads of babies with the ague. Idiots.

There's been word from Riga. The Leesma needs money. And men. One of us must go back.

'It should be you, Kuznetz,' Elephant says, with his little dark bushy face. Rat peering through a shithouse brush. 'You'll be wanting to see that flame-haired beauty of yours. Is she back, I do wonder?' Says it with a dirty smile, tip of one little yellow tooth hanging over his lip because he knows what happened. My girl vanished, just took off and vanished, and it drives me sick if I give any thought to it.

'It's to spread revolutionary consciousness amongst the dock workers and organise a strike,' Torch adds. I see the blinking fool take a sideways glance at his master to check he's done right and get a pat on his pointed skittle of a head. Elephant smiles again.

He smiles because he enjoys seeing me pulled in two this way, like the Tartars did to their enemies. I don't want to go back to Riga. Because of her. I'm better off here, like Velkis said, not know-ing where she is. Or whether she is. But still, it's what I want to be doing: mobilising the workers, educating them to see the obvi-ous, so the State just withers away. That's my anarchism. Not this. Skulking like a pack of Bessarabian bandits in the woods. Plotting little robberies and fires.

I'm ready to give them full cannons on their stupidity, how little they've done for the Cause since getting here, apart from finding this room and nearly getting us all arrested when we stole the printing equipment. But upstairs in the bookshop, the Litvaker stamps his foot three times on the floor. Dust showers on our heads. Means a customer has come in. Or police. So we all just go still and glare at each other until we hear the bell on the door and two more stamps.

Elephant wipes the dust from his eyebrows and says he's signed on at Schnurrman's, the Rubber Factory on Chesnut Road. Tomorrow Torch starts too. It's a big old place with a clock tower. So many Russians working there now they call it the Spasskaya. Here's the interesting thing: what looks like just one boy, a sickly type, carries the wages from the bosses car to the clerk's room.

But – back to Riga? I'll be thinking I've seen her everywhere, my heart seeking the shadows of her out and tricking my eyes. On every corner, a kvass stand where they know me, a gypsy cigarette-seller who'll ask me about her, maybe tell me some rumour about her.

Velkis had sent me on a little job. Cross to Kaunas with some twenty-rouble printing plates in a case of herring. Strange lot over there, I remember. Made out they weren't expecting me – or my 'herrings'. Point is I was only gone three weeks, and she knew how it was, how I couldn't always tell her when I'd be back. Still, this time, my girl had had enough. When I got back, she wasn't there. No sign of her anywhere. No one knew. Nothing. I waited so long outside the dressmakers they asked me if I wanted to model evening gowns for them.

Then Velkis: dark, heavy, priestly Velkis at the back of the dockers' tavern in his army coat. *You're letting this girl dilute your revolutionary fervour.* Loses the broom up his arse after a couple of vodkas. *She was just a girl, man. A fuck. Let go. Move on.* He tells me he's sending a cell to London. *Lovely irony to it, don't you think? The Tsar's Navy taught you such good English that you'll pass for an Englishman. Stay six months, a year. Forget.*

So I came. Riga – Hamburg – Tilbury on a ship sweet with the scent of dirty wool and sheep-shit. Never forgetting her one minute of it. Still not, now.

It's snowing when I come out of the bookshop. Only the end of October – early, at least for this damp, crowded little island. I walk out to the edge of the Marshes, away from the smoke and the dust and my confused mind. The snow is all pure white on the trees and the ground. Cools my fevered thoughts. I can fool myself I'm back, gone to the dunes around Ainava to catch hares in the holidays from the Naval Academy, met up with the old pack. Down to town, all glowing, sell the hares because our mothers won't cook *trayf*, forbidden meat. Buy vodka and beer with the money and pretend one of us has the balls to approach a whore. Bicker and joke around all night like that in the bright, fierce cold. Not sick and twisted-up yet. No soldiers hauling your little sisters away in a dog-cart. No Cause. No Struggle. No Fight. No *her*. Wish it was still like that. But history calls men.

When I got home the house was in darkness, cold, just a couple of tiny red pinpricks from the embers in the grate, smells of boiled pigmeat and beeswax. The old lady's nostrils whistling upstairs. But something else as I took off my jacket in the blackness and wrapped myself in camphor-smelling blankets. Thought it might be a cart, way over down the High Road, with a squeaking axle. Then she sniffed and I realized it was her. It was Leah: crying, high-voiced, quietly, in her room.

I put my arm out through the blankets into the heavy cold air and I touched the wall between me and her.

* * *

By late afternoon, images of four sheepish young men emerging from Tottenham Police Station in the company of their solicitor were being shown on Sky News. The on-site anchor even graciously mentioned a 'local newspaper' as being responsible for the break-through. Rex watched the broadcast on the flat screen in Susan's office, while her laptop displayed the ebb and flow of traffic to NNL's website. The 'I'm Innocent' page for Terry had drawn a modest audience, rising slightly as the story about the Muslim boys had gone online with it. By rights, the TV news coverage ought to be helping, too.

'If anyone would actually mention us by name, the stats would be through the roof,' Rex said. 'Maybe we should text Sky News and ask for clarification.'

Susan grunted sceptically. 'Most of the visitors we're getting are just click-throughs. Thirty seconds on the site, max. The BBC gets these kind of figures on a wet Sunday tea-time.'

'Of course they do,' Rex said. 'They're the BBC.'

'Exactly. And we're not!' Susan sighed. 'Sorry, Rex. Sorry. It's just… People can get this shit –' she waved at the TV screen '– on their watches now. Why do they need us?'

'It's called repositioning,' said Lawrence Berne, Laureate of the Ladders, as he breezed in, clad in a houndstooth jacket and navy slacks. 'All the big papers are doing it. Stop concentrating on news. No point, is there? You can't compete with Twit-book, or whatever it's called. So you give 'em all the other stuff. Debate. Lifestyle. Arts. Comment.'

'But mainly comment, huh, Lawrence?' Susan said, glancing at Rex. He said nothing. He'd never seen his boss so gloomy. Normally Susan was the one urging everyone on, filling the sails with wind even if there was little other than wind on offer. A lot of the time he was sceptical of her transatlantic, positive-attitude stuff. Right now, he missed it.

He remembered that Susan had said something about going to the bank. Perhaps her mood was connected to that. He was about to ask when she swept out into the main office to talk to the Whittaker Twins.

He turned back to the screen, where the newsreader formally identified the victims. They showed a holiday snap of the Bettelheims, all together, looking happy at an airport. The baby was wearing a bunny-ears hat. Rex found he had to look away.

'It's a shame Di missed your big scoop,' Lawrence said, planting himself in Susan's vacated chair. He examined his big, gold watch, which, like much else about him, seemed to belong to another time and place – a Rotary Club Luncheon, perhaps, circa 1984. 'She'll be somewhere over Riga by now.'

Rex frowned. 'Diana's coming back?'

'She's been back,' Lawrence said. 'Now she's gone again. Didn't you know?'

Rex felt an irrational stab of anger towards Lawrence, with his bouffant hair and perma-tan, but it didn't last. If Lawrence's niece hadn't contacted him, it was no one's fault but his own.

He had behaved badly out in Cambodia. So, perhaps, had she. But she hadn't made any promises. They'd had a brief fling in London, then Diana, a GP – his own GP in fact – had decided to go off and save lives in a Cambodian children's hospital. She'd suggested he visit. Furnished with a ticket paid for by his workmates, he'd done just that, only to find there was a motorbike-riding Norwegian doctor called Kjell in the wings and then, increasingly, centre-stage. There'd been an angry, somewhat unhinged night in a beer garden, swiftly followed by Rex catching a plane out of the place. He still shuddered at the memory of it.

He realised Lawrence was chuntering on. 'She mentioned you – said she was going to give you a bell...'

Rex began to pull out his phone. But he knew it was hopeless. He knew no one had rung.

'Did you ever meet Dr Kovacs?' he asked, changing the subject.

'He did a little talk once at the South Hornsey Con Club. About "Revolutionary Tottenham".'

'Revolutionary?'

'Yes indeedy. Proper hotbed this manor was. That lot who did the Outrage, they were some sort of anarchist cell from the Baltics, trying to raise funds. Then there was a hotchpotch of Bolshie sorts in the 1970s.'

'Oh yeah - that lot in Stoke Newington... The Angry Brigade?'

Lawrence winced, annoyed at Rex knowing something he was about to tell him. 'Yes, them and others. Anyway, it wasn't a great lecture. Or rather, it was just that – a lecture. Went right over most people's heads.'

'Particularly the heads of the South Hornsey Con Club, I imagine.'

'Indeed. Anyhow, he put everyone's backs up, then refused to stay for a drink at the end.'

'Kovacs said his book was going to clear up some of the mysteries about the Outrage.'

'Oh yes?' Lawrence replied with an air of studied nonchalance.

Rex pressed on. 'I was wondering if you knew what those mysteries might be?' Conversations with Lawrence were often like this: him indicating that he had something you might want to know, you having to stroke until he coughed it.

'Could be what happened to the money. Or that thing in the hopsickle.' Lawrence had his own, allegedly amusing way of saying certain words.

'Do you mean the hospital?'

'Yes. One of the robbers – Helfeld – was shot, but took two weeks to die. One nurse thought he'd said something interesting just before he popped his clogs, but another nurse thought not.' He shrugged. 'I'll dig around for you, iffley likey-doo.'

'Thanks.' That was the terrible thing about Lawrence: so annoying, but so useful.

'And if you want my four penn'orth on Kovacs, I'd say read *Murder on the Orient Express*. You know what happened in that don't you?'

'Everyone did it?'

'Exactly. Anyhoo, dare I suggest that the first port of call might be the pages of the good doctor's book?'

'It's still with the printers.'

'And the printers won't let you see it, even though it might throw light on a recent murder?'

Four recent murders, Rex thought, if his hunch was right. Not to mention an innocent man locked up. Lawrence had a point. Why hadn't he tried to get hold of the book?

He was rummaging for his phone when Susan appeared in the doorway. 'Rex,' she said. 'Mike Bond on your line.'

Mike Bond was Brenda the Receptionist's husband – and, until last year, a lifelong policeman at Tottenham nick. After a heart attack he had taken a job in the Coroner's Office, where he remained an obliging source of information for News North London. He claimed – Rex suspected truthfully – to be writing a memoir called *Coronaries to Coroners*.

'How's Terry?' was his opening gambit.

'Just about bearing up,' Rex said. 'But bewildered. Have you got any news?'

'Not on that,' Bond said. 'But I thought you'd want to know. The tests on the Bettelheim family just came back. It was cyanide poisoning. They all ingested cyanide.'

'Ingested it how?'

'We don't know. It metabolises very quickly, so it's hard to tell how it came in. One of their Tupperware boxes had very faint traces, but it had been wiped clean, so we don't know what else was in it.'

'So could someone have sneaked something into the food while they were having their picnic?' Rex said. 'Or maybe whoever prepared the picnic and wiped the Tupperware out afterwards, presumably the mum...?'

Mike Bond finished it for him. 'Poisoned herself and her family. Yeah.'

* * *

'Cut-back bitch! Cut-back bitch. *Rabbah* bitch! Bitch teef!'

He couldn't see Bird, but Rex could hear his latest rant from the top of the street. It was familiar stuff, but the location was new. Rex was walking down Langerhans Road, planning to have a look at Terry's house before going on to pick up the main east-west bus route towards Stamford Hill. It was a quiet street of terraced houses – no Council Offices down here. Perhaps Bird had started to terrorise individuals.

As Rex turned the corner, his suspicions seemed to be confirmed. Bird was sitting on the wall outside the blue door shared by Terry and the late Dr Kovacs, bellowing hoarsely at a slim blonde woman. She appeared to be struggling into a shabby leather jacket. Maybe she worked for the Council. Maybe she was just a woman.

'Cut. Back. Bitch. Teef. *Kurva!*'

Like quite a few locals, it seemed Bird had now adopted this universal Polish insult. Shouting it at Council buildings seemed forgivable. Cornering lone women on quiet streets, on the other hand, did not.

'Pack it in!' Rex shouted, at the top of his voice, and as he quickened his pace, the two figures, far off at the end of the road, turned. Rex got a flash of a punky, alternative-looking woman – curly, close-cropped hair bleached white, a neckerchief and an old biker jacket – before she turned away again. 'Leave her alone!' He half- expected Bird to get off his wall and lumber towards him, but instead it was the woman who moved. Still trying to get her jacket on, fast, in the opposite direction.

Outside number 324 was a large yellow board, inviting people to call Tottenham CID if they'd seen or heard anything. Rex remembered then that there had been a witness. A woman claiming to live over the road had called 999. Could that have been her, the woman with the brassy hair? He could do with talking to her, if he could find out who she was. For now he had to make do with Bird.

A pair of tiny yellow eyes stared at him. He wasn't sure if the man had any idea where he was. The stench of beer and piss was eye-watering. Rex was surprised. Bird was usually clean. Mad. Drunk. But hygienic, at least.

'Bird, you'd better move on. There was a murder here, you know.' Rex pointed towards the house, crime scene tape still around the front door. Bird didn't move.

'That bitch, that bitch,' the old man muttered, before suddenly roaring 'CUT BACK!' in Rex's face, prompting him to step back off the kerb in alarm.

'All right, fuck off to you too,' he said, as Bird staggered yeastily away. Alone, Rex stared up at the house – at the window of the room where Kovacs had died, at the front door with its missing corner of coloured glass. If he could just get inside, he might find some answers.

In the films people booted down doors and picked locks as easily as if they were picking their own noses. He knew it didn't work like that. Once, when his sister-in-law had passed out in the bathroom, he and his wife, Sybille, had spent fifteen minutes trying to smash the door down. Sybille had dislocated her shoulder. He'd broken a toe. At the A&E in the Royal Free Hospital, the nurses had assumed that the three of them had had some sort of alcoholics' fight.

House-breaking might be out of the question, but there was something he could do now. He took out his phone and looked up local printers. A large, Greek-owned business in Palmer's Green was the most prominent, and in days of yore, the old *Wood Green Gazette* had used them for leaflets and inserts. He hoped Dr Kovacs had used them, too.

A well-spoken young man answered. Rex explained his business. The young man said he'd have to ask someone else. Rex hung on to the point where he'd started to wonder if they'd forgotten him, when an older voice came on.

'I know you. Sat next to you at that Local Business Awards dinner-thing,' said the new man. Rex didn't remember the man, or the dinner in question, but it was a useful start. He restated his inquiry. The man tutted.

'Yes, we're handling it. As it's you, ordinarily, I'd say, okay – you could maybe see the typescript or the page-proofs. I mean, I can't see why not – the guy's not coming back, is he? But we can't find either of them.'

'You can't find the book you're printing for Dr Kovacs?'

The man cleared his throat. 'We've had a break-in. Some of our documents have gone missing.'

'So someone stole manuscripts from you?'

'Well – no – someone broke in and made off with all our computers. But yes, some of our open jobs seem to have gone, too.'

'And you're sure Dr Kovacs' book is one of them?'

'I'm not *sure* about anything right now,' the man said. 'The whole place is a bloody mess. But I certainly remember Dr Kovacs. He refused to supply us with an electronic copy, so we had to scan in every page of his typescript by hand. So if we do find it, or either of the two sets of proofs he rejected, or if our hard drive shows up in a branch of CashExchange, we'll let you know, Mr Tracey. But don't hold your breath.'

Rex apologised and hung up. It all sounded rather odd. A break-in at a printer's. The manuscript of a recently murdered man going missing. A man who had himself witnessed the killing of a young family, mere hours before his own death.

Then again, it was possible the various versions of Kovacs' manuscript hadn't gone missing. They might turn up amidst the detritus caused by the break-in. And desperate people were always breaking into all manner of places. He'd reported on a smash and grab at EazyLets the other day: someone had made off with a box of rubber bands. It was right to look for links, wrong to jump to conclusions. Rex decided to call back in a few days' time, and carried on his way eastwards, towards Stamford Hill.

He wanted more on the Bettelheim family: where they'd lived, how they'd lived, what could possibly have led to the murder by poison of the entire lot of them. He needed only the tiniest lead to get going. But it wasn't proving easy to procure one. In Mega Glatt Meats, the man who'd earlier been willing to talk to him now seemed terse and inhibited. Across the street, in a religious bookshop smelling delectably of leather and wood, an Arabic-looking old man in monochrome Hasidic garb simply sang, 'No, no, no,' putting up a blocking palm as Rex entered the shop, and kept repeating it until he left.

His spirits brightened when he saw Mordecai Hershkovits coming out of the Boots with a bottle of Benylin.

'My mum always used to say there was a bug going round,' Rex said, pointing to the medicine. 'But right now, I think maybe there is.'

Mordecai ignored this. 'Here for more *rechilus*, Mr Tracey?'

'What's *rechilus*? Gossip?' At a nod from Mordecai, Rex went on: 'I'm here because a lot of people want to know why a quiet, religious, peaceful family was fatally poisoned. I'm also here because on the same day another man was killed – a man who saw the Bettelheims die in the park. And right now an innocent man, my friend, in fact, is in prison for it. So no, I'm not interested in *gossip*, Mr Hershkovits. I'm interested in the truth.'

At first Rex regretted his outburst, but the little man seemed to be taking it in and pondering it. Then he sighed and said, 'Maybe they weren't so peaceful.'

'What does that mean?'

The short man glanced around and then leaned in close. 'Some people who live nearby have said it wasn't a happy house.'

'Arguments, you mean?'

'Chaya Bettelheim was…' He shrugged. 'I didn't know her but some people think… I tell you something *my* mother says. *A shotten zaal*. A hall of shadows. You know what I mean? There's a kind of darkness, around some people. Whether they're sick, or they're just unhappy, or it's kind of a curse… It's what some people think about Chaya Bettelheim.' He stowed the bottle in his navy Macintosh pocket. 'And some police seem to think the same thing.'

'They've been asking questions specifically about Chaya Bettelheim?'

'Yes... Especially one of the detectives who keeps coming down here. Whether she was a good mother, whether she behaved oddly... You would have to be a very stupid man not to see what they were thinking.'

'Where did they live?'

'On Riverside.' Mordecai gestured behind him. 'A nice road, by the river. I know a lot of people there. Nice people.'

'Anyone who'd talk to me?'

'I doubt it, Mr Tracey,' Mordecai replied, walking off and shaking his head.

Rex decided to ignore this gloomy prediction. He looked up the road up on his A-Z and set off towards it. As he walked up the hill, he wondered whether there'd been some kind of mass injunction on talking to him. Maybe the word had gone out and the shutters come down.

In the window of a shop laconically marked 'Travel', he glimpsed a young Hasidic blade. His skullcap was tipped cockily forwards; his feet were on the desk; his unlit cigarette was poised in his lips like a weapon. Somehow that sight tuned him in to many others, into the sheer variety of the place. Some of the men wore white stockings and the sort of buckled, archaic footwear that belonged at the Lord Mayor's parade. Others looked sharp, like Mordecai, in modern dark suits and fedoras. There were little boys in Batman T-shirts, and then there were long-frocked, wool-stockinged girls straight out of *Little House on the Prairie*. It was inconceivable that this place could have arrived at a single decision – about him or anything else. Mordecai Hershkovits himself was a walking contradiction, declaring that no one would help Rex at the same time as handing over the latest speculation. This had to be worth pursuing.

He kept going up the hill. 'Vegetables'. 'Travel'. There was something Soviet about the way the people around here named their businesses. Something otherworldly at any rate, a stubborn rejection of anything modern like branding or marketing. You just sold something, and the people who wanted it, bought it. He reached 'Vegetables' only to find that the place was shut, its grimy blinds pulled down over windows and door, the incongruous little van still parked up outside. The van really didn't fit. A grim museum piece of a shop, and the sort of vehicle young Shoreditch designers drooled over.

His phone rang. It was a woman. She informed him that he had five minutes to get to Wood Green Town Hall or he'd miss his slot for a Driving Test. Of course, even if he could have made it in five minutes, he now had no car to take the test in, courtesy of Terry's incarceration. Rex apologised – needlessly, since the woman on the other end of the phone clearly didn't care whether he lived or died, let alone whether he acquired a driving license – and hung up. He tried to feel something about missing his test – the culmination of three months' hard work with Terry, and many long years of doubt and questioning and entreaties to a God who ignored him. But there was nothing there. Other things mattered more. Perhaps they always had.

He was about to continue up the hill when a narrow PVC door at the side of 'Vegetables' swung open.

'Rex.'

The woman called Rescha stood there, wearing a long-sleeved burgundy top. She scanned the street, then motioned him to come closer.

'Not open today?'

She shook her head. 'He's sick.' She rummaged in a pocket of her wide, dark-green skirt. A smell of toast came from the interior of the house. 'The woman. Chaya Bettelheim. I thought you might want to know.' She handed him a piece of plastic. 'She dropped this inside the shop one time.'

It was an entry card for a Travelodge hotel room. Printed on it were the words: 'And Now Relax'.

'I meant to give it back to her, but she was never alone. I know what this Travelodge place is,' she added in a low voice. 'It's a hotel.'

'It's a chain of hotels. Five hundred of them, I think.'

She frowned. 'Oh.' Her skin was very soft, he noticed. And her eyes – had he ever seen sadder eyes? 'I guess it's not much use then.'

'Well, use for what?' he asked, politely. 'Yesterday, you said you were sure it could only have been some kind of accident.'

'Today I'm sure, too,' she said. 'But people are starting to say that it was her. Police are saying it, too. That she was a crazy person and she did it.'

'And you don't think that, Mrs, er –?'

She paused as a clutch of children walked by: all olive-skinned Hasidic girls. There was a willowy teenager and a smaller carbon-copy with pigtail. Perched on the teenager's shoulders was a laughing toddler with the same, almost Uzbek or Tajik features as her sisters, only buffered by baby-fat. Rescha followed them with such hungry eyes as they moved off up the hill. He wondered if she had children.

'Schild. I'm Rescha Schild,' Rescha said, returning her attention to him once the children had passed from view. 'Chaya Bettelheim had *tsuris*. Problems. She wasn't happy.' She looked at him.

'So you think I should find out why? Who will that help?'

'I thought it might stop people saying that she did it. Maybe even… I don't know. Okay, it was a stupid idea.' She shrugged, and then winced, as if the gesture physically hurt her. Rex sensed there was something she wouldn't say, something about the card that he was meant to understand, but didn't. He nodded thanks and put the item in his pocket.

'Was she your friend?'

She gave a faint smile, as if his question was a joke. 'She came in the shop. We had things in common.' She rubbed her shoulder. 'One of the customers today had your news… email thing on his telephone,' she added, suddenly. 'I saw about that man you work with. He was here with you yesterday.'

Terry had gone home by the time Rex came into the shop, which meant Rescha Schild must have been watching them. She and perhaps others. He wondered if she'd been watching him today.

'My friend didn't do it either.'

She seemed about to reply when a bell rang from the interior behind her. A hand bell, like something from an old-fashioned primary school. 'I'm sorry to waste your time,' she said, awkwardly stepping back into the gloom. The door slammed shut.

He took the little white plastic key card out of his pocket, stared down at it, then up at the blank, gauze-curtained windows above the shop. What had she been trying to tell him?

* * *

Riverside was a quiet street of scruffy semis, fragranced by the salty, muddy tang of the adjacent marshes. A bespectacled, jerky-limbed Hasid boy on roller-skates pointed out the Bettelheims' house. Its only distinguishing feature was a piece of plyboard over the front door, no doubt where the police had forced their way in. Apart from that, there was nothing to remark and no one to talk to.

Back at Turnpike Lane, he decided to go home for an hour or two. He headed for Get-It-In to pick up a couple of cold Okocim. The weather had turned cold again, the sky had gone a threatening brown, and the lights were on in the shops along the little parade opposite the tube station. Get-It-In smelled good inside, of baking bread and chopped parsley.

The owner, a bald, mahogany-coloured man called Kemal, acknowledged him with a gloomy, upward jerk of the head.

'You visit Tel-boy?' he asked. 'What prison?'

'Pentonville,' Rex said. He recalled his conversation with Terry in the police cell. 'You had some problems with Dr Kovacs, didn't you?'

Kemal's face darkened. 'Police was in here asking about today. I told them, yeah, yeah, sure, a lot of argy-bargy wiv that doctor.

Always in here, making difficulties. But no stabbing. You wanna know why it was me that didn't stab him?'

Rex wondered whether Kemal had said it exactly like this to the police. He probably had.

'I'll tell you why. I was Wood Green Crown Court all yesterday,' Kemal said as he put Rex's beers in a thin, candy-striped carrier bag. 'Seeing that wanker sent down.'

The word 'wanker' sounded mighty strange coming from Kemal, though the episode he referred to was all too familiar. A crack addict had robbed the place with a fake gun over a year ago; stolen ninety quid, and broken Kemal's jaw.

'He got seventeen munf. I thought your newspaper might have been there,' Kemal said with an aggrieved air. 'Or wrote something about it. You still write things or it's just internet nowadays?' He fiddled with the zips on his fishing jacket – a *de rigeur* item amongst all Turks over the age of fifty – and awaited a response.

Rex muttered an apology and, on discovering that he had no cash, handed over a card. Kemal looked at it.

'What you want me to do with this?'

It was the hotel key-card. Rex didn't know what to do with it either. He paid with his bank card and left. Kemal had a point: the robbery trial was pure local news, with a direct impact on the people Rex was meant to be working for. The recent murders were local too, but was it really his job to solve them? He was a journalist, not a detective.

Then he remembered Terry, gaunt and sweating in the cell, pleading for his help. He owed Terry a lot. When Rex had washed up on the shores of the *Wood Green Gazette*, his career on the nationals had been in splinters, he'd just had a nervous breakdown, and his wife no longer recognised him. Not that Terry had fulfilled any kind of spiritual role. He'd just driven Rex about, and talked shite with him into the grey hours over countless beers and takeaways. Yet he'd been more instrumental in repairing Rex's soul than any priest or psychotherapist. So how could he walk away now? How could he not try everything to help?

Making sure the hotel card was safe and separate from the rest of his wallet, he went back into the shop, purchasing from the surprised Kemal a large bottle of the most expensive vodka. It was a brand he'd never heard of, called Dynasty.

'This your dinner?' the Turk quipped gruffly, as he put the bottle in another bag.

* * *

It was a gamble, in fact, but one that paid off. Half an hour later, a bony, bearded Russian pulled up outside Rex's house on a motorbike.

'You look the same,' the man said, as Rex opened the door.

'You look different, Vadim. Where've you been?' Rex croaked, once he'd been released from a violent bear hug.

'Siberia.' Vadim grinned, displaying a row of tiny, perfect teeth.'

'Seriously?'

They went inside. 'Yes. Implementing multi-platform digi-sec systems for gas plants. Dollar wages, very good. But boring. I grew a beard because there was nothing else to do. Really. I only got back a month ago. Actually you were lucky that number worked – I'm just changing it over.'

'So you're back for good?' Rex asked, rubbing the sore patches on his arms.

'Set up my own company. Same thing for domestic.' He looked at Rex with a smile. 'You don't know what I am talking about, do you? OK. Basically, you are bastard Russian gangster, with bastard house in Hampstead, you pay me to put in very expensive bastard alarm system you can access and control from yacht in Monaco, or wherever. I had a revelation. You know, after Milda.'

Milda, a Lithuanian artist, had been Rex's girlfriend. She'd been Vadim's too, slightly later, and shortly before she died. He and

Vadim should have hated each other. But it hadn't worked out like that.

'I say to myself, Vadim, you never will be rich doing IT support for the London Underground. You must go back to Russia, broaden marketable skill-set and monetise emerging tech opportunities in London-Russian client base. See?'

Rex smiled. Milda's death had hardly resulted in a spiritual revelation. But it had worked miracles for Vadim all the same. His long coat was all leather, he realised, and wrapped around the man's sinewy wrist was the sort of watch Wimbledon champions donned for the cameras.

'Where is the card?' Vadim asked, sitting at the table and pouring himself a glass of vodka. Rex passed it across. The Russian tapped the card against his teeth – thinking, Rex assumed, rather than physically checking it for data. But you never knew.

'Depends if 128-bit or just only Crypt-Cab,' Vadim said, hauling a satchel onto his lap. 'How many laptops you got here?'

Half an hour after that, they were both seated at the dining table of the front room of Rex's small, terraced house, with two laptops, a smartphone and an unexplained flat, grey box, which had all been cabled together like some sort of devilish hi-tech bomb.

They'd discovered that the card had last been used on the afternoon of Monday 18th of April at the Borehamwood Travelodge, to open Room 29. After a brief chat-room consultation with someone calling themselves YURISEXDWARF#, Vadim was attempting to access the hotel's secure CCTV site. It was proving reassuringly tricky.

'Who is Yuri?' Rex asked, topping up Vadim's glass with more 'Dynasty' and taking a sip of Okocim.

'My friend. A premium hacker,' Vadim murmured, his fingers whirring over the keys like a swarm of cicadas. 'Actually he has very high position in Uralsib Bank, also.'

Rex tried not to give this too much thought.

'What was the date again?' Vadim asked.

Rex reminded him. As his Russian friend typed on, it occurred to him for the first time that 'Dynasty' could also be read as Die-nasty. And given the volume of bootleg on the streets of Tottenham, that might just be a deliberate joke on the manufacturers' part. This in turn made him wonder something else. If there was bootleg booze, could there be bootleg food too? Could that have been a factor in the Bettelheims' deaths?

Before he could give more time to this, the laptop screen magically parted into six segments, like a kaleidoscope, each showing a grainy, black-and-white view of the hotel precincts.

'See?' Vadim grinned, proud of his work.

'I don't know how you do it, Vadim.'

'Thank Lenin, not me. Serious, Rex. If you say to people, "you must be all equal", it makes them fight to be not equal. I read your Mrs Thatcher book when I was in Siberia. Great woman. But wrong. If you want to stimulate competition, you don't say to the people: "Go! Be competitive." You say, "No. You cannot." You are laughing at me?'

'No, I'm not. I just want to know – what's the time on this footage?'

'11pm.'

'Okay, so, go back to 2 o'clock.'

They watched the view over the Reception desk, speeded up so that every figure seemed to be a marionette. Two blonde girls in mauve uniforms did very little, it appeared, except eat biscuits and laugh at things on the screen of some kind of smartphone. A DHL courier came, with an envelope. Vadim chuckled.

'I saw a porno just like this in Siberia. Two chicks in uniform. Man in leathers. Ah well.'

He sighed as the courier took a signature in return for his envelope and then left. Then a woman came in. She was gaunt-looking and dressed in a long black Puffa coat. Her hair was tied up in a scarf. She glanced up at the camera, and Rex flinched. He felt as though Chaya Bettelheim were looking right at him. Berating him for spying on her. One of the receptionists handed her a plastic card-key – the one, presumably, that was now inside a laptop on Rex's dining-room table. They also passed her a large, buff envelope from behind the desk. It looked like the one the courier had left, though it was hard to be certain.

'Okay, watch second floor…' muttered Vadim. He enlarged the relevant view, and they watched the empty, flickering space for what seemed like an age until Chaya Bettelheim emerged ghost-like from the lift, carrying her package, and passed down the corridor. A view from another camera showed her using the key-card with smooth efficiency to open the door.

'That normally takes me ages.'

Vadim grunted in agreement. 'I think she'd had practice.'

But when? When had a woman from one of Stamford Hill's most reclusive Hasidic groups learned to check into a hotel with such apparent ease and confidence? What business did she have in this anonymous, air-conditioned conference centre at the bottom of the M1? And where did the package fit in?

'Wait!'

Vadim froze the screen. A man had appeared at the end of the corridor, through the fire door. His features were hard to make out, but he was tall and had a similarly gaunt look. He was dressed in a dark coat and a black fedora hat.

'Irish man, I sink,' Vadim quipped, clicking so that the scene played on. The man walked down the corridor, more cautiously, Rex thought, than she had, until he came to the door of 29. He didn't knock, but the door opened. He went in. Vadim gave a low whistle. 'What do you say in English? Forever the quiet ones?'

Rex struggled to think of an innocent, or at least a non-obvious explanation for the sequence he'd just seen. A strictly religious Jewish woman meeting a strictly religious Jewish man in a suburban hotel in the mid-afternoon. Nothing came to mind. Nothing besides the glaringly obvious. His thoughts returned to that strange encounter with Rescha Schild, hesitant in her doorway, wincing as if in pain. Perhaps it wasn't pain, but immense discomfort, because there was something she couldn't say, something she wanted him to find out, and it was this; the tawdry scene on the laptop screen in front of him. Why would she have wanted him to know that the murdered Chaya Bettelheim was having an affair, though? How that would that stop the gossip about her? 'Maybe we should see when they leave,' Vadim suggested. He fast-forwarded. The woman came out two hours later, and left the hotel. The man followed after a further half-hour, again exiting via the back stairs.

'Did they come back?'

'Key was only used once, when she went in.' Vadim said. 'I'll save these for you.' He clicked his fingers. 'Which Cloud you got?'

'Eh?'

Vadim tutted. 'USB then? DVD?'

Rex rummaged in his bag for the DVD he'd been given by the boys at Sylheti Stores. He didn't care if their video message got deleted. Better for them if it was. 'You want me to save these two video files on here?'

'Two?' Rex peered vaguely at the menu. One file was called 'Video Press Release'. He smiled at that – at these junior jihadis and their media-savvy lingo. The other was called 'Khutbah: Malik Waheed al-Shakhrah'. He didn't know what that meant, but there didn't seem any reason to keep either file. 'Not bothered,' he said. 'Whatever's easiest.'

'OK. Then we drive to Bore Ham Wood to see, yes?'

Chapter Three

Rex was awake early, because a delivery truck-driver had trusted in his satnav rather than in the bleeding obvious. As a result, between 6:30 and 7 am, over 30 tonnes of slowly reversing frozen chicken kievs were stuck down the narrow lane outside his house. Unable to ignore the mechanical voice that announced the same very obvious fact every twenty seconds, Rex abandoned his bed, made a large pot of Turkish coffee to wash his painkillers down, and switched on the news.

Between something about budgets and something else about a Junior Minister in an ill-judged fancy dress costume was a piece from Heathrow airport. Ashen-faced Hasidim were shown arriving on a flight from Sydney, greeting others with handshakes and the odd hug. It was a while before Rex clocked that they were Chaya Bettelheim's family, and that they were being met either by their own relations or by Yaakov's. He watched as an apple-cheeked young man from the arrivals party calmly approached the camera and asked to be left alone. 'We want the inquest to be finished with, so that we can bury our loved ones,' he said, in what sounded like a pre-rehearsed speech. Then a tall, striking, red-headed Hasid loomed, placing a large, commanding hand over the camera lens.

Rex was so absorbed by this scene that he didn't notice his phone ringing until it had finished. He picked it up to return the call, assuming it was Susan, who never slept and was no doubt glued to the same news bulletin. But it was a number he didn't recognise. No message. He was about to put down the phone when it rang again. Same, unknown number.

It was Terry. 'The gangs make you pay extra to use the phones,' he said, in a low, urgent voice Rex had never heard before. 'The only way to get round it is to get up before they do. So – sorry if it's early, like.'

'It's fine, Terry. How are you doing?'

'Me cellmate's got schizophrenia,' Terry went on. 'He doesn't wash. Just sits there all day, wanking into his tracksuit. It's fucking terrible, Rex.' He took a deep breath. 'Is there anything?'

'I'm going to talk to all your neighbours today,' Rex said. 'Who's been there the longest?'

Terry sighed at the memory of life before the hell he was in now. 'There's a Greek lady at 322. Sixty-odd, always sniffing about, that sort. She's all right though. On the other side, 326… I dunno, it's a girl. Woman, I mean. Hardly ever there. When she is, she's leaving or arriving with a suitcase. Does some sort of posh job.'

'Blonde?' Rex asked.

'Dunno.'

Rex felt the painkillers kicking in. At last. They seemed to act more slowly on him these days. As the relaxing, unlocking sense of warmth spread from his foot up to his arms and his head, he thought about what Terry was saying. He remembered the blonde woman Bird had been shouting at in the street. Was that the neighbour then? Had she been carrying a case? He couldn't remember. Her hair had certainly been blonde.

'What about over the road?' he asked. 'The person who made the 999 call said she thought something was going on over the road. That means someone opposite. Any idea who she might have been?'

'It's all just Polish kids over the road. And students. All rented out, like. Coming and going. I did remember something, though.'

'What?'

'I'm hardly ever around in the day, with the job and the driving lessons and that. There's only been two times. That day in January I had the shits, and… when I found him. And he had visitors. Each time. Two visitors, both times I was there. Not together, separate. He buzzed 'em in, then played his music.'

An hour later, Rex was sitting in the stuffy, over-trinketed sitting room of Number 322 Langherhans Road. Mrs Gia Christodoulou began by saying that she didn't talk to the press. She added that whatever the doctor got up to had been his own business, and that she wasn't one to judge or interfere.

But of course she couldn't help noticing things, and one of the things she had noticed was that Dr Kovacs had two regular visitors.

'Proper little United Nations it is,' she said, quickly adding that everyone was welcome as far as she was concerned, just as long as they didn't lounge about on the dole making bombs, and didn't force their women to wear bin-bags. Rex steered her gently back to the topic in hand.

'There's an old black man. He's round almost every day. Has been for years.'

Rex remembered seeing Bird outside the house the day before. Was it possible?

'Do you mean Bird? Wears a sheepskin coat. Drinks lager on the High Street.'

She flinched, as if the mere mention of such behaviour might sully the Doulton figurines and the Avon glassware. 'I don't know who does what where round here. If I go out, I keep my head down and get on with it. I certainly don't look anyone in the eye.' She briefly looked Rex in the eye. 'Well, you don't know if they might be someone with a knife or a gun, do you? So many crazies around.'

Rex felt a wave of sympathy for Mrs Christodoulou. His own mother had ended up like her: afraid, paralysed with anxieties that were stoked by the very newspapers she chose to read. Perhaps Mrs Christodoulou would have a happier outlook on the world if she'd moved northwards with the bulk of her fellow Greeks who'd abandoned Wood Green to the incoming Turks. Now, assailed by wave upon wave of fresh arrivals, she was like a miniature island-state, marooned and paranoid.

'Dr Kovacs had another regular visitor too?' he prompted.

'Long black coat, black trousers, all black, black, black hat.' She adjusted her hairdo, which looked like it had been glued in place, strand by strand. 'You know. Siddicks Jew. That's what they're called, isn't it?'

'What did he look like?' Rex asked.

'I already told you.' She picked up a tiny, yappy dog that had begun to eat Rex's shoelaces. 'A Siddicks Jew. I don't look at his face. I don't sit by the window all day. He hasn't been coming all that long. A year maybe. Not like the black one. Can I say he's black or do I have to say something else now?'

'I believe black still covers it. Were you close to Dr Kovacs?'

'Close?!' The tiny Greek lady looked scandalised.

'I didn't mean –'

'I know what you meant. No I was not close to him. He was a rude man. I discovered that in April 1994, when he killed off my fig tree by concreting over his garden, and I went round to complain. After that I never spoke a word to him. I was glad his wife ran off. Good on her, I thought.'

Rex had never considered the possibility that Kovacs might not live alone. 'He had a wife? Where did she go?'

'I don't know!' snapped Mrs Christodoulou. 'One day she and the kid was there. Next day they weren't. There was always rows. I guess she just had enough and went.'

'When was that?'

'Actually it was the day before he concreted his garden over.'

* * *

Vadim was driving. Rex had had to dampen the Russian's enthu-
siasm the night before, because he was needed at the office, but
they'd agreed a time to visit the Travelodge together. Vadim was
keen to show off his new car: a BMW, complete with German
number-plates and a German-speaking sat-nav too. This led to
some confusion, and they ended up severely lost in the Tottenham
Hale area. At one point they found themselves on Chesnut Road,
now a street of almost cottage-like council homes. Rex remembered
that the rubber works had once been here – Schnurrman's, where
the Outrage robbers had briefly worked in 1909, while plotting
their raid on the weekly wages delivery.

They passed down other streets whose names he vaguely recalled,
either because of the pamphlets on the Outrage he'd flipped
through, or because more recent crimes had taken him there. Scales
Road, where rows of bland, 1960s bungalows were broken up by
dramatic, fairy-tale trees. Marsh Lane, wide and windswept – the
Pumping Station on one side; on the other a vast, white Pente-
costalist tent, where in the summer you could see wild Nigerian
pastors blessing mobile phones and lifting curses.

They crossed the marshes that separated Tottenham from
Walthamstow, where the Outrage had had its bloody final act
after two deaths, 23 casualties and 300 bullets. Rex wondered why
Walthamstow hadn't claimed the Outrage for its own, along with
William Morris and East 17. Then he wondered why he and Vadim
were heading towards Walthamstow at all.

'Vadim, we're going the wrong way. This is east.'

Vadim struck the satnav a blow with the heel of his palm and
did a U-turn. The blow didn't cure the machine of its Teutonic
leanings, but within minutes they found themselves back on the
North Circular, heading in the right direction. West, towards the
Borehamwood Travelodge.

After seeing Mrs Christodolou Rex had felt fired up, certain
he was onto something. He'd tried the house on the other side,

Number 326, and finding it empty, left a note asking the occupant to call him when she returned. Now, though, he was starting to wonder. After his accident, Rex had been ill. And in the hospital where they'd looked after him, they'd told him that seeing links everywhere was part of the illness – a sign that his imagination was taking over from reality. Was that happening now? Perhaps things really were as simple as they looked from the outside, and Terry had killed Kovacs in a fit of unneighbourly rage. He hated to think it, but that possibility, he knew, had to be allowed in.

If anything could cast doubt on that terrible idea, though, he wanted to find it. And he sensed the doubt would come from Kovacs. The crabby historian had been there when the Bettelheims died. Not only that, but he had definitely behaved oddly, fleeing the scene in what looked like panic. Not to mention being found dead himself just a short time later. And someone, described by the old lady as a Hasidic Jew, had been had been a visitor to Kovacs' house. Surely these were real links, at the very least coincidences worth exploring, and not just figments of his imagination?

Yet what didn't seem to link in at all was the other visitor – the black man. Had Mrs Christodoulou really never looked at him, as she maddeningly insisted? Could anyone in the Wood Green area fail to recognise Bird, even if they didn't peer directly at him? Then again, what possible reason could a man like Bird have had to pay regular visits to Dr Kovacs' house? It seemed so unlikely.

Rex took a call on his mobile. It was the man from the firm who'd been printing Kovacs' book. 'We found a few things, but I'm not sure they'll be much use to you.'

'What are they?'

'Whoever did our place over dumped a lot of stuff in a skip down the road. There's a chunk of pages that are definitely from his book. And a sort of… notebook I suppose you'd say. Nice old leather-bound thing. Handwritten.'

'You're sure that belonged to Kovacs?'

'I'm sure. He parcelled it up with the manuscript when he sent it to us – wanted us to use some of the pages for the back-cover design. I should probably be handing it to the police, shouldn't I?'

'Well, I guess that's up to you,' Rex said, trying to mask his annoyance. Why call him, only to announce that he wasn't going to help? 'But I don't think they'll be interested. They think they've got their man.'

'Hmm,' said the man, after a pause. 'All right. I'll pop it in the post to you.'

Rex hung up as Vadim drew into a hotel car-park, abutted by a low, red-brick conference centre. Not far away, just beyond the tailored verges and the uniformly trimmed laburnums, the M1 roared. This was the real England, away from the tin-shuttered spice halls and teeming, tribal highways of Haringey. This world was corporate, dull, neat: a landscape of business centres and motorway exits. He was glad he didn't live in it.

The same two girls he'd seen in the footage were on the Reception Desk. Polish. Agnieska and Ewa. They were both pretty in a blonde way, and dismissive in a uniquely Slavic way that was rude yet without intending any personal insult. They didn't remember the woman, or the name Bettelheim. Besides, guest information was confidential. Lots of women came through here, they added – alone or in company.

'Do they all pick up packages at the desk?' Rex asked.

'Business people get things sent to here all the time,' Ewa said, in a voice that sounded as if she was trying hard not to open her mouth. 'We've got all the facilities.'

'A woman in a headscarf doesn't ring any bells?'

'Why doesn't she ring bells?' Agnieska asked innocently.

Rex and Vadim left the girls snickering amongst themselves, and snuck round the back, to the laundry. It was Vadim's idea. The cleaners and chamber-maids would hang out here, he said, something he knew from a stint working as a concierge in Frankfurt.

They'd be on less money than the receptionists. Which meant more willing to help. Or more easily bribed.

It was a good hunch. The laundry smelt strangely comforting: of starch and steam and women's sweat. It reminded Rex of his mother, who had done ironing for the neighbours. When he described the Jewish couple, a pair of African women in striped tunics cackled.

'We know them!' declared one, a motherly figure called Blessings. 'Stay two hours, and go. Two hours, and go.'

'What, they just…?' Rex found he couldn't say it. But the other woman, a tougher-looking, lighter-skinned woman called Gloria snorted.

'They don't have SEX!' she more or less sang. 'They jos' use the rooms.'

Rex was lost. 'What for?'

Blessings shrugged. Gloria displayed one gold tooth and then sucked it. 'Watch TV. Look internet. Drink mini-bar. They *use* everything. Just not the bed.'

'Why?'

Gloria and Blessings shrugged as one, not seeming that bothered, and hurriedly went back to folding towels and stacking carts as Agnieska from Reception appeared. Rex imagined she was here to turf them out, but instead she smiled awkwardly.

'I thought you might come in here,' Agnieska said, tightly. She spoke as if she were outside in a gale, without a coat. Maybe it had something to do with coming from a cold country. 'I looked up that name you said, Bettelheim. It's that woman, isn't it? From the family in the park?'

'Did she stay here under that name?'

'They came a lot actually.'

'They?'

'The husband and wife.'

'How you know they were husband and wife?' Vadim asked, sharply.

'The last time he was here, the man gave me this.' She handed them a card. It was for a jeweller's in Hatton Garden called J.R.R.S. The initials stood for Jewels, Resizing, Repairs, Supplies, and beneath that were the words: Yaakov Bettelheim, Senior Technician. 'He noticed my engagement ring was loose,' she said, twisting the silver band on her finger as she spoke. 'He said he could resize it.'

Rex asked if he could keep the card. She said she didn't mind. She was pregnant now, she added, bashfully, and the ring was getting tighter every day.

'Have you any idea why they would meet up in that room?'

She shrugged. 'To watch DVDs? That was what was in the package. You could feel it. Every week. DVDs.'

Why would a wife meet her husband in a hotel room miles away from where they lived to watch DVDs? Vadim and Agnieska seemed to have no more idea than he did. But perhaps Rescha Schild knew.

* * *

Rex returned to the office just after lunch. He was itching to go back to Stamford Hill, but it was Wednesday. Deadline day for the free paper, which consisted mainly of adverts and competitions, with the odd, filleted news or comment piece designed to lure people onto the website. Every Thursday morning he'd find copies of it strewn all over Ducketts Common. It made a mockery of the preceding night's efforts. It still had to be done, though.

Rex, Brenda and Susan took in turns to do the final layout. It was his turn today, which meant a slightly later stint. He enjoyed it, though, for nostalgic reasons, tending the mock-up like some priest on a vigil, eyes itching under the lights, the office smelling nutty with coffee and sweat as the minutes ticked towards to that magical point when you pressed the 'lock' button and the paper was 'put to bed'.

He switched on his computer. While it booted up, he watched Susan show some men out of her office. These days she was often cloistered in there with groups of men. Some were middle-aged, suited and hearty, with the look of local councillors. Others, like the group shuffling out now, were young and cool and studiedly scruffy. The specific purpose of these meetings was never explained, but Rex, like everyone else, knew generally why they were taking place. Because News North London was slowly, inexorably, going under.

'It's kind of like December without Christmas now, isn't it?' Susan said, stopping by his desk. As always, she smelt of fresh linen.

He knew what she meant. The constant updating of the website had taken the magic out of the process. The week no longer had a shape, no longer built to a delectable Sabbath-like point when you pressed a button and declared the paper ready. They might pretend that Wednesday was deadline day, but they all knew it was just a pretence. But he was surprised to hear Susan admit it.

'Did you see your Post-it?' she added.

He had not. Brenda understood Post-its in principle, but had not grasped the practical necessity of putting them where they would be noticed. This one was stuck to the side of Rex's monitor, towards the back. It said, in neat, Junior-School-teacher's handwriting: *A nun called round for you. No message.*

No message was necessary. He knew exactly who the nun was. And what she had meant to convey. So did Susan, who was still hovering by his desk, and Brenda, and the Whittaker Twins, and Lawrence Berne, and the thousand pairs of eyes that now seemed to be staring in at him from the sky outside. It was time to go up the hill. He could go tonight, once he'd sorted the paper out. Yes, that was what he would do.

He glanced up. Susan was still there, her mouth framing a question. It never came, though, because his phone rang. It was Mike Bond – Brenda's husband, the coroner. He was calling from somewhere outdoors, and Rex thought he could hear shouting in the background.

'Any more news on where the cyanide came from?' Rex asked.

'There is some news on that, but I can't tell you now.'

'What can you tell me, Mike?'

'I'm at the mortuary. The Bettelheim family's down here. It's all kicking off.'

* * *

One sign of change was the beggars, Rex thought, as the bus crept down the High Street towards the junction. They were definitely working harder for their cash. Where an outstretched hand or an indecipherable hard-luck story on a scrap of cardboard might once have sufficed, now there were active scams.

The gypsy girls, for example, had veiled up and donned rucksacks and clipboards to pass themselves off as pious Turkish students soliciting donations for wherever happened to be the current Islamic crisis zone. Further down, a man who used to sit outside ShoeZone in a dirty tracksuit was now swathed in a vaguely Afghan-looking array of scarves and waistcoats. He had also taken to waving what purported to be the stump of an arm at people, although everyone but the newest of newcomers knew this was just his old, perfectly intact limb, with a MaxiCoke cup from Burger King shoved over its old, perfectly intact elbow.

They weren't the only ones putting on an act, Rex thought. After all, most of the kids round here pretended to be Jamaican, even if their parents were Greek Cypriots. And if his last encounter with the Sunday supplements was anything to go on, the middle class lot up the road in Crouch End all wanted to live and eat and do up their flats as if they were Italians, or Japanese, or indeed anyone they were not. Perhaps that was what globalisation really meant. Anyone could be everyone they were not.

The bus turned right onto Turnpike Lane, and picked up speed as it passed under the railway bridge permanently festooned with Kurdish slogans and emblems of the PKK. There'd been yet another doomed attempt to turn the Old Pumping Station into a Mecca for fine diners. The current proprietors had resorted to painting enticing trigger words for the moneyed middle classes all over its windows, like magic charms or Pavlovian stimuli. *Veal bones. Truffle oil. Prosecco.*

The Pumping Station marked a geographical caesura. As you moved past it, you entered a region that was still scruffy but had more in common with the adjacent areas of Crouch End and Muswell Hill. Here you saw dads looking after babies. People who drove camper vans and made sourdough bread and learnt the ukulele. It wasn't so much about income, perhaps, as outlook.

Tucked behind the main thoroughfare, with Ally Pally looming up above, was the low, modern building that housed the mortuary and coroner's office. As he walked down towards it, Rex remembered another time Mike Bond had summoned him there – a dark night last year, when he'd had to identify the remains of a former lover. It was one memory among many. The truth was, his job often took him to Hornsey Mortuary, and often in response to a call from Mike.

He spotted Brenda's husband, his wavy white hair dancing in the light breeze, his grey suit echoing the saggy, surprised look of a body suddenly thin after decades of being fat. He was standing a little way from the building, talking to a WPC as a small crowd of black-coated Hasidim milled around the entrance. They seemed to be arguing both among themselves and with the uncomfortable-looking line of policemen who stood directly in front of the doors. In their midst Rex recognised the tall, muscular, red-headed man he'd seen on TV, greeting family members at the airport.

'What's the beef?' Rex asked, as he joined Bond. 'And don't say *kosher brisket.*'

'This isn't the time for jokes,' Bond replied shortly. 'This lot are really upset. They're not unlike your Muslims, see. Desert cultures – they want to bury the bodies as quickly as they can.'

'And the police won't release the bodies before the inquest?'

Bond nodded. 'And we can't hold the inquest until the pathologist has completed some tests on the Bettelheim boy.'

'The teenager? What tests?'

Bond shifted Rex away from the WPC and lowered his voice. 'Needle marks. Both arms. Plus, evidence of a nasty subcutaneous infection, which cleared up, but left some scars. No mention of anything on his GP's records.'

'They had a GP?' As he considered this, Rex caught sight of D.S. Brenard, standing over the road, talking earnestly into his phone.

Bond frowned. 'They're just normal people, Rex. Normal people with rules that sometimes bump up against ours.'

Something suddenly changed the mood of the crowd, and it surged forward. The tall red-head grabbed one of the door handles. Rex studied him. There was something odd about his face. It was strong-jawed, thick-necked. The face of someone who played sport, which in itself seemed somewhat unusual for a Hasid. But that wasn't it.

'Sir, I will arrest you if you do not desist,' said a young, sweating copper.

'Do whatever you like,' the man declared, in a loud, American accent. 'We're taking our dead!'

Rex began to film on his camera phone as a scuffle broke out. A hat was knocked askew, shins and groins were kicked, faces reddened. Incredibly, there was no swearing.

And then there was.

'For fuck's sake pack it in or I'll pepper-spray the lot of you!' D.S. Brenard roared as he ploughed into the thick of the brawl. It provided just the shock everyone needed. The crowd pulled back. The big red-head kept his hold on the handle of the mortuary door, then finally backed away after a warning glare from Brenard.

'Right,' Brenard said, with the controlled menace of a teacher in the playground. 'This is the situation. The mortuary is open between the hours of 8am and 8pm. During those hours, a maximum of two people will be permitted to stay in a room adjacent to the bodies. Between the hours of 8pm and 8am, I understand there will be a special kind of candle in a protective box, which will be kept lit out here, and which can be tended by as many of you as you like. The bodies, Mr Dordoff, will be released when the inquest is complete. Any further attempt to remove them before that time will be treated as a criminal offence.'

The voices of protest rose up again. This time, it was the flame-haired man, the one Brenard had called Dordoff, who roared for quiet.

'So it's only once a group of highly distressed people who've travelled halfway around the world come and beg, that you agree to some basic, humane concessions! Or perhaps it's only because the media are here?' he added, shooting a piercing blue gaze at Rex. The man didn't have a beard, Rex realised. That was it. He wore earlocks – impressively long ones. But he was clean-shaven.

'I apologise if we've been slow to respect your cultural needs,' Brenard said.

Dordoff ignored the apology. 'You have not been slow to come to our neighbourhood and spread suspicion and fear! These people are not only grieving over the sudden loss of their loved ones: they're dealing with lies, malicious lies, spreading through the community, that accuse Chaya Bettelheim of poisoning her own family! Where did those lies come from?'

Brenard held his hands up. 'The officer responsible for that ill-judged line of enquiry has been taken off the investigation. I am also authorised to inform you that there has been a development, and it now looks highly unlikely that Chaya Bettelheim... well...' The detective faltered as he looked at what were obviously the relatives of the dead woman. 'We are not pursuing that line of enquiry,' he concluded weakly.

There was a change in the crowd; a tiny, almost imperceptible slackening, as if a knot had been loosened. Dordoff removed his hat, and scratched under his skullcap.

'What is the development?' he asked.

'A forensic development. We have been able to conclude with certainty that the poison was neither present in the Bettelheim house, nor handled by any of the family prior to its being swallowed. I should add that it took time to arrive at that conclusion. Time we would not have had if we had immediately released the bodies for burial. We still need more time, and we're asking for your understanding.'

Rex sidled back towards Bond, asking quietly. 'Is that true?'

Bond nodded. 'And it wasn't exactly cyanide, either.'

'So what was it?'

Bond shrugged. 'We don't know yet. Something similar, but the symptoms are slightly different from what you see in industrial cyanide cases. There's not a lot to go on because it was absorbed by the bodies so quickly. We've sent off tissue samples to the poisons lab, but they're snowed under...'

Rex looked back towards the ruck. Brenard and Dordoff, who seemed to have been appointed the family's spokesman, were still eyeing one another tensely, but the rest of the group had moved apart, and people had begun to talk among themselves. Relations had been repaired, at least for the moment.

Rex realised he was standing next to the fresh-faced young man who'd spoken to the cameras on the news that morning before being usurped by Dordoff. He stretched out his hand. 'Rex Tracey. I work for the local paper.'

'Limburg, Moses,' came the reply, along with a handshake.

'Chaya's brother?'

'Nephew,' Moses Limburg said with a faint smile. He was a handsome boy, with rosy cheeks. 'Big families.'

Rex smiled back. 'Can you think of any reason why someone would want to harm Chaya and her family?'

Moses Limburg took a long time to reply. Finally he said softly: 'An example, maybe?'

'An example of what?'

Limburg seemed poised to say more when Dordoff loomed behind, clapping a brotherly hand on his shoulder. The effect was marked. Moses reddened. 'I – you get the wrong word when you use Yiddish all day, sorry. I meant like a spectacle.'

'A spectacle?' Rex looked from the kid to the tall man. Dordoff's face conveyed nothing.

'Yes, I mean, you know how terrorists do something to make a spectacle. To make everybody notice.'

Rex was still thinking about Limburg's reply when he got back to the office, armed with footage to upload onto the website. Had he really meant an example, but changed tack when Dordoff appeared? If so, what kind of example? And what role did the tall, athletic Dordoff have in it all? At the airport he'd waved away the cameras, to all appearances to protect the family. At the mortuary, he'd spoken on their behalf. Yet somehow he seemed more like an agitator. Then, as he ushered Moses Limburg away, more like a minder. Rex spent some time searching for Dordoffs and Daudovs on Google, but turned up nothing.

Oppressed by so many unanswered questions, he went out and spent too much money on baklava. The soggy pastries gave him a queasy, sugar-fuelled rush which kept him going through the afternoon dip, so that he was ready to lock the paper just before seven o'clock.

Alone in the building, he eyed Susan's office. It contained a tiny shower, a facility which, though no word had ever been pronounced on the topic, was accepted to be out of bounds to anyone but her. Rex had used it before a couple of times in the dead hours of the night, drying himself with his shirt, and feeling as though he'd done something indecent.

He felt sticky and grimy now, and he was just wondering whether the nuns in the convent would mind him showing up with the 'Jesus and Mary Chain' T-shirt he kept as a spare in his drawer, when the phone rang.

'Fancy a quick half when you've tucked him up in bed?'

It was Ellie Mehta, somewhere crowded and jolly. After something, no doubt.

'You think I'm going to trek over to some cunty joint in Hoxton at seven o'clock?'

'I'm just down the road in The Salisbury,' she shouted, above a clatter of glasses and a roar. 'Catching up with some old flatmates. Come on. I want to know how Terry's doing. I do care, you know.'

He missed all of that, the nights getting sloshed when the job was done. Lawrence's recent mention of Diana had made him realise how much he missed something else: the company of a woman. A woman's eyes. A woman's interest. Her otherness, and warmth, and smell, especially when she was close to you in the sudsy, glowing snugness of a pub-bar. Besides, he wanted to talk to anyone who might listen for a few minutes about the weirdness of the day, about the darkness that surrounded Terry and the Damoclean sword that seemed to hang ever lower over the job he loved.

But there was his wife. He had a wife to visit. And he'd promised.

'See you in half an hour,' he said into the phone, and hung up quickly.

In the event it was more like twenty minutes, and during that time Rex went through several changes of heart. All became clear, though, as he passed through the wooden doors into an arena at once sacred and everyday.

His favourite local boozer was rammed with young men in check shirts and elaborate whiskers, giving it the look of a Wild West saloon. Most had only been there to support a band whose early slot was now finished, and within ten minutes the cavernous Victorian drinking palace was almost deserted. He'd steeled himself for an encounter with Ellie's former flatmates, anticipating a mix of skinny, belligerent boys and tubby, flinty girls, but in fact he'd found her sitting alone at a little booth, with a pair of pints on the table in front of her.

He'd also steeled himself to resist her blandishments and not give away too much. She'd already asked about Terry. So he'd talk about Terry. Everything else was off limits. With Ellie, he'd found, it was best to set rules in advance.

He sat down opposite her. She began by saying she couldn't stop thinking about Terry, which no doubt was a preamble to asking him to get her a Visiting Order so she could go and interview him in Pentonville. But then she said she couldn't face seeing him. She would write him a letter instead. And she wanted to help in any way she could.

'So the story has nothing to do with it, then?' he said, then instantly regretted it. She looked genuinely hurt.

'We were all mates,' she said, patches of red appearing on her cheeks. 'I don't know why that has to change just because I work somewhere else.' She started zipping up her bag, lips tight. He recognised the signs.

'Sorry,' he said. 'We are mates. Sorry. I'm a twat sometimes. And you *can* help…'

'You are a twat,' she said, but stayed, and let him tell her about the mysterious 999 caller, and about Dr Kovacs' sinister concrete garden. As she listened, she kept rubbing her thumb with her index finger. Rex knew the gesture. She was itching to make notes.

'What does it look like round the back of the house? Nice, professional concreting job? Or something he did himself at midnight?'

Rex realised he hadn't looked. It was a good question. An ageing history lecturer was unlikely to be a dab hand at concreting. Or, if he'd just buried his family under the turf, to hire a gang of Wembley-Irish bhoys in to do the work.

Ellie went off to fetch another pair of pints, promising to do some digging of her own when she got the chance.

'Now tell me about Cambodia,' she said when she returned. 'We haven't had a proper catch-up since then.'

A catch-up. His wife had used that term, whenever she went off to have drinks with her friends. Because that's what they did. They caught up. Exchanged information about one another. What did men do? They either took the piss, or they competed to see who could piss the furthest, same as when they were twenty. Or fourteen. Or seven. God, he missed women. He missed his wife. He missed Milda, the strange, winsome Lithuanian artist with whom he'd often drunk in this very pub before her death up at Alexandra Palace. He'd been with someone else the night they found her body. With Diana…

'Cambodia… Well, she seemed very pleased to see me. We had a great few days – visiting the temples, going on the lake. Nice.'

'Nice in a knickers-off way?'

'Nearly.' Even the mere mention of knickers made him feel how empty and sterile his existence had been since then. The nearest he got to ladies' underwear these days was walking past it to the booze aisle in Marks and Spencer. 'She said she needed more time…'

'Oh.' The tone of that single syllable amply conveyed Ellie's view that 'needing more time' was not cause for optimism. A woman understood that, clearly, whereas a man, or at least this man, had little chance of doing so.

'She had to go back to work at the hospital, and I went off round the country. Up north. Over into Laos.' He smiled. 'I even found an opium den.'

Ellie made an impatient gesture, not interested in this detail.

'So, then I came back. We arranged to meet in this nice colonial-style bar in Siem Reap. I had a white suit on, and I was smoking at the bar, and I'd lost some weight, and I felt like I was in a film.' He sat back on his beer-stained velvet stool, for a moment back in the orient, hearing the whirr of the fans, feeling the chill of the glass on his fingers, sitting on that terrace at the edge of the black, throbbing jungle night, so dense and fragrant and steamy it felt like a bathroom. 'And in she walks, looking absolutely beautiful.

And with her was this fucking great Viking in cut-off jeans. When I'd arrived he'd been away in Bangkok learning some new surgical technique or something…'

He took a morose swig of beer.

'So they were on a break and she was having doubts and then you came along…' She filled it in, effortlessly.

'The worst thing is, he's not a twat. He's interesting. Quite funny. Certainly not thick.' He remembered Kjell explaining the different idols in a temple on Wat Bo Road as in the background a choir of monks softly chanted through the incense smoke. He remembered longing to pick up the nearest joss-stick and stick it somewhere unforgivable.

'Sounds like he has a massive ego more devoted to saving the world than devoting itself to her… and when she's had her jungle fling with him…'

'I can confidently expect her to put her dreams behind her and come back and settle for the local journalist with the fucking limp? Right.'

He'd said this a little too savagely. People turned round, and the barmaid stopped taking glasses out of the washer.

'Rex, come on. She's out there, on her own. What's she meant to do? Light a little candle in front of your picture every night? Most people… most people want a shag every now and then. Everyone. Even those nutters down in Stamford Hill do it once a week. On the Sabbath. Did you know that? That's why you see hundreds of Bulgarian gypsies flogging roses up and down the road at lunchtime on Friday.' She chuckled. 'To all the rabbis on a promise.'

It seemed a little out of the blue, this sudden reference to the story they were both trailing. But it was a welcome diversion from the sad topic of his sex life.

'The people of Stamford Hill are freakier than you'd imagine.' He pulled the keycard out of his pocket, and told her what he'd discovered at the Travelodge – that before their deaths Yaakov and

Chaya Bettelheim had paid regular visits to a hotel, apparently to watch DVDs together.

'Rude DVDs?'

'I don't know. According to the staff nothing else, you know, went on in the room...'

'Maybe they watched rude DVDs, then rushed home and did it through a sheet with a hole in it.'

'I don't buy that sheet thing. Anyway, it is just possible, Ellie, that sex has nothing to do with it. Perhaps they just... watched films.'

'Why go all the way to the Borehamwood Travelodge to watch *The Muppets*?'

'Maybe because they're not supposed to have anything to do with—'

'– muppets?'

'Modernity. DVDs. Naked flesh. Bad talk. I don't know. Aren't they a bit like the Amish?'

'Who are constantly in the news for various kinds of illicit shagging. Trust me. This has got sex all over it... Or else they were Mossad agents, picking up instructions from their spymaster. Or Hezbollah agents, posing as Jews.'

'You really think that?'

'It's got to be weirder than a married couple going to a hotel in the afternoon to watch Hollywood blockbusters. You can have that tip for free.'

* * *

Rex may not have possessed the sharpest of street instincts but, living where he did and coming home so often in a befuddled state in the small hours, he'd developed a personal checklist that more or less worked. As he neared the parade with the hairdresser and the driving school, his checklist told him that the group of boys on the pavement outside it had more than a casual relationship with bother. Was it the faint, bonfire whiff of skunk weed that trailed behind them? The skewed trousers, the studied, rolling gait? Or the way one of them, meerkat-like, repeatedly swivelled this way and that in search of danger or opportunity? At any rate, the clues stacked up enough for Rex to hang a right and walk down Langherhans Road. Terry's road. A longer route: duller, darker, but also, he hoped, safer.

It had been an odd, truncated evening with Ellie. He'd become drunk in an unusually short space of time, it seemed to him, and started talking about himself with uncharacteristic intimacy. She'd gone quiet, begun to fiddle with her phone, and then suddenly declared a need to be getting on home, even though it was only half-past eight. She'd talked a lot about sex too, which wasn't exactly like her. Rex wondered if she'd been drunker than he'd thought. He hoped she'd was okay getting home. He should have made sure.

A guilty sense of unfulfilled obligations was still with him as he passed Number 324. He remembered Terry's words under the migraine-lights of the holding cell. 'I didn't do it. I need your help.' He had achieved little so far. But what else could he do? And then there was the ever present, never adequately fulfilled duty he owed his wife.

He stopped at 326, the house where he'd dropped the note. No lights on anywhere. Peering through the letterbox, Rex saw his note where it had fluttered down onto the parqueted hallway. She hadn't been back.

A blue, wavering light glowed from the front room of 322. Mrs Christodoulou had the TV on loud. By the sounds of it she was watching the worst sort of programme for a nervous old lady living on her own: a cop show.

However, safely enveloped as she was in sirens and terrible dialogue, Mrs Christodoulou wouldn't be alarmed by the sound of him creeping round the back of Number 324. The house was detached on the right, Kovacs' side, and a narrow passageway led to a rickety wooden gate that fell open at a touch of its pitted, flaking surface. As the door swung back, a security light on Mrs Christodoulou's wall flashed on, illuminating the garden-facing side of the gate. Rex saw that it was covered in scratches and cuts, as though it had been hacked with something sharp. He wondered if the police had noticed it. He took a picture with his phone.

Up some steps at the back was a narrow garden, divided, ridiculously, into two even narrower strips by a low chicken-wire fence. Most gardens round here were split up, but generally their owners had done it sensibly, horizontally, affording each occupant a relatively private patch of their own. The straight-down-the-middle approach here breathed pettiness and dispute. Rex could picture Dr Kovacs insisting on this millimetre-precise division to some poor co-resident who'd fled years before Terry arrived.

Terry's patch looked wild: grass and bush mostly, overhung by a massive, blossoming sycamore on the side belonging to the mysterious, absent female neighbour. Kovacs', by contrast, looked like the top floor of an NCP car park: a flat, concrete space, with a stack of breeze-blocks in one corner. He wondered what type of personality did that to a place that could have flowers and fruit in it. Someone who didn't want the responsibility? No, that was Terry, and if you were like that, you did what Terry had in fact done – just leave nature to claim it back. Something else had motivated the concrete. An inner bleakness? Or an external secret that needed hiding?

It was a bright, chilly spring night, the light from the street lamps bouncing back off the cloud to tinge everything orange. He paced the length of Kovacs' concrete strip, noting that it was uniformly smooth. A professional job then. He turned and looked back at the house.

Dr Kovacs had lived alone. But a light was on in his house.

A window was open, too.

On both sides, below the ground floor windows, there was a recess where the tip of another window disappeared into the ground. The house had a basement. That explained why he'd come up those steps after the gate.

A light was shining from the strip of window visible above ground.

Terry had never mentioned a basement.

Keeping to the edge of the garden, Rex crept towards the house and bent down to peer through the basement window. It was a low room, spanning the whole of the bottom part of the house, and was lit by a single fluorescent strip. He could see the edge of a simple, wooden table, with what looked like box files on it. Elsewhere, all around, stacked in piles from the floor to the wooden beams, were dull brown archive boxes, some named, others numbered. There was a bottle of beer on the table, among the files. And the curling remnants of a doner kebab in its paper. Was someone living down there? A squatter hiding out, reading through Kovacs' archives out of sheer boredom? Unlikely. But someone had been there, and recently. He remembered Mrs Christodoulou talking about Kovacs' regular visitors – a black man, and a Hasidic Jew. Did they have some business down here? Rex straightened up. He reached in his pocket for his phone to call the police. There was a glint of reflected movement in the screen as he held it up, then he heard a grunt behind him, then a dull thud, before the searing pain in his head gave way to falling and blackness.

* * *

When Rex woke up, the throbbing head and the stale-bread taste of last night's beer made him think he had a hangover. Instinctively he put out a hand for the glass of blackcurrant squash he always placed on his bedside table before going to sleep. He touched dusty, cold concrete. The surprise forced his eyes open, only for the light to send twin ice-picks of pain into each socket. He screwed his eyes shut and felt something hard being shoved between his lips. A bitter-tasting liquid washed into his mouth.

Warm, flat beer. *Zubr*. The one Polish beer he refused to drink. He spat it out in alarm and tried to sit up.

'Sorry. It's the only liquid I have to give you. Thank God you're okay. I got you in through the window all right but then you passed out again. I thought I'd killed you!'

A figure swam into focus. It looked like one of the boys from the pub, holding a beer bottle. Skinny, in super-tight, pigeon-grey jeans and a red check shirt. Facial hair best suited to an Edwardian Sea Lord. And a pair of large, brown, doleful eyes that seemed faintly familiar.

'Were you in the pub?' Rex asked slowly, each syllable producing a new and surprising level of cranial discomfort.

The boy shook his head, obviously confused.

Rex realised they were in the basement, which did indeed extend all the way under the house, though there were no signs of Terry's possessions among Kovacs' boxes and files. He noticed a row of dictionaries along a wall shelf. Latvian-English. Yiddish-English. Russian-English. A grotty basement, but a serious workplace. He sat up and leaned against the cold, damp wall. It felt a little better. He touched his scalp gingerly. It was moist. He winced.

'Sorry. I thought you were a burglar.'

'How do you know I'm not?'

In answer, the boy held up a business card taken from Rex's wallet, which lay on the table.

'Rex Tracey, Reporter, News North London.'

'And who are you?'

'Sam Greenhill,' the young man said, pulling up the chair. 'This is – *was* – my Dad's house.'

Rex nodded. The effort made him feel nauseous. That was where he'd seen those eyes before – on Dr Kovacs. Large, heavy-lidded, somewhere between Prince Michael of Kent and an old, sad bloodhound.

'I thought you were under the patio,' he said. 'You and your mum. That's why I was in the garden. Then I saw the light on.'

The boy frowned. He looked to be about twenty, with an ungainly, uncertain manner, as if he'd somehow landed in his body quite recently and wasn't used to it. 'Why would we be under the patio?'

'Something a neighbour said. About your dad concreting the garden over and you and your mum disappearing.'

Sam snorted. 'Disappearing? We went to live with my gran in Chigwell.'

Rex suddenly remembered that the boy had lost his father. 'I'm sorry about your dad...' Sam made no reply. 'You'll have had a visit from the police, I take it?' he went on. 'You know the next door neighbour's in custody?'

'The bald Geordie bloke. A mate of yours, yeah? Since you both work for that news... thing?'

Rex almost smiled. Not a paper. Not a website. Just a 'thing'. The boy's verdict was more useful than the advice of the dozens of focus groups and social media consultants Susan had shelled out for. Nobody knew what the fuck they were, anymore. And that was the problem. He forced his attention back to the conversation.

'The bald Geordie bloke says he didn't do it. I believe him. That's why I'm here – to find out who did. Any ideas, Sam Greenhill?'

Sam shook his head. The side-parting barely moved. Brylcreem and whiskers and pigeon-leg jeans. What a look. 'I don't really care who did it, to be honest. Dad was a bastard. Mum moved out with me when I was two, and he never had any contact with me at all. Never sent a birthday card. Never gave her a penny, either, even though he was loaded. That's why I'm here. To see if the fucker left a will, and if we're in it.'

He waved a hand at the open box files. Rex noticed ink stains on the boy's fingers, in many colours.

'Any luck?' Rex stood up. He felt a little dizzy, but more or less stable. He took a step back and felt something sharp dig into his back, just below the shoulders. Turning round, he saw a ghastly little iron hook protruding from the wall just below the beams. He touched his back tenderly. The hook had pierced his suit jacket.

'Yeah, sorry, I should have warned you. It's got me a couple of times, too.'

'What's it for, hanging hams off?'

'Probably just to cause a bit of pain,' Sam said. 'Anyway, I can't find anything resembling a will. It all seems to be about his book. Pity. I was hoping to go back to my mum with some good news.'

'She knows you're here?'

Sam laughed, his face briefly becoming almost beautiful. 'She'd totally kill me. I know why – there's a *process*. They try to find out if he lodged a will anywhere, and if he didn't – and there are no closer next-of-kin – we can apply for probate and all that… But mum needs money now. Her business is going down the spout. Up the spout… whatever.'

'What business?'

'She sent me to a good school and now she's paying my course fees, and she deserves something, you know? She deserves something. It's a jeweller's, in Hatton Garden.'

Rex asked the name of the jeweller's. He wasn't surprised by the answer. J.R.S.S. The place where Yaakov Bettelheim worked as a Senior Technician – at least according to his business card. More and more strands were threading their way between the Bettelheims and Dr Kovacs. Was Mrs Greenhill the link?

Or… was it her delicate-featured, handsome son, with the skinny jeans and the ink-stained fingers? Rex was pretty sure that Terry's origins and accent hadn't been mentioned in any of the media stories, and the single photo being circulated was an old one, from last year's *Wood Green Gazette*, in which Terry had a reasonable head of hair.

So if Sam Greenhill knew that the accused was 'a bald Geordie', then he knew far more than he was letting on.

Chapter Four

Brenda had brought in her celebrated ginger flapjacks this morning. She baked twice a week, bringing a portion of the produce into work in a tartan tin with a picture of a Scotch Piper on the lid. There was a lot more produce these days, probably due to Mike, Brenda's husband, being on a strict diet after his heart-attack.

The toasty, gingery smell gave Rex hope as he came through the doors. Hope which vanished as he saw Brenda at the Reception desk with Lawrence Berne, cheeks bulging. They were poring over something, and they froze as he walked in. Whatever it was, Brenda pulled it out of sight swiftly.

'Ginger-jack?' she asked, thickly, proffering the tin.

'I'd rather see what you were just looking at.'

'My sonnet about the roadworks on Laker Street,' Lawrence said, hastily. He was wearing a tie with little golf-balls on it. 'I loved the cuts you made. It must be very tricky, editing a sonnet. If I was wearing a hat, I'd take it off to you.'

Brenda chuckled, as she invariably did at Lawrence's jokes, however poor. Frowning, Rex went up the stairs to the main office, where he soon discovered the secret.

SECRET LIFE OF TRAGIC PARK PARENTS

That was the headline. Underneath it was the byline: Ellie Mehta. And in a paper for which, as far as Rex had known, she didn't even work. Her first splash for her new bosses, he assumed, as he read through the article in the copy of *The Times* Susan had left open on his chair.

'She stiffed you good and proper,' Susan said, for once visibly rattled. 'What did she do – come on to you?'

Rex blew his nose. His cold had at last shown its hand, the early sore throat and chills giving way to rivers of snot and a permanent light-headedness. Not to mention the sore-headedness resulting from last night's encounter with Sam Greenhill. 'Come off it, Susan. The last time anyone came on to me was VE Day. We met in the pub. I thought she wanted to talk about Terry, but…' He remembered how the conversation had been steered towards Stamford Hill, and how easily all that Class A information had tumbled out of his drunken mouth into her greedy, heartless ears. A flush of shame crept from his wrists to his throbbing scalp.

'The little cunt,' Susan said. The word sounded twice as ugly in her polite, East Coast accent.

'On the plus side, no one has to waste any more time wondering what the Bettelheims were up to at the hotel.'

Ellie knew full well what they'd been up to. After the pub she'd gone to the Travelodge herself and proved so persuasive or obnoxious that someone there had talked. Unhappily for Rex, and very happily for Ellie, another envelope had arrived in the post for the Bettelheims that same afternoon, and they'd let her have a look. 'Meet The Parents' and 'The Bourne Identity'. The DVDs all came from a charity called Hayim Hadoshim. It meant 'new life' in Hebrew, and it helped people from strict religious backgrounds to find a new existence outside them, and to understand the modern world. The Bettelheim family had been planning to jump ship. Perhaps that was why they'd been picnicking in the park that day: dipping a toe in the water of this other world in which they were hoping soon to immerse themselves. Perhaps it explained other things, too.

Ellie hadn't been drunk at all. She'd got him drunk, though, and then wrung him dry before disappearing into the night to finish her story. Maybe that was why she'd been fiddling about with her phone. She'd been recording him. Or letting her boss know she was onto something.

'I've been having an interesting discussion with Commander Bailey,' said Susan. 'He's in charge of the North-East Division of the Met, and he'd very much like to prosecute you for hindering a murder enquiry.'

'How have I hindered it?'

'By not telling them what you'd found out.'

'Well they know now.'

'Later than they might have done.'

'A technicality.'

'Not the way Commander Bailey sees it.'

Rex sat down, and stared at the article. It was illustrated with a picture of some modern-looking, dark-clad Hasidim, who were neither the Bettelheims nor even members of the Dukovchiner sect, nor indeed anything at all to do with the story. But one thing still didn't make sense.

'Hang on – how do the police know this story is anything to do with me? It doesn't mention me.' The story very carefully didn't mention him, in fact

'Jesus, Rex. Can't you work that out? Bailey did the old "reveal your sources" line on Ellie. And she revealed them. She didn't just steal your story. She landed you in it too. Did you fuck her one night and leave without saying thank you or something?'

'I assure you I would say a full and very sincere thank you to anyone who slept with me. You realise this opens up a whole new set of possible motives for the Bettelheim murders?'

'How?'

'If leaving the sect is something so serious they have to creep off to a motel to prepare for it, then maybe… maybe someone else didn't want them to do it. Or wanted to punish them for trying.' Make an example of them, he thought, suddenly recalling the words of Moses Limburg outside the mortuary. 'Yesterday, I met the nephew –'

Susan held up her hand. 'If you've got something, tell the police. This whole episode has made me realise something, Rex. We're supposed to be about local issues, and we've been losing sight of them. Look –' She reached behind her for a fresh edition of the free paper. 'Page one – Finsbury Park Poisoning. Page two – Inside Stamford Hill's Hasidic Community. Page three – Kovacs Murder. It's page four before we get to the dog shit on Duckett's Common, page six before the Literacy Bus closure. And this is the stuff people care about! The stuff that affects them every day.'

Rex sighed. There had been a time when he'd have argued with her. For many years he and Susan had tussled in this very room over whether 'issues' or 'stories' were what people wanted. At this moment, though, he was pleased, relieved even, to hear a little of the old Susan.

'I don't mean we stop digging for Terry. We don't stop for a minute,' Susan said, addressing the mostly empty room as if it were some hushed, packed-out stadium. 'But we don't have to publish a daily update, and we don't pretend we're in the business of solving murders. Readers will soon stop caring if we do. We need to give them what matters to them.'

'Kiddy-fiddlers,' Lawrence said, as he breezed into the room with another flapjack in a tissue.

There was an embarrassed silence before Susan said, 'I beg your pardon, Lawrence,'

Lawrence sat down. 'My old mucker in the Council, Soapy Dave…' He paused, evidently hoping to be asked about the hilarious circumstances whereby Soapy Dave had come to be called Soapy Dave. No such enquiry came. 'Soapy Dave says some private company is applying to turn the old West Green library into a halfway house for ex-cons. A hundred yards from Flint Street Community Primary.'

Susan made a celebratory circle of thumb and forefinger. 'A1, Lawrence. Let's roll,' she purred. 'Let's freakin' roll.'

* * *

By lunchtime, Rex was munching a warm cheese and spinach borek on the top deck of a 341. He was bound for Hatton Garden, the old jewellers' quarter on the edge of the City. This was in no way, he told himself as he surreptitiously wiped his fingers on the seat, a defiance of Susan's orders. She'd specifically said to keep digging on Terry – and after last night's meeting with Kovacs' son, he had every reason to dig in his ex-wife's shop.

Susan had also charged him with turfing up some more straightforward, local interest stories, and he'd spent a productive morning doing just that. After the events of the last few days it had felt rather comforting: ringing up mistrustful Primary School Headmistresses; hobnobbing with the burqa-clad mums down at the playground, making his English extra clear so that they could understand his questions about the dog shit. It was familiar, what he'd done for years, what he was, he supposed, since he survived by doing it, very good at.

Yet something had kept nagging at him throughout these investigations. It was like the thirst he felt for an ice-cold Okocim, intensifying from mid-afternoon until the moment he snapped the first ring-pull back and poured the stuff down his throat. Or like the ache that passed in a Z-shaped meridian from his damaged foot to his right lung and up to his left eye before he'd swallowed the first of the day's codeine pills. Perhaps it was just another addiction, this need to be out there searching for something forbidden and forbidding. He'd wrapped it up and locked it in a basement of his soul when a decade on the nationals as an investigative journalist had come to an abrupt end. But then the questions surrounding his ex-girlfriend's death had forced him to revisit that basement last year. Now it was back again. A hunger he couldn't ignore.

As he read Ellie's piece for a third time, he found he also couldn't ignore what had happened outside the mortuary, and that strange choice of words from Chaya's nephew. He'd said 'example' because he'd meant to say it, Rex was certain of that, and only back-tracked when the imposing Dordoff came near. Before that, Rescha Schild had tried to convey something important to him about the Bettelheims, but seemingly been too afraid to say it outright. Did she – this woman seemingly on the edge of the group herself – know what they had been doing up at the Travelodge? Or know why they had been killed? Take it to the police, Susan had said, if you think you've got something. But what did he have?

He gazed out of the window. The bus was circling Newington Green. He could get off by the Primary School, change buses and be at the door of 'Vegetables' in ten minutes. He changed his mind, though, and stayed on. He felt almost certain now that the murders of Kovacs and the Bettelheims were connected. There was Kovacs' behaviour at the park, for a start, and now he knew that the man's ex-wife had worked with Yaakov Bettelheim. Somehow that felt like the angle of entry. Somehow, also, for all his doubts and theories, it felt as if poking round Stamford Hill was never going to help Terry.

Hatton Garden looked much as it had done on the blustery spring afternoon in 2001, when he and Sybille, his wife-to-be, had gone in search of wedding rings. A wide, quiet, blossom-lined street, more like a Parisian suburb than a jewellers' district just off High Holborn. The shop fronts were mostly the same. They probably had been since the 1970s. Why update them? People were always going to want diamonds, with or without fancy modern signage.

He couldn't remember where they'd bought their wedding rings, only that the man who sold them had been eating tomato soup throughout the transaction, which had amused Sybille and irritated him. Perhaps it had even been on the site of the present-day J.R.R.S., with its wide, green awning and the black-and-gold tiled motif around the bottom of the window and the door. He pressed a buzzer, and was admitted into a cool, dazzling room of pinks and whites and golds.

Much of the colour emanated from a pleasant-looking, slightly overweight Indian lady, whose sari-draped form was not only rainbow-hued, but also situated next to a vast and fussy floral display on the counter. He suspected that the other lady – angular, severe, black-haired in the puce cashmere twin-set – was Mrs Greenhill.

'I was wondering if someone could take a look at this ring,' he began, tugging at the gold band on his finger.

The ring wasn't coming off, but it didn't matter because Mrs Greenhill said, 'You can stop with the act. My son told me about you and I've seen your picture on the internet.'

Rex was about to speak, but she went on: 'I've got nothing to say about George. Nothing I'd trust you with anyway. So if you don't mind, we're very busy.'

'I'm not here about George,' Rex said, having prepared himself for this outcome. 'I'm here about Yaakov Bettelheim.'

The Indian lady made a tutting sound, the sort of noise people make at sad stories on the news.

'He did work here, didn't he? I'm not... I'm not here to make any trouble for anyone.'

'You leave that to *The Times*, do you?' said Mrs Greenhill.

'You saw that rubbish? That photograph? Who were they meant to be? Some Lubavitchers from Manchester? Pathetic!'

Mrs Greenhill showed just a flicker of surprise at this tiny amount of inside knowledge. It was enough for Rex to take the plunge.

'My name used to be Treski,' he said. 'It's a village in Latvia, I think.' This little speech contained two lies, which he'd prepared just over an hour ago. He sensed Mrs Greenhill's appraising glance. He'd undergone similar scannings in Glasgow and Belfast, as people weighed up his surname and his schooling and his physical attributes in order to determine what side of the religious divide he came from. He'd always managed to pass for Catholic up in Glasgow, perhaps because he was. Now, he could almost feel Mrs Greenhill giving him the benefit of the doubt, her disbelief thawing millimetre by millimetre.

'I just want to tell people who Yaakov was. Not Yaakov the Hasid. Yaakov the mensch. Yaakov the workmate.'

'He was a lovely man,' said the Indian lady from her corner, as she stacked salmon-pink display trays in a pile.

'He was,' Mrs Greenhill said, lightly brushing one, exquisitely made-up eyelid. 'Never late. Never off sick. Never – not even when that little boy went missing…'

'Micah Walther?'

'Yaakov and his friends were out all night looking for him. Still turned up here on the dot and did his shift.'

Mrs Greenhill had been pretty, Rex realised, before a quarter-century of single motherhood took every spare pound of flesh away. She'd probably been one of the great beauties of a certain year's crop of marriageable Chigwell maidens. How had she ended up with Dr Kovacs? 'Do you think it was true – that Yaakov and his wife were planning to leave?'

'I wouldn't have been all that surprised. He must have had a bellyful of all that… *mishegoss* silly business with the divorce. You know about *gittin and agunot?*'

'Gittin and… sure,' he lied.

'Well he had all that going on, for years, over a *get*. You see, Yaakov Bettelheim used to be a Belzer Hasid. Lots of them up there in Manchester. And Montreal – that's where his first wife came from. But then he moves to London, and he decides he wants to go over to the Dukovchiner, and his wife doesn't want to. So he asks his Rebbe, I mean the old Dukovchiner Rebbe, not the business they've got now, for a *get*.'

'The business...' he echoed. It was a technique. You zoomed back in, on the thing you really wanted to know about. In this case, the mysterious new Rebbe. Sometimes it worked. Not this time.

'Hmm. And the Rebbe says yes, sure it's fine, you're divorced, here's your *get*. But the Belzer Rebbe says *she's* not divorced. So she's *agunah*. A chained woman. Can't marry. And you know what these Belzer are like.' She held two bejewelled hands either side of her head, like blinkers. 'Very, very Old Country. People kill over that sort of thing.'

'Is that what you think might have happened? The ex-wife might have done it?'

'Well, no, not her, sweetheart, she died. But I wondered if maybe one of her family did it, in revenge. I like Hasidim, Mr Tracey. Back there, it's all Hasidim in the workshop, because they're honest and they work hard. And it's a filthy job many of them do, you know – all those chemicals – but you never hear one of them complaining, never see them taking a day off. The only thing is, some of them can be very clannish. Very vengeful. It's a weird mentality, all that. It's Jewish, Captain, but not as we know it!' Mrs Greenhill added, paraphrasing Star Trek with a faint laugh.

Rex replayed a snatch of what she'd just said. *A filthy job. All those chemicals*. He was about to ask more when a phone rang in some back part of the office and she said, 'Oh, there he is now,' and went to answer it.

There was silence in the shop. Rex took it all in. The place reminded him of an aristocrat's flat he'd visited once, in Knights-bridge. Money, fabulous, unbelievable quantities of the stuff all around it, but inside everything faded, a little bit worn, twenty years out of date. Hatton Garden was like that, too. There were vaults, he knew, underneath its pavements. Men were said to walk the streets with packages worth millions, but behind the reinforced doors there was just old wallpaper and the scent of pine air-freshener. The Indian lady, who'd been kneeling down behind one of the glass display cases suddenly spoke.

'Everything is close up,' she announced. 'That is what you need to say in your newspaper. Like in India, some castes of people we wouldn't let inside the house. But we need them. To bury the dead. Take the rubbish away. Same thing here.' She pointed towards the back of the shop. 'Those people in the black hats. They write the special scrolls, don't they, for the doors? Slaughter the meat. Circumcise babies. You need them, see? But you do look down on them. You do.' She touched her left eye. 'I see. I've been here ten years.'

'So you know Sam?'

Mrs Greenhill returned just as the Indian lady was about to reply. 'I'm going now, Mrs G,' she said, gathering up a light beige jacket and a handbag. 'Anything you want?' She turned to Rex as she opened the door. 'Sam's a good boy to his mummy,' she said, flashing an ingratiating smile in the direction of her employer.

'I thought so too,' Rex said when she was gone. 'Breaking into a murder scene isn't the cleverest thing to do, but it takes a lot of nerve.'

Mrs Greenhill rolled her eyes, acknowledging both her son's folly and Rex's compliment. 'If Sam had told me beforehand he was looking for a will, I'd have told him not to bother. George wrote to me a year after I left him and said he was leaving it all to the Goldsmiths College library. The whole fortune. Anyway, after my phone call, I don't need it anyway.

'It was good news?'

'I've been waiting a month for him to make up his mind about buying the place. Indian chappie. We get a lot of business from them' – she made a sweeping motion around her neck, miming necklaces – 'because of all the gold they have for their weddings and that. That's why I hired Reena. He's going to keep her on, he says, when he takes over.'

'New adventures ahead, then,' Rex said. He noted that she'd said a month. If that was true, it ruled Mrs Greenhill out of a money-motivated murder. Not her son, though. If Sam hadn't known that a buy-out was on the cards, he might have killed his father in vain. That, combined with the boy's comments about Terry, made him worthy of another look.

From the way she'd started stacking up boxes, Mrs Greenhill made it apparent that she wanted to end the conversation. Rex had a few more things to ask, though.

'Was there really a fortune?'

'Well, he wasn't Roman Abramovich, no, but he had quite a bit. His family up in Liverpool had been wealthy. They supplied things to the port and the docks, stuff for shipping and loading and all that. And he inherited it all.'

'But he just lived in a little half-house in Tottenham.'

'Well, that was his philosophy. He was the kind of man who'd spend five thousand pounds on a record player, but just have bits of cloth nailed to the pelmet instead of curtains. He wasn't mean – he was even quite generous, you know…' She paused and showed him an oblong ring, an emerald surrounded by diamonds. 'Bought me this. Not for our engagement. Just because we saw it. That's what he was like. Some things, I guess the things that matter to most people, like having a nice house and nice food to eat, he just wasn't bothered about. He'd have a Renoir on the walls and eat beans cold out of a tin. I mean – he didn't really have a Renoir but… he spent fifteen grand on his watch.'

Rex recalled the dandy shoes, the muted sense of power given off by Kovacs' old Rolex. 'Eccentric.'

'No… That's too nice a word for George. Clever. Very clever – he could learn a language in six months. And sharp. His lectures were actually very funny.

'You went to them?'

'I was one of his students.' She sighed. 'My little rebellion I suppose. All the other girls were marrying nice accountants and lawyers with prospects. He was like this fiery intellectual with fancy tastes and a Beatles accent. Silly. It was all right for a year. ... Then we had Sam. He shut me out completely. Left me little notes on the table. 'I can't stand your shrieking common voice.' That was the last one he wrote to me, before I grabbed Sammy and left. He wanted it to be just him. His books. His teaching. His writing. He said to me once, it was my fault – *I* should have known, the men in his family were no good as fathers. But how could I have known what his dad had been like, or any of the rest of them? His parents were dead when he met me. All I knew is, he came from Liverpool, and they'd had a big business. That's all he knew, as well, to be honest. There was meant to be some big mystery about them. I don't know what. Something to do with a diary. He always said he'd spend his dotage finding out.'

'Did he?'

'I wouldn't know. He cut off completely. Never saw Sam. Never showed any interest in seeing him. Now –'

She came out from behind the counter, with the obvious intention of ushering him out.

'Can I just ask, did your – did Dr Kovacs have any contact with anyone else? I mean, any family or friends?'

She gave a small laugh. 'He didn't even invite them to our wedding. Everyone there was someone from the university – a colleague. He didn't have anyone. Sad, really.' For a moment her face looked genuinely full of pity, before a shadow passed across it. 'It was his own bloody fault, though. He used to say, "I can't be around other people because I'm too clever, and they're all so stupid." What's the use in being clever if it makes you alone like that?'

Her question hung in the air for a few seconds as she twisted a ring around on her finger. Then she started moving over towards the shop door. Rex stalled for time, pretending to fiddle with his coat buttons. Someone had paid regular visits to Kovacs. And a neighbour had bothered to call the police when they thought he was being harmed. Who?

'He seems to have some sort of social life nowadays, mind you,' Mrs Greenhill added, 'But I doubt it's what you or I would call friends.'

'So you have had some contact with him then?'

She sighed. 'My Mum died early last year. She made me promise I'd contact him one last time... try and make him have some kind of contact with his son. So I went over there and saw him. Must have been... May? Something like that. I ended up feeling sorry for him. His rigid little life and all its routines. Walking all that way for his groceries every morning.'

'Walking where?'

She didn't seem to have heard. 'He made a joke when he opened the door. He said – you're the former Mrs Kovacs. Now I'm the former Mr Kovacs.'

'What did he mean by that?'

'Well, I don't know – but he was quite a changed man. Much thinner. Smaller, somehow. He'd had three heart attacks, he told me, so he'd retired early, summer of 2012, and he was okay, but his doctor had told him to exercise. So he could only see me between eleven and twelve, he said, because of that, and all the things he was busy with. He was well stuck into writing that Outrage thing by then... and he'd taught himself Latvian, and now he was learning Yiddish. He'd just got back, with his little bag of shopping, when I arrived at his door.'

'From where?'

'Stamford Hill. He had a favourite little fruit n' veg shop there, he said, and he liked being the first one through the door so he knew he was getting fresh. Just like a little sad old man.'

* * *

By mid-afternoon, he was back in Tottenham. At the Police Station, the desk-boy with the huge tribal bore-holes in his ears recognised him of old and buzzed him through. Limping painfully, he climbed two flights of exquisitely tiled stairs towards the hot, bright attic occupied by C.I.D.

Tottenham nick was meant to be closing, all its staff moving to some new-build palace of light and space just off the Seven Sisters junction. It never seemed to happen, though, and the cops remained stuck in a Victorian museum piece. There was even a fern motif running along the decorative walls and curved banisters. It was the only Police Station people actually asked to come and visit.

Halfway up the stairs, Rex felt his phone buzzing. He didn't recognise the number, but thinking it might be one of the people he'd been trying to find all day, he answered it.

'Rex, the nuns say you haven't been up to visit in three weeks.'

He felt a flush of guilt and annoyance. 'It's only just over a fortnight, Aurelie,' he said, flushing again, this time in embarrassment at the lameness of his response.

'I am in London now, visiting for a few days,' his wife's sister said. 'Why don't you come up?'

Rex sighed. He was used to his sister-in-law's angry, impetuous demands. One of them, one festive winter night, had come close to destroying his marriage before he destroyed it himself. But the chaotic, slurred tone of the old Aurelie was gone. The woman on the phone sounded clear. And determined.

'I can't. I have to work.'

'This is not what Sybille deserves, Rex,' she said, before hanging up.

He continued up the stairs. The call had unsettled him. She had sounded so positive and forceful, as though she were standing right by his ear. Normally, talking to Aurelie was like talking to someone lost at sea.

Upstairs, behind a desk laden with yellow folders, sat D.S. Brenard, neat and slight in his shirtsleeves. He had a day's growth of stubble, Rex noticed, and his eyes looked sore.

'If you're after a quote about the bloody nonce hostel next to the school, ring the Press Office,' he growled.

'You know something, D.S. Brenard. Until yesterday, you were the only police officer I'd never heard swear before. Now you're at it all the time.'

'All four kids, wife and mother-in-law off with the flu, and me next,' D.S. Brenard said, like someone reciting a list. 'Five open GBH cases on my desk. This afternoon – four thefts, one arson, a suspected firearms, and a bloke going round trying to push women into the traffic. No problem – for twelve CID officers. Except I'm losing two, two more have got the frigg... the flu, and half the rest are on a course. *Honour killings. How to spot the signs.*' A grim chuckle turned into a paroxysm of coughing.

'Maybe I can take up the slack,' Rex said, pulling up a chair.

D.S. Brenard eyed him balefully. 'What are you after?'

'Quid pro quo.'

'If you're withholding information about a murder investigation then I'm not doing any quid pro quo with you, Rex. I'm going to get on the blower to Commander Bailey and he's going to personally come down here and fuck you.'

Rex held up a hand. 'I'm not withholding. I'm offering something I have only just discovered and confirmed in the last 24 hours.'

'Which is what?'

Rex told the Welshman about his encounter with Sam Greenhill in Dr Kovacs' house. He also told him about his efforts to contact Sam Greenhill after leaving Hatton Garden that afternoon. No sign of him at his art college – indeed, he'd missed an important presentation that morning. No sign of him at the digs he shared up in Palmer's Green. And every sign that he'd been at his father's house before the evening Rex found him there.

Rex fished out his mobile. 'Someone's had a go at Kovacs' garden gate.' He showed Brenard the picture he'd taken. 'It could have been someone practising stabbing up Dr Kovacs before they did it for real. Could have been his son.'

It wasn't the best photo, and Rex had the distinct sense that he was being humoured. Nevertheless, D.S. Brenard nodded and made a note. Then he folded his pad over. 'Thanks. Anything else?'

Rex smiled. He'd deliberately saved the best for last. 'Actually, yes. Dr Kovacs wasn't present only when the Bettelheims died. He also frequented the same shop as the Bettelheims. And I've got reason to wonder if the owner of that shop…'

'If you mean Yitzhak Schild, he's not the owner, his wife is,' Brenard interrupted. 'Are you about to tell me Schild used to visit Dr Kovacs' house?'

Rex nodded, numbly. 'How did –?'

'Door-to-door enquiries in Stamford Hill. Schild told one of our officers that he and Kovacs were friends.'

'You believe that? Not exactly natural soulmates, I wouldn't have thought.'

'Well, whatever you're thinking, Rex, on the Monday afternoon Dr Kovacs was killed, Yitzhak Schild was waiting at his rabbi's house to speak to him about a religious matter. As verified by his rabbi's assistant, Mr Simeon Dordoff.'

'Dordoff. That would be the same Dordoff who was at the mortuary yesterday?'

Brenard nodded. 'His official title is a gabbay. Means kind of a right-hand man to the rabbi.'

'Apparently it's Rebbe…' Rex recalled the conversation in Mega Glatt Meat Mart, when he'd been told that the Dukovchiners' new Rebbe had forbidden them to eat meat, then that they were without a leader. 'Anyway, I wasn't even sure they had one,' he said.

D.S. Brenard smiled tightly, revealing networks of wrinkles. How old was he? Perhaps anyone with four children would look old. 'You don't know quite as much as we do, then, Rex, do you? Incidentally, before you go off at right angles again, Schild's got a solid alibi for the morning too. Allergy Clinic at the Homerton. His wife was serving in the shop alone most of that day, except for the period when you went in there sniffing about. Which we also know about.'

Rex sighed. 'Customers?'

'Eh?'

'Who came in the shop?'

'Only about half a dozen people all day. I can't see how that place can keep going, let alone make the payments on that van.'

Brenard flipped through his notebook, while Rex pondered this brave new world where everyone owned their motor vehicles on the drip. Even so, the van seemed an odd choice for a business like 'Vegetables'.

'Right. Here we go. Customers. First one was Dr Kovacs. He was the first one every morning, apparently. Bought some biscuits. Next was a couple of Mormon boys about ten forty, trying to save her soul.' He gave a thin smile. 'Bit late to the party, I'd have thought.'

'What about the Bettelheims?' Rex asked. He suddenly wondered if they had crossed paths with Kovacs earlier in the morning on the day they had all died.

'They were customers sometimes, but Mrs Schild didn't see them that day.'

'Was Bird ever a customer?'

'Who?

'I don't know his last name. That black bloke who's always pissed and shouting at people on the High Street. You know the guy I mean?'

Brenard nodded.

'Well,' Rex continued, 'according to the Greek lady who lives next door to Kovacs, he might have been another regular.'

'How would the Greek lady next door to Dr Kovacs know that this Bird visited a fruit and veg shop in Stamford Hill?'

'Sorry. I mean – she told me a black bloke used to call round at Kovacs' house, just like Yitzie Schild did. And on Tuesday lunchtime, I saw Bird outside the house, shouting at a woman. A blonde woman.'

'He shouts all over the place, doesn't he?' D.S. Brenard said. But he made a note. 'Can't quite see him and Kovacs being pals.'

'Trust me, Dr Kovacs and anyone being friends was a bit unlikely. He was a nasty piece of work.'

'So we're told. Not least by the man we've got in custody for murdering him,' D.S. Brenard said. There was an awkward silence.

'What did this blonde look like, then?'

'Medium height. Arty-looking. Sort of bleached, short hair. Leather jacket. She ran away when I shouted.'

Brenard put his pen down. 'Well I'd run away if I had you and Bird shouting at me in the street.'

'Terry didn't do it,' Rex said. 'And given that I've just given you two useful leads – I know you think they're useful because you don't bother writing them down if you don't – how about a little exchange of intelligence?'

D.S. Brenard took a deep breath. Rex hastily continued. 'What about the Muslim boys? I single-handedly brought you them, D.S. Brenard. Come on. I just want to know if you've had any joy finding that 999 caller yet? Not to publish anything, I swear. I'm trying to help out a friend. You said yourself, you don't blame me for that. And I have of my own volition just told you everything I've recently found out, so eager am I to co-operate with your investigation. Is that not so, D.S. Brenard?' Rex realised he didn't know the man's first name.

D.S. Brenard gazed at him for a while, then tipped his head back and scratched his neck. An exhausted man, the rings under his eyes forming a motif with the sticky circles left by coffee mugs on his desk.

'No joy. The caller had what sounds like an Eastern European accent. Then again, it could be Spanish or South American.'

'Can I listen to it?' Rex was good on accents. He was the only member of the News North London staff who could tell a Turk from a Kurd.

Brenard chose not to dignify this request with an answer. 'The call came from a payphone at the bus station,' he continued, 'but the CCTV's been out of order since January. The caller said she lived on Langerhans, and she thought there was something going on over the road. We sent two lads in uniform to every house on both sides of the road, without any positives. But…'

He rummaged wearily in a drawer. Rex was expecting him to bring out a file, but instead it was a packet of pills. The packet turned out to be empty. D.S. Brenard's reaction to this discovery was so pitiful that Rex offered him two of his own. Brenard necked them without water.

'There's a trio of possibles,' Brenard continued. 'The lady next door at 326 – a Miss Martell – some sort of human rights lawyer, always flying off to Cameroon or Rwanda. It could have been her – her office say she was in the country Monday and took an afternoon flight to Kigali the day after. But she doesn't check in all that regularly, so we're still waiting for confirmation either way.'

So was the blonde woman Bird had been shouting at Miss Martell, as she made her way from a First World trouble-spot to one in the Third? She'd rushed away, struggling with her coat. Had she had luggage with her? He couldn't recall.

'I don't think it was her,' Brenard went on, 'because the caller said the disturbance was "over the road". There is, however, a Polish law student who lives on the other side of the road. She's gone back to Krakow because her dad died. And there's also a Brazilian massage therapist, who regularly visits Birmingham for reasons not clear, or allegedly not clear, to the girls she shares a house with. We're trying to trace all three, currently without success. And you're running an appeal, aren't you?'

'We could add the information you've just given me.'

He screwed his eyes shut and opened them again. 'Do that – it might just improve your reputation in police circles. Commander Bailey has told everyone to make you a focus of special interest. You know what that means?'

'It doesn't sound good.'

'It means there's a bottle of single malt for the first person to nick you.'

D.S. Brenard was in the process of cracking the first smile Rex had seen him crack in a long time, when his phone rang. As he listened, the smile quickly faded. Then he slammed the receiver down and covered his face with his hands.

'Fuck fuck fuck,' the detective muttered, quietly, into his palms.

'What is it?'

'The arrival of Typhoon Shit.' D.S. Brenard took his hands away from his face and gazed at Rex. 'You want a Scotch?'

'Not got any Welsh then?'

'Ha ha,' Brenard said, pulling a bottle and a pair of glasses from his bottom drawer. 'You want a laugh, mate, try this. Anwar Hafeez, aka the misunderstood Muslim medical student you brought to us under suspicion of crimes against perfume, has just been picked up by the anti-terror unit. Blueprints to the service corridors of Shopping City and a bomb-making manual in his college locker. You know what that means?'

'He's a terrorist?'

'I imagine he's just another wanker who's been spending too much time on the Al-Qaeda website. Anyway, I couldn't give a fuck. The point is what it means here. For me. Terror Alert upgraded to 'Severe', all leave cancelled, every officer with a pair of boots diverted to stop-and-fucking-search, and those bell-ends from Anti-Terror crawling all over the shop.' He held up a glass.

'Fucking bloody sodding pissing cheers.'

* * *

Rex surveyed the busy, drizzle-sprayed High Street from his kneeling position on the Whittaker Twins' L-shaped desk. Pushed up against the single window in the News North London office that actually opened, it offered the only vantage point.

The twins neither remarked upon his presence on their desk, nor enquired as to what he was doing, nor indeed gave any sign of having noticed that he was there. The ad-selling pair never ceased to astound Rex in their complete indifference to the people who surrounded them. They came in at 9, in their identical, ill-cut Byrite suits, and sat at their desks until exactly 5. Yet, awkward as they were when face-to-face with their fellow creatures, over the phone this milky, bulbous-headed duo could bewitch any business in North London, regardless of economic circumstances, into taking out an advert or two. They seemed to charm revenue out of thin air. Rex knew that, no matter how good a journalist he was, or had been, what kept him in work was the Whittakers. The Whittakers knew that too, but they were beyond lording it over him. Beyond anything, in fact, with their identical Tupperware lunches and their school shoes. Where on earth had Susan found them? Was it on earth at all?

Rex's gaze travelled up and down the crammed, frenetic, push-chair and burqa-filled High Street. He'd already walked the length of it, from Morrison's to Turnpike Lane tube, without finding what he was looking for – though he had seen ample signs of what Brenard had called 'Typhoon Shit'. A walk-through metal detector in the entrance to the Morrison's. Stop 'n' Search teams playing tip-out-the-rucksack with every bloke whose skin was darker than a cup of tea. Bad moods everywhere.

Perhaps this was the true point of terror. Not blowing a hundred people's limbs off but making hundreds of thousands of lives more frustrating and difficult than they would otherwise have been. And if that meant more young men made angry enough to become terrorists themselves, then so much the better. He wondered whether the adolescent chippiness of Anwar Hafeez would ever have crystallised into a bomb plot if it hadn't been for his short, intense encounter with the Anti-Terror Squad after the perfume incident in the park.

As he watched a pair of Somali boys sulkily doing up their trainers after a street-search, it occurred to Rex that few people would have minded Shopping City being blown to smithereens. So long as the place was empty at the moment of destruction, Anwar Hafeez would probably have been in line for having a primary school and a library named after him. Not that new libraries were a common occurrence these days.

As he pulled his head back in, Susan was ushering another pair of visitors out of her inner sanctum. Today it was suits – white hair, double chins and pin-stripes. Was that a good sign? He doubted any of the visits amounted to a good sign.

Susan forced a smile as he went into her office. He'd just sent her a draft of the new police appeal for information and it was on her screen, he suspected, unread.

'Tell me why a man like Dr Kovacs would hang out with Bird?'

Despite her evident fatigue, her dark eyes widened. 'You mean shouty Bird on the street Bird?'

'Shouty Bird not on the street, as far as I can see. Constantly out there, rain or shine, with his lager – except on the one day I need to speak to him.'

'What makes you think he was pally with Dr K.?'

'The next-door neighbour said he used to have two visitors all the time. A skinny black bloke, and a fat Hasid.'

'Sounds like the start of one of Terry's jokes.'

They were quiet for a moment as they contemplated their incarcerated friend's fate. 'A couple of days ago,' Rex went on, 'I saw Bird sitting on the wall outside Kovacs' and Terry's house. It might just be coincidence. Bird sits on a lot of walls. Anyway, here's another thing. Kovacs used to go to a vegetable shop in Stamford Hill every morning. He liked to be the first customer there, every day, apparently, and it was the same shop frequented by the Bettelheim family. And he was friends with the man that owns it, Yitzie Schild. A fat Hasid. If the skinny black bloke *is* Bird, what would three men like that be doing with each other?'

'The mind boggles,' Susan said drily. 'I'm also wondering why a man who lives on Langerhans Road, with a dozen, brilliant, cheap Turkish and Bangladeshi fruit and veg stores within a five-minute walk, chooses to go over to Stamford Hill every morning. Did he ever live there?'

'I don't know.'

'Didn't they tell you in the fruit and veg shop? Rex?'

Rex didn't answer. Susan's point not only made sense, it troubled him. Rescha Schild clearly knew about Kovacs' murder. But she hadn't mentioned anything about him visiting the shop. Why was that?

Before he could say anything more to his boss, a breathless, flustered-looking Brenda came in.

'You need to come down to Reception,' she said, supporting herself on the back of Rex's chair. 'Someone's here.'

'Who's here?' Susan said, standing up.

'You just need to see,' said Brenda urgently, starting to cough.

Rex couldn't help himself. Whenever people said things like this to him – that there was someone here, someone waiting for him, a message, a package, a present – he had the thought that it might be his father. He didn't have a father. He'd never had one. Which of course explained why a part of him always expected one to show up.

Today, what had showed up was Terry, in baggy jeans and a shapeless blue T-shirt. Huddled into himself on the orange foam seating at the bottom of the stairs, he gazed up at them.

'Free at last!' he said, but there was little joy in his voice.

Susan opened her arms to him, expecting him to stand up. When he didn't, she bent and hugged him awkwardly around his neck. Rex patted his friend on the shoulder as Brenda came back down, blotchy-faced, wiping beads of sweat from her brow.

'Let me guess. They've arrested someone else.'

Terry just stared up at him with dull eyes. 'Not to my knowledge they haven't,' he said. 'I've been bailed on medical and compassionate grounds.' He lifted up and clanked against the floor a metal crutch that Rex hadn't noticed. 'I've got multiple sclerosis, haven't I? I can barely walk.'

* * *

I thought she was crying again this morning. Heard a sobbing sound from her room. But she went down the stairs before me, carrying her pot with a muslin over it and I knew from the stink that followed her she was vomiting. She looks unwell. Always wants to sleep. Never eats. Mind you, I never much want to eat the stuff Missus Cutter destroys in her kitchen. She cooks everything until it bends. I'd kill for a simple bowl of kasha.

The old lady had already gone to her work at the laundry, and I thought to ask after Leah's health, but going back in from the yard I saw the sign. Elephant's idea: if they want to meet me, they throw a little ball of red wool, over into the Cutters' yard. Stupid idea. First reason: a rat or a dog might have it away before I've seen it. Second reason: Missus or Leah might see it and keep it for darning, throw it away. Third reason: anyone following E or T follows them right to my back yard. Once upon a time I'd have carried on fighting, insisted we use a chalk cross on a busy street, like we did in Riga and St Petersburg. But I've given up. Let Elephant have his small victories.

Today he hands me the message to decode, although I know he's read it himself, and shared it with Torch. They come inside the bindings of Hebrew books, sent upstairs to the Litvaker. It says that the committee has given approval to the robbery. Funds are to be returned to the struggle, to Riga. By me. Elephant raises his eyebrows when I've finished reading it, going over my face to see my pain. There isn't any. None I'd let him see.

'Time I went back,' I say, flat as a June sea.

'Plenty more knaidlach in the soup, eh?' he says.

I didn't answer. You know why this little turd thinks he has power over me? Because in prison, he was the one in charge of the shit bucket. That's true. The apes conferred a little power on the monkey, and he started to think he was one of them. He's no more an anarchist than I'm the miracle-working rabbi of Rujiena. I begin to wonder how many anarchists are left. Sending me their orders. 'The committee approves'. Like the navy, only in the navy there were a few men you could respect.

So I say we need to go over to the place and have a good look, work out how it's to be done, what routes are to be taken away. So we set off down the High Street in the slush. Hot coals and horse-dung smells. The pair of them walk with their shoulders hunched and their collars up and their hands in their pockets, swivelling about to check the street as if their necks don't work. Pricks. Like the famous clown double-act in the Yiddish Theatre – the pompous fool and the cry-baby – and this week, they're being burglars. The more they try to escape everyone's attention, the more everyone notices them. I kept back, minded my own business, bought chestnuts from a girl with a barrow and concentrated on them.

Then we stopped. The factory right opposite us, across the road. Schnurrman's, the rubber works, sending its rotten-egg, charred-corpse smell all about the place.

'There's the gate,' says Elephant.

Torch takes his knuckle out of his mouth just long enough to say: 'And just to the left of the stairs for the workers, see, just there… that's where the cashier's office is. The car docks there when it's come back from the bank.'

They might as well have been saying Kaddish for all I was listening. For they'd as good as signed their death warrants. Mine too.

'And you've not yet mentioned what lies opposite the factory,' I says. 'The building whose windows we're standing by.'

And they looked at each other, and then at the building behind us, for, I honestly think, the first time.

In this part of the world they call it 'the Nick'. It's the police station.

Baruch ata, Adonai Elohainu, Melech ha-olam… Blessed art Thou, Lord our God, King of the World, who put all that time into creating man. And ended up with this pair of turnip-tops.

* * *

It had been a long time since Rex had had a houseguest. In fact, he wasn't sure it had ever happened, although he possessed a sofa that turned relatively easily into a bed, and enough towels in the back of his wardrobe to accommodate a large family. These were relics from the time when he'd lived with Sybille, and people had overnighted in their Camden flat in a proper, grown-up way, kitted-out with sheets and flannels and even dressing-gowns.

Terry had arrived with nothing apart from the clothes he'd been wearing, which stank of Dettol and rolling tobacco, a watch, and a St Christopher medal, which slid about in the awful, clear plastic property bag he'd been given on exiting Pentonville's Remand Wing. So, leaving his guest gazing blankly at an episode of 'Murder, She Wrote', Rex had gone over to Terry's house to collect a few things.

There was mail in the shared hallway, both for Terry and for Kovacs. He divided it up, placing the dead man's letters on the little table with the equally dead cactus on it, and keeping hold of Terry's. As he sifted through the mail he remembered him that the printers had promised to send the bits of Kovacs' book they'd salvaged from the skip. He made a note to chase them.

As he was locking Terry's flat, Rex saw a third door at the far end of the little hallway. He went to investigate. The door was stiff, but it opened. He peered in. Wooden steps led down to the basement. The unlocked door suggested the space was communal, but had Terry ever been down there?

He returned to his friend's unaired flat. The place smelled of man – a scent both sweet and brackish, with shaving foam prominent among other less easily recognisable odours. Rex wondered if his own house smelled the same.

He tried to concentrate on the task in hand: finding things that a man might need while he awaited... what? Trial for murder? Paralysis and slow death? Both?

He found he was grabbing items almost without thinking, like that game show where they had three minutes to stuff a shopping trolley with goods. With an effort he calmed down, gathering clothes and toiletries more methodically from the tidy, almost Spartan home. It didn't help. His thoughts swung from Terry's sad circumstances to the gruesome slaying that had taken place just on the other side of the hall.

So far his own investigations had done nothing but turf up more questions. Who were Kovacs' visitors? And who had called the police, with possibly vital information about the murder? And were the two regular visitors the same two visitors Terry said he'd heard arriving on the day Kovacs was killed? Where did Sam Greenhill fit in? And Dr Kovacs' lengthy trips to the vegetable shop? Had he crossed paths with the Bettelheims there?

Back in the present, Rex wondered about books. What was Terry reading these days? His normal fare was war photography. To his surprise, Rex found a cheap edition of the Koran – photocopied, by the looks of it – on his friend's bedside table. He pulled out the bookmark: a leaflet, of the sort peddled daily on the High Street, raging about drone strikes and British troops. Rex put the bookmark back, and left the Koran where it was.

He rushed back through a fine drizzle to find Terry exactly where he'd left him, staring from the sofa at the very same supermarket-based game show Rex had been thinking of earlier. He thanked Rex vaguely, but showed no interest in what he'd brought. The same was true for the cup of tea Rex made him, which sat growing a skin in a blue Istanbul souvenir mug. Rex decided it might not be the time to ask about Terry's bedside reading matter, or the basement, although he was curious about both.

Susan had told Rex to take as long as he needed. In reality, though, he knew he had to get back to the office. He was just contemplating how to broach this when Terry turned away from the screen and looked at him.

'Go on, go,' he said. 'I'll be all right. I'm just sorry you'll have to walk back to work instead of driving.'

'Yes, well, I could have taken my test if you hadn't got yourself charged with murder.'

Terry gave a wan smile. Rex sat down again. 'We're going to sort this out, Terry. Trust me. There's a lot of stuff that needs looking at. For a start, what spooked Kovacs so much at the park? Who called 999? What about the son? And Kovacs' visitors? I think one of them might have been Bird.'

Terry frowned. 'The one who's always outside the Council mouthing off? Get fucked.'

'I don't think anything is quite what it seems.'

Terry turned back to the TV, which now showed a woman in a white bikini diving for pearls. Rex waited for a comment about pearl necklaces, or where Terry might wish to go diving, or at the very least, a chuckle.

Instead Terry said, in a low, quiet voice: 'I was planning to go back to Thailand, wasn't I? In the summer. Shit.'

He left Terry with two promises he might actually be able to keep – to bring home a Turkish takeaway from the Pamukkale, and a DVD of 'Dr No', Terry's all-time favourite film.

The drizzle had gone, leaving in its wake a cold, faintly promising dusk. The birds were doing a sort of springtime evensong, and the air smelt of mingled blossom and charcoal from the nearby kebab-houses. Rex was walking back towards the office along his quiet street of terraced houses, staring up at the cloud-streaked, pinkening sky and wondering where to buy or borrow a copy of 'Dr No', when someone suddenly emerged from the shadows. It took him a moment to realise who it was.

'You frightened me,' he said.

Rescha Schild, wearing a short, belted gabardine mac over her shoulders like a cape, gave a short laugh. 'I can't be the most frightening person round here, can I?'

'Probably not. Are you visiting someone here…?'

'Visiting someone, yes,' she said, smiling again and biting her bottom lip in a way he found rather appealing. 'I was looking for you. I went to your office, and the big lady there told me where your house was, but I got a bit lost.'

'I hope it's not to give me another tip-off. The last one got me in a lot of trouble.'

She frowned, adjusting the raincoat over her shoulders. 'A tip-off?'

'The hotel card. Why did you want me to have it? Did you know what Chaya Bettelheim and her husband were doing?'

She took a deep breath, fiddling with the coat again. Why wouldn't she just do it up? 'I had an idea. And I had an idea that some people would have been very angry.'

He remembered what Chaya's nephew had said at the mortuary. *An example*. 'Which people would be angry? People like Dordoff?'

She tucked her hair behind her ears. 'The Rebbe is having a tish tonight. They haven't had one for many months. Lots of slivovitz. You might hear something, or see something.'

'About Dordoff?'

She shot him a pained, almost angry look. Because he was wrong? Or because he shouldn't keep saying aloud what she plainly wasn't prepared to. He supposed she was giving him a useful lead. But something stopped him from trusting her.

'Why didn't you tell me that George Kovacs was a regular customer?'

She looked up, puzzled. 'You didn't ask. Anyway, we weren't talking about him. What does it have to do with the Bettelheims?'

They had, in a sense, been talking about Kovacs, because she'd mentioned seeing Terry on the street. But she had a point. The two incidents were inextricably linked, to Rex. There was no reason why they should be to her.

'How long was he a customer of yours?'

'Not so long. About a year. He met Yitzie first, at the hospital, last winter. They both go to a… heart clinic. He wanted someone to help him practise his Yiddish.'

'Why was he practising Yiddish?'

She frowned. 'Perhaps to do with research? He told Yitzie he was writing a book, about that robbery. I don't know. After that, about a year ago, he started to come in the shop, buy some cookies, some fruit, talk to my husband, then go.'

'Every day?'

'Every day. Early. He liked to be the first through the door. But some weeks he didn't come. He went away a lot. To Liverpool, once or twice, I think. But mostly abroad. Latvia, a lot of times, he said. Also New York, then Sydney, and Canada, Hungary…'

'Did he say what he was doing in all those places?'

She shrugged and winced again, as he'd seen her do in her doorway.

'Are you all right?' he asked. 'You look uncomfortable.'

She nodded, waving a hand vaguely over the upper part of her body. 'I get some pains. It's a hard job. Lot of lifting.'

'I still think it's odd. George Kovacs was almost a friend of yours, but you didn't mention it to me.'

She laughed, a bitter sound. 'I'm a woman. You know what every Jewish man says in the morning when he gets up? "Blessed are you, Lord our God, who has not made me a woman."'

Rex laughed slightly, but he realised she was serious.

'So I don't have male friends, Mr Tracey. Why I didn't you tell you something. You didn't ask.'

'But you're telling me about this thing – the tish – tonight.'

She shifted the mac across her shoulders again. Like all Hasidim, Rescha looked like someone from another era. But hers wasn't 18th-century Poland. She looked more like a woman from the Sixties. Alice band, lots of eye make-up, long legs. 'I want the truth to be found out. And the police won't find it.'

'Why are you so sure of that?'

'Have you heard what they are doing over by us? A policeman walks into one of the *shtiblach* – that's like a prayer-house – finishing his hot dog. They send two officers – two men – to ask questions at the Girls' School. They didn't even ring the Principal first to say they want to come. So nobody will talk to them. So soon they'll go away and give up and say, "the community did not get justice because the community has not co-operated." Same as they did with Micah Walther, same as they do whenever one of the black boys gets stabbed or shot. You aren't stupid, Mr Tracey, and at least you try not to offend people.'

'I don't know. I've had complaints.'

She didn't reply, just looked him up and down, as if appraising potatoes in her shop. 'The tish is tonight. About nine o'clock, in the new shtib they've found. It's Number 7, Bruce Grove. If you're bothered, you're bothered.'

She nodded curtly and veered off left towards the bus station. No van, he thought, as he watched her stockinged legs march briskly away in their flat lace-up shoes. Was that because of the Sabbath, or because she couldn't drive it? Yitzie had said it belonged to her, though – as did the business, according to Brenard. There must, he thought, as he turned right onto the teeming High Street, be a lot of tensions in that household. A lot of tensions in her community, too. The woman seemed convinced that the Bettelheims' killer was one of her own kind. There must be a reason why she was so sure.

* * *

It was an old part of the borough, or at least a part of the borough that hadn't been bombed or turned into council blocks. Bruce Grove featured a mix of Tudor castles, Georgian villas, early Victorian alms houses and Edwardian music halls – many either rotting into the ground, or taken over on short leases by one doomed venture after another. The Portuguese bakery was one that had lasted, given fresh life by a new wave of incomers from Brazil. The Snooker Hall, too, with its sinister, windowless frontage, seemed to endure yearly stabbings, shootings and arson attempts, without ever quite becoming extinct.

From his vantage point in the harsh, almost chemical light of the railway station exit, Rex watched groups of Turkish and Caribbean men heading into the Snooker Hall, and checked his watch for the eleventh time. Lawrence should have arrived twenty minutes ago. He wondered if he was going to have to visit the tish alone.

That didn't really matter, of course, but he'd been surprised by Lawrence's tepid response to the venture. When Rex had suggested that a practising, Yiddish-speaking Jew would be a useful guide to the proceedings of the tish, he'd expected Lawrence to be flattered. Instead, he had said, rather irritably, that his Yiddish was rudimentary, and whatever Judaism those 'black-hatters' practised was a long way removed from his own. The man who routinely referred to himself as a 'daft old Yid', made endless quips about bacon sandwiches and had a repertoire of stories about Uncles called Solly and disastrous bar-mitzvahs had seemed almost insulted to be linked to the Hasidim living out their own, very Jewish lives, barely a mile away from him. Rex was reminded of what the Indian woman had said in the jeweller's shop on Hatton Garden. Perhaps there was a kind of caste system in operation, with the pious of Stamford Hill right at the bottom.

In the end, what had persuaded Lawrence was the address. Number 7 Bruce Grove was a listed building. Once home to the Quaker scientist, Luke Howard, it now boasted a blue plaque, though in these straitened times, no organisation, civic, charitable or cultural, would take responsibility for maintaining the building. For a while some Trinidadians had run a bar in the basement called Port-of-Spain, which was overlooked by the authorities until it exploded in flames, taking a chunk of the rear ground floor with it. According to Lawrence, the building still contained a lot of original coving, and a magnificent spiral staircase. It was the prospect of seeing these that had winkled him out on this chilly, breezy night.

Or perhaps not, since Lawrence was distinctly not where he'd said he'd be, and not answering his telephone either. Between clutches of short, stern-looking men clutching pool cues, Hasidim flitted by on their way to the tish. At one point there'd almost been a crowd of them, filling the still evening air with footsteps and cigarette smoke and barely-voiced twitterings of Yiddish. Then the crowd had become a trickle before dwindling to nothing. Rex wondered if the tish had already started. He sent Lawrence a final, curt text and went on his way.

The building was screened off behind a high, wooden hoarding. The official route in, it seemed, was to heave apart two huge ply-board panels, and clamber through the gap before they sprang back together. Rex did that, then picked his way across a rubble-strewn forecourt and mounted the stone steps to the entrance. The metal anti-squatter door had long since been prised off, and he walked into an empty, crumbling hall lit by a thousand flickering tea-lights.

Stronger light shone from a doorway to the right of the hall, behind the vast, carved staircase, and there was a rumble of male voices in the dank, mineral-tinged air. He was about to head towards it when he heard a cough and a mutter behind him. He swung round.

Dimly, in the dancing light of the candles, he made out two men in a corner, on the other side of the central stairs. One was slim and dark, the other fat and blond. Apparently they hadn't seen Rex, and the dark Hasid was handing a small, canvas bag to the blond one. It clinked and clattered as the blond man rolled it up and stowed it in his dark overcoat. The transaction had a furtive air to it, confirmed when the two men noticed Rex. The dark man hurried away, looking down to avoid eye contact. The other man stared at Rex, transfixed, lips moving silently.

'Hello, Yitzie,' Rex said.

'Wh – why?' was the best response the man could muster.

'What's in the bag?' Rex said, pointing to the man's pocket.

'Nothing,' Yitzie growled. 'Books.'

He pushed past Rex, who blocked him.

'Tell me about your friendship with Dr Kovacs. Did he lend you books too?'

Another group of men came through the main doorway, sporting high, circular fur hats and long, velveteen coats. With surprising swiftness, Yitzie pushed Rex into their path and almost ran towards the brightly lit room. By the time Rex had made his way inside, Yitzie had secreted himself in the heart of the black-clad throng filling the long, thin room. Clearly he was a man who didn't want to talk. But why?

A thought struck him as he walked towards the main room. That Yitzie might have been his intended target. Too afraid to name her husband outright, Rescha had pointed Rex to where she knew he'd see him, find him doing something incriminating. But what had he been doing?

Rex had done enough research on the internet to find out that tish was Yiddish for 'table', and in Hasidic terms, it referred to any occasion on which a Rebbe ate in public with his followers.

He couldn't see a table, though, or a Rebbe, only a sea of men in coats and hats. The crowd was an amorphous tide of black, seeming to surge forwards and backwards in the shimmering light of myriad flames. It contained a multitude of noises. Here two red-faced men bellowed drunkenly at each other across the room; there, people softly murmured prayers while they rocked back and forth on their heels. Somewhere a melody was being played, a repetitive sea-shanty of a thing, picked out on a hidden guitar or banjo, while a dozen or so people sang and clapped along. The smell in the room was incredible: the medicinal whiff of strong alcohol, the moth-balled coats and hats, the sweat and the hair and cigarettes and candles and the fungal damp of the old building combining to make Rex feel almost drunk. A hand patted him on the arm, and he looked round to see a pale, freckled and beaming face, ringed with earlocks. Its owner handed him an open bottle of some straw-coloured liquid.

'Drink!' the face commanded, slapping him on the arm again. He took the bottle and swigged. He felt as if he'd swallowed a plum pudding with a stick of dynamite in it – fire exploded across his body and he bent over in a paroxysm of coughs. When the tears subsided, he saw a circle of men around him, old and young, smiling and nodding approvingly, felt a host of hands patting him gently across the back and shoulders. Someone offered another bottle and he drank again. This time they laughed and clapped.

Dimly, through the rush of intoxication, he registered how surprised he was. He hadn't expected to be made welcome. In fact he'd expected to be thrown out as soon as they realised he was among them. As more friendly hands guided him towards the middle of the room, he realised he wasn't the only un-Hasidic attendee. He spotted Vik, the famously grumpy man who ran KumarKabs on West Green Road: shiny of pate and gazing around benevolently, he now resembled an Indian god on a mantelpiece. Elsewhere Rex thought he caught a glimpse of a black leather cap stuffed with rasta dreadlocks. Clearly, the Dukovchiner weren't as reclusive as people said.

Invisible from the edge of the room, a long, thin trestle table stood in the centre. It reminded Rex of the birthday parties of his childhood, decked out with a paper tablecloth, and cardboard cups and plates. A handful of men sat on folding chairs, mostly ignoring the meagre spread of small, silvery fish and some kind of thick potato-cake. They were all singing, or humming, and stamping their feet to the melody coming from elsewhere in the room. All except the tall, muscular, red-haired young man who might have passed for a Welsh rugby player, and who gripped Rex in a handshake only just the right side of assault.

'Hello,' he said, bending down to Rex's ear over the hubbub of voices. 'We didn't get a chance to speak before. I am Simmy Dordoff, the gabbay.'

Once again it occurred to Rex that Simmy Dordoff cut a remarkable figure. About six foot four, he had the physique of a young farmer, now crowbarred into a perfectly cut, charcoal grey waistcoat and trouser combo.

Bidding for equal attention with the man's mountainous physique was the magnificent set of copper-coloured ear curls, which performed a dinky curtsey each time their owner moved his head.

'Where is the Rebbe?'

Simmy beamed and held up a massive finger. 'Coming. Now can I ask *you* a question? What brings you here?'

'I heard you don't have these dinners very often,' Rex shouted back. 'I thought I should see it.'

Simmy chuckled and shook his head, the ringlets flinging out like Cossack dancers. 'A tish isn't a dinner. It's *dvekus*.'

Rex looked confused. 'Dvekus means cleaving,' Dordoff explained. 'It's a moment when a Rebbe and his followers come together in joy, and we all join with God.'

In the room, it felt as if a dial was slowly being turned, bringing the intensity of the singing and the clapping and the stamping to the brink of some sort of tipping point. A chant had started up, made up of short syllables that grew ever longer. He wondered whether Moses Limburg, or any of the Bettelheims' other relatives, were here. It wouldn't be easy to spot them in the crowd.

Simmy Dordoff smiled. 'You feel it? Every time Jews gather together to do this, we're making something happen.'

'You're certainly making a lot of noise.'

Dordoff laughed heartily. 'It's *tikkun olam*. We're repairing the world. Not just with the singing and dancing. But every time we joyfully fulfil any of the six hundred and thirteen commandments.' He joined finger and thumb in a circle and put it close to Rex's eye. 'Our first Rebbe explained it this way. Each one of them is like a grain of mortar and one day, when some Jew, somewhere, has completed the last one of the trillions of commandments that need to be fulfilled, a chasm in the created world will be filled again.' He cast an arm around the room. 'Which Jew will it be? Somebody here, maybe, singing a holy song? Or a member of the faithful in Brazil, or Yemen, or Birmingham, Alabama, putting on tefillin and reciting the morning blessing. We don't know. Isn't that a wonderful thought?'

'It depends what happens when you've filled your chasm up,' Rex shouted.

'Then creation is repaired, the Messiah comes, God is united with the lost side of His nature and…' Dordoff shrugged, beaming still. 'We don't know. Enough of our prophets and holy men say it will be good for us to know that it will be good and we should all try to make it happen.'

'So actually, it would happen sooner if there were more people out there doing what you do. Does that mean you try to convert people?'

'You thinking about it?'

'Too painful. Seriously, though. Do you go out there, trying to get new members?'

'We live our lives. Sometimes people are attracted to the way we live our lives and they ask to join us.'

'Like Yaakov Bettelheim,' Rex said, remembering what Mrs Greenhill had told him at the jewellers.

'Yes, like Yaakov Bettelheim,' Dordoff confirmed, a little bit too quickly, to Rex's thinking. 'Here –' He reached onto the table. 'You wanna frank?'

Rex took the tepid frankfurter. 'I thought you guys had given up meat?'

The smile wavered before returning full-beam. 'Who said?'

'Bloke in the butchers.'

Dordoff nodded. 'Okay, okay. And did anyone tell you we never go out at night, and we haven't got a Rebbe and we've got horns and tails?'

'Erm… Some of the above.'

Grinning enigmatically like a conjuror, Simmy Dordoff removed his fur hat, then lifted the skullcap underneath it. 'See them?'

Rex smiled. 'People seem to have some funny ideas about you lot.'

'What people? Gentiles? No. You mean Jews. In fact, you mean other Hasidic Jews. You know why? Because we won't take sides. Everyone else – Satmar, Lubavitch, Belz, Ger, Bratslaver, Skverer – they want to know, where do you stand on Israel? Where do you stand on adoption, and conversion, and Islam, and changing your socks on the Sabbath? They want to know, all the time, what side are you on? Who are you against? And we say: against nobody. With God. We haven't stopped buying and eating meat! But the community here expects that everyone will buy from either Mega Glatt or Mehadrin. Because you see, where you buy your meat from, says which kosher slaughter board you side with, which of the officiating rabbis you support. So it ceases to be anything to do with God's law, and becomes about money, and politics.' He laughed. 'We refuse to play the game! We don't eat a lot of meat, it's true. When we do, we get it from Antwerp!'

Rex nodded, half-admiring, although the solution seemed in some ways as perverse as the problem. 'Whose idea was that?'

'The Narpal. Our Rebbe.'

He seemed about to say more when the noise in the room suddenly cut dead. Silence swelled and filled every corner like a balloon. The men parted and through the middle of them, someone pushed a tiny, wizened child in a wheelchair.

'The Narpal,' whispered Simmy.

The Narpal had minute, twisted limbs, and was propped into a sitting position by an array of velvet cushions. As he came closer, Rex saw that the figure in the chair was actually a young man, with a fuzz of downy hair on his chin and upper lip. He gazed at the world through thick, fishbowl spectacles, and his head and fingers jerked, periodically. Rex had seen the Narpal before, he remembered – freed from his afflictions, in the idealised line drawing on the tiled wall of Yitzie Schild's shop. In the reverential silence, Rex watched as the young Rebbe was wheeled around the table, stopping by each man for a moment of communion that seemed to take place entirely without word or gesture.

'You want to meet our Narpal?' Simmy asked softly.

'I'd like that. What does Narpal mean?'

'It's an acronym, Mr Tracey. From the main syllables of *Na-ar ha-Plaot*. Boy of Wonders.'

'Wonder Boy?' Rex found it hard to suppress a smile.

'You think it's funny?' Simmy asked, but he said it in an amused way, as if he found Rex as strange as he knew Rex found him. 'The last Rebbe chose him as his successor even before he was bar-mitzvah, because he knew.' Simmy tapped the corner of his eye. 'He knew there was something special about him. You would call it holiness.'

Rex recalled the fraught exchange he'd caught between Yitzie and his wife in the grocer's shop. Maybe not everyone agreed that this sick young man was holy.

'And everyone's happy? I mean, happy to have a very young and sick man as a leader?'

'He isn't so young. He is eighteen. Anyway, we can't help it if some people only look on the surface,' Dordoff replied, now less friendly.

'What about the Bettelheim family? Was that why they were leaving the sect? Why Moses Limburg told me they had to be made an example of?'

The smile vanished completely.

'Are the Bettelheims' relations here tonight, Mr Dordoff?' Rex went on.

'They're with the bodies at the mortuary,' came the stony response. 'Or as near as you'll allow them.'

'Not me, Mr Dordoff. I just wondered why Moses Lim–'

The Narpal came near. Rex caught a sharp, sweet hospital smell familiar to him from the long months of visiting a wife in a coma. He saw a cannula attached to the young man's wrist with a pink length of plaster. It was plain that the Narpal was very ill, and yet there was something arresting about him. Perhaps it was the softness of his skin, and the tapered beauty of his extraordinarily delicate fingers. Or was it simply the almost palpable love and awe radiating in the direction of this twisted, poorly human from a packed roomful of men.

Two vastly magnified, ice-clear blue eyes stared right up at Rex. Ridiculously, he felt himself bowing. The Narpal murmured something and Simmy Dordoff bent down low to catch it.

'He says you knew God, but now you hate Him,' Simmy said, straightening up.

'Well, that applies to 99% of all Roman Catholics,' Rex quipped. In truth, though, the comment made him nervous.

Dordoff merely relayed this to the Narpal, and then brought back a response. 'Very soon, you will witness a miracle.'

After that pronouncement, the Narpal was wheeled away. Rex wondered whether he would have a silent moment of communion with everyone in the crowded hall. But then another chant started up, gradually snaking its way through the place until everyone seemed to be joining in. Simmy Dordoff took a deep swig from a slivovitz bottle and passed it to Rex.

'This kind of song is called a *niggun*,' he said. 'It's a word for melodies we've kept in our hearts from the time of the Great Temple. Enjoy.'

'You never answered my question about the Bettelheims,' Rex said. But Dordoff was already striding off in the wake of the Narpal's chair, leaving Rex alone in the crowd with the bottle. He passed it to an old man and tried blearily to focus on the scene around him. Perhaps he could find the young man – Moses Limburg – and get him to say more.

He didn't think he liked Simmy Dordoff much. It wasn't just because of his steely response to questions about the Bettelheims. Even before that, Rex had been unnerved by the dazzling teeth and the American smiles, and the long Press Release-type statements. Whatever else Hasidism might be, this particular branch was beginning to seem a little like a cult.

But what did that mean? On one level, this was just a bunch of men getting pissed and singing songs and venerating a boy in a wheelchair. Nevertheless, there was something remarkable about it, like the three Kings kneeling before a baby in a stable. There was a kind of spirit in the room, which he'd interpreted as friendliness when he first came in, but whose full and proper name he now realised. It was love. But did God have to be involved?

And could all those wise, mystical words that Dordoff attributed to him really have come from the twitching, twisted form in the chair? Was the Narpal truly a Wonder Boy? Or were other, stronger people using him for their purposes? Was that what Rescha Schild had meant him to see?

He became aware of a disturbance on the other side of the room. A man was shouting, in a high-pitched, hoarse voice, on the edge of tears. The singing died and the black sea parted, revealing a very unholy scattering of fag-ends and bottle-tops across the floorboards. The shouting came from a livid-faced man with a straggly beard, while another, much bigger man struggled with his arms. The second man was Yitzie Schild.

'Micah!' the man was shouting at the Narpal and Simmy Dordoff, who were now surrounded by a protective semi-circle of onlookers. 'Voss veystu? Voss veystu?' To Rex, it sounded half-question, half-accusation, repeated over and over in a fraught, breaking shout – the sound of a man on the brink. And if Lawrence had shown up, he'd have known what was being said.

The chant started up again, at first softly:

Ce, Vce, Kovce, Dukovce, Ce, Vce, Kovce, Dukovce, Ce, Vce…

It grew louder and louder with each repetition, almost as though it was being wielded as a weapon against the man. Rex saw Simmy Dordoff give some sort of command to Yitzie Schild, and the big man dragged the other from the room. The tone of the struggle wasn't quite clear: was Yitzie looking after him, or chucking him out?

Rex pushed his way out after them, the dream of sacredness pierced by this ugly little scene, like a fight at a wedding. He didn't know any Yiddish, but he knew the name Micah. Micah Walther. The boy who'd vanished six months ago. Was the man was his father?

A scuffle was taking place on the forecourt by the time he got there – not Yitzie doing anything to the man, but Yitzie trying, with limited success, to avoid the wild thrashings of the man, who'd armed himself with a rotting floorboard. Rex realised that his face wasn't flushed as he'd first thought, but almost entirely covered in a port-wine birthmark. Rex's appearance was enough for the man to drop his weapon and escape through the flapping panels of the security fence.

'Wait! Can I talk to you?' Rex shouted, but by the time he'd squeezed himself out onto the Grove, the man had vanished into the night. He started to push his way back through the boards, and saw that Yitzie had been joined by Simmy Dordoff in the doorway. He could tell at a glance that Simmy Dordoff did not want him back in.

Under normal circumstances, Rex would have been inclined to put his head down, place one shoulder forward and, insofar as any man with a limp could charge, charge his way back in. The reason he didn't do that now was because his phone rang. It was Lawrence.

'Where the hell were you, Lawrence?'

'Where the hell were you, more like? I must have called you five times at least. I'm at the North Middlesex. With Terry.'

'What happened?'

'I found him unconscious on the floor of your living room. He's taken an overdose.'

Chapter Five

'I just thought Bertha could do with a little run around, and as I drove down your road I saw the light was on, so I thought perhaps you were still there, and might like a lift...'

Save for a pair of exhausted young Indian doctors nodding off over their toasted sandwiches, Rex and Lawrence were the only customers in the new hospital café. Before the overhaul, it had been a mere hatch. Now it was a bright, plastic-clad restaurant, run by a Brazilian family and decked out in that nation's distinctive cheese 'n' onion livery. Rex sipped his coffee and tried to overlook Lawrence's reference to 'Bertha'. Lawrence had names for his cars, his suits, even for various items of luggage. On the other hand, irritating as he was, he had just saved Terry's life.

'I looked in through the windows and saw him. He'd been sick and there were pill packets all around him.

Lawrence dug in the pocket of his checked sports coat and handed Rex a packet. They were his codeine pills. Rex had taken to buying them on the internet, from India, after his new GP had advised him to try meditation classes to cope with the pain in his foot.

'Quite a stockpile you've got there.' Lawrence gave him a meaningful look.

'I'd have hidden them if I'd known he was suicidal.'

'I know. I know.' Lawrence said. 'But why have you got so many of them?'

'So I don't run out,' Rex said, realising, as he said it, how he sounded. Lawrence, to his credit, pretended not to have heard.

Terry had been given an opiate blocker on his arrival at the hospital, and his vital signs were now approaching normal. He was sleeping it off, on a bed in a corridor just behind them. It would have been a different story if the pills had contained paracetamol along with the codeine.

The man behind the counter put a TV on. A fuzzy football match appeared on the screen, along with near-hysterical Portuguese commentary. The two young doctors stirred.

'I did a bit of digging on your Outrage doodah,' Lawrence said.

'Yes?'

'Yes.'

Rex stifled a sigh. He wanted to take some of the pills, but he didn't dare. 'Please just tell me, Lawrence.'

'Well, if you recall, there were two perpetrators of the wages-snatch. Josef Lapidus died during the chase. Paul Helfeld was shot by the police during the chase and he took two weeks to die. He was coming out with some very queer stuff, according to one of the nurses in the hospital...' Lawrence paused and smiled. 'It was this hospital, actually. Fancy that. Anyhoo... one of the things he kept saying, or asking... well, it's disputed, because he was delirious with meningitis, and he was talking in a language that wasn't his first to a nurse in a similar predicament. So anyway, according to this one nurse, he was going on about Vulcan.'

'Vulcan?'

Lawrence, who'd been trying to cut a cheese toastie in half with a plastic knife, finally gave up.

'Have you noticed they've taken away all the proper knives and forks? It's the same in the Jerk Chicken place. And the Good Taste Café. I'm thinking of doing a few verses on it for next week's paper.

"Terrorists growled, and cutlery withdrew…"'

'Lawrence. Vulcan? As in the Greek god?'

'Roman. God of metals and mining, frequently depicted with a bad foot. Like you.'

'Yes, well, the only divine thing about my foot is that I sometimes think God did it to me. What exactly did this guy Helfeld say about Vulcan?'

'As I said, opinions differ. According to one nurse, he asked whether Vulcan had got back to Riga. According to another, he said his mother was in Riga.'

'Riga, Latvia?' Kovacs had been there, Rex recalled, and learnt Latvian, so this could have been an angle he'd been exploring.

'Yup. It was part of the Russian Empire at the time, of course. Apparently the nurses told the local bobbies, but they didn't think it was important.'

'Well, they were probably right weren't they? Even if he did say "Vulcan" then he just meant the other guy he did the robbery with, didn't he? Like a codename for him?'

'Josef Lepidus.' Lawrence shook his steely curls. 'I don't think so, because he'd seen Lepidus shot dead on the chase.'

'So he got confused. The man was dying from a bullet wound after all.'

'Yes, he might have been confused. Then again no one ever found the money.'

'So there could have been a third member of the team?'

'It's a thought. And it might have been what George Kovacs was going to reveal in his book.'

Rex ran his fingertips over some sugar crystals on the table top. It was plastic, with a log pattern. What if there had been a third man, who'd somehow taken the money back to Riga? Did it really matter? Perhaps to people interested in the events of January 1909, but not, as far as he could see, to those more worried about last Monday.

'I did find out a bit more about the group Helfeld and Lepidus were involved in. It was called *Leesma*. Latvian for 'the flame'. It stayed active over here for a couple of years. They were key players in the Siege of Sidney Street in 1911. You know about that one?'

'Was that the one where there was a massive shoot-out and Winston Churchill came down to have a look?'

'The very article. Thing is, there's plenty of whatnot about the Leesma's activities over here. Chuff-all information from their homeland, though, largely because Lenin got rid of all the anarchists and then Stalin got rid of virtually all the records. There was one thing, though…' He held up a finger and rummaged in his black leather satchel for an iPad.

'There is a website…' he said, typing something into the browser bar. The screen went black, then two words shot in from opposite sides of the screen to make the message "Black Flag". 'It's a sort of anarchist hangout. Some rum coves on here, I can tell you…'

He clicked on a profile in one of the site's forums to reveal three burly young men in balaclavas, displaying an array of knuckledusters and knives on a table.

'Boy Scouts, all of them, I'm sure,' Rex said.

'Indeed. But you also get lots of free-the-web hacker-types and flat-earthers who just believe in the philosophy. And…'

He scrolled down a list of discussion topics on the site, ranging from 'Bakunin on the Church' to 'Top Ten Ways To Disappear'. He found what he was looking for and turned the device towards Rex.

On a forum about pre-revolutionary Russian archives, there was a request for information about people suspected of involvement with the Leesma. The request had been posted eleven months previously by one 'KovaGN15'.

'Sounds like our George,' Rex said, looking up.

'Read on, MacDuff.'

The conversation which followed this query seemed to confirm the identification. Someone calling themselves GoldVlad had offered information, but asked for a research fee. KovaGN15 had agreed to this, and there'd been no further communication until the autumn, when GoldVlad had re-appeared, abusing KovaGN15 and warning other site-users to stay away from him. It wasn't clear whether the research had been done or not, but KovaGN15 had responded, and there had ensued several months' worth of toing and froing cyber-abuse. During the final exchanges, GoldVlad was accusing KovaGN15 of assorted deviant sexual practices, and KovaGN15 was calling GoldVlad a ponderous cretin. The ponderous cretin had had the last word, though, signing off with the following words:

Watch you're back, Kovacs. If I can fined one girl in Russia I can fined one sad cunt in N15.

'Not exactly a gifted writer, is he?'

'Kovacs had his problems, too,' Lawrence pointed out. It was true. KovaGN15's posts looked as if a gang of cats had been let loose on a keyboard – random capitals, punctuation marks and symbols dotted throughout. Rex remembered the printers complaining that he'd refused to send an electronic copy of his book. The man obviously hadn't been at ease with computers. Yet he, and this GoldVlad had chosen the internet to conduct their very public spat.

That was less important, though, than the timing of the whole exchange. The very last message had been posted on Saturday the 28th of February. Two days before Kovacs was murdered. Rex stared at Lawrence.

'When did you find this?'

'Just this afternoon. That's another reason I came over in the car – I wanted to show you and Terry. You realise what it means? Someone else is on record, making threats against Kovacs, just before he died.'

'So if we can find out who this GoldVlad is…'

Lawrence chuckled. 'He's made that rather easy for us.'

He clicked on the profile name and they were taken to another page. GoldVlad had not included a photograph but he described himself thus:

Research Associate in Russian History at Goldsmiths, University of London. Genius. Black belt. Exile.

'Goldsmiths. That's where Kovacs taught.' Rex stared at the profile page. 'So the guy happily puts his sodding job title next to his death threats. Do people really not understand what the internet is?'

'My youngest went on Twatbook or whatever it's called to complain about her boss at the bookshop and then had a fit when she got sacked. They think this stuff is just like talking. They don't realise it stays around forever.'

They were interrupted by a pretty Chinese nurse. 'Your friend is waking up. You can take him home once the doctor has given him the all-clear.'

* * *

Everyone in a stew this morning. Missus Cutter being sick now, clutching her bonnet, saying the slightest noise is a torment. Leah, looking pink and plump, growing weary of her mother's demands. She's got better and she's got plump, that girl. Not in a bad way. In a way like they say in Yiddish *zaftig*. Like a peach you want to bite. But she's breathless on the stairs, going up and down for her mother. I've noticed that.

Could be Tuberculosis. Could be this smog. Everyone's suffering. I've got a cough I can't shift, though I've been trying the Old Country way – raw garlic, glass of vodka, glass of tea, one after the other. In the streets, though, no one seems to notice the poison that's hanging in front of their eyes. They only complain about the cold. And until you've done the dawn watch on New Year's Day going up the Neva, you don't know cold. It's not cold that I mind.

I was going about in that filthy smog all day. Work. Post Office. Work. Ferry Lane Working Men's Library. Coughing and coughing. The librarian looks at me, open-mouthed. Funny, he reminded me of my sisters when the Recruiting Officer came to call. No idea what creed we were of course: no money for fine candlesticks or challah-covers in our house. Anyway, who'd think this fine brood of blue-eyed Lettish dune-dwellers might have the taint of Abraham about them?

'Bright lad, Mrs Kuznetz. Top marks in the exam. And sharp, you know, in his interview, sharp as a kike peddler.' My sisters' mouths drop. Mother slaps them. Recruiter slurps tea through his ginger moustaches, none the wiser. Certainly not wise that the father to the lot of us was one kike peddler, now deceased.

Ivanhoe by Sir Walter Scott. What a book. I hate it, all those knights and castles. A man called front-of-beef and a Jew moneylender who drools over gold. Velkis picked it for our most private correspondence. Only to be used in dire emergency. I telegraphed him a message last week. This week, the reply. *I will come when mother is quite well. Regards, your brother William.* Like the arithmetical hocus-pocus those vain young scholars perform on the Torah. Gematria, it's called. But ours has real messages. You turn each of the letters of those words into numbers and the numbers point you to the pages and the lines of the dreaded Sir Walter Scott, and there's your answer.

Velkis was a teacher and a poet, I believe, before he discovered a talent for slitting postmen's throats and exploding railway bridges. Still likes to fill his messages with metaphor and symbol.

So it comes out as: Sailor tells Captain how to sail ship, ship hits rocks.

The joke of it is, if the boss sent a message like that to Elephant and Torch, they'd be scratching their heads like a pair of Tartar whores ransacking their crotches for lice. Wouldn't get it at all. I, on the other hand, get it fully, even though what it means is – I'm the sailor, and they're the Captains, and they know what they're doing, and I'm to follow, quiet like, never mind the Police Station next to the factory or any other example of their thundering dunder-headedness. A rebuke. Just like sending me here to work with the pair. That had nothing to do with getting me away from the girl. That was Velkis – jealous. I'm the one who can hold a room. I'm the one who can change minds. And the more I changed, the more the boss hated me for it.

I despair of our organisation. Leesma is not pure any more. Half of us are informants. And I suspect the other half are policemen. That explains why they are so stupid. Anyway, I've decided. I don't care if it is a suicide mission. I won't be dying.

Speaking of informants, I had this feeling I was being watched. Not in the library. Of course they were watching me there, spluttering like a clogged tender among the bookstacks. I mean in the streets on the way back to the Cutters'. The smog plays tricks, of course. It's so heavy and dark, it can almost feel like a person at your neck. Still. I know what it is to be followed.

Got it wrong, though, sometimes. All those weeks I spent in Riga, on the trail of the one I thought was on the trail of me. Same flash of red as I turned my head, no matter whether it was the fish-market, the book-market or the clothes-market. Or a gate would creak. Or there'd be this sweet smell outside my door, above and through the dog-piss and the pickles. Heaven filtered through hell.

All thoughts of this following business vanished, though, when I rounded the corner. Leah at the door of the house, flushed, wet-faced, calling out. Missus Cutter flat on the hearth rug in her nightgown, pale as holystone, vomit on the floor.

Run for a doctor!

Leah begs. I can't run of course. But there's this police sees me. Big lad with a country face and a silky moustache. Old Bill they call him round here, though he's a young fellow, and P.C. William

Tyler's his proper name. Sees me hobbling and says he'll run for the quack.

Off like a wolf on a goose he was. A good lad. Torch and Elephant will go on about the 'truncheon-bearing lackeys of the hegemony' but that's just because they've read it somewhere. I've nothing against the police here. Just working lads, most of them, and I've seen Old Bill slipping a penny to the odd, hollow-cheek beggar child with a hacking cough.

They took Missus Cutter to the Prince of Wales Infirmary. It's just Leah and me now. Playing house. At least, she thinks that's what I'm doing because when we got back from the hospital, I washed the window that looks out onto the yard. Before, you could only see a glimpse of your own face shining back at you from the blackness. Such a dirty town. Worse even than Sosnovy Bor, where they light the whole port with herring oil and you come away with black, greasy, fishy dust all over your clothes, reeking like a whore at dawn.

'Aren't you going to do the rest of them windows, Mr Smith?' Leah asks me. And, I think, asks with a bit of sauce in it, too. Weeping for her poor mama a few hours before. Now doing the innkeeper's daughter dance with the lodger. She's to go to an aunt at Highgate tomorrow, while her mother's in the infirmary. A good idea, too.

No, Miss Leah, I need a view of the yard, because that's where my friends will be placing a secret signal, any day now, for us to begin a most audacious robbery of the Bank of England.

See, I actually said that. Like I was teasing her back. Must be losing my mind. Time she went to her auntie's, like I said.

*   *   *

The next morning, Rex took an overground train – a new, strange, wide, orange-liveried thing with concertina sections between the carriages. It was mostly empty, the commuters who packed it out during the week being all tucked up in bed. Rex pictured them, this alien tribe, having languid, hungover weekend sex and consuming tea and biscuits under their duvets in their gadget-filled flats. There were times when he envied them: the people with the straight jobs and the other-halves, the eat-in kitchens and the holiday plans. He'd almost joined them, once.

The overground line was high up, and he looked out onto attics and top floors, mobile phone masts and advertising hoardings. It was no uglier than his own patch of North-East London. But it wasn't his, and nowhere seemed less his, less familiar or capable of sustaining life, than the place that lay across the Thames but was, incredibly, still called London.

This attitude, he remembered, had been a point of contention with his wife, who, at various points during their truncated marriage, had suggested moving out of their Camden flat to something bigger in the south, where she had lived for years in the dense yet strangely barren areas of Rotherhithe and Bermondsey. Rex had stubbornly resisted, without being able to provide a single solid reason for it. He just didn't like south London. Something bad happened to him, he said, every time he went over the water.

'Bad like getting into bed with me?'

It was what she always said in response to this argument, half-joking, sometimes following it up with a pinch of the soft flesh under his ribs. Suddenly he remembered it all, their life together: that quip, her incongruously rough, physical way of showing tenderness, the night they'd first fallen into her hard, lumpy, pine-smelling bed. It all came back, sharply, painfully, as the tannoy said 'change here for Bermondsey'. He got up and moved seats to take his mind somewhere else, away from what he'd lost forever.

He tried to concentrate on the Goldsmiths campus map he'd printed up last night. He'd established that the library and the history faculty building were open on Saturdays, but of course that was no guarantee of the person called GoldVlad being there. Even if he was, confronting him might be a very bad idea. But Rex knew that if they put their findings to the under-resourced, overworked and increasingly short-tempered D.S. Brenard, nothing might happen for days, or even weeks. It had to be worth a try.

In the event of something bad happening on this particular trip across the river, there was a pre-written text, addressed both to Lawrence and Terry's phones, ready to go at one push. That had been Lawrence's idea. Since leaving the hospital, Terry had adopted a numb, blank look, speaking only to say that he was fine, that he felt fine, and that he didn't want another cup of tea.

At the North Middlesex hospital, they saw too much self-harm. Too much to be able to do more than patch up those for whom it was still an option, and send them home. In the car on the way back to Tottenham, Lawrence had tentatively suggested Terry might want to talk to someone. Their gaunt, grey-faced friend had shown a sudden, brief flash of passion.

'Talk about what?' he snapped. 'I just took too many of those painkillers because it hurts all down me neck and me back. I didn't know how strong they were. What's there to fucking talk about?'

Instinctively, both Rex and Lawrence had acted as if they believed this explanation one hundred percent, but from that point on an unspoken pact existed between them to keep Terry under permanent watch.

Rex had left the two of them at his house. They were planning to spend the morning in Kovacs' basement, looking for further clues as to what he'd been working on. He doubted Terry would be doing much looking. Most likely he'd be sitting at that wooden table, perhaps in torment, perhaps just utterly empty and numb. Still, it was better he did that with someone's beady eye on him.

The train arrived at New Cross Gate. Fittingly – for Rex's prejudices at any rate – what had been a fine, almost sparkling drizzle in Tottenham was driving rain in this part of town.

Ten minutes later, soaking wet, and with his foot sending arthritic spars of agony up as far as his inner thigh, Rex took shelter in the doorway of the very un-historic-looking History Faculty and popped a couple of pills. He had brought the entire remainder of his supply with him, to keep it away from Terry.

A beautiful, Latin-looking woman in a tight angora jumper sat at a desk in the Faculty Office. She wore a thick, cloying perfume, and a coloured scarf was wrapped around her neck.

'I'm looking for one of your research associates,' he began. 'I'm not sure of his name, but it might be Vlad, or Vladimir.'

'Why do you want him?'

'I'm down from Lincoln for a few days,' Rex said, hoping that the way he said 'Lincoln' might convey 'University of'. 'We're working on similar turf and he suggested we meet up.'

'Okay,' she said slowly. 'But we don't have anyone called Vlad or Vladimir.'

'Ah… It's just that Vlad is the, sort of, nickname he uses on some of the websites I've met him on and–' He trailed off, noticing her raised eyebrows.

'You've come to see someone you met on the internet?'

'Well, not like that, but…'

'Not like what?'

'We share a research interest in Russian pre-revolutionary anarchist movements,' he said sternly.

'I see,' she replied, with the ghost of a smile. 'You must mean Tim. He's upstairs in the research office. Room 119.'

GoldVlad, aka Tim, turned out to be a pale, very fat young man in a UCLA Sports Department sweatshirt. His haircut was similarly ironic – shaven at the sides and foppishly long on top, rather like the North Korean leader's. A huge bag of Japanese rice crackers sat on the desk in front of him. He was alone in the room, flipping idly through a learned journal when Rex introduced himself and bluntly stated his business. A look of alarm came into Tim's piggy eyes.

'Shit, look,' he said, in a faint West Country accent. 'I shouldn't have said that stuff to Kovacs, I know, I just lost it a bit when he wouldn't pay up. I've been expecting the Feds ever since I heard about him being killed.'

'Pay you? So you did do some research for him?'

'Yeah. We agreed a fee... God, must have been back in February last year, but his initial request drew a blank, pretty quickly. Then he said he had some others, and one job sort of kept turning into another, and then at the end, he said he wasn't going to give me the full fee because I hadn't sorted out the first request for him. Twat.'

'Is it normal – for people to hire historians to do research for them?'

'It's not abnormal. Most big libraries have a few researchers you can hire if you don't want to do it yourself.'

'But why would a historian not want to do it himself?'

'Are you really not from the police?'

'I'm a friend of the man who's currently the main suspect in George Kovacs' murder. If I hear something the police ought to know, I'll tell them, Vlad. If I don't think they need to know it...'

Tim nodded and sighed. 'It's not Vlad. It was V-lad. I'm from a village in Cornwall. Virginstow.' He lumbered over to a bookshelf and fetched a folder.

'Pre-rev Russia wasn't his area. He had a bit of the lingo, but unless it's your specialism, you don't know where to go, where to cross-refer, what source to trust.'

'So it was a complicated job?'

'Not really.' Tim opened the folder and gave it to Rex. 'Most of it was straightforward 'Who Do You Think You Are?' stuff.'

Rex looked at the pages in front of him. They seemed to be copies of some old census or register, written in a tiny, sloping, old-fashioned hand.

'He had you tracing his family?'

'He got in touch initially because he wanted to know about people who'd been suspected of involvement with a Latvian terrorist group between 1905 and 1909 or so. I said I could help him. But as I say, there just wasn't anything. The records weren't there. So I got back to him about a month or so later and told him and he said, all right, something different then – tell me about this woman.' He tapped the pages in the file. 'Rosa Brandt. She was from a very well-off Jewish family in Riga. More of a dynasty, really. All the men were important rabbis, married to the daughters of other important rabbis, stretching back hundreds of years. Kovacs wanted me to find out what happened to her.'

'Did he say why?'

'Dunno. A relative maybe? It wasn't very interesting.'

'I'm guessing she married an important rabbi, and had lots of little important rabbis?'

'Well, that was the only odd bit. She married a grocer…' He rummaged through the folder. 'Immanuel Feigenbaum. They emigrated to Whitechapel in London in January 1911.'

'So for some reason, instead of being married off to an illustrious rabbi, she married a grocer and moved.'

' Yup. They had at least one kid…' he shrugged. 'I don't know. I sent him all the records but they didn't seem very interesting. I got the impression he thought that, too, because that was when he started trying to talk the price down. As you know.'

'I know your response to it.'

Tim blinked. 'Look. I'm really ashamed of what I wrote. But you don't expect your old tutor to skank you, do you?'

'I wanted to ask you about that. How come he knew you already, but you hooked up on that anarchist forum?'

Tim reddened. 'He didn't remember me. I doubt he'd have approached me if he had.'

'You didn't get on?'

'He tutored me for two years, before he retired. Made my life an absolute misery. Lots of people's lives. Honestly, a tutorial with him was like, I don't know, being interviewed by the Stasi or something. He was really demanding, mega-critical… And nasty with it. Shouty. He'd had all these heart attacks, so when you were getting it in the neck, you were always thinking was he going to pop his clogs. Hoping, I'm afraid, quite a lot of the time.'

'I guess you weren't fond of him then.'

'More like, no but yeah,' Tim said. 'I mean – he made me into a historian. If I'd had someone softer, I might not be here doing research. I mean, I'm dyslexic, so lots of people just assume I'm thick and don't bother with me. He wasn't like that. He kept on at me, all the time. So I do respect him, in a way. Respected him. I kept wanting to tell him, you know, when we were messaging over the research, like, do you know who I am? That kid you used rip to shreds – do you know where he is now? I kind of liked him not knowing, though.'

He caught a hint of something in Tim's eyes then – pride, and also a kind of steeliness. Something that came, perhaps, from being the tubby boy in the tiny village school, Tim who was teased for reading slowly. He was angry. But no killer.

'And you really have no idea why he wanted to know about this Brandt woman?'

'No idea. As I say, I think he just lost interest. When I told him I'd found the shop he didn't even acknowledge it.'

'The shop?'

'The Feigenbaums sort of disappeared off the record for a while. That's normal – there were shiploads arriving into the East End every day. After I'd tracked them to Whitechapel it took me quite a long time to find what happened next. A few months of enquiries anyway – all over the summer. Kovacs seemed to be getting impatient at first, like he really wanted to know. Then I guess he lost interest. When I told him what I'd finally found out – must have been September, I think – he didn't reply for about two weeks, and then he started trying to talk the price down. That's when we stated slagging each other off on Black Flag.'

'And what did you find out?' Rex asked, struggling to sound patient.

'Feigenbaum was dirt poor. But somehow, maybe because of his wife's family or something like that, he managed to buy a grocer's shop. In Stamford Hill. I tracked it down. It's still there.'

* * *

Rex sipped a can of Coke as he walked back down Langerhans Road. He couldn't remember the last time he'd gone into Get-It-In or any of the other comparable shops in the locality and not emerged with a can of Polish lager. But he'd come off the train feeling strangely trembly, and somewhere through the fog of codeine and pain and hangover, he sensed his body telling him it wanted something very specific.

Some people's bodies were always telling them things. His wife had regularly claimed hers told her it needed salted peanuts. For the first time Rex believed that might have been true. His body had definitely wanted sugar. And the minute he provided it, it felt better.

He went round the back of Terry's house to peer in through the basement window. He was about to shout a cheery greeting, then saw that Lawrence was on his own, picking up sheaves of paper scattered all over the floor. Rex climbed in through the window and asked what had happened.

'Terry had a bit of a…' Lawrence said. 'Well, I don't know quite how to put it.'

Rex surveyed the scene. Kovacs' carefully labelled document boxes had been up-ended or thrown across the room. The floor was covered in notes, some of them typed, many scribbled on strange triangles of brown greaseproof paper. A wooden chair lay smashed in the corner.

'I think my youngest would call it a total thermonuclear melt-down,' Lawrence said, placing another sheaf of recovered notelets on the table.

'Where is he now?'

'Upstairs. The catalyst was that – thing on the wall over there.' He motioned to the hook that had skewered Rex when he'd been there with Kovacs' son. 'He kept walking into it and jabbing himself in the back, and in the end, he just… sort of lost it.'

'It's had me before now,' Rex said, going over and touching the needlessly sharp, malevolent point.

'Me too,' Lawrence said. 'And judging by that patch on the floor, it's got someone really badly at some point.'

Rex looked down. It was true. In amongst the papers, there was a rusty brown blood-stain in the shape of Cyprus. He wondered how long it had been there.

'I don't blame him. It must have been horrible for him all these years, knowing you're sitting on this time-bomb, just waiting for something else to stop working.'

Rex frowned. 'Terry already knew he had M.S.?'

'He's had it for over a decade. It's the relapse-remission kind, apparently, but I doubt that was much consolation when his leg stopped working in the cell.'

'It's not my leg,' said Terry's voice from the top of the stairs. 'It's these bastard shooting pains up my back and neck.' He picked his way slowly down the stairs. Rex went across to help but Terry waved him away. 'Fuck off,' he said, but gently, as he came into the room.

'Sorry,' he said to Lawrence. 'I wish you hadn't seen that.'

Lawrence acknowledged this with a brief, vague gesture then went back to tidying up the room. Rex felt an urge to do the same thing, but then thought that would only make Terry feel even more awkward.

'Did you manage to find anything useful before you did your impression of a cyclone?'

Terry smiled faintly. 'We did, actually. Don't know what it means, but...'

Lawrence straightened up again putting a few more papers into the lidless box.

'The... storm didn't hit this one. He seems to have been trying to find someone.'

'Let me guess. A family called Feigenbaum, who came to Stamford Hill in 1911?'

Lawrence and Terry exchanged a puzzled look. 'No, actually,' Lawrence replied. He pushed the box over to Rex. There were electoral roll searches, photocopies of birth certificates and wedding licenses, press cuttings, correspondence. But he knew what Lawrence meant him to see. A page cut from an old edition of their own newspaper. A picture of a boy, gap-toothed, cheerful. Micah Walther.

* * *

On Sunday mornings, much of North London had a hangover. Or if it didn't have a hangover, it was pretending to have one, by not getting out of bed, or looking slightly unwell, or doing everything at a snail's pace. The one proud exception to this rule seemed to be Stamford Hill, whose bright-eyed, well-rested residents had stepped straight through the sacred curtains of the Sabbath into their full working week. There was a long, excitable queue outside the baker's. At the street corners, hat brims bowed and raised in conversation. In the covered shopping arcade, a gang of coffee-skinned Yemeni Jews unpacked dates and avocados from crates filled with straw.

Even at 'Vegetables' there seemed to be some business going on: an old, stooped, bird-like lady was filling a tartan shopping trolley with spinach while a boy in an embossed apron went through a long list with Yitzie Schild at the counter. When Rex walked through the door the customers seemed to conclude their business in a hurry, and left.

Yitzie gazed open-mouthed at him across the counter. Rex could hear a clock ticking and the rasp of the big man's breath. Clearly he wasn't going to speak first.

'Does the name Feigenbaum mean anything to you, Mr Schild?

Yitzie adjusted his skullcap and blinked. There was a long pause, while Rex perused the long, dirt-filled crack tracing the shape of a river across the tiled wall behind. 'Fig tree,' Yitzie said finally.

A cute answer. But then Rex had suspected for some time that Yitzie wasn't as spaced-out as he looked. 'Was it your mother's name, by any chance?'

'Her name was Schild.' Rex made a face, but the man went on. 'I am not playing a trick with you. She had the same name as my father before she married. And after.' He shrugged. 'It can happen.'

'So…'

'Feigenbaum was my wife's name,' he blurted out. 'Rescha's name.'

So it was Rescha's family who had come from Latvia to this shop. Rosa Brandt, daughter of a distinguished line of grand rabbis, had ended up married to a man called Feigenbaum in a poky Stamford Hill grocer's. Was that also the kind of thing that could happen? Or was it unusual enough to arouse the interest of a historian like Dr Kovacs?

Rex looked into the man's pale, watery eyes. 'Did Dr Kovacs ask a lot of questions about her family?'

He moved the skullcap to one side of his head. 'Some.'

'Did you like him?'

'He came into the shop every morning. Early, every morning, just as we opened. Bought some fruit, some cookies. And he talked to me. So I talked to him.'

'Every morning since when? A long time?'

The skullcap moved back, high up on the crown of Yitzie's head. 'Not such. A year, something like that. I met him before that at the Healthy Heart Clinic,' he added, confirming what Rescha had said. 'He was learning Yiddish. He wanted to practice. So we talked. Just this and that. About my shop. My wife.'

'And Rescha's family?'

'Sometimes, some little things he wanted to know. Rescha said he asks too many questions, he doesn't like us, he's just studying us. I said if that was true, how come he gave me his keys to look out for his house when he went away?'

'Where did he go?'

The skullcap went to the other side of Yitzie's head. 'Liverpool. About a month ago.' Yitzie patted his breast pocket slowly and proudly. 'Before that, Riga. Australia, America… A very great traveller,' he said, as if somehow he shared in the glory of Dr Kovacs' trips abroad. 'He asked me to make sure the heating went on in his house. And sometimes, I went when he was there'.

'To talk Yiddish?'

'To talk Yiddish, and to fix things. I know how a lot of machines work. You see?'

Rex did see. Or thought he saw. The realisation that Kovacs' attention had passed for friendship in Yitzie's eyes made him feel immeasurably sad. In front of him was someone so lonely that they regarded switching Dr Kovacs' heating on as a kind of an honour. But what had Kovacs wanted from him? Just Yiddish practice? More information on Rescha? Or something else? Rex remembered the boy's photograph in Kovacs' box file.

'Did he ever mention Micah Walther?'

Yitzie looked surprised by the question. 'No. Why would he?'

'Did you ever see a black man at Dr Kovacs' house?' Rex went on, ignoring the man's question.

Yitzie's eyes widened. 'Once or twice. One time, I fixed the record player and he was arriving as I was leaving. And he called once when George was away. Rang the doorbell, and when I answered the door, he said the record player was good now. Then he just walked away.'

'The record player was good now,' Rex repeated, thinking aloud. 'Do you mend other things for people?'

Yitzie said nothing.

'What about the man at the tish? The man who gave you a bag?'

The skullcap moved again, orbiting Yitzie's damp scalp like a planet around a sun.

'Okay, have it your way,' Rex said, moving to the door. 'I won't pester you any more, Yitzie. I'll just make one phone call.'

He hadn't specified 'to the police', or 'to the council' or 'to the tax-man', because he didn't know which, if any of them, would be remotely interested in Yitzie and his bags. The significant thing was Yitzie's reaction. The big man barrelled around the counter so fast Rex almost thought he was going to be thumped. Instead, Yitzie turned the shop sign round, locked the door and pointed, panting slightly, towards a strip curtain at the back.

'Come.'

Rex followed his large rear-end up a short, dingy flight of stairs, lined with wooden vegetable crates and egg-boxes. At the top was a landing, also dimly lit. Its yellowing dado walls were adorned with tracts and solitary Hebrew words etched and burned and stitched into pieces of wood and tapestry. Wheezing, Yitzie led him through a door, and up a further wooden staircase into a little workshop in the roof. It had a sour reek that almost made his eyes water. It reminded Rex of his mother polishing horse-brasses at the local pub.

'Give your ring,' Yitzie grunted, motioning towards Rex's hand. Not entirely coincidentally, Rex was wearing his wedding ring that day, pricked into observance by another call from the nuns. A little taken aback, he pulled it obediently off his finger. Yitzie rolled it round and peered at it.

'A Chester assay mark. 1909. From your family?'

'My wife and I bought our rings second hand.' He watched as Yitzie padded over to the workbench with the ring. 'What are you doing with it?'

'See.'

Rex watched as Yitzie dropped his wedding ring into an aluminium bowl that was, via a Heath Robinson arrangement of crocodile clips and wires, connected to a power-supply. Whistling through his teeth, Yitzie added scoops of a fine-grained powder to the bowl, followed by a glug of clear fluid from a canister, and finally what was unmistakeably a lacing of maple syrup.

'Is this a joke?'

Ignoring him, Yitzie stirred the mixture with plastic tongs and switched the power supply on. It buzzed loudly, and he twiddled with a dial until the sound went away. A smell rose up, another one Rex remembered from long ago: hot metal and grease, the whiff of train-sets.

'I clean things,' Yitzie said, as a timer ticked away. 'In here, I have everything for cleaning gold and silver, diamonds, rubies…' He ran a proprietorial hand around the shelves. The place was like an alchemist's workshop. Butter of Antimony. Karo Syrup. NH3. 'The man you saw was giving me these. Wanted me to make them good for his wife's 50th birthday.'

He pointed to a rack hung with an assortment of necklaces and bracelets.

'We are not so different, you see. There are men who love their wives.'

Surprised by the comment, Rex looked directly at him and their eyes met. Yitzie blushed. The timer pinged off, and with obvious relief Yitzie fetched Rex's ring out of the pot and laid it on a wad of white cotton wool. To Rex's eyes it didn't look any different.

'So if this is all you do, why did you run away when I saw you at the tish?'

'I worked at a jeweller's until I got sick. So I tried to set up…'
He paused for breath. Yitzie wasn't mentally slow, Rex realised, just
not a well man. 'I tried to set up my own workshop here, but the
Council said no. Too much of dangerous chemicals. No license.'

'So you did it anyway.'

'I am very careful,' Yitzie replied. 'I got so many allergies these
days. Most things set me off. But these materials here… They don't
do anything to me.' He sprayed something onto the ring, wrapped
it in the wad of cotton wool and scrunched it up in a massive fist
for a few seconds before handing it delicately to Rex like a sweet-
meat. The ring was very bright now, brighter even than when he'd
first bought it with Sybille. It felt like putting on a different ring.

'It's how I knew Yaakov Bettelheim. And Toyve Walther
– Micah's father. We all worked together in this business.'

'In Hatton Garden?'

Yitzie shook his head. 'Yaakov went to work there at the end
but before it was a place in Homerton. That's where we were – me,
Yaakov Bettelheim, Toyve Walther.'

Rex remembered the red-faced man at the tish, screaming at the
young Rebbe. Being held by Yitzie. And the file in Kovacs' basement.

'Why was Toyve so upset at the tish?'

Yitzie paused, visibly thinking. 'Angry over his boy.'

'Angry with Simmy Dordoff?'

'Just – angry. Angry because his boy is gone. It is hard to lose
a child.' The big man fiddled with his skullcap. 'I told him when
Rescha served him in the morning, don't go to the tish. It won't do
you any good.'

Yet the man with the birthmark hadn't seemed angry in a general
way. He'd behaved with violence towards someone in a wheelchair.
Why?

'Do you know why Dr Kovacs might have been interested in
Micah Walther?'

Yitzie shook his head. 'He had a lot of interests. A great mind.'

Rex asked for the Walther family's address. Yitzie wrote it down, silent and hesitant, as if he thought he was doing the wrong thing.

Rex considered the bulky, odd man before him, who'd known everyone who was either dead or missing, and kept a row of dangerous poisons up here in his attic.

'The police were thinking the same thing as you,' Yitzie said, following Rex's gaze. 'I have just put this place back in order after they searched it.' He returned a bottle of clear fluid to the shelf. 'I have not been charged with any crimes.'

'Yitzl, voss machst?'

They turned in alarm at the high voice in the doorway. Rescha stood there in her vintage raincoat, holding a carrier bag with a Hebrew logo. Rex smiled. She didn't smile back. Yitzie growled something in Yiddish, his wife snapped a response, and with a sulky, chastened look the big man lumbered off, wheezing, down the stairs.

'Sorry to intrude,' Rex said. 'But your husband offered to show me the workshop.'

'Is there anything else you'd like to see?' she asked awkwardly.

It was clear that Rescha wanted him gone. Rex walked slowly to the doorway. 'I was wondering why Dr Kovacs was looking into your family history. Rosa Brandt, who became Rosa Feigenbaum, and moved here? What was she – your great-grandmother?'

'Great-great. He was looking because I asked him to.'

'Oh.'

The answer was so simple, so obvious. Rex didn't know what else to say. He stared at the blue bag in Rescha's hands. He couldn't read Hebrew, but he recognised the shapes of the letters from somewhere on his travels around Stamford Hill. Two words of three letters. Both starting with the same rather beautiful character, somewhere between a 'W' and a crown.

Then Rex remembered something from his recent talk with Yitzie. 'But your husband said Dr Kovacs came here, asking questions and you didn't like it.'

'Yitzie's got you in a muddle. They met at the hospital. Started talking Yiddish together. Then he started to come here a few months later. And I guess it was just his way. To ask a lot of questions about people. You know, not like they are people, but something he has to find out about. I mean – at the hospital, he saw a Hasid so he thought, 'Right – you can teach me Yiddish.' Why else would he have been interested in Yitzie? He just wanted something. To help him with his book he was writing, or… I don't know. Yitzie is right, I didn't like it. Especially not at first, because I hardly knew the man. But later, as it went on, I thought, okay, if he wants to stick his nose in, maybe he can help. I never knew much about my family. I was curious.'

It made sense. And it was backed up by what Tim, the historian, had said. Kovacs had wanted information about terrorists. Having failed to get any, and having already engaged the researcher's services, he simply put him on to tracing Rescha's family.

They went down the stairs in silence, Rex aware of her supervisory presence just behind him. As she opened the door to let him out, he asked, 'Did you ask him to find out about Micah Walther as well?'

Like Yitzie, she seemed genuinely baffled by his question. 'Micah? No.' Then, as a lorry thundered by on the road, she suddenly leaned in close and asked, in a very different tone of voice. 'Did you go? On Friday?'

Rex was surprised. He'd have thought Yitzie would have told his wife. But perhaps they didn't share much. 'I did. I saw Micah's father.'

She seemed to nod, a gesture so faint, so tightly controlled, it was if she had a gun to her back. Then the hand-bell sounded from within, and she shut the door on him without another glance.

Waiting for a bus, he tried the number Yitzie had given him for Toyve Walther. There was no reply. The bus came – and it was empty. Or at least, the bottom deck was, because a young man with a cut-up face and no socks was sitting right at the front, his gaunt frame giving off the odour of rotting cheese. Rex discovered it too late, and stayed put, breathing through his mouth as the bus drove westwards through the quiet streets. His trip had answered many questions. Kovacs had started making this trek over to Stamford Hill to learn Yiddish from Yitzie Schild, presumably to help him with his research for his book. Rescha had asked for something in return – some information on her family background. He'd set his researcher on the task. End of story. Or it would have been, if he hadn't had a file on Micah Walther, the missing boy.

* * *

The Sisters of St Veronica of Jumièges had outposts in Krakow, Sydney and Santa Monica. However far-flung the locations, they all fulfilled the same function as the house tucked away in a patch of woodland at the edge of Alexandra Palace. Nuns lived there, along with a handful of people who needed to be cared for in quiet, humble seclusion.

Rex knew that some people went there to live out their final weeks. The nuns – many of whom apparently dwelt in a sort of limbo world between the supernatural and the real – never seemed to attach much importance to this. Perhaps it was because they thought dying wasn't really dying. But sometimes Rex would arrive to see scary, yellow oxygen cylinders in the damp, earth-smelling porch. And on the narrow wooded path leading from the convent's front door, he occasionally came across red-eyed, bewildered visitors trying to find their way back to Muswell Hill.

As for the long-term residents who shared the premises with his wife, Rex saw little of them: the handles of a wheelchair here, an outline shrouded in blankets in front of a window there. He supposed a better man would involve himself in the life of the place, get to know the others and their families, participate in tea-parties and fun runs, and send the nuns religious cards on their name-days. He'd never been able to. Partly this was due to his innate aversion to joining in. But mostly it was because he tried, when he wasn't sitting in a chair right next to his wife, to pretend that she wasn't there, and that it wasn't his fault that she was. He preferred to scuttle in and out at specific times, greeting the familiar nun who'd always open the door to him, and then proceeding by the swiftest route to the room where Sybille always spent her evenings, in front of crime shows on the TV.

So he was alarmed, this Sunday evening, when the door wasn't opened by the usual, tiny, brisk Belgian nun called Sister Florence, but a little girl in a red velvet dress. 'Where's my daddy?' said the little girl, as if Rex had done something with him.

'Erm,' said Rex. Before he could say anything better, Sister Florence came bustling through the doors.

'It's okay, your daddy will be back in a minute,' she said in a soothing sing-song, before guiding Rex away down the corridor with the cobwebs and the forever peeling paint. Once they were some distance away, she said, in a low, pastille-scented whisper, 'Her brother is with us. So young. The family would do anything, but… Very sad.' She paused in front of the door to the TV room. The corridor was warm and damp, as always. In his dreams the walls of the place ran with water, like a cave. 'Tonight, a surprise.'

She opened the door. He went in. Surprise was a wild under-statement. His wife was standing by the window.

She turned, and her face was as beautiful as it had ever been – smooth and pale, with its exquisite sweep from cheekbone down to jaw. She saw him.

'Hello Rex,' she said. She'd been in a wheelchair since 2003, but now she walked across to him, the scent of Mitsouko, her perfume, in his nostrils. His heart thumped. His mind seemed to have been squeezed into a funnel, to have risen several feet above his head, so that he had a clear vision of himself, in that shabby little convent room, embracing his wife, his miraculously healed wife, for the first time in years. How could it have happened?

'It's been too long,' she murmured. He felt the warmth of her next to him – the silk of her blouse, the brush of her thighs beneath her skirt. Blood rushed to and from his thundering heart, he became hard as he thrust his lips towards hers. She was his again. He remembered what the Narpal, the sick young Rebbe had told him at the tish. *You will see a miracle.* He wanted to laugh. But it was true. Miracles were true.

Two firm hands pushed against his chest. 'Rex? Are you ok?'

Something, a change in the light, a tiny movement of her body, was like a key turning. It turned and the whole picture broke up and dissolved. Flushing with horror, he realised the mistake he'd made.

'Aurelie, I...' He faced his sister-in-law and swallowed. She smoothed her skirt down. 'You look so...'

Last time he'd seen her, she'd been bloated and red-faced, forever having emergency haircuts to hide the self-loathing chop-jobs she did on herself with nail scissors when she was drunk. Now he saw his wife's elder sister as she'd always been meant to be. Beautiful. And just like his wife.

'I got some help,' she said, smiling, a faint flush on her cheek-bones. 'I don't drink now.'

'Where's Sybille?'

'She is in her room, getting changed. I wanted to talk to you alone before she comes in.'

'Okay,' he said warily, pulling up a chair.

She did the same, sitting neatly, legs folded to one side. Unzipping her neat, maroon-coloured handbag, she took out a photograph and passed it to him. It showed a fat, beaming man outside an ornate but semi-derelict villa. 'He is a Captain in the Sûreté,' Aurelie said. 'We are getting married in August, in Corsica, because he comes from there. This is the house we are going to live in. St-Aubin. Just outside Paris.'

'Congratulations. That's great news. Lovely house.' He still felt desperately embarrassed.

'I want Sybille to live there with us.'

'No.'

'Rex – allow me to talk.'

He was reminded again of his wife. Though it was never intentional, he'd often interrupted Sybille: her jokes, her stories, her questions. Her life.

'I know you don't have any reason to listen to me. I was crazy for years.' Aurelie went on. 'But not now. It's a new life. A different life. And I can make a good life for Sybille as well.'

'She has a good life.'

'You don't come to see her for weeks. The nuns tell me. You come, once a month maybe, you stay half an hour and you go. She's in this place, which is falling down the hillside, onto a shitty part of London, only because it is near to you but you don't even come any more.'

Anger replaced bewilderment in his veins. 'How often did you come, when you were doing a bottle of Grey Goose every day before lunch? How involved were you then in Sybille's life?'

Aurelie blinked, as if absorbing a series of light blows. 'You are right to say that. And I am not saying that it's your fault.'

No one needed to say it was his fault. The obvious never needed saying.

'You can't make her well again, Aurelie.'

'And you can't repair things by keeping her here. She might live twenty, thirty, forty more years, just like us, no one knows. How should she spend them? Here, in front of TV shows, with some old nuns? Or with her family?'

The bright, high-pitched chuntering of Sister Florence could now be heard as she wheeled Sybille into the room. 'They haven't switched it on yet, Sybille. I don't know why.' The door swung open. 'With these "Foyle's War" we cannot follow the story if we miss the beginning! Will you switch it on ITV please?'

Aurelie said a few, short, incomprehensible words in French to Sister Florence. The nun reddened slightly and left the room.

'Ask her,' Aurelie said. 'Ask Sybille what she wants.'

He turned to his wife, and took hold of a cool, slim hand. It felt slighter and bonier than the last time he'd seen her. He cleared his throat, which seemed to tighten up in the dusty micro-climate of the convent, and asked her where she wanted to go.

She didn't answer. She'd lost an eye, and the one remaining had had no sight in it since a scaffolding pole shot through the passenger side of the windscreen into her head. Still, as he did every time he came here, he found himself gazing into it, peering into the sightless well in search of something lost.

'You have to understand the start,' she said at last. She said it very quietly. As he and Aurelie craned forward, he was reminded of the Narpal, and how desperate everyone had been to hear his utterances. 'They show you all these things to lead you astray. But in the beginning is where the answers are.'

Aurelie glanced at Rex for clarification. Rex sighed. 'She's talking about *Foyle's War*,' he said. He leant forward to switch on the TV. The glum, wartime detective had already started on his mystery. 'Can you get this in Paris?' he asked harshly. 'Because that's what'll probably decide it.'

'Rex,' his wife said reproachfully. She did this, sometimes. Echoed the words and the gestures of her old self – squeezed his hand or giggled, as if she was still there. He found those moments, those ghosts of an old, normal life, especially hard to bear. Harder than her silences or her weird utterances.

Later Aurelie walked with him back up the path to the bus-stop. It was a light, spring evening, fresh and full of a kind of promise. He felt irritated by it. He wanted it to be dark and icy, something to give him an excuse to go home with a bottle of raki and shut himself away.

'For now anyway it's still just talking,' she said. 'The house won't be finished until next year.'

'What does Inspector Clouseau think of your plan?'

She smiled and touched his arm. She was taller than his wife, he realised. Or maybe it was just shoes. 'His name is Eric. He wants me to be happy. And I… you might not believe it, but I want you to be happy, too, Rex. I want you to have a chance of it. I don't think you will allow yourself, and Sybille is the way you prevent it from happening.'

It wasn't the first time someone had said that to him. Not even the first time a beautiful woman had said it to him, standing on this very hill. And they'd all been right, at the same time as all being wrong.

They fell into silence, gazing down at the flat valley-floor of Tottenham below. He wondered where in that blue-grey confusion Rescha and Yitzie's shop was, and where the Bettelheims had lived, and if all those separate lives were, or had been, as complicated as his. He supposed they must have been. Perhaps more so.

'You really thought I was her?' Aurelie said suddenly. He nodded, and as awkward as he felt, he admired Aurelie for bringing it up. Most people would have been too embarrassed to mention the fact that their brother-in-law had just shoved a semi-erect cock at their midriffs. Maybe it was because she was French. Or maybe ex-alcoholics just had no embarrassment left.

'You see how we are made to repeat our mistakes,' she said, as the 144 bus approached. 'Unless we do something to stop it.'

He thought about that, as he sailed down Muswell Hill on a virtually empty bus. It wasn't just her comment that struck a chord, but his wife's. *You have to understand the start.* Because if he traced the roots of the accident that had shattered so many lives, he came to an event a few weeks before it.

It was mid November, 2003. He'd been ill, with tonsillitis, and he'd made a bad patient. Rex's mother had never really mothered him that much; and lacking a father, he'd had to play the man of the house from a young age. Consequently he was uncomfortable whenever circumstances rendered him needy. Over the years, some of his girlfriends had accepted this and withdrawn, but the one who became his wife never had. The kinder Sybille was, the fouler her patient behaved, until, on the evening his voice returned, the resentments of the past week spilled over into an argument.

He'd returned to work the next day and come home late that evening to find Aurelie passed out on the sofa. He'd lugged a spare duvet over his sister-in-law and gone to bed himself, waking some hours later to the sensation of his wife's cool fingers dancing up his thigh. Half-conscious, he'd rolled onto his back and given himself over to the reconciliation, before realising, just on the threshold of pleasure, that it couldn't be his wife, because his wife was away for the night.

He'd sprung away, hints of semen and saliva and stale booze in his nostrils, and Aurelie had staggered out of the room like a shot fox. The next day everything had seemed almost normal when his wife returned from her conference in Leicester. But something had been said, or perhaps only divined. Whatever it was, it was enough to ensure that the coolness between Rex and his wife lengthened and deepened. Ensuring that, a full fortnight after Aurelie had gone, they were still not entirely reconciled.

At the end of that fortnight was a Press Awards dinner, where he'd had too much drink and had driven them home. In the car their bickering teetered on the edge of some bigger quarrel which had never come, because he'd crashed the car. The breathalyser said he wasn't drunk. What could explain that other than God, intervening to show that He could? To show that only He knew the numbers and the natures of everybody's sins.

Chapter Six

Rex dreamt of the past and thought he was still there when the alarm went off. The radio was playing some irritating jokey single of years gone by, and warm sunlight was streaming through the bedroom windows. Downstairs, someone was frying bacon. All these things made him wonder briefly if he was still living in a basement flat in Camden with his wife, or perhaps even at the place he still sometimes thought of as home, his mum's council house overlooking the pea-fields.

It was Terry, he discovered, at the hob with a spatula, his bad leg kneeled up on a folding chair, humming as he flipped curling pink rashers in the pan.

'Bacon sarnie?'

'Ta,' Rex said, as he poured a coffee from the pot. His new house-mate had underestimated the properties of the Turkish coffee Rex bought from the nearby shop, and created a brew with the consistency of French onion soup. But it was good to see Terry up and about.

'Brain food,' Terry said, hobbling to the table with two thick sandwiches on a plate. 'I'm tackling Mentioned Volumes 1 and 2 today.'

'Mentioned?'

Terry shuddered as a mouthful of the super-charged coffee went down. 'As in all the people who got mentioned in the inquest. People who tried to stop the robbers and that.'

At first Rex didn't understand, then he realised Terry was talking about the Outrage. It was odd that he was suddenly so interested in it. 'Did you know Kovacs had a little archive down there?'

Terry shook his head. 'The deeds said the basement's communal. But when I realised he'd set up his own little office down there I left it alone. I knew he'd only kick off about it.'

At that moment the front gate swung open and a squinting D.S. Brenard walked into the little courtyard that was Rex's garden. The Welshman looked uncomfortable, even more so when he saw Terry.

'Oh. Well. If you're here, you're here.' He stood in the hallway, rubbing the back of his neck, then followed Rex into the living room, while Terry poured another coffee in the kitchen.

'The Bettelheim inquest is tomorrow,' Brenard said.

'Ah.' Rex said. 'Thanks.' There was a pause. 'Was that what you came here to tell me?'

'Erm. No. I caught up with Sam Greenhill,' Brenard said. 'He admits he's been to Kovacs' house. Not the day of the murder. In October. Got himself all fired up to confront his dad, but he says he rang the wrong bell, and then Terry came out, and he scarpered.'

There was a silence, while Terry came in from the kitchen. Rex was struck by how ridiculous they looked, all standing up in the centre of a room, three guests at a very bleak party.

'What are you muttering about?' Terry asked.

'Well…' D.S. Brenard looked like he had toothache.

'Do you remember someone calling round and scarpering five months ago? A kid? In the autumn? Looked a bit like George Kovacs?'

Terry shrugged.

'Are you disputing Greenhill's statement?' Brenard asked.

'I'm not disputing it,' Terry said. 'I'm saying I don't remember. There's all sorts knock for us. Gippos with dishcloths. God squad. I don't remember. Five months ago?'

'He gave a pretty clear and consistent account, and his Oyster-card does show him making the trip. October 9th. A Wednesday.'

Terry shrugged. The date meant nothing to him.

'And not making the trip any other time?' Rex asked.

'Not making the trip any other time.'

'Well there you go,' Terry said bitterly. 'I must have done it. See you in court.'

'He's not making any admission of guilt,' Rex added hastily. 'He's upset.'

'I'll speak for me fucking self,' Terry snarled, limping into the kitchen.

Rex showed Brenard out and walked back into the kitchen. Suddenly Terry's face was close – close enough to smell the bacon and the coffee. 'What are you, my fucking nursemaid?' Rex could feel the heat of his friend's sudden, terrifying rage.

'Tel –'

'My name's not Tel!' he roared, shoving him across the room. Rex skidded and fell to the floor. Terry charged out into the living room like a rampaging animal. On the floor, Rex realised he was genuinely afraid. He felt a surge of relief when Terry finally hobbled out of the house, an unzipped holdall flailing over his shoulder. His friend was gone. He hoped it wasn't forever.

* * *

The Walther family lived close to Seven Sisters in a place called Sanchez Dwellings. It had the cramped, crazy look of the very earliest, philanthropic attempts at flat-building, with rows of tiny front doors opening onto walkways, and black-painted iron staircases criss-crossing the whole frontage like a child's scribbles.

Children were the most obvious feature of the place, too. Sanchez Dwellings seemed to be occupied entirely by Hasidim and even though it was a school day, it was crawling with children.

Small boys with flying earlocks were belting up and down the metal staircases while their sisters played quieter, more co-operative games in the shabby grounds. It must be painful, Rex thought, for the Walthers to have lost a child and yet stay in a building that was teeming with them. Or perhaps it was a comfort.

His phone rang as he was climbing the stairs to the third floor. A huddle of boys stopped playing marbles and stared.

'What time will you be in?'

It was Susan, her tone abrupt and urgent. 'In time for conference,' Rex said defensively. 'I haven't forgotten.'

'That's comforting,' Susan said, and hung up. As Rex put his phone away, he realised the little boys were mimicking him, holding their fists against their ears. He was, he guessed, a complete alien in their midst.

He'd rung ahead and asked if he could call in. Even so, he felt a little nervous as he knocked on the Walther family's front door. Toyve seemed happy to see him, though, guiding him through a hallway packed with bikes and kids' scooters to a messy, rather stuffy little living room that faced the back. There was no TV, but otherwise it seemed that a Hasidic household looked much like that of any other low-income family with a lot of kids. There were shoes and school-books everywhere, and the place smelled comfortably of fabric conditioner and frying.

Toyve, the man of the house, was evidently preparing to leave for work, but he insisted that Rex sit down on the huge, sagging, wine-coloured sofa that dominated the room.

'You will be the first guest to sit on it,' he said, self-consciously.

'You just bought it?'

'A donation from Beit Chesed. It arrived this morning.'

Toyve's wife, a sturdy, almost Arab-looking girl appeared in the kitchen doorway. 'It's a bribe.'

'From who?'

'It's too big,' was all she'd add, before handing a fat, happy baby to her husband and going off to make tea.

Toyve sat opposite Rex on a folding chair and jiggled the child on his knee as they waited for the tea. His red-stained face crumpled with pleasure every time the baby laughed. He looked very different from the raging bull Rex had seen at the tish.

'I don't want to upset you but I need to ask some questions about Micah.'

Toyve nodded, glancing at a picture of the boy on the wall. 'It's okay,' he said, in a high voice with a very faint Germanic accent. 'We want to talk about him. It's the silence that makes us angry. As you noticed.'

'Is that all you were angry about?'

'Some people are silent because they know nothing. Some people are silent because they know something. That's what I am angry about. And anger is *bitul Torah*, Mr Tracey. It means, taking time away from the Law.'

'What people are keeping silent? The Rebbe?'

Toyve made a face. 'You know what the Maggid of Voydislav said?'

'I'm afraid I don't,' Rex said.

Toyve smiled, revealing large, grey teeth. 'When there is a weak King, then there is a strong Servant.'

'Simmy Dordoff?'

Toyve nodded as his wife came back in with the tea. She took the baby from her husband and stayed in the doorway.

Rex sipped the tea, which came in a little glass with a handle. It was good: black and strong, with a thick slice of lemon in it. 'So what does Dordoff know?'

Toyve's wife murmured something to him. In response, the man reached up and stroked her hand. For a moment, Rex might as well have been non-existent as the family gazed at one another, bound together by a very obvious, very deep kind of love. Rex looked away, but not because it embarrassed him. It hurt him.

'A few months before Micah disappeared, they asked the boys to come forward to give some blood for the Rebbe. Just boys.'

'A blood transfusion?'

Toyve shook his head. 'Not blood, I think. They wanted somebody to give…' There was another short, whispered conference with his wife. 'Bone marrow. Yes. A special treatment in Antwerp – they thought it could make him well. Well, not make him well, but maybe… make him stay alive longer. It had to be an exact match, they said, but I don't know what they were matching.'

'So Micah gave blood?'

'Micah gave his blood – just to be tested. And then a few weeks passed, and it was his fourteenth birthday. He was our eldest. *Is* our eldest.' Toyve paused and smiled. 'We gave him the Rashbam's *Commentary on the Bava Batra*. Have you read that?' He cleared his throat. 'Then Dordoff came here to tell us – Micah's blood was a match. I mean – I guess he had the right kind of… whatever it was. So they sent him for more tests.'

'He went to Antwerp?'

'No. First here. A private place – in St. Albans. But this wasn't like giving blood. They were taking… taking small pieces of bone from inside his arms and his legs. Very painful. After he went two times, they said they wanted him to go to Antwerp, but Micah said he couldn't do it any more. I tried to argue. I told him about the Ilui of Kotzk, you know, and the pain he endured to become a great Talmud scholar, but Micah…'

'It was too much for him,' Toyve's wife suddenly interjected in a low, husky voice. 'Have you got children?'

Rex shook his head.

'When you do, you'll see. You can't let them hurt. You would let yourself hurt. So we said, okay, you don't have to go any more.'

When you do. Because everyone in this woman's world had kids. Except Rescha and Yitzie Schild.

'So we told Dordoff that Micah wasn't happy to go on,' her

husband said. 'And he was quite....'

'Angry?' Rex knew he'd spoken out of turn, and instantly regretted it. It hadn't unduly influenced Toyve Walther, though, because he just shook his head slightly.

'Not angry. Annoyed. He kept following Micah – catching up with him after school, at the *kollel* where he was studying, at the *shtib* when he was praying, trying to persuade him. And then one day, that was it. Micah was gone.' He cleared his throat.

'And Dordoff wasn't around when Micah went missing,' added Toyve's wife, her tone becoming more agitated. 'He was in Antwerp. He even admits he was in Antwerp.' Toyve reached up and patted her arm.

'So you think...' Rex prompted.

'He knows something.'

'But did the Rebbe have the treatment?'

Toyve shrugged. 'He's still alive.'

'So... you must...' Rex stopped himself, remembering the sage words of his first editor. Victor Eastwood of the *Lincoln Daily Despatch*, with his hairy tweed jacket and his permanent smell of TCP. A small-town genius. *Don't tell people how they feel. Ask them.* 'How does that make you feel towards the Rebbe?'

'Sometimes I wish him dead. Then I remember that that won't bring Micah back. But it's hard... You know, you are told to love your Rebbe, but... I've started to pray somewhere else now.'

'Is that what the bribe is for?' Rex asked, patting the sofa. 'To stop you from leaving?'

Toyve closed his eyes and gave a small, internal, mirthless chuckle – the gesture you make when someone is a long, long way from the truth. 'Nobody is bribing us, Mr Tracey. Nobody.'

Toyve's wife abruptly handed the baby back in order to withdraw to the kitchen, and from the vigour with which pots suddenly began to be washed and put away, Rex guessed he'd upset this family enough. He still had questions, though.

'Did you tell all this to George Kovacs?'

Toyve frowned. 'George…? Ah. Dr Kovacs. How do you know about that?'

Rex didn't answer, but how noticed Mrs Walther had returned to the doorway.

'He came to ask us some questions. But not about Micah. About Anshel Walther.'

'Who's he?'

'An ancestor of mine. I didn't know about this, but Dr Kovacs said that he got a reward for trying to stop some robbers a hundred years ago.'

Rex caught the sigh before it left him. Kovacs hadn't been interested in Micah. Just the family. For his book. 'The Tottenham Outrage.'

'Yes. He didn't collect it. The reward, I mean. Kovacs was very interested to know why. I couldn't really help except to tell some stories from my grandmother.'

'They used to say that Anshel was a naughty boy,' said Mrs Walther, with a smile. 'Went to prison a few times. So maybe he didn't pick up his reward because he was doing something wicked.'

'Or he only stopped the robbery because he was somewhere he wasn't supposed to be.'

Rex nodded. 'Did Kovacs say why he was so interested?'

Toyve shrugged. 'He was writing a book, wasn't he?'

Rex stood up, thanked them for the tea, tickled the baby and left.

As he was picking his way through the children at the bottom of the staircase, Toyve Walther caught up with him.

'I am late for to work,' he said. 'Also, because you started to talk about Dr Kovacs, I forgot to say something. After a while, when everybody stopped looking for Micah, Dordoff began to ask Eytan.'

'Who's Eytan?'

'Eytan Bettelheim, Yaakov and Chaya's son. He was the same age as Micah. They wanted him to go for the tests, same as Micah did. He went for some. Yaakov, his father, told me the tests gave him an infection in the bone. I told them about the pressure Dordoff had put on our boy and... I worry maybe I made them too afraid, and that's why they were going to leave.'

Rex thanked him. He asked if he could ask one more question. Toyve said he didn't mind.

'Have you ever thought about leaving? Coming to...' He didn't know how to put it. 'My world?'

The birth-marked man looked upwards and sniffed the air. 'If we left, we would have to move away, and then if Micah came back, how would he find us? His room is here. His clothes...' The dignified man rubbed his nose, evidently trying to ward off tears. 'We have to believe that he is alive.' He looked at Rex. 'Is that a good... what would you call it... a good... line for your newspaper?'

'I'm glad you told me,' Rex said. 'But I won't be putting it in any newspapers.'

Walther nodded. 'I didn't think you were going to ask me that question. I thought you were going to ask me the question all the *goyim* and the *freie yidn* ask me. How can you still believe in God?'

'And what do you say to them?'

'You don't remember what Rabbi Reuven of Vitebsk said, when the soldiers mocked him after the death of his wife?'

Rex shook his head. Toyve seemed to live in a world of scripture and mediaeval rabbis, and to assume everyone else did, too. Then again, perhaps everyone else did, around here.

'He said: *God gave me sorrows. He also gave me shoulders.*'

As Rex left the grounds of Sanchez House he saw a dirty white van slowly driving away. It had a design of a paint-pot and brush on the side and some Hebrew letters – Rex recognised the ornate crown-like letters again. He also recognised, leaning out of the passenger side, and watching him impassively, the figure of Simmy Dordoff.

* * *

A day she stays at her aunt's in Highgate. A day and a night and back on Friday morning. 'Oh my auntie's got sick now,' she says. 'And she doesn't want me to catch it. So I shall just have to stay back here with you, Mr Smith.'

I can smell lies like only a liar can, like the old sailors knew when the wind was about to change. Long before I joined the Leesma, I had a nose for them. The over-long explanation. The too-fervent assurance. The detail too many. They have a smell. It is the smell of an onion gone bad in a forgotten corner of a ship's galley where the rats piss and the cook flicks his toenail clippings.

Remember that lisping old dame of an orderly in the infirmary, where I'd lain, soaked in my piss and sweat for weeks while the polio twisted me up like a love-letter in a flame. 'I've seen the mark of the covenant in your flesh, sir. Couldn't help but see it, sir. But don't worry. I won't tell anyone.'

My cock he wouldn't. Two days out of my sick-bed, the Under-Lieutenant has me in on my sticks. Squid, was what he reminded me of, with his long head and his tiny spectacles and his tentacle hair. 'You'll be aware, Midshipman Kuznetz, that persons of the Hebrew faith are barred from service in the Holy and Imperial Russian Navy.' Service ended. Pension denied. You can keep your boots. Except one of them doesn't fit you now, cripple.

I didn't mind the girl lying so much. Nice to have someone in the house anyway. Friday was my free day this week, so I helped her take down the net curtains and haul the washtub out of the yard. It felt how being a married couple might have.

We found a bee as we took the curtains away. Alive, just. A bee, abroad in January – bad omen, the old fools in my village would say. Leah wanted to kill it, but I stayed her hand. First time I'd ever touched her skin.

Remembered when I first touched Rosa's. Grabbed her in the dark outside the printer's. She screamed, but I wouldn't let go. *Why are you following me?* Just remember how cold it was, thick snow falling into the wells of all the thousands of frozen footprints, but there was still this little bead of sweat or tears going right down to the end of her little nose. *I-I-I saw you talk. To the Porters' Association. And then to the sail-makers. And then the soldiers. But they wouldn't let me in there. I know your name. I'm just a girl. I'm nothing, I'm no one.* And she started crying.

'And I'm just a cripple,' I said. 'Pleased to meet you, No one.'

And she looked at me, all earnest, as earnest as only a young woman can be and she said, 'I think you are beautiful.'

Took me right away, that touch did, and when I came back, Leah was staring at me.

'Where did you go?'

'Bees have more wit than man, so you leave him be,' I said.

'Leave the bee be?' she goes. 'What do you mean anyways, Mr Smith?'

So I tells her, that brilliant, beautiful passage from Proudhon about the hive. Perfect illustration of a harmonious society without division or tension, each contributing its skills and its strength towards the benefit of the whole, without coercion, fear or force. And if tiny insects can create a living machine of such perfection, imagine what beauties, what earthly paradises men could effect.

She listens all the while, her head tilted on one side, just like Rosa used to do. There's a long quiet as I'm finished, me looking at her, her at me. Smell Coal Tar soap and rosewater. Don't know if she's going to kiss me or join the Movement. Or both. Rosa did, after all.

Then she says, 'You have some queer ideas for a gas fitter from Goff's Oak, Mr Smith. Talk like no Hertfordshire man I ever heard, neither.'

Felt a little chip of ice enter me as she said that. Not because she hasn't listened. But because she's playing with me. Question is: playing like the village-girls used to, all knowing but unknowing? Or playing because she knows something? Could she be the one that has been following me?

'Well, you spend twenty-five years sailing the world with a pack of Balts and Huns and Chinamen,' I said – an answer well-re-hearsed. 'If you mind how I talk, I'll keep quiet.'

'I don't want you to,' she said. I could hear my heart beating. And hers.

Then the fucking door knocker goes, shocking the very salt out of my blood. She goes to it. It's Mr Parks. Shows him into the front parlour. I can hear their voices in there, low and quick, so after a bit I crept over and listened.

'A very responsible position. House attached,' he's saying.

'Bradford,' she says back. 'I don't even know where it is.'

'So come and see, Leah. I've handed my notice in and I'm going there tomorrow. To see the mill and the house.'

'I just don't know.'

'Your mother approves it.'

'How do you know that? Cuthbert, have you gone to see her behind my back?'

I had to stuff my fist in my mouth then. Cuthbert Parks. What a curse he must have been to his Mama, to have carried him and laboured him into this world, and after all that to have gazed down at his little pink face and willed the name of Cuthbert Parks upon him. Never had a chance.

I missed what was going on in there for a bit, then heard.

'But you know how I feel,' Cuthbert Parks is saying. 'Leah...'

'I didn't want that!' she says, agitated. He says 'Leah' again and she squeals. I'm in there like a toothless babushka on a soup-bone.

'You. Out!' says I, grabbing the moist boy by his tweed coat and hoisting him up. Even crippled, I'm strong.

Leah said nothing, red-faced, sobbing or – I think, maybe – pretending to sob a bit more than the real thing as I shove and drag Cuthbert Parks into the hall.

'You have no right. This is not your house.'

'Not yours neither,' was the best I could do, as I pushed him out into the fog. Could have done better in Russian, or Yiddish, or Latvian and three other tongues. So as I go back in I think to myself, must get better at cursing in English. Then I think, no reason to, is there? I'm going back. The thought makes me sad. Sad and angry.

I let her alone a while, and she went up to her room. Carried on cleaning, and then darned some socks. She came down with a new dress on, blue with flowers, very pretty.

'Where did you learn to be so good with a needle?'

'The Navy. An Englishman taught–'

See, I'm getting like an old hull when the tar's worn thin. Letting just tiny dribbles in at first. Then a proper spout you can catch in your palm. Before long, sunk to the sea-bed. I'm letting things slip, because I'm getting too easy here, with this girl. Who else but an Englishman would teach the fucking Englishman George Smith in the English fucking Navy?

Luckily, she hadn't heard, or hadn't made anything of it if she did. She seemed bored, so I made tea. Remembered to put milk in. Played her a game of chequers on the pinewood set I carved in Yakutsk. Then in spite of the fog we took a walk. We stopped by a bill for the Yiddish Theatre and for a moment she slipped her arm through mine and said: 'So strange that Jews' writing of theirs. Like little crowns and forks. I'd love to know what it says. Probably telling them all to rise up and murder us in our beds.'

I wondered again, then, is she testing me out, this apple-cheeked petticoat? I had the sense again, all the way on our walk, too, nice as it was to walk abroad with a pretty girl again, that I was being followed. Maybe because it was her. Following me. And am I getting too soft? Has loving one, and losing her, ruined me for this endeavour?

I know what Velkis would have done. Pushed the little chit straight up the alleyway between the cobblers and the Temperance Hall. Cut her a second mouth before she could scream out of the first one.

Maybe I should have done that.

For good or bad, I didn't. We bought two penn'orth hot chestnuts off an Italian woman and walked back slowly. I started to think I'd been imagining it. Enjoyed being with her. For the first time started to think, too, that another girl could be better than Rosa. That girl always wanted a fight. An argument. If not about the inherent weaknesses of dialectical materialism then about why did I look at that shiksa's arse as she went by and was one girl not enough for me. Leah isn't like that.

Maybe I felt a bit guilty for thinking that about Rosa – like it was a betrayal. So I was a bit quiet as Hartington Park loomed up out of the icy, woolly mist and we were there almost by our door when she stiffened next to me like a farm dog on a scent.

Parks was waiting outside the door – frozen blue by the looks of him, blowing his fingers. He holds them up as we approach, like a tart admiring her nail-paint and says, 'Look. This is important. Please. I have something to tell you.'

So we let him in and I ushered him straight through to the back. No fancy front room for Mr Parkses this time.

And he looks pale and grey, as he says, 'I went up the hospital to talk to your mother, Leah…'

'To tell tales on me and get her to stick her nose in so I'd go with you to the north, you…'

He holds up a hand to stop her.

'She's died. Leah. She died this morning.'

I can hear her starting to cry. Can feel that I ought to do something. Comfort her. Keep that wet-lipped woodlouse from comforting her. But I can't. Because I've been staring out of the window and seen a little ball of wool fly over the yard-gate, a graceful dive like a gull after scraps.

The job is on. Tomorrow.

* * *

Back at the office, Rex discovered that Dordoff wasn't the only one watching him.

'She's after your hide,' Brenda said without looking up. Enthroned behind the reception desk, she was munching on gözleme while reading a magazine.

By the time Rex reached her office upstairs, though, Susan was shuttered up in yet another meeting. He could hear men's voices, and, unusually, a lot of laughter.

Rex switched on his machine and searched for marrow + transplants + Antwerp. Along with a great many research papers written in Flemish, the results included the website of a clinic called Senticel, replete with videos of treatments at work in the bloodstream and pictures of improbably beautiful nurses. You could email them, fax them, Skype them, even book a live video-chat to discuss anything from repairing spinal chord injuries to warding off degenerative disease. He opted for the telephone.

'I'm calling on behalf of Simeon Dordoff,' he said, as a polite, Chinese-sounding woman replied. 'It's about the treatment.'

'What is your relation to Mr Dordoff please?' replied the woman. It seemed he'd got the right place.

'I'm a colleague in the rabbi's office. My name is Mr Schild,' Rex lied. 'Yitzhak Schild. Mr Dordoff asked if you could fax another copy of Micah Walther's test results.'

There was a pause. 'I'm sorry, who?' Rex repeated the name. There was another pause. He thought he could hear typing. Then he heard a muffled conversation. The woman came back on. 'We don't have any results for a patient of that name.'

'He's a potential donor, not a patient.'

'We don't have any results for a donor of that name.'

Rex hung up. Did that mean Micah Walther had pulled out before this clinic became involved? Or that they'd known him under a different name? Or perhaps they just weren't telling him. They certainly knew Simmy Dordoff.

He made a few notes. He wrote down 'Arms' – remembering what Mike Bond had told him about the unexplained marks on the Bettelheim boy. He wrote down 'Pressure' too, the word Toyve Walther had used. How much pressure, and what kind, Rex wondered. He remembered what Sister Florence had said to him the night before, about the sick young man at the hospice: *they would do anything.* Was that true of Dordoff and his community, as well? The Narpal was gravely ill. The community desperately wanted him to stay alive. And this desperation to prolong his life had perhaps forced them to seek dangerous cures. Families had panicked and pulled out. Had something gone wrong? Something which meant some people knew too much, and had to be silenced. Perhaps Dr Kovacs had found something out, and that was really why he'd made all those trips over to Stamford Hill. Or whilst he was talking to people like the Walthers about his book, seen something he wasn't supposed to. Something that meant he had to be killed.

He was so deep in his thoughts that he didn't notice Susan standing in front of his desk.

'I'm assuming that's a page of ideas for the next edition.'

'The terror crack-down,' he said quickly, surprising himself. 'You know – stop and search, plastic bloody cutlery everywhere… I heard someone called the cops yesterday because they saw a couple of blokes with beards whispering in ShoeZone. There's got to be mileage in all that, hasn't there?'

Susan gave a slow nod, with a very faint smile. 'It's lucky for you, Rex, that you're enough of a *chachem* to be able to come up with a brilliant idea on the spot, even when you've clearly been devoting all your attention somewhere else.'

'What did you call me?'

'A *chachem*. Ask your friends in Stamford Hill, next time you're there. But before you go, listen to me. We need an A-class output this week. Print and web. Top stories, the absolute best local issue stuff we can get. I can't tell you what that meeting was about, but it's important. Really important. Everything hinges on it.'

After looking up *chachem* on a Yiddish-English website, and being flattered to find his boss was calling him a genius, Rex took her at her word. He spent the rest of the day interviewing people on the High Street. The bearded whisperers were the tip of the iceberg. Everyone had tales to tell: a young father-to-be missed the first ultrasound scan because the bus was late after the police had decided to search every single backpack and shopping bag. A stallholder down in the covered market section of Shopping City who'd had his entire stock impounded because one DVD had a picture of the Twin Towers on it. Rex almost wondered whether it would be worth doing a special pull-out 'Wood Green War on Terror' supplement.

By four o'clock, his foot was in agony, and he'd retreated to The Seagull, a chain pub at the very top of the High Street, to wash down some painkillers with a pint of Tyksie. They had the stuff on tap there, which was about the best thing that could be said for the place. The clientele, by and large, were the sort of men who kept a different mobile phone in each pocket of their long leather coats.

They were small-time hoods. More accurately, a large number of them were men who did fuck-all, but derived a mysterious satisfaction from pretending to be small-time hoods. None of them were terrorists, though. Rex had a hard job believing anyone was, in this neck of the woods. The DVD stallholder, a thin, anxious Pakistani now reduced to gloomily sipping tea in the pots and pans outlet next door, had summed it up perfectly: 'I'm here twelve hours a day, six days a week. What I'm not paying in petrol and taxes I'm giving to my ex-wife so I can see my kids for four hours on a Sunday. When have I got time to build a bomb? By the time I get home I'm so tired I can't see straight.'

He'd let Rex film him – and Rex was planning to put it on the website. Not just because Susan was almost indecently obsessed with what she called 'embedded video', but because it said exactly what Rex and everyone else in the borough seemed think. For most people life was just too hard, too hard and boring and tiring, to want to spend their precious scraps of spare time building bombs or listening to inflammatory sermons or even being that interested in global injustices of any kind. Terror was a hobby, a luxury.

His phone rang. With a spike of dread, he saw that it was Terry. He took another sip of his beer before he answered it.

'Rex, I – I'm sorry about before. I just – I keep losing it. And with the wrong people, an' all. I'm sorry.'

'It's okay,' Rex said, although he wasn't sure if it was. Terry had really frightened him.

'I just called 'cos, you know, I bet Susan's on your case about stories and… I've got one for you. It's Bird.'

'What about him?'

'He tried to break in next door. To Kovacs' house. I didn't see him – I was downstairs. First thing I knew was all these cops show up. He was pretty wild and they tasered him. Took him off in an ambulance.'

'Right… Thanks. Nice one. I'll see you later.'

'Aye,' Terry said. 'Inshallah.'

Inshallah, he thought, as he waited for a 144 towards Edmonton. Like *kurva*, the Polish insult that so many people had adopted, you heard the Arabic phrase for 'God willing' from a great variety of mouths, Islamic and otherwise. He'd never heard it before from Terry's, though. Perhaps he'd picked it up in prison.

Outside the newly refurbished and extended North Middlesex they'd erected a huge sign with the words: 'We're back in business'. Unfortunately, the bevy of nurses and doctors whose photographs they'd used to illustrate this legend looked so forbidding that it wasn't clear what the business might be. In a recent 'Laureate of the Ladders' column, Lawrence Berne had suggested it might be debt-collecting.

The new interior was gleaming and impressive, in a way, although some of the changes seemed a little patronising. The Geriatric Unit had now become the 'Elder Care Community' and the old Clap Clinic had turned into something vaguely entitled 'Encounters'. But it was in the main male ward, still named after Danny Blanch-flower, that Rex found Bird.

To his immense surprise, he also found the Whittaker Twins, Mark and Robert, in their wonky suits and their Clark's Skuffaway shoes, seated in a pair of high-backed chairs either side of the black man's bed.

'He goes to our church,' explained Robert.

'Sometimes,' added Mark.

Rex blinked. He'd had no idea the Whittakers had a church. Then again, he didn't know anything about them, except that they sold advertising space very well. That was all anyone knew.

'They've given him something to sober him up,' said Robert.

'Cunts,' Bird added.

'I can see how you might feel that way,' Rex said, looking round for another chair. There wasn't one. In fact there was a sign saying 'No More Than Two Visitors Per Bed', and a tiny, very angry-looking nurse at the end of the room who, Rex guessed, was the kind to be quite keen on enforcing the rule. He felt rather strange – woozy and a bit short of breath – but he'd just have to stay standing and get on with it.

'How did you know Dr Kovacs, Bird? Can I call you that? Is it your real name?'

'It's his stage name,' said Mark Whittaker.

'Bird Curton,' said Bird, proudly.

'He was a jazz trumpeter – weren't you?' Robert coaxed.

'I made a lot of record,' Bird said, his eyes suddenly welling up. 'Record with everyone. Barber. Brubeck. Lyttleton. DeVries. George had all of them.'

'Dr Kovacs had all your records?'

'All of them. He was my friend. He try an' help when I lost my flat. Tried to get me to stop drinking.' Bird chuckled, causing a tubercular-sounding coughing fit. 'He didn't mind, though,' he wheezed, finally, as beads of sweat shone on his brow. 'He said me welcome at his drum, drunk or sober, so long me naa sick 'pon the carpet or piss on em floor. Let me sit in the cellar when he was away. Showed me a way in, through the window.'

'Is that what you did today?'

'I tried! Some blood-clat lock it now!'

Terry and Lawrence, Rex thought, protecting the little archive in a way its creator, oddly, never had.

'He tried to break a window at the front,' Mark Whittaker said. 'The Police saw him.'

'Oddly vigilant,' Rex said. He'd have said more but found he had to grab on to the little clip-on table attached to the bed. He felt as if the floor was lurching, and he wasn't sure how much this was to do with the painkillers, and how much with the utter weirdness of what he'd just heard. Kovacs had a friend. A real friend. And the friend was Bird. Bird who sat on the high street, drinking Navigator super-strength lager and hurling abuse. The mysteries of the universe surely knew no bounds.

'Why were you trying to get in today?'

'Want to see what that bitch had taken. I thought maybe she take some record of mine.'

'What bitch?'

'Cut-back bitch,' Bird said, leaning back on his pillow and squinting at him. 'All bleeding down her back. When he was away. When George gone some place away me walk past, and me seen this cut-back bitch come out his place. Blonde hair.'

Rex remembered what Bird had been shouting at the funkily-dressed woman in the street, the day after the murders. *Cut-back bitch. Teef.* He'd thought it was something about budgets, naturally assumed it, because the cut-backs were on everyone's mind and because Bird's particular bugbear seemed to be the Council. But Kovacs had been dead a day when he'd seen Bird outside.

'He hadn't gone away, Bird. He was dead. I saw you shouting at her – do you remember?'

Rex remembered. He remembered the woman running away, her biker jacket half-on, half-off. Had she been bleeding, as Bird said? He remembered the dried blood on the floor of the cellar – but that could have come from anyone.

'Cut. Back. Bitch!' Bird suddenly bellowed. The Whittakers winced. The tiny nurse came bowling down the ward.

'Now what's all this nonsense about?' she asked. She looked up at Rex. He expected she'd direct her fury at him, but her face suddenly crinkled up in concern.

'You don't look at all well.'

'I'm fine,' Rex said, as a strange sucking sound filled his ears, and his vision dimmed.

He felt better outside, with the drizzle on his face. He rang D.S. Brenard, and told him what Bird had just said, about the woman with the cut back.

Then he sat on a wall for a while, taking deep breaths. There was nothing seriously wrong with him, he was sure. It was just a cocktail of things: the sweetish stink and the heat of the hospital, and the strange revelations from Bird, and his own tiredness. And the painkillers. He was definitely overdoing it on the painkillers. He needed to cut down. Maybe he wouldn't have any more tonight. Just lager.

In a huge new Polish supermarket on West Green Road he bought six cans of Okocim Mocne. His route back home took him right past Terry's house. He had the idea of calling on him, to see if they could arrive at some sort of peace and understanding, then dismissed it. It was partly that Terry had genuinely scared the shit out of him. It was also on account of discovering that the woman next door at 326 was back. At least, her lights were on.

He rang the doorbell. It was a ponderous, electronic 'ding-dong' chime. Was that what Terry's doorbell sounded like? He couldn't remember ever hearing it. He tried to recall the woman's name. Brenard had told him. Something to do with booze...

'Miss Martell?' he asked, remembering just as a freckled woman in a white dressing gown with a towel turbaned around her head opened the door.

She didn't look pleased to be disturbed. He decided to cut to the chase.

'Sorry, I just wondered – have you been at home recently? Were you here on Monday the 4th of April, or the day after, on the Tuesday?'

'The police asked me that,' she said in a clipped Kiwi accent. 'And I had a note through the door from some reporter, asking me the same thing.'

'That was me. Rex Tracey.'

She nodded, in a not-especially welcoming fashion. 'The answer is not much. On Monday, I was in Clerkenwell, attending a workshop of the offices of an NGO until the late evening of the Monday, I got back here very late, packed, got a taxi to Heathrow around 1 am and flew to Kigali via Paris.'

A lock of her hair suddenly tumbled out from under the turban, dangling on her chest. He stared at it. Miss Martell drew the robe tightly across her front.

'You're a red-head,' he said. 'I mean... I don't suppose... Have you ever been blonde?'

'Fuck off,' Miss Martell said, as she slammed the door in his face.

He could have dealt with that a lot better. But he'd gathered, at least, that Miss Martell wasn't the person who made the 999 call, or the woman Bird had been shouting at.

He turned to see Terry standing in his doorway, bloodshot and red-eyed, but definitely grinning. He invited Rex in and ushered him to the back of the house, into the kitchen, which was full of the sharp, fruity tang of skunk weed. Much of Kovacs' archive was spread across the table. Terry sat down with a pained grunt, and Rex realised he'd been walking without a stick.

'Leg feeling better?'

'I've been doing a bit of internet research,' Terry said, leaning forward and taking a smouldering joint out of the ashtray. 'This stuff helps. Helps a lot. If I was in California, I'd be getting it on prescription.'

Rex poured a glass of Okocim and passed it toward Terry. Terry shook his head, taking a deep draw.

'Helps you concentrate, too,' he said, in the strangulated voice of someone trying not to let precious smoke out of his lungs. 'I'd never be able to wade through all this stuff normally. Here – look.'

He laid the joint back in the ashtray, and lunged abruptly across the table for one of the files. There was a strange sort of energy about him. Better than the listless, hopeless Terry of the past few days, certainly, but still, odd.

'See this, right. As well as trying to find out about his own family, Kovacs was looking into what happened in Tottenham just after the Outrage. There were dozens of people down for little rewards for trying to help stop the terrorists…' Terry continued to rummage, then with sudden force, threw the box down and reached for another. Kovacs' notes, tiny ink inscriptions on those strange, brown triangles of grease-proof paper, fluttered across the table.

'A Mrs Mary Ann Cawley got a quid for chucking a potato at the robbers as they scarpered. A Mr Aldred got three pound, three shillings to make up for the loss of his pony…'

'A Mr Anshel Walther?'

Terry looked up, puzzled. 'Yeah, he was one of them… How do you know about that?'

'That's why Kovacs had that picture of Micah Walther. He wasn't interested in the boy. Just his family. They couldn't tell him much about their ancestor, except that he was a bit of a wrong'un.'

Terry nodded. 'That makes sense. Kovacs was chasing up two people who were mentioned for bravery, but didn't collect their rewards. He put a note next to Anshel saying 'not suspicious'.'

'Meaning the other one was?'

'George Smith. Gas-fitter by trade. Terry squinted, quoting from the notes: "Who most pluckily and despite his own disability wrestled with the robbers without regard for his own safety." He was down to receive £25 at a ceremony at Tottenham Council Chamber on 13th March 1909.'

'Big reward in those days.'

'Yeah. The Walther bloke was only down for a hundredth of that – five shillings. And here's a tiny note in the *Wood Green Gazette* from the day after.'

Rex took a sip of his beer and peered in.

> Despite a fine luncheon being laid on gratis courtesy Messrs. Cattini Caterers and various civic dignitaries present, the award could not be made, since Mr George Smith did not appear.

Rex looked up. 'He never showed up?'

Terry chuckled. 'Never showed up anywhere, man. The Council just left it at that, but Kovacs did all sorts to try and find out what happened to him. Parish registers. Military records. Court transcripts. Prisons. Couldn't work out what happened.'

'Probably not too easy to track down someone called George Smith.'

'Maybe not. He did find out something, though. In his statement to the police, Smith said he lodged with a Mrs Cutter and her daughter at 7 Scotland Green. But according to the records, that house burned down, with no casualties.'

'So you mean he gave them an address that didn't exist?'

Terry slammed the table irritably, making Rex jump. 'No! I don't mean that! Just listen to me, man, will you? The house burned down on Saturday 23rd January 1909. See? Same day as the Outrage!'

Rex nodded uncertainly. He couldn't see what it all meant, or why Terry was so agitated.

'If that nurse in the hospital got it right, there was a third man, codenamed Vulcan, whose job it was to take the money back to Riga. That explains why no money was found. Right? That's why Kovacs was so interested in the two guys who never picked up their rewards. If that man – Vulcan – was George Smith – or someone claiming to be George Smith – that would explain why he disappeared without picking up his reward. The hero was a villain!'

'So what's the house burning down got to do with it?'

'I don't know!' Terry gave him an almost disgusted look. 'Maybe he needed to destroy evidence or something.'

'Isn't it more likely that George Smith the gas fitter was just George Smith the gas fitter – and the reason he legged it without picking up his reward was because he'd burnt his landlady's house down? What happened to the landlady and her daughter, anyhow?'

'I don't know, man! Jesus. Why are you so fucking determined to pick holes in it?'

'That's the process, isn't it, Terry? You have a theory, and you test it to see what's wrong?'

Terry didn't reply. Suddenly drawn into some byway of his own internal debate, he'd started scribbling fiercely on a notepad. Rex watched him uneasily. He didn't want to shoot Terry's ideas down, but he didn't understand why they were so important. None of this frenzied research was helping explain why Kovacs, or the Bettelheims had had to die. Terry seemed to have become obsessed with the thing for its own sake, and perhaps that was all right in the circumstances. But Rex didn't feel comfortable with his friend's new, twitchy energy.

Leaving Terry's house, he tried the Greek lady on the other side – Mrs Christodolou. Eyeing his carrier bag of beers with great suspicion, she said she'd never seen any women going in or out of her neighbours' house, blonde or otherwise, but then she didn't look, because she kept herself to herself.

On the way home, Rex wondered if he should perhaps do more of the same himself. Keep his nose out. Let Terry do what he needed to do. He couldn't help worrying, though. Worrying, and wondering why his drinking companion of five years and the only man who'd ever joined him in a medicinal shot of vodka at breakfast-time, wouldn't have a beer.

Chapter Seven

The inquest into the Bettelheim murders was held at Wood Green Crown Court, in a stuffy room rendered even less bearable by the number of people in it, and the heating which couldn't be switched off until the end of April, regardless of the specific weather conditions. Rex found it hard to stay awake, and after he'd given his own statement, he occupied himself with making a note of all the people he recognised. The relations were all there, of course, along with Yitzie Schild and Mordecai Hershkovits, and a number of faces he'd seen either on the streets of Stamford Hill or at the wild celebrations of the tish.

D.S. Brenard was present too, red-eyed and sniffling amidst the police contingent. Next to him was a severe-looking but rather dashing officer who sported assorted medals and epaulette flashes. Rex wondered if this was Commander Bailey. As he scanned the rest of the room, he noted two conspicuous absences. It was understandable that Terry hadn't been called: the criminal proceedings against him presumably cast doubt on his testimony. But where was Dordoff?

Everyone in the room knew exactly where the long, ritual intonement of statements and questions was heading. The coroner was a tanned, Spartan-looking old man who spent his weekends running up hills, and whose pronouncements always brought a strange note of refinement to the grim catalogue of human demises being categorised at Wood Green. '*This gentleman's unfortunate fondness for crack cocaine...*' was a phrase that regularly featured in his verdicts, along with, '*a rather regrettable use of an automatic firearm.*' From his seat in the separate Press Area, close enough to yank Ellie Mehta by the hair, Rex noticed a number of his fellow journalists sitting up straighter and smiling expectantly as the coroner began his closing notes. No doubt they were hoping for a nice Dickensian phrase to liven up their copy.

None came, today, though. *Unlawful killing by poison – and by person or persons unknown.* 'A sad matter,' was the coroner's only gloss on the subject. As chairs scraped and people stood, Ellie turned to Rex, opening her mouth to speak. He cut her dead, walked away, and caught Mordecai Hershkovits by the sleeve.

'Doesn't change much, does it?' Hershkovits said, putting on his wide-brimmed hat.

'It means they can bury the bodies.'

'And the police can stop investigating,' Hershkovits said loudly, throwing his voice in the direction of the medalled officer. 'Not really a coincidence, is it? Suddenly they're happy to have an inquest now that they need all their officers on the street stopping terrorists.'

'Would you rather we didn't bother to stop the terrorists, Mr Hershkovits?' said the policeman.

'Have you actually stopped any terrorists since Anwar Hafeez?' Rex asked. The senior-looking policeman eyed him beadily, before executing a military turn on the heel and stalking out. Rex saw D.S. Brenard shaking his head as if to say, *bad move.*

'You had any luck finding the mystery blonde?' Rex asked Brenard, as they filed out.

'Bird's been discharged from hospital but no one can find him,' Brenard said. 'He may have told you he saw a blonde bird coming out of Kovacs' house but if we can't talk to him, there's not much we can do.'

'You could try and test that patch of blood in Kovacs' cellar.'

'Someone went to the house and took a sample yesterday,' Brenard replied coldly. He walked away.

Outside in the sunlight, Rex found himself next to Hershkovits again. 'I didn't see Simmy Dordoff here today.'

Hershkovits shrugged. 'I expect he's at the kollel still.'

'What is that – a sort of study place? Is that really what people do all day? Just study?'

Mordecai laughed. 'We *work*, Mr Tracey, same as you. Dordoff's firm is doing up some of the rooms at the study-house.' He went off, shaking his head and chuckling to himself.

Not wanting to waste a minute, the Bettelheims' relatives had booked a funeral, to take place at Abney Park Cemetery in a couple of hours' time. Rex planned to attend, mainly because they desperately needed some photographs for the website, and in the absence of Terry, he was the only one who could get them. As Susan had reminded him, half a million people had lined the streets when the victims of the original Outrage had been interred at Abney. It was the least they could do to cover this more recent crop of burials.

It also gave him an excuse to root out Simmy Dordoff: the kollel was only a short distance up the road. He walked out of the court house, past the Driving Test Centre where only a week ago he'd thought he'd be taking a test, and caught a bus.

On the way, his telephone rang. He didn't like answering it on buses. Whenever he said, 'Rex Tracey', people turned round and stared. He let it ring off. But then it rang again – same number. He answered it.

'I heard from Latvia,' said an eager, west country voice. It was Tim from the university, aka GoldVlad. 'The registry place in Riga got back to me today about a request I made a while back. They told me someone else had been asking about the same person – Rosa Feigenbaum née Brandt.'

'Kovacs, I assume?'

'No, I mean – someone else right now.'

Terry. He wished the guy would just relax.

'Anyhow,' Tim continued. 'Rosa's dates don't add up. I mean, when she turned up here in the UK, she had a child who was fourteen months older than her marriage certificate…'

'Meaning she had a child by someone else before Feigenbaum married her.'

'Exactly. The other thing is… Do you know what a *mamzer* is?'

'A what?'

'A –'

The line went dead. He tried calling back. It was still dead. He jotted down the word *mamzer* as the bus swung right at Seven Sisters. So Rescha's ancestor had got pregnant by one man, and then married – or more likely had been married off to – another. Did it mean anything? It was hardly an unusual story. It could have been his own story, in fact, if his mother had married.

His thoughts returned to the woman with the blonde hair. He was encouraged that the police were testing the blood spots. But they'd obviously had no luck finding the mystery 999 caller, or tracking the person he'd seen with Bird outside Kovacs' house. The only person who knew anything about that woman was Bird. And Bird, a normally ubiquitous sight on the streets of Wood Green, seemed to have disappeared.

The study-house was on Cazenove Road, where a row of smart, stuccoed villas faced brown council towers. On the council side, from a low block that had probably once served as a community centre or a Youth Club, the sound of youthful chanting drifted through open windows.

He peered inside one, and the energy and movement almost made him stagger back. The small room was packed with boys and young men in white shirts and black trousers. Some were absorbed in texts, swaying to their own rhythms as they chanted aloud. Others were reading together, or deep in argument, as a pair of older, white-bearded men wandered round with pointers, listening and occasionally intervening. It was like looking in on a beehive, or a factory.

'Want to study Talmud?' asked a voice at his shoulder, startling him. He turned around. Dordoff. He was in white overalls, and covered in plaster dust.

'How can anyone learn anything in that noise?' Rex asked.

'We've always had to learn in difficult circumstances,' Dordoff replied. 'With pogroms and wars and Holocausts all around us. These places are the engine-houses of the Jewish spirit, Mr Tracey.'

Dordoff motioned to him to follow, and they went round the back of the building, where there was a row of allotments, complete with plastic tunnels and rickety greenhouses. At their far edge a slim, narrow building was being vigorously sanded down by a crew of Hasidim in overalls. But for their skullcaps pinned to their dust-frosted heads with hairclips, they could have been any bunch of workmen, anywhere. They even had the radio on loud – tuned to the BBC World Service.

'I was expecting to see you at the inquest, Mr Dordoff.'

Dordoff shouted to one of his workmates to turn the radio off. 'We're packing up early so we can get ready for the funeral. That's of rather greater importance to us.'

With the radio off, the sound of the chanting seemed louder. Dordoff led Rex towards the building. They stood for a moment in the doorway, looking out on the flapping, creaking greenhouses and the tilled soil.

'Studying and gardening,' Rex said. 'A strange combination.'

'For you, maybe. Is there something you want, Mr Tracey?'

'What's behind the whole home-grown veg thing? Is it about staying healthy?'

'Partially. Dukovchiner believe we should look after ourselves, and not depend too much on... well, be self-reliant.'

'Why? Aren't you expecting the Messiah to come at any moment?'

Dordoff snorted. 'In the meantime the world imposes its demands.'

'Such as?'

Dordoff led Rex over to the little greenhouses, and motioned to Rex to join him.

'Lima beans, oca yams, peanuts, sweet potato, courgettes, cassava…'

Rex peered into the warm, musty little sheds, where trays of soil, enlivened by the odd green shoot, stood on metal bookcases. The wind rattled the glass in the frames.

'You eat all of it?'

'Sure. It's easy to grow. Easy to harvest. There are tutorials all over YouTube. You have to be a bit careful preparing the cassava, but it's all high in calories, very nutritious. And if we ever get a surplus, we sell it to the Nigerians and the Brazilians on Philip Lane.'

Rex remembered the strange-looking veg in Rescha's shop – the speckled beans, the long, hairy yam-like things. 'Do you sell to Rescha Schild?'

'Kind of. She distributes it to participating members, sells it to the rest. You look surprised.'

'I just got the impression she wasn't very involved with your activities.'

Dordoff smiled thinly. 'Her vegetable shop is certainly involved. We're growing potatoes and carrots, too. Some here. Some in our other allotments down Mannock Road. Near to you. You see, the more mixed your diet, the healthier you are. And the less you rely on one crop, the less likely you are to starve.'

'You're very modern, aren't you, Mr Dordoff?' Rex asked, noting uncomfortably the reference to his address. 'YouTube, market gardening… Transplant clinics.'

Dordoff didn't show any surprise. 'Life is precious. That's not just *Hasidus*. It's a central tenet of the Jewish faith. We are even commanded to break many of the other commandments if doing so will save a human life.'

'So in some cases, even murdering someone would be okay, if it allowed someone else to live?'

'No. No, of course not. Absolutely not!' Dordoff laughed, incredulously. 'Is that what you think, Mr Tracey?'

Seeing Dordoff here, in his overalls, surrounded by his vegetables, Rex realised what had perpetually bothered him about the man, and indeed, a lot of the Dukovchiner he'd met. Generally speaking, few Hasidim looked healthy: they looked as if they had bad diets, and spent too much time indoors. The Dukovchiner, by contrast, seemed to be bursting with health and strength. Was it because of their vegetables? Or their faith? Neither, he then realised, seemed to do much good for the Narpal.

'I came here to ask about Antwerp. Specifically, to ask what were you doing there, in the city where Senticel has its main treatment centre, when Micah Walther went missing.'

'Antwerp has a sizeable Hasidic population, Mr Tracey, including members of my own family. I was on family business.'

'You obviously know what Senticel is, though.'

Dordoff gave a small inclination of the head.

'But you didn't take Micah Walther there, to undergo some medical procedure he didn't survive?'

Dordoff shook his head, as if he couldn't quite believe the insult he had just been dealt. He seemed about to walk off, but then changed his mind. 'You know what Mr Tracey. There's no reason why I should, but I'll tell you who I sat next to on that flight to Antwerp. Or better yet, I'll ring the person I sat next to on the flight to Antwerp and he can tell you in person.' He had started to sound angry, though to Rex the outrage seemed a tad overdone.

He pulled a phone out of his overall pocket and dialled as he spoke. 'His name is Meir Russberg and he works in a diamond dealership on Pelikaanstraat. We had a very interesting conversation about Rabbi Simeon of Chelyabinsk. Wait.'

Dordoff handed the phone, in loudspeaker mode, to Rex, who took it somewhat sheepishly. A voice answered: 'Russberg.'

Rex cleared his throat. Dordoff's co-workers had stopped work and were quietly watching. 'Hello Mr Russberg. Did you travel on an aeroplane to Antwerp in October last year with a man called Simeon Dordoff?'

There was a pause. 'Who are you?' said the voice. Dordoff leant in and explained, in a mixture of English and Yiddish.

'Aah. Yes. Yes I did.' The voice said. 'City Airport to A.I.A. We talked about our favourite subject. Rav Simyon of Chelyabinsk.'

Rex frowned. 'So you have known Mr Dordoff for some time? I mean – prior to the flight?'

'Of course! He is married to the niece of my cousin's husband, and we were in the yeshiva together for a year as boys. In Gateshead. I was making a joke, you see. At the yeshiva there was one topic we especially did not enjoy, and it was the vision of Rav Simyon of Chelyabinsk. Ha!'

Rex asked his final question, knowing full well what the answer would be.

'Simmy was alone. Until he bumped into me at the departure gate, that is…'

He handed the phone back to Dordoff. 'But the Rebbe is having treatment in Antwerp, isn't he?'

'I don't have to discuss that with you,' Dordoff said, turning his back.

Rex might have left it that, if his bus back to Wood Green to pick up a camera hadn't been diverted and he hadn't chanced to find himself outside the premises of KumarKabs. On the pavement the assorted drivers – an exclusively Turkish and Somali crew – had arrayed themselves on stools and boxes, amidst a scattering of sunflower seeds and fag-ash. They didn't look busy – a good time to make enquiries.

He felt more or less sure Dordoff was telling him the truth. It was really only a twitch, a tiny, possibly paranoid vibration on his radar that made him wonder whether the whole phone conversation had just been a little too convenient.

After all, this Russberg was a relative of sorts – and relatives were, generally speaking, more ready to lie than friends or strangers. And Dordoff had said some words to the man in Yiddish.

Vik Kumar was a thin balding man with thick, overhanging eyebrows, and a famously forbidding manner. In addition to the cab firm, he owned a row of shops off White Hart Lane, a restaurant, and a small block of flats. He was forever receiving awards from the Haringey Chamber of Commerce, but neither they, nor his growing fortune, seemed to make him any happier.

Over the years Kumar's mood seemed to have rubbed off on his drivers, who had themselves become renowned for their unwillingness to converse with their fares. Many customers, of course, favoured Vik's cab-firm for exactly that reason.

Since the night Rex had seen Vik at the tish, and apparently enjoying himself, he'd wondered several times what could have brought this noted local mogul into the orbit of the Dukovchiner Hasidim. He had a hunch, though – and it was a hunch strengthened by the fact that Vik and many of his drivers were today sporting dark suits and ties.

'Do you drive a lot of those Hasidic Jewish guys about, Vik?' Rex asked, as he went into the office.

Vik looked up. 'Why?'

'I saw you at that celebration of theirs the other night on Bruce Grove.'

'We're doing the cars for the funeral this afternoon,' Vik confirmed, spitting a wad of khat into the bin at his feet.

'Ever take them to the airport?'

'Sometimes.'

'Do you remember taking anyone to City Airport in October last year?'

Vik chuckled sardonically, displaying green, khat-stained teeth and tongue.

'All right – silly question,' Rex admitted. 'But could you maybe check your logs and see if anyone did a fare from Stamford Hill to City in October?'

Vik squinted at him, then spat again. 'You joined the Old Bill now?'

'Yeah, Vik, they fast-tracked me. I've joined the brand new Mini-cab Driver Persecution Unit.'

That earned a vague smile from Vik, who rummaged on some shelves under his desk and produced a greasy, cloth-backed book with assorted Post-its fluttering off it like wings. The man said nothing as he flipped through it. Rex looked around. The ply-wood-panelled walls, the Spurs Calendar, the smell of fags and deodorant reminded him of the places he'd had his hair cut as a little boy. Suddenly, without looking up, Vik bellowed, 'Jock!'

Jock turned out to be a huge-eyed Somali whose suit and shirt billowed around a coat-hanger body. He had the look of an eleven-year-old in September, during his first days at secondary school.

'Says here you took one of those Jewish guys to City Airport on October 12th. That was your first day here wasn't it?'

Jock nodded. Vik made a gesture towards Rex, as if to say, be my guest, he's all yours.

'I just wondered if he was alone?' Rex asked.

Jock looked at Rex eagerly but blankly, not understanding.

'DID HE HAVE ANYONE WITH HIM?' shouted Vik, who'd learnt a thing or two about communicating with foreigners.

Jock nodded vigorously. 'Yes, yes. With him, yes.'

'Fuck. They just say yes because they think that's the answer you want,' Vik complained, rolling his eyes. He took a deep breath and addressed the driver again. 'Are you – ARE YOU JUST SAYING THAT OR DID HE REALLY HAVE SOMEONE ELSE WITH HIM? ONE PASSENGER OR TWO PASSENGER?'

'Two passenger,' said Jock. 'I know, because ask if Daddy.'

'What do you mean?' Rex asked.

Jock held up long, twiggy fingers as he illustrated his point: first one, then another. 'Man. Boy. Two passengers. So I ask if Daddy. Says no. Boy says no. Want my Daddy. Crying boy.'

* * *

We met at dawn on Saturday by the High Cross. Three Jews with their prayer books on a Sabbath morn – nothing odd about that. Something odd about Elephant, though, those matching catkins on his brow waggling up and down constantly, a thin, maddening little smile on his puss whenever he looks at me. A man who knows, and wants others to know he knows, only not know themselves. I begin to wonder if you could build Kropotkin's perfect beehive, when it might contain such wasps.

I cannot fault him on his planning, though. Military. Clever, the choice of the day. Half the police at the station will be on duty up in the city for the Lord Mayor's Parade. And many of the rest will find their big policeman's boots drawn away towards the White Hart Lane area, where the Tottenham Hotspur Foot-ball Club are playing a morning match because of the worsening smog.

Also – extra money at Schnurrman's. Bonuses paid out on the last Saturday of the month. Could be two hundred coming from the bank. A fortune.

The factory's fired up by the time we meet: awful stink just hangs there in the fog. We talk it all through, smoking to ward off the damp creeping cold, switching to Yiddish when English people come by, to English when we see Jews. Not many of either on this dark, savage morning. I tell of my plans for making it back to Riga: Felixstowe, not Tilbury, on Danish papers to Lubeck, maybe German for the final leg, if I can get them. Elephant listens throughout. That smile. Begging to have it wiped off him by my five friends.

I'll own to it, though. There is something liberating about the act we are about to commit. Something swooping and soaring, and nature-defying. Like when we were boys on the dunes, and we'd put our coats up above our heads in a gale to feel the wind picking us right off our feet. You feel it feathery and light right up your arse, and in the twitching tip of your cock. The promise of violence, gunfire, striking out, explosions, mayhem. We all felt it. Smirking, hinting Elephant. Twitching, spot-picking Torch. Soon, we who had been in chains would be flying.

We split up. I am George Smith, after all, heading from my lodgings to my place of work when I see the commotion and do what any decent citizen of the borough would do. But I don't want to go back to the house. Don't want to see anyone until it's done with.

I have to be coming south down the High Road when it happens. Need to be seen making that journey, so I stay up around the High Cross. The cold is too much, though. If I stay two hours on the streets, I won't be doing any heroics, I reckon, I'll just be dead. Nowhere open at this time. Nowhere I can sit.

Then it strikes me to go in a prayer-house. Can't go in the grand new synagogue because of course there's a shomer outside, demanding to see your subscription book is all up to date. Remember the old shomer joke they tell now from Shanghai to Cape Town: *Okay sonny, you can go in and find your daddy. But don't let me catch you praying.*

So I follow two swinging-locked little bony Hasid boys to one of their assemblies. Not a *shul*, a *shtib*. A room. So much noise in there, with them jumping up and down and singing and flinging their curls back and forth like pendulums – no one notices the terrorist at the back. No fire in there, but hot bodies and candles make it better than the street.

I recognise words and lines from my past. The Aramaic. *Yikum purkon min shemayo.* May Deliverance arise from Heaven. Amen to that. I can't find the ecstasy these fellows seem to be enveloped in. Enough to bring back memories, though. Mama's face as I limped home, discharged from the Navy. *You're going to Riga to work on a newspaper? What is a newspaper?* Left in anger. Next time I went back, everyone gone. House burned down. Soldiers took my sisters away, to do what soldiers do to people's sisters. Mother, grandfather, five other Jewish families – run through with sabres. Outside the beer shop I meet cross-eyed Osip. He tells me, oh yes my dog still pulls at the leash and tries to go over to that plot. To lick the earth where all the blood spilled. So I kicked cross-eyed Osip's fucking cross-eyed dog with my good leg and fell in the street, and they all came out of the beer shop and kicked me – kicked me out of the village for good.

So I'm not much good with grief. What was Missus Cutter to me? I was relieved when Leah ran upstairs to her room, leaving me and Parks together. 'Tell her I'll postpone my trip to Bradford,' he says, 'To help with arrangements.'

'She doesn't need help,' said I. 'She has her auntie. And me.'

His eyes narrowed and his cheeks pinked up prettily but he didn't say anything. Just went out, slammed the door, like my sisters used to do in a girl's rage.

I only went to a synagogue once or twice before, but I was sure their rites had a clear end to them. A point when everyone stood up and nodded to one another and left. But these Hasids just carried on at it. One chant ends, another begins. No wonder they're so thin, I thought; they spend their whole days like this, meeting God so violently.

I nearly believed again myself when Rosa said those words to me outside the printers that night. Believe a lot in *words*, of course, Jews. God spoke creation into being. Rabbi Loeb spoke words over his clay golem, and turned it into the scourge of Prague. Those Hasids follow some man, a sort of a witch, whose power came from knowing the names of God, and uttering them. And what power there is, what unlocking power there is in a girl calling an ugly man beautiful.

Like she'd uttered an incantation over me. She untwisted me. I wasn't the man with the two mismatched legs, I was the man I'd been before: sailor, man you'd think twice about, man you'd try catch the eye of. She grew me, that girl, and in the time we had together, I grew her: taught her to see, to look, to question, to be angry.

So full of memories, I nearly missed my time to leave. Hurrying out of the shtib, I resolved to myself – I would find her. Go back to Riga, do whatever it took.

Walked slowly down the High Street on the railway side, opposite the turning to the rubber works, feeling faint and trembling, sweeping either side of me for police or followers, near gagging with the factory egg-smell. Still a lot of the normal Saturday folk have not come out, stallholders and strollers and beggars and pickpockets and tarts, all of them staying in their berths out of the fog and the cold, so I have a clear view a long away ahead. I can see the grey cap and the blue cap of Elephant and Torch, outside the photographer's.

They're just staring over the road to the factory. All the time I look at them, that's the only place the pair of stew-pots look. You're standing outside a shop, I want to scream. One of you at least, look in the fucking window! They might as well hold up a placard like those Votes For Women women do: We're About To Do The Factory.

I take out my watch. Twenty to ten. Listen for a car engine, but there's nothing. Stomach coiling up now, like rope on the quay. I'm close enough now to see a little way up Chesnut Road and to the gates of the factory. Schnurrman himself has come out, peering round anxiously in his fur-collar coat, checking the gold watch in his waistcoat pocket.

I have an absurd thought. What if some other cell has been at work for months, planning this in tandem, and they're robbing the car up the road, outside the bank, this very minute? Almost makes me smile.

Then I hear the engine. The car is coming. Elephant and Torch hear it too. Schnurrman, heavy shoulders relaxing, trots back inside his tower. Quick for a fatty, I think. The car swings in. Elephant and Torch cross the road.

There's a barber who of a Friday papers half his window with the Yiddish news, so the devout can see without exactly reading and the poor can learn without paying. I linger there for a minute, like I'm reading about the Tsar's ban on music in Russian cinemas, when I'm really looking at the reflection of events on the other side of the road. Then I realise. I'm George fucking Smith. I don't read Yiddish newspapers.

I hear the car engine stop. I cross the road. I hear a car door open. A shout. Two shouts. I hobble into Chesnut Road, towards the factory gates. A stout woman from the corner greengrocer's is doing the same.

They're rolling on the ground in the gateway like schoolboys – Elephant, Torch, and a clerk with a heavy case. The clerk calls out. A driver gets out of the car with difficulty, and Elephant shoots right at him. The bullet hits his coat, but glances off it. Button maybe. A lucky coat.

They've got the bag off the clerk, and I can see Elephant whipping the money out, ready. I'm about to do my bit when a policeman's whistle sounds. 'Stop! Police!' A copper comes running down the road. Torch points right at the man and fires at his chest. The copper jumps back, dead, instantly. As his helmet rolls off I see it's the lad they call Old Bill. PC Tyler. They'll hang us all twice for that.

All the planning gone out with the bilge-water. These men are maniacs, I think. Shooting unarmed men. Shooting a big, honest, stupid country lad like PC Tyler.

So I scarce have to pretend I'm an honest man, outraged, as I hurl myself at Elephant and knock him and his bag to the floor.

Compared to him, I am honest. I get in a good couple of punches to his nose and his eye. He never stops smiling. He seems to reach up and embrace me. I feel a thick parcel being stuffed inside the special fold I'd sewn into my coat the night before. I can smell the gunpowder on him – a sweaty, smoky, below-decks smell. We roll on the cobbles and he whispers in my ear, like a lover.

'Tell you a secret, Vulcan. When you went to Vilnius, the boss sent your Rosa away. Called her in to the Dockers' tavern and told her you were never coming back.'

We stopped rolling. I stared at him, hands round his neck. He smiled that smile.

'The girl was a bad influence on you. And we needed a good English-speaker for this job. Velkis paid the fare and she went back to her family without a backward look. The rabbis sent her straight away again, I heard. To Canada. So you don't waste any time looking for your lost love.'

I pulled my fist back. I was going to take out that little rat-tooth that drooped over the bottom lip. But just then I caught a blow from the side. Torch. My ears whistled. My sight cleared in time to see their two arses, haring away with the bag.

The woman from the grocer's hurled her biggest potato after them. 'I'll want reimbursing for that,' she said, uselessly, to the corpse of PC Tyler, as more of his fellows came running out of the station house. I felt the thick wad of money at my belly and I resolved something, there and then on the bloody cobbles. It wasn't going to Riga. Nor me.

* * *

For the rest of the week, Rex asked no questions about Dr Kovacs, or the Bettelheims, or Micah Walther. On his way to and from the office, he kept an eye out for Bird, in the hope of finding the man in a moment of clarity, and asking him more about the woman he'd encountered at Kovacs' house. He never saw him, though, nor, to the best of his knowledge, had anyone else in the area. Those efforts aside, he concentrated on the paper. Susan's message about bringing out an 'A-class' edition had sounded more like a plea than the usual pep talk, and he'd taken it to heart.

There was plenty of other local news, as well, what with some misguided soul spraying FUCK TERISTS [*sic*] in pink letters on the exterior of the Noel Park Sikh Gurdwara, and a sit-in protest by a splinter group of the Flint Street Primary School Action Committee at the offices of the Council Planning Department. The police had reacted with the heavy-handedness typical of the past few weeks, and several of the mothers who'd been objecting to the siting of a hostel for convicted criminals next to the school had ended up with criminal convictions themselves. One had ended up with physical injuries. There were lawsuits and inquiries in the offing.

Susan's outrage was almost matched by her delight that Brenda's eldest daughter had managed to film some of police brutality on her mobile while visiting the Council Offices to apply for a permit to cut down a tree. The footage on the News North London website had had nine thousand hits, and a copy on YouTube had almost as many.

Then there was the government leaflet that had been slipped through the letter-boxes of every home in Haringey. 'Communities', it said, had a 'duty' to report suspicious behaviour to the anti-terror hotline. Everyone knew what 'communities' meant. It meant Muslims. And the list of what to look out for was almost comical. False passports. Mood swings. Spending a lot of time in internet cafés or with new friends. Adopting a new name or nickname. Not to mention personality changes, obsessive behaviour and constant lying.

'Now I know what was wrong with my first wife,' Lawrence said, when he saw the leaflet, and Susan liked his joke so much she turned it into a cartoon and put it in the middle of the homepage.

Rex found it hard to share in her delight. Of course, in an abstract sense it was good that they had important, local stories to tell, and that people were noticing. He didn't see how that made any real difference, though, if those people weren't paying money to read them. And the meetings in Susan's office hadn't stopped. Those, he felt, were a surer indication of failure than web stats were of success.

The other thing was that Terry had shuffled in early on Wednesday afternoon, clearly stoned, to say he felt better and wanted to come back to work. There'd been much fanfare. Brenda had dished out cake, and even the Whittaker Twins had attended a little 'Welcome Back' tea party. The next morning, however, Terry was nowhere to be found, and he remained that way for the next two days.

On Friday afternoon, after three days of increasingly fine weather, Brenda invited Rex to a small barbecue party she and Mike were throwing on Saturday in honour of their anniversary. Rex, on his way out to a dentist's appointment, hesitated, and, as Brenda was wont to do sometimes, she took it the wrong way.

'Feel free to say no if you've got better plans,' she said huffily.

'I haven't. I mean, I have got plans, for earlier on, but yes, I can come in the afternoon. I mean – I'd love to, thank you,' he said.

Brenda gave a queenly acknowledgement. 'What are your plans for earlier?'

'It's Purim on Saturday,' he said, heading off before she could probe. The fewer people knew about his plans for Purim, the better.

* * *

Saturday dawned as bright and warm as the days before it – the perfect weather for his scheme. He'd laid off the lager and the painkillers the night before, and felt better than he had done in months as he made his way towards the bus station and the 55 route towards Stoke Newington.

The florist on the station parade was doing an amusing deal. 15% off if you bought flowers, chocolates and a 'Sorry' card all at the same time. He thought it would make a good filler piece – especially if they could interview a few men taking advantage of the deal – but his zeal was diverted by a familiar sight. Outside the shop, on a bench, Bird was back, can in hand. He was drunk, of course, but not yet shouting drunk.

Rex sat down next to him, placing a two pound coin on the wood between them. Bird eyed it. 'Do you remember that woman you saw at George's house?'

Bird took a breath. 'CUT –'

Rex stopped him. 'Yes. Her. Did she say anything to you?'

'She cut her back.'

'Did she say that, or did you just see it? Did she speak?'

Bird finished his can, threw it, then belched. This wasn't getting anywhere.

'Get off me,' the old drunk said, displaying a hall of yellow teeth.

'She said get off me? Why? Did you touch her?'

'Push her back,' Bird said, pocketing the coin. 'She try teef George's yard, so me push the white bitch. Get off me. *Kurva*!'

'Wait a minute. She said that?' He'd heard Bird shouting this Polish epithet before. Assumed it was just part of his routine. But what if it wasn't?

'Bitch. *Kurva*!'

'She shouted that at you? Was she Polish?'

'Uh.' Bird gazed vacantly at him, then caught sight of two teenage girls giggling as they walked by. He lumbered after them, roaring curses. They obligingly screeched and tottered away. Rex sighed. He had more questions to add to the pile. No answers. He just hoped Stamford Hill would be different.

Pausing by the top of Langerhans Road, his camera knocking against his chest, he felt a short pang of sorrow that he wasn't doing this with Terry. In the first place Purim in Stamford Hill was a photographer's gift. In the second place, Terry was the natural accomplice for Rex's real mission, because he never minded taking risks, and he was loyal, brave and strong. At least, the old Terry had been.

Rex hadn't had much chance to read up on the traditional yearly festival of Purim. It had something to do with the Jews living in ancient Persia, and how they'd outwitted an evil official and avoided a massacre. Its chief point of interest for Rex right now was that the descendants of those Jews, specifically the faithful of the N16 area, celebrated the avoidance of the massacre in a very public fashion. This meant there'd be periods of this High Holy Day when everyone was outside. Which meant Rex could be inside the Bettelheim house, undisturbed.

What he'd learned from the improbably christened Jock at KumarKabs had convinced him this was a vital lead. His instincts had been right. Dordoff had lied. He had not travelled to Antwerp alone. He had taken a boy with him. And that boy, it seemed pretty clear, had not come home. Now, some months later, Dordoff was back, putting pressure on a new family to give up their son. They'd refused – and they'd all died. Dr Kovacs had died too, possibly because he had known or seen or found out about it. There had to be some clue, something the police had missed, in the Bettelheim house, linking them to Dordoff. He felt sure of it. All week Rex had had dreams about finding it, whatever it was. Dreams like the dreams he'd had as a boy, in which he'd ridden a bike or swum before he'd actually been able to do either.

The first hint of the festivities was a trio of little boys, running along the road in cowboy gear. They met up with some little earlocked pirates, then stood obediently at the kerbside as a procession passed down Stamford Hill. It was made up of walkers and floats and the odd, random, horn-blaring Volvo or people carrier, festooned with ribbons and flags. The noise was incredible: some sort of Israeli folk-pop was blaring out from speakers on the opposite side of the road, mingling with cheering and whistle-blowing and loudest of all, the strange, grating sound of the thousands of wooden rattles being twirled by everyone from fat babies in their pushchairs to wispy-bearded scholars. It was remarkable. Remarkable to see this quiet, somewhat sombre community suddenly exploding into life, and with such conviction, as if they'd just been pretending the rest of the year, and this was what they were really like.

He took some snaps, partly for the website, but also because it would help with his alibi, if he needed one.

He spotted a group of little boys, done up not as super-heroes or figures of modern legend but in outsized pin-striped suits and ties. One had a big briefcase, another carried a toy mobile phone, a third waved a rolled-up umbrella about.

'They're being you,' said a voice at his elbow. It was Mordecai Hershkovits.

'What do you mean?'

'Look.' He pointed to another group clad in tracksuits and rugby tops. 'They're pretending to be *goyim* – gentiles. For these kids, that's fancy dress.'

'What's with the rattles? Did Spurs give you a job lot?'

The little man looked at him pityingly. 'If you think they still use rattles at football matches, Mr Tracey, then you are more out of touch than any of the people here. It's to blot out the name of Haman. That's the tradition. When we read out the story in the synagogue, everyone makes a big noise with the rattles whenever Haman's name comes up. And then they carry on making it, all day.'

'Boo-hiss, sort of thing. I get it. Is everyone here today?' Rex added, wondering if the likes of Yitzie and Rescha and the Walthers were amongst the jubilant crowds.

'Some people do their own thing,' Mordecai replied. 'Your Dukovchiner friends opted out of everything, basically, when the new Rebbe took over.'

'Why?'

He tutted. 'You still haven't worked it out? The other Hasidim thought the Rebbe was too young, that other people were manipulating him. There was a bit of a *broiges*. A row. Then the Dukovchiner basically said, Okay, you go your way, we'll go ours – and pulled out of everything.'

Rex was a little annoyed. If Mordecai had been so forthcoming a couple of weeks ago, he'd have understood a lot more. 'Pulled out of what? Parades?'

Mordecai chuckled. 'Not parades, no. How do you think all these people have ten, eleven children and just run little shops and bake bread and sell religious books for a living?'

'I thought you were a chartered accountant, Mordecai.'

'I am. And yes, we've got lawyers and property developers and some doctors. But there are a lot more who make only a tenth, a twentieth what a doctor makes. It's all kept together by charity. Like a little Jewish welfare state. One charity for children's clothes, another for schoolbooks, another if you need a lift to the hospital or a funeral… Everybody gives, everybody receives, whatever Rebbe you follow. Except if you decide not to give –'

'– you don't receive.' It was starting to make sense. The disapproving reactions when he asked about the Dukovchiner. Dordoff and his cassava garden, or whatever it was – they had to grow food because the free, charitable supplies had dried up. Yitzie and Rescha's forlorn, empty shop. And the sofa at the Walthers' house – not a bribe from Dordoff, as he'd thought, but an entitlement that came on joining another group.

'Exactly.' Mordecai followed Rex's gaze to a vast, papier- mâché figure making its way slowly down the hill. 'You recognise him?'

Rex did recognise the swept-back quiff, the broad, drooping moustache and the military tunic. It was either the bloke who ran Konak Kebab and Grill on Westbury Avenue, or it was someone he'd learnt all about in A-level history.

'Why is Stalin in your parade?'

'He was a modern-day Haman. Another person who plotted to destroy the Jews, and failed.'

Rex shook his head. 'You really do live with your history, don't you?'

Mordecai's chest swelled. 'We *are* our history.'

Rex bade goodbye to Mordecai and picked his way across Stamford Hill. The crowds and the raucous atmosphere disoriented him, and it was some time before he found his way to Riverside. A few sparrows and gulls were the only signs of life. Even the single house with the name of Allah stuck over the door was silent. He wondered if they'd gone to the parade too.

He was still thinking about Mordecai's parting shot. *We are our history.* Perhaps it held a message for him. He'd been ignoring everything to do with the past – Kovacs' box files and brown paper triangles, the stuff about Rescha's ancestors – assuming it had no bearing on recent happenings. But what if he was wrong? Here, the past clearly wasn't past. Was that what linked the historian's death to the others?

Like many of the properties in this part of Stamford Hill, Number 11, until recently the Bettelheims' family home, had a tiny yard at the back, reached by a narrow alleyway. Even a man of Rex's physical limitations found it easy to force his way inside.

He'd been half-expecting to find that the relations had cleared the place, or put up metal shutters to keep out the squatters, but it seemed they'd been too busy or grief-stricken to take such practical steps. He found a rusty spanner on a pile of bricks next to a boy's bike, and used it to smash the glass in the kitchen door. He found himself in a Marie Celeste situation. Though it had obviously been dusted and tested and searched by the police, the house was still very much a physical record of what its occupants had been doing before they left it forever.

Immediately he was surprised by how grubby the place was. It smelt of onions and cooking fat, and the lino was sticky as he walked across it. The Bettelheims hadn't owned much, and what household goods they possessed – kettle, toaster, oven – were on their last legs. Here was another sign that the charity support network had ceased to function.

He found himself thinking about his mother. She would have instantly condemned the woman in charge. In Rex's mother's world, as in this one, kitchens were always the responsibility of women. Perhaps the women round here had condemned Chaya Bettelheim. Some had hinted that she was a bit mad. Disordered kitchen, disordered mind. Maybe there was some truth in that.

But he felt there was more of a collective madness going on. The Dukovchiner had opted out of everything the community had to offer, and as a result life had become hard. People – at least two families – had started to leave the fold. Could that have given rise to desperate measures? Harsh penalties, publicly carried out, to deter others from slipping away? Was that what Moses Limburg, Chaya's nephew, had meant when he said they'd been killed as an example? Was such a thing possible, here in Stamford Hill?

Rex climbed the stairs, and entered the musty smelling master bedroom, with its strange arrangement of twin single beds. In a drawer on the chipped dressing table, he found a small cloth bag. Inside it were seven tiny wrist-bands, all from the Homerton Hospital. Chaya Bettelheim had had only three living children. He recalled something Rescha had said, about her and Chaya having some things in common. Had they both lost babies?

The boy and the girl, Eytan and Simcha, had shared a room looking onto the yard at the back. It was the cleanest, tidiest one in the house. Rex wondered if that was because they'd been responsible for it, instead of their mother. They had twin beds and a bookcase, upon which there were a few educational games, with pictures of 1970s children on their boxes. Hand-me-downs, he guessed. On the floor was a rug, with a moon and stars and a space rocket on it, and for reasons he couldn't quite understand, the sight of it made him sit on the floor and cry.

From down there, he noticed something shoved deep under one of the beds. He pulled it out. A briefcase. Unlike everything else in the house, it was smart and new. It was also locked. He took it down to the kitchen in search of a knife.

The catches gave way easily, and inside he found what amounted to the contents of a Hasidic teenager's school bag. There were school-books and a weighty, brown-paper-backed tome in Hebrew, pens and pencils, and a ball made from the red rubber bands that the postmen dropped all over the city. There was also a passport. A brand new one, in the name of Eytan Bettelheim. A tubby lad, with lively eyes, according to his photograph.

Rex then tried all the kitchen drawers, and a deep cupboard in the hall that smelt of boot polish and housed only raincoats and shopping bags and a folder full of old bank statements. He went back upstairs to the bedrooms for another look, and even scoured the baby's room and the cupboard under the sink, where he found only a spider and a dried-out flannel.

Then at last, behind the sofa, he discovered a concertina file, with all the family's important documents stuffed into it. There were birth certificates and insurance policies, P45s and rent books. All the paperwork that every citizen – even a family as unworldly as the Bettelheims – was deemed to need.

But no other passports. So unless the relations had taken them, and he couldn't imagine why they would have, the only family-member to have owned a passport was Eytan. Who, according to Toyve Walther, was being pressured to travel to Antwerp.

Rex returned to the kitchen, noticing for the first time that the Bettelheims had the same decorative scheme going on as Yitzie and Rescha Schild: a few photographs on the walls, but mostly tracts and bright images of the Menorah and the Star of David. Pushing the sticky highchair aside and sitting at the table, amid the toast crumbs of the Bettelheims' final breakfast, he began to go through the briefcase again, more thoroughly.

There was no diary. No calendar obligingly marked 'Antwerp'. No airline ticket. He did, however, notice, in one of the felt-covered corners of the inside, a tiny corner of bright paper peeping out. As he pulled at it, a whole cardboard bottom came away.

Rex had had the odd secret place as a boy. A cavity round the back of his dressing table, into which he'd occasionally stuffed packets of cigarettes and the odd bit of erotica. The chubby Eytan Bettelheim's secret vice, it seemed, had been sweets: in particular, judging from the sea of wrappers, Blueberry Hubba-Bubba, Zega-Zoids, Fizznuts and CherryBomz. But these weren't what caught Rex's attention. He was too preoccupied with the other items in this hidden museum: dozens and dozens of almost transparent, brown, grease-proof paper triangles, exactly like the ones Dr Kovacs had at his house. He sniffed one. It smelt of vanilla and sugar.

He stuffed everything back inside and rammed the case under his arm, heading out of the kitchen door into the yard. He knew where he should go next, but to his astonishment the tiny form of Mordecai Hershkovits bowled through the gate.

'Shame you didn't stay and listen to me,' he said. 'You'd have found out who foiled the plan to kill all the Jews.'

'Who?'

'The King's wife, Esther, and her uncle – Mordecai.'

Rex had no time to respond to this before two much larger bodies marched through the gate. One was D.S. Brenard. The other, complete with ribbons and a swagger stick, was the man Rex had clocked as Commander Bailey. They both wore an expression poised somewhere between fury and glee – one that over the years Rex had discovered was unique to policemen in the act of nicking someone.

'You're not going to believe this,' Rex said, as the briefcase was taken from him and plastic cuffs were fixed around his wrists, 'but I was just coming to see you.'

'And I'm Tom Jones,' said D.S. Brenard, encouraging him through the gateway with a knuckle in the back.

Back at the station, they chucked everything they could at him. Breaking and entering. Burglary. Vandalism. Obstruction. Commander Bailey even discussed the possibility of bringing Accessory After The Fact charges: from his talk with Vik Kumar's driver up to his arrest on Mordecai's tip-off, Rex had had evidence pertaining to a murder and chosen not to give it to the police.

In the cells, between an assortment of ponderous interviews, Rex considered Commander Bailey. The man was an anomaly. Rex had a theory – one he'd developed, tested and more or less proved during his long years as a reporter – that all young policemen were bastards. They were either officious prefect types, or they were straightforward thugs. Those who stayed in the force long enough to become old policemen became lesser bastards, over time, until in the end they were usually all right.

Commander Bailey, on the other hand, seemed to be travelling in the opposite direction. He had the dark, passionate looks of a Victorian romantic hero, and Rex suspected that he'd had romantic ideas about becoming a policeman, turning angrier and more sarcastic as these fell away.

'Tell me again what motivated you to break into the Bettelheim household.'

'I thought I might find a clue relating to what Toyve Walther told me. Something to prove Eytan Bettelheim was being pressured to donate bone marrow to the Rebbe, as Micah was.'

'I see. And would you mind explaining one more time how exactly this donated bone marrow works?' Bailey asked, with heavy irony.

'I don't know. I'm not a medic, am I? I've read that a transplant can cure certain conditions. And Micah Walther's father told me they were under some pressure to donate it to the Rebbe.'

'What kind of pressure?' Bailey asked.

To that, Rex could only shrug.

'And you know for certain that the Rebbe has actually received this treatment, do you?'

'No, I don't. I asked, but Dordoff wouldn't tell me. I do know that the Rebbe is very sick, though.'

'Well that would suggest he hasn't had a transplant, then, wouldn't it?'

'Or he had it, and it didn't work.'

'In other words, it suggests nothing useful. Nor does the whole scenario you've described. If the Bettelheim boy was needed to donate his bone marrow, then why kill him and his family?' Commander Bailey put his hands together and leant across the table. 'How would that help to make the rabbi better, Rex?'

The gesture towards intimacy and the use of his Christian name were not coincidental, and not unfamiliar to Rex. Psychiatrists talked to you like that, and mental health nurses – anyone, in fact, who suspected you were stark, raving mad. And wanted you to know they suspected it.

'I don't know,' Rex repeated, aware how many times Bailey's questions had forced him to say this. 'Perhaps they knew something about what happened to Micah at the clinic in Antwerp, and they were going to go public with it. Or because they were going to leave the fold, they couldn't be trusted to keep the secret, and Dordoff was frightened…'

Bailey was silent, looking at his notes. 'Sacrifice of the first-born. Is that what you're really getting at, Rex? Like Abraham binding Isaac to the rock? The Old Testament on the streets of Stamford Hill?'

'No, that isn't what I'm getting at,' Rex replied coldly. 'The idea that the Dukovchiner would sacrifice their children for perverted religious reasons hadn't occurred to me, Commander Bailey, because I'm not a medieval anti-Semite. I'm a journalist who has discovered some information – information that ought, under usual circumstances, to be of interest to you.'

'So why not give us that information right away, instead of waiting to be arrested?'

Rex wondered at the man's eyes, with their almost absurdly long lashes. Once upon a time, girls must have fallen in love with Commander Bailey's eyes. And probably fellow coppers in the locker-room had ripped the piss out of them – no doubt adding to the man's general free-floating rage and disappointment.

'D.S. Brenard will confirm that I've consistently passed on information to you. In this case you simply got to me before I got to you. Which I'm guessing wouldn't have happened if I hadn't bumped into Mordecai, and he hadn't done his secret policeman act and followed me.'

Commander Bailey's head moved ever so slightly, as if conceding a point.

'Why are you so desperate to nick me for something when I'm telling you Dordoff lied!' Rex almost shouted. 'I've proved that he lied about going to Antwerp alone.'

'You've told us that a Somali man called Jock at a cab-rank told you a man who may have been Dordoff wasn't alone when he took the cab.' The sarcasm was back on full setting again. 'Not exactly proof. Though perhaps journalists have a different understanding of the word.' Bailey permitted himself a chuckle, before gathering up his papers and clicking his biro off. 'Okay. Thank you,' he said, standing up.

'So I can go?'

Bailey fixed him with a cold gaze. 'You'll remain in custody until we've made some checks, and sorted out the grains of truth from the make-believe and the hallucinations, Mr Tracey. That might take a while. In any case, you broke into a house and took property – we can still have you for that.'

'Then I want my lawyer. I want Bernadette Devlin.'

'I gather she's gone to Guyana for a fortnight, which is why there are several people ahead of you in these very cells, waiting for a locum solicitor. Good luck.'

The door slammed shut.

Chapter Eight

He woke up in the night, sweating and shivering. The slightest movement caused goosebumps to break out and his guts were churning. He was still in the cell. Its walls were throbbing. Had he seen a lawyer? He felt sick. He called for help.

Luckily a doctor was close at hand, patching up the man in the next cell who'd spent the afternoon and evening hurling himself against the walls. It was the same one Rex had seen taking swabs at the park almost a fortnight ago, boy-faced and snub-nosed. His first question was: 'What sort of usage are you on?'

'Usage?' Rex said dimly.

'You're not injecting, and that's good. But you're going through pretty severe withdrawals. You're "rattling",' he added, proud to have thrown some street-argot in.

'I-I'm not a bloody addict. I just take p-painkillers,' Rex shivered. 'For my foot.'

The doctor raised his eyebrows. He gave Rex a tiny diazepam pill and two paracetamol. He said they would help him sleep. They didn't. Rex spent the entire night awake, going through the names in his head and trying to see the connections. *Kovacs. Terry. Toyve Walther. Micah Walther. Eytan Bettelheim. Simmy Dordoff. The Narpal. Smith. Kovacs. Yitzie.*

Somehow it became light, and there were bangings and clatterings in the corridor outside, along with smells of coffee and toast.

He felt the tiny release from boredom a long-haul air traveller experiences at the first intimations of an in-flight meal. D.S. Brenard – an unlikely air hostess – brought in a blue plastic plate with scrambled eggs and toast on it.

'I hear you had a bad night,' the detective said, sitting at the end of the narrow built-in bed. 'You want to sort that pill thing out, mate. It's bad news.'

'I guess I'll be able to get the hard stuff in prison,' Rex said, trying a sip of the coffee. It was surprisingly all right.

D.S. Brenard shook his head. 'Come on. You know we're letting you go. We'd have let you go at 2am, but to be honest you looked so sick at that point, we thought you'd be better off in here.'

'Why 2am?' Rex grimaced as the coffee reacted with his grisly insides.

'Because that's when we charged someone with the murders of George Kovacs and the Bettelheim family. Thank you for the leads.'

Rex sat up, letting the blanket fall. Instantly his skin broke out in sweats and shivers but he didn't care. 'You got Dordoff? Is he talking?'

Brenard shook his head. 'We got Yitzhak Schild. And he is definitely talking. In fact he's coughed to the lot.'

'Yitzie? I don't get it.'

'Simeon Dordoff was cast-iron. The kid he travelled to the airport with was his nephew – his sister's little lad. She'd run off to Israel because the husband was a bit of a bad lot, but she hadn't got the youngest out. Dordoff was spiriting the kid onto a dawn flight to Ben Gurion via Frankfurt before he caught his own plane to Antwerp…'

'So his alibi guy – on the phone – was telling the truth when he told me Dordoff travelled to Antwerp alone.'

'Dordoff was nervous in case there were legal comebacks from him taking the kid without the father's consent, and we let him think there might be for a bit, so he'd give us anything else he'd got.

And he did. He told us he'd been asked to lie about Yitzie Schild's alibi. Turns out Schild wasn't consulting the rabbi on a religious matter on the afternoon Kovacs was stabbed. Dordoff doesn't know where he was.'

'So you went back to Yitzie?'

'He folded right off. We didn't even say anything. It was like he'd been expecting us. Told us he baked a batch of cookies, put cyanide in them and held onto them, biding his time.'

'Didn't you say you'd searched his place for cyanide? Anyway, I heard it wasn't cyanide that poisoned the Bettelheims. '

'He had a bit hidden away. And it was cyanide, the Poisons lab think – just very poor quality. You know, kind of cheapie knock-off, probably from the old Soviet Union or somewhere like that. Fits with the kind of outfits Schild worked in.'

'The Schilds definitely sell biscuits in their shop?'

'Fresh. Every morning. That's what that brown-paper stuff in the kid's case is. They wrap them up in that. What happened, we reckon, is the kid bought some and gave them to his mum, who put them in a Tupperware box for the picnic and shoved the wrapper in the bin. Collection day is Monday round there, which was why we never found it when we searched the house.'

Rex recalled his first visit to the shop. A pyramid of things in brown cones. He should have connected them to the triangles he'd seen at Kovacs' house, with notes scribbled over them. Presumably he'd begrudged spending a few pennies on Post-it notes. Yet – it still didn't make sense.

'But Rescha Schild said they hadn't been in that day.'

'She said that because she hadn't seen them come in the shop that day. There were ten minutes or so at the start where she had to take a call about the mortgage. It all checks out. He saw two of the Bettelheim kids coming in – the older one, the lad, bought a bag of cookies every day, apparently. Schild just decided that was his moment, like, fished his poisoned ones out and sold them to the kid.'

'I thought Dr Kovacs was the first customer every day.'

'On the Monday he wasn't, probably because the last part of St Ann's Road had been closed off due to a burst water main. He'll have had to cut south down to Amhurst Park and go back up the hill again.'

Rex was silent, recalling Dr Kovacs' complaint as they'd sat at the café. *An unexpectedly long walk.* Another event that was out of the ordinary that day – the kid, Eytan, instead of wolfing all his cookies straight away like normal, selflessly contributed them to the family picnic. Probably because he had his sister there spying on him.

'But what about the passport? Eytan Bettelheim had a passport. No one else in his family did.'

'He'd won a scholarship. He was going to spend six months at a yeshiva in Israel. It's like a special religious school, but… a lot broader than the kind of education he was getting here. We think maybe the family were going to join him later. Finally escape the fold.'

Rex asked the final, crucial question. 'But… I don't understand. Why did Yitzie want to poison the Bettelheim kids?'

'Revenge. They were going to leave, and that meant the kid, Eytan, wouldn't help the Rebbe.'

Rex nodded. It made sense. And yet it didn't.

'That wouldn't have helped the Rebbe though, would it?'

'No. But Dordoff confirmed they still need a donor. So Yitzie was sending out a message to everyone. *Don't let us down.* Point is, Rex, he's coughed.'

'So what about Kovacs?'

'Kovacs saw Eytan and Simcha Bettelheim coming out of the shop with the biscuits. Then he saw them all dead at the park, with the remains of the picnic all around them, and he twigged. Instead of calling the police, he rang Schild. Maybe it was the historian in him, wanting to check the facts himself. Or maybe he just got some kind of kick out of knowing something no one else did – the power… I don't know. He wasn't a nice bloke by all accounts, was he? Anyhow, Schild panicked, went round there and did him in.'

'With Terry's knife?'

'Says he found it in the front garden. We haven't tested the knife, but there are soil traces in the handle.'

'What about the garden gate? Remember it's got those massive knife-gouges on the reverse side. How do you explain those?'

'They don't tell us anything, Rex, other than that, like me and probably 99% of the garden gate-owning population, Kovacs needed to give his a new coat of paint.'

'Did Yitzie say anything about the gate?'

'No he didn't, and we haven't asked him. I'm not his defence brief, bach!' Brenard said, slipping into dialect. 'In any case, there isn't a defence, is there, since the man's coughed? End of. You know your problem, Rex? You think too much. That's what made you nuts in the first place!' There was an awkward silence, before Brenard added, 'I didn't mean that. Sorry. Do you want a lift home?'

Rex sighed. 'Can we have the siren on?'

The lift never materialised, because as Rex was being ushered out, Terry was limping into the station foyer in his blue tracksuit bottoms and stonewash jacket. The two men performed a sort of awkward dance, all the more awkward due to the audience of local constabulary, before they finally managed a sheepish embrace.

'It's 8:50,' Rex said, looking at the clock over the duty desk. 'So, Tel, by the time we get down Green Lanes and park, The Salisbury will be doing breakfasts. I reckon we start with two bloody marys and stay in there until closing time.'

Terry looked uncomfortable. 'I don't really want alcohol to be honest.'

In the car, he elaborated in the same low, almost toneless voice. 'I might be in the clear. But this has been the worst thing I've ever gone through, man. There've been times when I've…' He put a hand up to his mouth. 'Well. I reckon you know… And I' – his voice contorted

– 'I HATE those bastards in there for what they fucking did to me. I hate them, man. And I can't just go, you know, howay, bit of a mistake that, let's have a couple and forget about it. I can't. I can't forget it. I'm too fucking angry, Rex. I'm just… full of hate. Sorry.'

'Fair dos.'

'And can you please stop calling me Tel? I've put up with it for years, man, and, actually, it's time to be honest about it, right. I really don't like it.'

'Okay. Sorry.'

They drove back towards Wood Green in silence. Rex had so many things to ponder, but the pain in his foot and the shivering-feverish thing were taking over most of his consciousness. Maybe the pub would have been a bad idea. Especially given the way his putative drinking companion was behaving.

To Rex's surprise Terry parked up outside his own house. 'I'll… see you then,' Rex said, as they stood awkwardly on the pavement. 'Tomorrow?'

Terry sighed. 'I dunno. Susan says I can stay off for a bit. I'm thinking of going to Riga.'

'Riga?'

Terry shrugged. 'I've just really got into this Outrage thing, going through the files and that. I want to carry on with it. I want to know what Kovacs was going to say in his book.'

Without thinking about it, Rex laughed incredulously.

'What's so funny? Oh, thick Tel, is it? Geordie Tel doing something that involves his brain cells? Yeah. Bit of a laugh. Let me tell you something, kidda, there's things you don't know about. Things I'm involved in, that are going to make a difference…'

Rex put his hands up. 'Terry. Terry. Sorry. I'm not… I wasn't laughing at you. It's just a surprise. I mean, you hated Kovacs, and now you're really into his book. It's just…'

Terry tapped his forehead. 'I've beaten this bastard MS before. By being tough inside. Staying focussed. That's what I'm doing now. If you want to take the piss, go ahead, but I'm doing what I have to do.'

An aeroplane roared overhead. 'I'm not taking the piss, and I'm sorry if it sounded like I was,' Rex said. 'I'm glad. What will you do in Riga?' he added, hoping to divert things into calmer waters.

For the first time, Terry smiled. 'When I popped in work on Friday night, Brenda give us this envelope to drop round at yours.'

'So you opened it?'

'It wasn't sealed, man! They dropped it off.'

'Who did?'

'The printers. I just had a look. I was going to tell you! Anyway, it's not like you're interested in any of it, are you?'

'I don't know. Can I see?'

By way of an answer, Terry opened the front door and let him in. Downstairs in the basement, he showed him what had arrived. As the printers had said, there were about a dozen pages of Kovacs' book, mostly from the index, and a small, old leather-bound booklet. Rex walked gingerly across the space, avoiding the evil wall hook, and picked it up. It smelled damp. He flipped through the pages – written in a sloping hand with ink that had turned a rusty colour with age. He couldn't decipher a single word.

'I looked some of the words up on Google and it's Latvian. I thought I'd go over there and see if I could get a bit translated.'

'You know you could just go down Green Lanes to the Baltika Supermarket and the lady in there would tell you what it said.'

Terry just sighed, and held the notebook out to Rex. 'Do you want it?'

'No, I don't. I'm happy for you to have it. I just –'

Terry stood up abruptly. 'Right now, Rex, I don't think we've got anything else to say to each other.'

* * *

Made sure to hang around and give my statement. Copper who took it, big, tree-trunk Irishman, weeping openly about his mate PC Tyler. 'You're a brave maaan,' he says to me. Wanted to be sick on his boots, I did, for the deceit. What a fucking mess. Supposed to be grabbing a bag and getting out of there. Instead they skipped off down the road, letting off shots like it was a fairground game.

The street was like it had woken up from a dream. People poured out from shops and houses, the fog lifted. Everyone in little clutches, trading rumours for facts. 'They've slit the King's throat and now they're going for the Lord Chamberlain,' I heard one wobble-chinned dame saying, with the utmost authority.

Up the street, two big fellows had got inside the barber's and torn down the Yiddish papers. Didn't take long to start. No one was leaving Schnurrman's. All the workers just looked out through the topmost windows, wondering if they'd be safe to go home, even though it was them who'd had their money taken, not the mob of English outside. The chimney stopped belching smoke.

I refused the assistance of a medical gentleman. I reckoned he'd have enough to do, the number of guns I saw coming out of the houses: pistols, rifles, one old goon with a musket from round about Napoleon's time. Some more will fall today, I thought, for sure. Besides, I didn't want anyone patting me down, not with the baby in my coat.

So I left the commotion and got home. Started shoving what I could in my sack. Leah comes down in her nightdress, face like a fruit pudding she'd been weeping that much.

'Where are you going, Mr Smith?'

'I –' I lost my words for a minute. 'I have to go to my family. My wife is gravely sick.'

Then a voice comes from behind the kitchen door. 'Your wife in Goff's Oak is that, *Mr Smith*, or in Russia?'

Parks. Been in there all the time.

'George – sorry. He pushed his way in and he made me –'

I nodded to her to be quiet.

'I saw you, just now, fighting those robbers. Mighty heroic. Not so many people know what I do, Mr Smith. That you've been walking up and down the High Street with that very pair these past six months, in and out of the Yid bookshop and the library. I've seen you. I've been watching. So now you're going to tell me just who you are.'

I looked at him, not sure what to do. My pistol was still outside in the yard, under a water-butt, wrapped in rags. Then there was a noise – noise like a gong, and before my eyes, Parks simply crumpled to the floor like his legs were cut from under him. Behind him stood Leah with the coal shovel.

'Let's get out of here before he comes to!'

I looked down at Cuthbert Parks. 'He won't be coming to or from, Miss. You killed him.'

She started weeping and I shook her.

'Get upstairs, get dressed and put some clothes in a bag. You'll go to your aunt's.'

She hesitated and I roared at her. 'DO IT GIRL!'

While she was banging away up there, making little sobbing noises all the time, I set to, arranging the body where it would need to go, hunting in the cupboards for all the things I needed. Those clowns might have shat all over the robbery. But Grigoriy Kuznetz still knew how to set a good fire, a proper blaze that left no traces of whatever you wanted no traces left of. Not even traces of a Mr Cuthbert Parks.

So I got it going and I hauled the girl into the street. Reckoned we could cut south towards Hackney, avoiding whatever chaos might be underway in Tottenham. Then she drops it on me. Moist-eyed in her cheap little coat with the stuffing come out of one sleeve and a bit of soot on her cheek.

'Take me with you, George,' she said. 'Please.'

* * *

It was almost dark when Rex woke up. He didn't feel hungry but his stomach was rumbling, so he got up, in clothes cold with sweat, and shuffled into the kitchen. He drank orange juice straight from the carton. Once that had cleared the clag in his mouth, he bit into a cold, slightly curling lahmacun from two days before.

As he sat munching the cold, stiff, fatty bread at the table, he remembered how he'd been cowering under it not too long ago. His mind kept going back to Terry. He hoped he'd be okay. He'd never seen him like this before. Maybe he just needed time.

And maybe the same was true for himself, he thought, as he poured himself a shot of raki, watching as the water worked its milky magic inside the tulip glass. In time, perhaps just a few more hours, some similar chemical transformation would take place inside the corridors of his mind, and he'd accept that what was, simply was.

He'd read about a serial killer once – a good-looking young American boy, who in all his interviews and statements had only given one explanation for the trail of deaths he'd left behind him: 'I guess there's just a meanness in this world.' Could Yitzie's actions be explained in the same vague way? He was an odd man, slow and unhealthy, and trapped, Rex was pretty sure, in a loveless, sexless marriage. No doubt he was the object of people's scorn and contempt. Perhaps that had all just built up. Things did build up, and then they came out, in odd ways. And he had suspected Yitzie before. Had thought Rescha had been trying to tell him something about her husband: to warn him, or show him where he might find something that pointed to Yitzie's guilt.

It did seem very strange, though, that Kovacs could have worked out what had happened just from seeing the Bettelheim kid with his biscuits, and then the family dead in the park. The man must have had an inordinately suspicious mind. That, or Yitzie had already said something to him, about seeking revenge, or deserters deserving some punishment.

He tried to imagine Yitzie, in the shop, behind his trays of cassavas and beans, promising death. The man had a quick temper, Rex had certainly seen that. But every time he thought of Yitzie, he saw him at the tish, pulling Toyve Walther out of the room. That was a far more ambiguous scene: he'd seemed to have been acting on Simmy Dordoff's orders, but he'd also seemed concerned for the man he was chucking out. The image kept coming back to Rex, and for reasons he didn't grasp, it bothered him.

He poured himself a second raki and drifted into the sitting room, not sure what to do with himself. He wasn't good at relaxing at the best of times. He didn't fancy Sunday night TV – a mix of rural, retro police dramas and earnest programmes about Islam – but thought there might be something on the news about the arrests, so switched it on.

He couldn't remember when he'd last watched a DVD, but someone, presumably Terry, had hooked the player up to the TV, and when he flicked the switch, the disc that was inside the machine started playing.

He was about to eject it when he saw what was on the screen. Shaky, barely audible footage of some kind of lecture. A fierce, clean-shaven man in sports clothes before a crowd of men kneeling or sitting cross-legged. A talk at a mosque. The talk the boys said they'd been to, before going to Finsbury Park. Recorded on the disc Anwar Hafeez had given him. He'd assumed Vadim had saved the CCTV footage over it, but obviously not.

He turned the volume up. Over the buzz, he could make out what the man was saying. He spoken in an intense voice with faint hints of Dewsbury or Sheffield.

'Terror has nothing to do with the Twin Towers, brothers. Terror has nothing to do with bringing down aeroplanes full of people. Terror is about what you can do with people's minds, and how all those frightened minds add up to a frightened nation.'

The camera, inexpertly operated, swung down to a pair of trainers as another voice raised a question or an objection that was inaudible. It swung back up to the main speaker as he gave his reply.

'I dress like this, brother, because they do. Haven't you understood anything? Go round the place in a beard and bullet-proof jacket, and they'll be on their guard. Do you want to bring terror to them or dress up as a terrorist? Same with your targets. Forget rush-hour tubes and packed-out sports stadiums. It's not an episode of 'Homeland'. People are already on their guard in those places. People already expect something to happen. No. Think normal. Think about the lone wolf. The sole operator. The lone wolf's terror starts on the night bus, at 2am on a Sunday morning, in Enfield Lock. His terror starts in the local baker's or the sweet-shop after school. The places people feel safest – that's where he will strike. Push a Jew under a bus on the High Road. Stab some *kuffar* soldier on the jogging track in the park. Let them know, as individuals, nowhere is safe.'

He remembered what the detective had said about 'some nutter' pushing people into traffic. He also wondered whether Sky News had been so daft when they suggested the Bettelheims' deaths were a terror incident. Wrong, of course, in light of the perfume, and Yitzie's confession. But based on this film, justified. The DVD needed to go the police, he thought, but not before he'd made a copy.

Then, suddenly, he stopped. Stopped listening. Stopped thinking. Just stared. As the speaker carried on, the cameraman had moved to the side of the room, and from his new position one of the attendees stood out in a way that was both recognisable and, to Rex, terrifying.

It was Terry.

He paused, skipped back. It was still Terry. Wearing the same awful, stonewash Eighties jacket he wore just about all the time. He had certainly worn it on the day they went to the park.

He'd even mentioned that he'd been somewhere else in the vicinity earlier on in the day, Rex now remembered. And hadn't answered him when he'd asked where. Now he knew why.

Rex sat back, his heart banging. Then the banging was outside him. He looked around him in alarm. Someone was banging violently at his front door, shaking it in its frame. Trying to smash it down.

He pushed himself back in the sofa, ridiculously, as if that might stop him being seen. The hate sermon still played on the TV screen. Vadim had left the DVD on the coffee table, Rex now remembered. So the only person who could have put it in the machine was Terry. Had he left it there on purpose, for Rex to find? If so, why not mention it?

The hammering on the door got fiercer. It could only be Terry.

Rex jumped up, and crossed into the kitchen, grabbing the largest knife he could find. Sybille had once cut her hand on it, he remembered, preparing soup.

'What do you want, Terry?' he shouted, in a high, nervous voice, from just behind the front door.

The banging stopped. 'Who's Terry?'

He pulled the door open.

It was Rescha Schild, red-eyed and agitated. 'Can I come in?'

'Of course.' She walked into the sitting room and perched primly on the edge of an armchair, clutching her tan handbag close.

'Do you want tea – or… I'm drinking raki. Would you like some?'

She shook her head. He sat down opposite her, feeling his heart rate slowing down. He rode out the silence, as he'd been taught to do, waiting for her to speak.

'I need your help,' she said finally.

He tried not to show any reaction. Since she'd arrived, he'd suspected what was coming. 'You think Yitzie's innocent?' he said.

There was a pause, during which she seemed to process his question. She shook her head violently. 'No! I know he did it. He's a crazy person. I've been frightened to live with him for years. He has these rages and...' She collected herself. 'No. He is not innocent. Do you believe that?'

'I don't know. He's confessed, hasn't he, but... there are some things I don't understand. Anyway... you said you needed my help?'

She looked at him. 'I haven't got anybody to talk to.' A tear formed in one of her eyes. 'I just haven't got anybody. I know you don't really know me and... actually for me to be here, alone with you, is an outrage. It would be an outrage, but I'm already nobody to them all now. And I just... I feel like I can talk to you. I don't know why, but I like you.' She bit her lip.

He didn't know what to say. His heart was still thumping. In the end, he said the most banal thing imaginable. 'I was thinking about getting a takeaway.'

She wiped her eye and smiled. 'Chinese food?'

'You eat Chinese?'

She laughed. 'Of course. There's even a kosher Chinese restaurant.'

'I don't think the Wing Lee Loi is kosher.'

'So I'll have spring rolls, vegetable fried rice and Chinese greens,' she said. 'And nobody's God will be offended.'

He went through the motions of ordering the Chinese and making tea. Rescha didn't leave his side for a moment, and he kept up a nervous, trivial chatter throughout – about his house, the wonky door on the kitchen cupboard, the vintage Paris photos he had put up throughout the house, Paris itself... Daft as it was, he sensed it might be doing her some good. If Yitzie was as crazy as she made out, perhaps his wife never got to have this simple, boring kind of birdsong conversation with another human being.

She didn't eat much, then offered to wash up. She seemed amused that he had a dishwasher. They went into the kitchen to look at it.

'Why would a man on his own need a dishwasher?'

'It was in the house when I bought it. I wasn't planning to use it, really. I just started, and then I found I couldn't stop.'

'Like Yitzie,' she said enigmatically. It was the first time she'd mentioned him since arriving three hours before.

'What couldn't he stop?' Rex asked, shutting the dishwasher door.

She raised a hand. 'Hitting. Afterwards, he'd be horrified. But then he'd do it again.'

'Why did you stay?'

'It's my shop,' she said, simply. 'My house.'

'You could have reported him,' he said, as the water began to surge through the machine. 'If not to the police then to the shomrim or someone like that.'

'We have nothing to do with the shomrim. And Dordoff? As far as he is concerned, Yitzie is a mamzer, and I am a mamzer, so we're already halfway to being savages.'

He recalled that word, from the interrupted phone call with the young academic, Tim. 'What's a mamzer?'

'Bastard,' she said.

He blinked. The word sounded so surprising, coming from her.

'Both kinds of bastard,' she added. 'It can mean, like an insult – you bastard. But it really means something else. If a woman is married, and she has a child by another man, then the child is a mamzer. When the mamzer grows up, they can only marry another mamzer. And the children they have, they will all be mamzers, too. And their children.'

'And that matters?'

'The old rabbis said no, it only affects who you can marry, nothing else. But what's written and what's done in every corner of every community are two different things. If you want to borrow some money, maybe someone on the committee will say, ah, but it's a mamzer. If you want, maybe, to get some important kind of job, like to be the gabbay, or look after the shtib, then, if you're lucky, no one will stand in your way, but if you're unlucky, somebody, maybe more than one person, will say, let's have the other guy, he's not a mamzer. You see?'

'I think so.' It sounded like the Indian lady, Reena, in the jeweller's had been right. There was a caste system, with the Hasidim at the bottom. And the mamzer below even them, like some sort of an Untouchable.

They went back into the living room. The conversation faltered. It was late. They were both very tired. He started to make stretching gestures. She got the point, though not in the way he'd expected.

'I don't want to go back there,' she blurted suddenly. 'I'm afraid. I know there's nothing to be afraid of now, but...'

'You can stay,' Rex said, adding quickly. 'Down here. This turns into a bed. Or... or you could have mine and I'll... No.'

Deep in the night, he heard her cry out. He guessed it was a bad dream. Some time passed, he might even have fallen asleep again, but then he woke up at exactly 4.11 am, to hear her sobbing and repeating, 'No, no, no' in a muted, throaty way that sounded as if she was still asleep. It didn't stop.

He was aware of the great taboo surrounding her. A married Hasidic woman, in bed, in his house. He could almost feel the forbidding electricity as he went down the stairs towards her. His shadow loomed in the orange light that came through the glass in the front door from the lamp-post outside. It made him feel like an attacker.

He looked around for a way to make a noise. Something to wake her out of her dream. He hit the door with the flat of his hand. She became silent.

'Rex?'

He cleared his throat. 'Are you all right?'

There was no reply. She switched the light on and opened the door. She was fully clothed, grey in the face, hair sticking to her forehead.

'Every time I close my eyes I see them. The children. The poor children…' She more or less collapsed into his arms, and he folded them round her. She stayed like that for some time. He started to pat her back, but she winced and pulled away.

'Sorry. I didn't mean to –'

'No… It's just that… *He* hurt me there.' He thought of all the times he'd seen Rescha wincing and standing awkwardly, shuffling her upper garments about as if they hurt her. Now he knew why.

He made tea, and they sat in the living room, she on the folded down bed, he in the armchair. They looked out as the synthetic hues of the London night ebbed away into a grey, still dawn.

'I used to love this time when I was a girl,' she said. 'I could be completely alone. I felt as if the world was mine.'

'I guess you didn't get much time on your own in a Hasidic household.'

'Actually I had a lot. It was just me – and my father and my grandfather. My mother died when I was eight. I had to do all the things that a woman does, without any help. And there was never any money.'

'What were your father and grandfather like?'

'My father was just weak,' she said. 'Just like a little mouse. My grandfather stank. He stank of tobacco and vodka and pickles-vinegar, and he never washed properly. He sat in a chair in the kitchen, with the Hebrew newspaper, swearing at things he read, or laughing when there was an obituary, and it was somebody he knew. And when he'd finished the paper, he got drunk and he swore about the *Kaliker*.'

'The what?'

'The Kaliker. It means, a disabled person. I never knew what he meant. He just used to get drunk and say that the Kaliker had ruined us all, he'd made mamzers of us all. There was a man with a bad leg who lived down the road, a Jew like us, a butcher, and when I was very small I used to think my grandfather meant him. But he didn't. He meant someone a long time ago. I mean – I'm not sure, but I think he did. And that man, the butcher was a nice man. One of the few people who would smile at me.'

'You must have had friends.'

She gave a hollow laugh. 'I see the girls walking past from the Beis Rochel sometimes. Those good little Satmarer girls with their modest uniforms and their quiet voices and all their study-books. You think that's what they're like all the time? You think they don't whisper, before the lesson, about fat little Malkah, and Brachele with the spots and Rescha who smells like an ashtray with the holes in her stockings? No. I didn't have friends. I just had books. Not Jewish books. Jane Austen. Georgette Heyer. The Brontë sisters. There was a lady who ran a kind of junk shop, near to Church Street, and she'd get boxes of books, and if they were falling apart she'd give them to me for nothing. And I'd read them through the night and the pages would come out and I'd hide them in this little... gap in the skirting board. They're still there. In the wall of our bedroom.' She laughed. 'All those heroes and heroines. All that love. In a hole in a wall. Like the prayers people write and put in the Wailing Wall. I never thought about that before. I was praying for a rescue, I guess. It never occurred to me to do what Micah did.'

Rex frowned. 'Micah Walther? What did he do?'

'He ran away. Everybody knows it. Nobody will say it. Every few years, it's what one or two boys do. The parents don't want to face up to it, they would rather say their boys have been stolen from the street. But it's what happens. They run away.'

'Why?'

'Because they look at their big brothers, and their fathers, and they see how their lives are going to go, year after year, without any change or difference. Like being stuck on a bus, going up and down the same street forever. Get up. Morning blessing. Wash hands. Blessing for washing hands. Eat. Blessing for food. Friday – Sabbath. Sunday – back to work. Rosh Hashanah, Yom Kippur,

Sukkot, Simchas Torah, Hanukah… It's a timetable for your whole life, that never stops. Never changes. Then they look, out of the bus windows, at the goyishe boys the same age, all the things they do, all the places they go. Looking into a future that can be anything. How can they not want the same?'

'Where do they go?'

She shrugged. They fell silent. Rex wondered if she was thinking what he was thinking. Of the sadness of it all. The lives she'd described. The grief of the Walther family, still sweetly faithful, tortured by the hope that what they knew, at heart, wasn't true. And her, Rescha, a lonely child, hiding all that longing in a wall, waiting for better times, yet receiving only the next instalment in some endless ancestral curse.

She sipped her tea. 'I don't know anything about you, Mr Tracey… Rex.'

Rex shrugged. 'Not much to tell. My life was a bit like yours maybe. We didn't have much money. It was just me and my mum. She was very religious. Catholic. She was trying to make up for the great sin in her life, which was having me. She wasn't married, you see. She wouldn't tell me who my father was. A bit like your Kaliker, I guess. A mystery man who ruined us.'

'Was it unhappy?'

He thought for a moment. 'Not really. We got on. We were close, in a way. I always felt I was missing something, though. A father, maybe. Or God. When I was young I was always trying to be more religious, joining the catechism class, going on retreats…' He stopped. 'I don't suppose you know what those are, do you?'

'I can guess,' she said. 'Religious things.'

He nodded. 'It didn't make any difference. I always felt like He was there for everyone else, but He'd left us alone.'

'That's what I felt,' she said, quietly. 'But why did you stay alone? Why aren't you married?'

'I am,' he said.

She didn't say anything. The silence between them felt like noise. She seemed to wobble and shimmer in the half-light. He needed more sleep.

So they parted again and he lay upstairs, as the first cars of the day fired up. Distantly, he could hear the lorries beginning to drop off their stock at the big shops on the High Street. Sleep didn't come. He had too many thoughts, about Terry and this sad, gentle, woman downstairs, so exotic she might have been a bird from Java. His foot throbbed, and he thought about being crippled. And cripples in general. The Kaliker in Rescha's grandfather's rants. Vulcan, the lame god, after whom the terrorist seemed to have been codenamed. Then there was Terry, and himself. And Yitzie – certainly crippled in some emotional, psychological sense, if not by his health. Yitzie stayed in his mind as he drifted off to sleep, an image of the big man, his mouth open, grappling with the birthmarked Toyve Walther in the doorway of the old house on Bruce Grove. Why couldn't he get that out of his head?

* * *

Through the strong, hallucinatory sleep that finally took hold of him, he became aware of Rescha talking to someone. A one-sided conversation. She must be on the phone. Did she have her own phone? He forced himself awake and went downstairs, only to find that she'd tidied the bed away, unloaded the dishwasher, opened a window to air the place and left him a note. There was a twenty pence piece on top of the note.

I made a call with your telephone. Here is some money to pay for it. YITZIE was attacked in the prison last night. I am going to see him. Thank you.

He sat at the table in his T-shirt and boxer shorts, and thought about the note. She must have called the prison. Now she was going to visit him. It seemed a strange thing to do, for a woman who'd expressed relief that her husband was gone, a woman who'd spent years in fear of the man's rages and his fists. But feelings were complicated. Maybe there was some loyalty still there. Maybe that was why she'd written his name in capitals.

He rang Susan. In the old days Monday conferences had always been at 9.30 am sharp. Now, they were a bit of a movable feast. She took a long time to answer, and when she did, her voice sounded as if she was dragging every last syllable out with pliers.

'I can't really see the point in having one this morning,' she said. 'Maybe things will be a bit clearer by this afternoon.'

'What things?'

'You might look into this freak going round pushing women into the road,' she said, ignoring his question. 'See if there's anything worth putting on the site.' She hung up.

As he stood in the shower, he felt Rescha's presence. Perhaps it was just because the toilet seat was down. It hadn't been down for a long time. He remembered her talking about the butcher who smiled at her. *A Jew like us.* Somehow it seemed rude to use that word. Jewish was okay. But Jew? Who else had he heard recently, using that word?

The sermon… He rushed downstairs, naked and still half-covered in soap. With trembling hands, he pressed play, then rewind. In his haste he missed the right bit, and had to scan forward again. Then it came. *Push a Jew under a bus… Stab one kuffar…*

He knelt in front of the screen, the soap drying on his body. Someone was pushing people into the traffic. D.S. Brenard had mentioned it. Now Susan. People had listened to that sermon, and were following its loathsome recommendations.

What the hell had Terry been doing there?

He dressed in a hurry and almost ran through the tiny alleyway that connected his road to the main streets leading south from the station. People – sober commuter types who had little to do with the wild, unmoneyed Haringey of the daytime – glanced nervously at the agitated, unshaven man limping swiftly down the road.

He reached Terry's door and pressed on the bell. No one came. He tried again. Then he lifted the letterbox flap and called through. He reached in his pocket for his phone, but he'd left it in his house. He pressed the bell again.

'He left in a cab,' said a voice behind him. He turned. It was Miss Martell, the red-headed Kiwi next door. Flushed and track-suit-clad, she was carrying milk and newspapers. Her pleasant face hardened when she recognised him..

'Gone to Riga has he?' Rex asked.

'He said Gateshead…' She took her keys out and opened her own front door. 'By the way – there's no point ringing the bell. I was mates with the girls who lived there before. It's never worked.'

She slammed the door shut. Rex stayed where he was. Had Terry lied? Changed his mind? Or had Rex, or the neighbour, got the wrong end of the stick?

He pressed the doorbell button again. Sometimes, in London, you didn't hear the doorbell go if you were outside, because of the racket. But it was quiet on Langerhans Road at this hour. Miss Martell was right. The doorbell didn't work. It had never worked.

In which case, Rex suddenly realised, Sam Greenhill couldn't have rung Terry's bell by mistake, as he'd told Brenard. Dr Kovacs' son had known what Terry looked like, but he'd lied to the police about how he'd found out. Why would he do that, unless he had something to hide?

Chapter Nine

As a student, Rex had shared a small terraced house in Manchester with three other young men. They'd all been studying anthropology, which was somehow fitting, given that, on the domestic front, they had more or less competed with one another in savagery. All were from respectable backgrounds; it was as if Rex and his co-tenants were engaged in a collective attempt to strip away the last traces of decency and reinvent themselves as abominations. During one party, someone had drained the toilet and put plants stolen from the nearby town hall gardens inside it. They'd kept it that way until the end of the year, pissing in the bath, and shitting at the pub. No girls ever stayed the night, unless they were unconscious. He had known Sybille back then. Loved her and pretended unconvincingly not to. She had never gone near the place.

He'd imagined art students at the rented end of Palmer's Green would be living a similarly dehumanised home life, possibly even wilder, turbocharged by those new, synthetic drugs that were apparently so easy to purchase on the internet. But Sam Greenhill's residence was bright and neat. As the young man showed Rex in, he noted the obligatory Nepalese and Peruvian textiles, a Bob Marley poster, and what looked like the top of a shisha pipe poking out from behind the sofa. But the place was orderly and clean. In the kitchen, two ponytailed girls were making cupcakes with the aid of a cookbook. Sam himself, facial adornments trimmed down to a modest goatee, appeared to have been studying hefty textbooks at a table.

'Glanville Williams?' Rex queried, lifting up the nearest book. 'I didn't know he'd written much about art.'

'How do you know him?'

'I did a year of law,' Rex lied, putting the famous handbook back on the table. Sybille had been a lawyer.

Sam Greenhill nodded glumly. 'Well, I did a year of art. I'm switching to law next year.'

'Why the switch?'

'Because if I carry on pissing about pretending to be an artist, then I'm going to carry on being dependent on my Mum. And I want to pay her back. I know she's selling her business but that won't leave her with much when she's paid everyone off. She deserves a better life.'

Sam seemed to mean it. There was only one problem. 'A murder conviction isn't going to help your career at the bar, Sam.'

Sam's eyes widened. He scurried across the room and shut the kitchen door. 'I never murdered anyone! What are you on about?'

'Terry Younger's bell doesn't work. It never has. So when you said you'd gone round, a few months before your father's death, and rung the wrong doorbell, you were lying. I'm guessing, however, that you did go there, and you rang your father's doorbell – the one you'd intended to ring. Am I right?'

The boy paled, and nodded. 'I'd plucked up my courage to go and see him. Well, it was Lou,' he added, gesturing vaguely towards the kitchen. 'My girlfriend. She encouraged me. So I went, and rang his bell, and he wasn't there.'

'But you saw Terry?'

He made a face. 'Well, that would have been a better explanation than the one I came up with. But still not true. I went back another time. On the day he... The day my father was murdered. Very shortly before, from what I can gather. It was just a coincidence. I needed some lino blocks, like desperately, for this assignment, which I'd left and left because I'm… basically, I'm better off doing Law because I'm shit at art anyway. So I rang round everywhere, and the only place that had them was this art shop in Muswell Hill. So I went. Louise lent me her Oystercard because I was broke.'

'Which was why the police found your first visit in October on your Oystercard history, but nothing to say you'd gone back a second time.'

Sam nodded. 'So I was up on the hill, and it's nowhere near a tube, and I got on a bus down toward Turnpike Lane, and I realised I was back near where my dad lived. So I got off at the bus station, and I had another go.'

'And he was in this time?'

Sam's face flushed. 'It was about eleven. He was in. And…'

In the pained silence that followed, Rex supplied the words. 'He slammed the door on you?'

Sam Greenhill shook his head. 'No. He invited me in. Offered me a cup of tea. It was like… Like the way I'd sort of fantasised it might be. For years, I'd imagined my mum might be wrong and maybe he might have changed and he'd be an all right bloke and… Whenever I was angry at her, I'd pretend, like, there was this cool dad out there and he'd understand and…'

'I did that, too.'

'Thing was – when I met him, he seemed like he was for a bit. Okay, I mean. He wasn't warm or emotional or anything like that – basically, he just seemed really nervous. Really on edge. But so was I.'

Not nervous because he was meeting his son, though. Kovacs would have just seen the Bettelheims dead in the park. Had he called Yitzie by that stage?

'So we talked a bit. He said one thing that was weird. I was already thinking about swapping to Law so I told him and he laughed and said, "I don't think they'd let you in with your ancestry."'

'What did that mean?'

'I don't know. I asked him what he meant, but he didn't say. He just looked at his watch and he said, "Well you've seen me and I've seen you so, let's leave it there. And don't come round again. It's not safe." And that was it. Bastard.' Sam's voice wobbled.

'That's what he said – it's not safe?'

'I guessed he just meant – well, Tottenham can be a bit dodgy, can't it?'

Rex said nothing. Perhaps Kovacs had been trying to protect him. He'd seen the Bettelheims dead in the park. Had he already made his call to Yitzie? Had he been expecting Yitzie at the door, found Sam and invited him in? That seemed unlikely. It was more probable that he'd come home, and had been pondering what to do, when his long-lost son suddenly appeared at the door. What had he meant about Sam's ancestry, though? Presumably it was Kovacs' ancestry as well.

'Did you see him make or receive any calls while you were there?'

Sam thought, and shook his head. 'I just left. I was so angry at him. I went round the back. I saw the gate was open, and I had this stupid idea of getting a brick or something and chucking it through his window. I saw some breezeblocks, but I wasn't sure I could chuck anything that big. And then I saw a window was open. It was this guy's kitchen. So… I don't know why I did it, I just stuck my head in, to see if there was something there I could grab, and I saw this… there was like this big ugly wooden knife, that had got down between the back of a kind of tea-trolley and the wall and I just grabbed it. I was just doing that when the bloke came through. He was stark bollock naked, and he was talking to himself kind of grumbling, and wiping his eyes with a towel. I just legged it. I heard him shutting the window so I guessed he hadn't seen me.'

'But you'd seen him. And heard his Geordie accent.'

Sam nodded. 'So now I had this knife. But… by then I'd kind of calmed down a bit. I had a go at the garden gate with it a few times. You know – just stabbed it up a bit.' He made a sheepish face. 'Then I ditched it. Chucked it in the bush in the front.'

'And you didn't see or hear anything else before you left?'

Sam thought. 'Only your mate praying.'

'My mate what?'

'Well, not him. He had one of those call to prayer things on his phone. Muslim thing. I heard it go off just as he shut the window.'

Ten minutes later, Rex was sitting on the narrow red seat of a southbound bus stop, within sniffing distance of the parsley and the tomatoes on the trestles of an adjacent shop called Super-Turk. Bursts of hot sun gave way to dark cloud, and the weather echoed his confusion. He thought he should ring Terry. He had his phone in his hand, working out what to say, when it rang. He didn't recognise the number.

'Rex.'

He sighed. 'What do you want, Ellie?'

She was on a busy road somewhere. 'Don't hang up. I know I owe you big time. And I've got something for you. Friendly prison admin lady I know told me Yitzhak Schild was beaten up in Pentonville this morning.'

'I knew that already.'

'Yeah, well what you definitely don't know is the experience seems to have brought about a change of heart in Yitzhak. He's retracted his confession. Says he didn't do it.'

Rex took this in.

'You still there? Does it even the score, Rex? Are we okay?'

He hung up.

He got on a bus. It was rammed with tiny Greek-Cypriot widows and their shopping trollies. He had to stand, leaning his forehead against the filigreed metal of the rail, hoping it might cool and calm his mind.

Sam Greenhill didn't do it. Yitzie Schild was now saying he didn't. That didn't mean he wasn't guilty, of course, but the change of heart meant something. He realised he'd never been quite sure of Yitzie's guilt in the first place, or at least, not understood his apparent motives. And the less plausible they seemed, the more his suspicions seemed to rush elsewhere, like blood going into a numb limb.

From the outset he'd assumed Terry's innocence. He'd accepted it in the way he accepted that his foot would hurt every time he put it on the pavement, or that someone would always be digging a hole on Green Lanes.

Once he'd let in the dreadful, heretical thought that Terry was hiding something, others flocked to the cause. Memories he'd ignored, episodes he'd struggled to see in a harmless light. The violent rages and the mood swings. The entirely different Terry who'd been much in evidence of late.

Rex thought back to the 'How to spot a terrorist' leaflet they'd all laughed at in the office. It didn't seem quite so funny now, given that one of their own colleagues had attended a sermon from a notorious hate-preacher. He'd also kept a copy of the Koran at his bedside, given up alcohol, responded to a muezzin's call and all in all seemed to have a whole alternative existence going on.

There's things you don't know about. Things that I'm involved in, that are going to make a difference…

What the hell had he meant by that? And why had he claimed he was going to Riga and then headed to Gateshead?

Them freaky ones up in Gateshead.

Rex remembered Terry had said that at the park. And Dordoff and his relation on the end of the phone had studied there. Of course. There was a large Jewish community up in Gateshead. A big yeshiva.

Some of those who'd attended that sermon were carrying out its instructions on the streets of Haringey. Was it possible that Terry was on the brink of doing the same, up north?

He remembered more of the puzzling encounters he'd had with his friend over the past weeks.

They don't listen do they? Dressing up like that.

Terry had said that in the park, watching the Muslim boys in their camouflage and Eastern-looking trousers as they parroted the preacher they'd all just heard – Terry along with them. It wasn't that Terry had a problem with their beliefs, only the fact that they were drawing attention to themselves. Whereas he wasn't. He was, to all but those who'd known him especially well, the same old Terry.

What if the link between the deaths of the Bettelheims and Dr Kovacs wasn't Yitzhak Schild? What if it was Terry? Was it possible?

He rang Terry's number. It went straight to voicemail. The Cypriot Grannies got off, as one, at Shopping City and he found a seat. He managed to search for Gateshead and Jewish on the tiny screen of his telephone, and found the number of the yeshiva.

That was useless, though. What could he tell them? There was only one person he could call. He wasn't sure he would listen, though. He wasn't sure he'd blame him either.

'Where are you?' asked D.S. Brenard urgently, after Rex had explained why he was calling. To his surprise, the policeman seemed to be taking him very seriously indeed.

'On a bus, crawling past W.H. Smith's.'

'I'll be at your house in ten minutes,' was all Brenard said before hanging up.

He was true to his word, and as Rex finally turned onto the little lane that led to his house, no less than two cars were pulling up outside it. One contained Brenard. From the other stepped three burly, crew-cut, unsmiling types, who looked like rugby-players in borrowed suits.

'Who are your friends?'

'ATU,' Brenard said sullenly. 'Anti-Terror Unit. We have to call them in if there's anything terror-related.'

'You'd better come inside,' Rex said. He surveyed the flat-nosed bruisers bulging in their suits. 'Earl Grey or Darjeeling, gents?'

He didn't make any tea, of course, just dumped his orange carrier bag in the hall and switched the DVD player on.

'I thought this might explain the person pushing women into the traffic, and I was going to look into that. Then I heard Terry had gone to Gateshead – there's a large Jewish community there – and, well, he's been very odd lately.'

The terror-goons didn't speak, just played and replayed bits of the DVD. One of them was wearing very strong aftershave.

'Odd in what way?' Brenard asked.

'Very aggressive. Very secretive.' Rex listed everything he could think of, before faltering at the final detail. 'He's...' As he was about to say it, he realised how bizarre it seemed, and how little it fitted with the theory of Terry-as-terrorist. 'Right. He's become obsessed with the book Dr Kovacs was writing. Trying to piece it together from his notes. It's more or less all he talks about. That's why he was going to Riga.'

'Why he *said* he was going to Riga,' one of the ATU men pointed out. 'Not a bad cover. His friends think he's obsessed with one thing. Really he's obsessed with something else. They often have a cover – a fake girlfriend, a new businesses – something that explains why they're not around.'

Rex was silent. It was a convincing theory. After all, he'd never actually seen Terry doing any research. And when he'd been looking over the files with Lawrence, he'd had a fit and smashed a chair. It had just never seemed... *right*.

He and Brenard looked at the TV screen, where the wobbly footage of the sermon was just beginning.

'Thing is,' Brenard mused, 'apart from being a moody sod and being at that... talk or whatever it is, he hasn't done anything, has he? Unlike the bloke who's been shoving women into the road.'

'Is he on there, too?' Rex asked, pointing at the TV.

'That's one of things we're looking for, isn't it?' said another of the ATU men tersely.

'Problem is,' Brenard added, 'we've got no useful images or descriptions. We know he has a big beard, which covers just about every trendy Media Studies student in Haringey these days. Also, there's no definite indication that he's doing what he's doing in the name of Muhammad or what-have-you.'

'Is there any pattern in the victims?'

'Not clear. He's done it three times so far. One African lady, one Greek, one…' Brenard winced. '…Welsh. My wife, in fact.'

'Jesus. Is she okay?'

'She is. She does think he shouted something like *Allahu akbar* as he shoved her in front of the number 55 to Baker's Arms. But her mother, who was with her, thinks he shouted 'Get back!', which is making for an interesting atmosphere in my house right now. So then we looked back at the other two. The African lady was wearing a large cross as she went down Philip Lane. The Greek lady was standing at the corner of Amhurst Park and Stamford Hill and…'

'Might possibly have been mistaken for Jewish?'

'It's a theory. Or enough of one for Commander Bailey to call in our colleagues and… Ah.'

The goons had stood up and appeared to be ready to go. The largest one had a red face and a bullet-shaped head. With the DVD in his hand, he advanced on Rex as if he was about to rugby-tackle him.

'Do you want a receipt?' he asked, in a surprisingly posh voice.

'Keep it,' Rex said.

The goons trooped out. D.S. Brenard looked at him.

'We'll have to put a search out for Terry. And do me a favour, Rex. Don't contact him. If you hear from him, or you find anything else, call me. You understand?'

'I understand.'

'Good. By the way. We got the results on the blood patch. No matches. But I'm instructed to thank you for the –'

Brenard stopped speaking because someone else had just walked through the door.

'Rex, who were those–'

It was Rescha Schild, laden with carrier bags and boxes from the shops on Wood Green High Street.

She fell silent when she saw Brenard. Rex observed the policeman's eyes narrowing, pondering, hunting for the angle and the possible wrong-doing. When nothing came to mind, he gave a curt nod and stalked out.

'Why was he here?' Rescha asked anxiously, as she put the bags down.

'It's about Terry.'

'Your friend?'

He felt a prick of sadness as she said that. Was Terry his friend? He looked at all her shopping.

'Did you win on the scratchcards?'

She looked puzzled and he realised his last sentence had meant nothing to her. 'I mean – what's with all the shopping?'

She sat on a chair and pulled a brand-new handbag out of one of the carriers. It was bright green. It matched the scarf she'd put on round her neck, he realised.

'I'm leaving,' she said excitedly. 'I've got a cousin… well, maybe not a cousin, but she's some kind of relative. She left. Went to live with a goy. Years ago. She lives near Paris. I can stay with her for a while, she says. So!' She patted the bag happily. 'That's what I'm going to do. A new start. New everything. Do you like this bag?'

'It's… it's very unlike your other one,' was the best Rex could manage, as Rescha began to empty stuff out of the old shabby tan bag onto his table. 'Rescha – are you sure you should do this so suddenly?'

She looked at him. 'What's sudden? I dreamt about leaving since I was eight years old.' She busied herself with the handbag for a moment, fussing with the zip. Still looking down, she said, 'Actually I was wondering… could you help me?'

'How?'

She looked up. 'I have a passport – because we were all planning to go to Dukovce about eight years ago. It didn't happen. Anyway,

I don't… I've never been out of this part of London. I'm serious. I know there's a train, now, to Paris, but I don't know how to get on it, or buy a ticket. Could you help me?'

'So you're leaving Yitzie.'

Her eyes flashed. 'He did those… terrible things. Why do I need to stay?'

'But he's pleading not guilty.'

She didn't look surprised that Rex knew. 'He got beaten in there. He's realised what prison is going to be like for an old man who's been able to bully people all his life. So now he's changed his story. You want me to tell you all the things that man did to me? You want to know what he was really like?'

She had become agitated. Rex held up a hand in surrender.

'It's easy to get a ticket. I'll show you.' He went over to the little desk in the corner of his living room and switched on his laptop. 'You can have this, if you like.' He took a slim, red, plastic-backed book from the shelf above the desk. 'It's got all the maps of Paris in there.'

She stowed the A-Z in her new bag, nodding thanks.

'What exactly happened to him in there?' Rex asked, as they waited for his seriously outmoded machine to be ready.

Rescha made a sort of facial shrug. 'He shouted at some boy in the canteen. Because of his allergies, you know, there's a lot of things he can't eat. Eggs, milk, wheat – he can't go near them… The boy didn't like the way Yitzie spoke to him.'

Rex showed her the booking page on the Eurostar website and asked her where she'd like to sit. She stared from him to the carriage layout map, with something like panic in her eyes, until he chose a seat for her. He booked a ticket for the following morning, and printed up the slip she'd need to take with her.

'Where are you going after Gare du Nord?' he asked.

'I'm going to Paris,' she said, frowning.

As he walked to the office, twenty minutes later, he felt uneasy. Rescha Schild wasn't his responsibility. But all the same, he wondered how she'd cope on her journey. Did she even know how to get to St Pancras? He'd told her, of course, and she'd nodded, but all the while looked like a frightened child trying to seem otherwise, something almost pleading in her eyes. She ran a business, he reminded himself. But it was a business in the fenced-off 19th century village of Stamford Hill. She'd made it to Pentonville to visit Yitzie, as well, but prisons made things easy for outsiders. Every step of the way there was someone barking orders at you. He'd given her his phone number. Told her she could call him. But would she know how to?

The office was locked. Even the lights in the foyer were off. Some sort of call centre had recently moved in next door, and two young men who worked there, dressed in cheap suits and short woollen coats, were having a smoke outside. They were often there, and Rex always thought they looked like old pictures of recruits from the trenches, with their sallow skin and their underfed faces. He made an enquiring face.

'They all left about an hour ago,' said one young man helpfully.

'Anyone say anything?' Rex asked.

The young man ground his fag out with a pointy, buckled shoe. 'Fat cow had a right gob on her.'

'My wife, you mean? Yes, she's having a hard time coping with the diagnosis.'

When the boys had scuttled, red-faced, back inside, Rex rang Susan. 'What's going on?'

She sighed. 'I've decided, in light of the uncertainty, not to bring out a paper or update the site for the moment.'

'What uncertainty, Susan?'

'I've been hoping for a rescue plan. That now looks unlikely. I can't really say any more. Have a few days off, Rex.'

'They aren't going to be days off exactly, if I haven't got a job to come back to, are they?'

'No.'

'Have I got a job to come back to?'

'I don't know. Look, Rex, I really can't say anything else right now.'

'What do you mean, you can't *right now?*'

'I can't right now,' she repeated. 'I'll be in touch soon.' She hung up.

He drifted towards Shopping City, although there was nothing he wanted in there, and never was. He felt dazed, stunned, and for once, he knew it was nothing to do with the pills. There seemed to be nothing, no single person nor institution nor corner of his existence upon which he could still depend. If Shopping City had magically transformed from a gaudy brand-name behemoth into a replica of the Istanbul Spice Market, he wouldn't have been that surprised.

It had not, of course. The old Turks were still frowning on their benches in the main hall, with a bewildered air, as if the place had somehow sprung up around them. Upstairs, the young mums were still cursing at their kids in the buggies, and their other kids out of the buggies. The plastic gangbangers – in reality mostly students at the old tech college – were still showing off their exaggerated walks and their elaborately shaven hairdos outside the sports shop. Wood Green was carrying on as per, completely indifferent to the existence or otherwise of Rex, and News North London.

Suddenly he had an idea. He went into the Primark and bought himself a cheap, folding cagoule. It wasn't his sort of thing, but Rex had spent many a spring in Paris, and he knew it was always raining.

In the atrium a small crowd was gathered in front of the big Sky News screens. As he descended on the escalators, Rex's heart flipped. He could see the emergency vehicles on the screen, the yellow incident tape. He'd already pictured the ticker-tape legend: Gateshead Siege.

But it was only the Junior Minister. The one who'd worn the SS outfit to the Constituency Fancy Dress do. This time he'd crashed his car into a tree. Wasn't expected to survive. It didn't seem right to chuckle, but Rex nearly did, his relief was so great.

He felt an urgent need for sugar, so he went into Istanbul Dondurma. It was a lavish, tinted-glass anomaly of a place, stuck between a famously rude, malodorous newsagents and a Pound Shop, with welcomingly soft banquettes and vintage Turkish pop playing quietly in the background. Over rocket-fuel coffee and a chewily fragrant bowl of orchid ice-cream, Rex took out his phone. He considered defying Brenard and ringing Terry again. But he didn't know what he would say.

He'd become more adept at using his phone, and he used it now to book himself a seat on the same train as Rescha. If he didn't have a job, he'd need to start selling pieces freelance. Ellie had said she owed him. She could put in a word, he was sure, and for starters he could offer her boss a nice big feature on the Hasidic housewife beginning a new life for herself. It wasn't exactly mercenary, he told himself, because Rescha plainly wasn't able to get to Paris without him. He would help her, she would help him.

He left a message for his sister-in-law to tell her about his trip, then, as the ice-cream parlour filled with an excitable crowd of headscarved student girls in search of a post-lecture sugar rush, headed home.

* * *

Passing Get-It-In, he fought and vanquished the urge to buy beers. The truth was, he felt lost and alone without a job to do. He wondered whether that might be true of all the other lost souls of the area, like Bird Curton, all the ranters and twitchers and Special Brew prophets. Maybe they'd all be fine if they just had something to do. And maybe he'd be joining them, if he didn't.

Back at home, he tried to ring Rescha. He didn't have a number, though, and Vegetables was, unsurprisingly, not listed. He came up with a cunning plan to look at the shop on Google Streetview. The number, or at least *a* number was on the sign, he remembered.

But on the image that appeared on his laptop screen, three tall men sporting round, high fur hats obscured the number on the shop sign. He was thinking about heading over to Stamford Hill to find her when he noticed the wad of receipts and bits of paper she'd taken out of her old bag. He sifted through them idly and saw one with an address on Stamford Hill. It was clearly a shop receipt of some kind, and its name was written in Hebrew letters. Two sets of three. Were they the same letters as on the sign at 'Vegetables'? He went back to the computer image. Same deal: the three amigos in their huge, beaver-fur *shtreimels* made it impossible to tell. He rang the number anyway. No one answered.

He went to the cupboard under the stairs where he thought there might be an old canvas holdall. He was just hauling it out when he heard his landline ringing.

It was Rescha.

'Sorry,' he said. 'I'd have left a message but you haven't got an answer-phone.'

'Yes we have,' she said. 'Anyway, you haven't rung me.'

'Oh, I thought…' He trailed off into silence.

'Are you still there?' she asked.

'Yes, yes, I am. Actually, I've been trying to ring you. I'm going to come to Paris. Tomorrow. So – I might as well help you find your way around.'

There was a pause before she said, 'Yitzie is dead.'

He scrabbled for some words to say. All he could find was: 'I'm sorry. What happened?'

'His heart was bad – you knew that. He had a massive heart attack in the prison.'

'So… you'll want to stay and make arrangements, I guess.'

'I want to go. Yitzie wasn't stupid. He knew he was sick, and he knew we didn't have much money. Even after everyone else stopped, he carried on paying into the *Chevra Kadisha*. It's like a funeral… association. They'll bury him. They don't need me there. I don't want to be there.'

'Oh. Okay. So… I can meet you at the station, if you like, or…'

'I really don't need you to come,' she said, tersely. 'I know how to get on a train.'

'I never said you didn't,' he replied, puzzled by her reaction. 'But you seemed pretty helpless when you were sitting here in my living room an hour ago. And I've booked a ticket. You can ignore me if you prefer but it might be a bit awkward because I got the last seat left and it's right opposite you.'

There was silence. 'I don't want you to.' After another pause, she snorted. It sounded like a laugh. 'I can't stop you, though, can I?' Her tone had softened, he thought. 'I'll see you at Waterloo.'

'Rescha, didn't you listen to anything I told you? It doesn't go from Waterloo anymore. It's St Pancras. Look – make your way to Turnpike Lane tube tomorrow morning. You know where that is – you just catch the 55 bus opposite your shop. Eight o'clock should do it.'

She agreed and hung up. As he sponged the mould off his hold-all, he found himself cringing. He'd played that badly. She might well, in some sense, have wanted his help, but a recently widowed Hasidic woman was hardly going to leap at the offer of going to Paris with a strange man. Her reaction hadn't been strange. It was entirely reasonable.

Hours later, though, soaking in his favourite seat at the back of The Salisbury, he found the episode still troubled him.

* * *

The next morning, while packing his bag, Rex tried to work out whether the feeling in his stomach was related to the beer and raki of the night before, the pine disinfectant with which he'd scoured his holdall, or pure excitement. He was going on a trip – something he hadn't done since Cambodia.

He felt oddly optimistic, as if this short journey would mark a break, a break with whatever he wanted to put behind him. He'd fallen into a routine of loading up his pocket with whole strips of pills every morning before he went out. Today he broke off only four pills and put the rest in the kitchen cupboard. It was a start. He had to start somewhere.

The radio was on, and he stopped to listen to the half-hourly news round-up. There were still some things he was not ready to put behind him. He'd done the same half an hour before, and half an hour before that, as well. But there was nothing. Something about Calais. Something about the Junior Minister, now dead. But no terror in Gateshead. No arrests. No sieges. He wasn't sure what else he could do, except wait. And hope.

He was almost out of the door when his phone rang. It was Aurelie returning his call.

'Have you booked somewhere to stay?'

He realised he hadn't.

'You are very welcome to stay with Eric and myself,' she said, in her musical, yet precise English. 'I will email to you a map where we are.'

Rex still hadn't worked out how to open attachments on his telephone. He put down his bags and returned to the ancient laptop in the corner as he spoke to Aurelie.

'I do have to tell you, though, Rex, I am now even more decided than I was before about what to do with Sybille.'

'How come? I mean, has something changed?' he asked, as he watched the screen change colour.

'Sometimes, I think we underestimate her. I mean, the things she says – we think they mean nothing, but she is really trying to say something to us.'

Rex didn't answer. He'd spent years thinking that. Thinking that, because he'd hoped it, longed for it to be true that his wife was still his wife, communicating with him. He'd stopped, because he'd had to.

When he didn't answer, his sister-in-law went on. 'When she said about understanding the beginnings. I think she meant that for me. She meant for me to understand that we must go back to the beginning of our relationship as sisters and to start again. Sybille wants to come to France to be with me.'

He was familiar with the mental contortions, the wild leaps one had to make to believe that Sybille was speaking sense, that she cared. He was familiar with the let-down, too, the disappointment when the truth dawned. He didn't want to shatter Aurelie's fragile self-confidence, so he simply said that they could talk when he got there.

The email had come through and as he waited for the machine to open the map, he wondered how he'd really feel, being in Paris. He hadn't been since the accident. It hadn't happened there, of course, but the city was so bound up with his old life, his time with the Sybille who'd lived, rather than the Sybille who simply existed. He felt uneasy about going there with Rescha. But why? It wasn't as if he had feelings for her.

A strange noise shocked him out of his thoughts. A ring-tone he'd never heard before. He scanned the room, wondering if a visitor had accidentally left some device. Then he saw an icon on his laptop screen. TELBOY69 was Skyping him. Should he answer?

Gingerly, he clicked on the green telephone icon. He'd never used it, although he remembered installing the software, at the behest of his workmates, before he'd departed for Cambodia.

A blurry image came through. It was Terry, viewed as if through a cheese-grater.

'Rexington!'

Rex felt a flood of relief, quickly morphing into anxiety. 'Terry. Where the fuck are you?'

'Riga. I told you. Look –'

Terry rotated the laptop and pointed it out of his window. Rex caught a glimpse of bell-towers and pinky-red roofs.

'Your neighbour said Gateshead.'

'I stayed the night at me mam's and caught a flight from New-castle the next day.'

'Jesus.' Rex let out a long sigh.

'What?'

Where would he start? 'Nothing. What's going on over there?'

'This Professor at the university is helping me translate the diary. It's his all right.'

'Whose?'

'Grigoriy Semyonovitch Kuznets,' Terry said, sitting back, proudly. 'Otherwise known as George Smith. Later known as Janos Kovacs.'

'Eh?'

'They're all the same person, man. Kuznets the terrorist became George Smith the hero, and then Janos Kovacs.'

'Kovacs?'

'Yep. Our Kovacs – *Dr* Kovacs – discovered he was descended from Janos Kovacs, who was really Kuznets – the missing third man of the terrorist group.'

The former George Kovacs. That's what Kovacs had said to his ex-wife. Not because he'd become ill. But because he knew he wasn't really a Kovacs. And she'd mentioned a family mystery, hadn't she, about a diary? He just hadn't made the connection.

He tuned back in to Terry, who was still excitedly talking.

'Anyway, look, I want you to know. I've packed all that crap in.'

'What crap?'

'The skunk. I thought it was helping with me MS, and it was, for a bit, like, but it was messing with me head. I just got so obsessed with… I had this idea, that if I could spend every minute stoned, and going through all Kovacs' stuff, I wouldn't get…' He took a deep breath. 'I tried to kill myself. I think you know that, don't you?'

'Yes.'

'I was just so scared of going back to that, like, state of mind… Anyhow, I didn't dare take any weed on the plane and after a couple of nights on the beers, I just feel… I feel like I was in a nightmare, but I've woken up. Sorry.'

'You don't have anything to be sorry for,' Rex said, thinking that he was the one who ought to be apologising. He cringed at the thought of the goons he'd called to his house the previous day. 'But – you're still carrying on with the research. I mean, you haven't given that up?'

Terry gave a pixelated wink. 'Well, you wanna see Professor Eglitis, man.' He mimed something. A pair of coconuts? No, it was obvious what Terry was on about, and what gender Professor Eglitis was. Rex listened to him enthusing about her extraordinary properties, and those of Latvian women in general, and the exceptional quality of Piebalga beer, without really listening. He was just delighted to have woken from his own nightmare.

He realised he should ring Brenard and tell him Terry had been in touch. He didn't want the Latvian version of the goon squad kicking Terry's hotel door down. But then he remembered why this whole thing had started. The DVD, showing Terry at the hate-sermon. There were things that still didn't make sense.

'Terry –'

The image of Terry had turned to smudges, the audio to something reminiscent of whale-song. Then Terry returned, mid-sentence.

'It's funny, man. Even though I couldn't stand the bloke. I've had this funny feeling he's been behind me, all along, telling where to look…'

The sound went, the pixels turned to large block of colour and then the screen went dead.

Rex sat back in his chair, thinking over the conversation that had just taken place, searching through the shock for his own feelings.

He ought to have felt relieved. He did feel relieved. But he wasn't happy. Why wasn't he happy?

He got up suddenly, went to the bin and pulled out the sheaf of receipts and mint wrappers that Rescha had taken from her hand-bag. He found the receipt with the Hebrew on it, and rang the number. This time, a faint, scratchy voice answered, unused to the telephone, he suspected, and certainly unused to enquiries of this kind. Nevertheless, he found out what he needed to know.

His sister-in-law was right, he thought, as he closed down his laptop, without printing out the map. Sybille did have useful things to say. The message wasn't for Aurelie, though. It was for him. *You have to understand the start. They show you a lot of things to lead you astray.* It applied to the TV shows she and Sister Florence were addicted to, for sure. It applied elsewhere, too.

He waited outside the establishment alleging itself to be a Thai Health Club. Occasionally, as on this morning, you might spot a vast, disagreeable-looking lady opening up the place who might, possibly, once have been a native of Siam. She was definitely the only Thai thing about the place, though, and it wasn't promoting health. As he stood waiting, a car horn beeped, and kept on going. He sighed. He wished he really could get away from this place for a bit, with its macho posturing and its edginess.

Rex looked around in irritation for whichever testoster-one-pumped numpty was currently using his car-horn as an attack weapon. To his surprise, he saw that Rescha Schild had parked her arty little silver van outside the station. It was her doing the beep-ing. She was waving to him, too.

'Rescha,' he said, crossing the road. 'What are you doing? We're getting the tube.'

'You didn't hear? There was an accident in France and there are no trains through the tunnel. It's blocked. I thought we could drive.'

'Drive to Paris? Rescha –'

It didn't matter, though, he guessed. He got in, fiddling with his mobile phone. He sent a text. He fiddled some more before putting it in his jacket pocket and doing up his seatbelt.

The interior of the van smelled new, with top notes of citrus and earth. Rescha was back in Hasidic navy, he noticed, but was driving in her stockinged feet. She set off confidently, turning onto Wood Green High Street then heading north.

'I hope you don't need me to navigate,' Rex said, 'because I'm useless.'

'I know how to get up to the M25,' she said. 'From there we just go round to Dartford and get on the M20 to the Kent coast. Easy.'

'Right.'

Many of his recent encounters in Stamford Hill had been like this, he thought. First he'd be entranced by the mysterious, forgotten-world character of the place: the Yiddish, the blunt shopnames, the men in their gaiters. Then he'd be pulled up sharp by the sight of someone with an iPad or a kid eating chips. Rescha, too, was both: Old Country and This Country. Hasid and Haringey. He couldn't work her out. And she'd known it.

By Wood Green tube there were big digital signs: Junction 25 of the M25 was closed. Everyone was being diverted east, through Tottenham. With a click of the tongue, Rescha swung the van right onto Lordship Lane.

'If I'd made it over there a couple of weeks ago,' Rex said, pointing to the Driving Test Centre, 'I could have shared the driving.'

'Why didn't you?'

'The Bettelheims and Dr Kovacs got murdered.'

She braked suddenly at a zebra crossing. A stout Caribbean lady walked over it, glaring all the way.

'Sorry,' she said under her breath, and carried on.

He sat back, waiting, looking out of the window, as the usual sights whizzed by. A newsagents. A Turkish grocers. A bookmakers. A Polish grocers. A satellite installer. Another Polish grocers. It all looked so… London. So Tottenham. He could hardly believe it had ever looked any other way. Things could be made to look different though. Anything could look like anything else – depending not just on the skills of the deceiver, but on people's readiness to be deceived. What had Terry said? *Behind me all the way. Telling me where to look.*

'Where do you think Micah Walther's gone?' he asked. 'You think he'd stay in a place like this? Or go right out of London?'

'I don't know,' she said. 'London is a big place.'

'That was when I started to doubt you,' Rex said. He waited for a response, but none came, so he carried on. 'When you came to my house, and you told me what had really happened to Micah. Because you were telling me the truth. That is – what we have good reason to believe is the truth. I've looked up the statistics. I've seen how many Hasidic boys run away every year. But before that, I had this whole fantasy going, a whole dreadful story taking shape in my mind about the sect, and how it was taking healthy boys to keep its sick Rebbe alive. And I started to think that, I realised, because someone had been making me. It was you.'

He glanced across. She still said nothing, just changed gears before a roundabout, eyes on the road.

'My friend, Terry, said something to me about feeling as if he was being pointed in the direction, shown where to look. And it made me realise someone was doing that to me. And when I went back and I thought about all the times I'd seen you, I realised how you'd done it, and why you'd started. You started because I saw you outside Kovacs' house. Didn't I? You ran away, and I never thought it could have been you because the woman I saw had a very fashionable short hair cut. It never occurred to me that something like that could have been a wig until I talked to the people whose receipt you had in your old handbag. Sheyner Sheytel. Beautiful Wigs. They told me they'd got some quite remarkable-looking false hairdos to sell to the ladies of Stamford Hill.'

When Rescha didn't respond, he went on. 'Because of your disguise, you probably thought you were safe until you saw me back in Stamford Hill that afternoon. You'd seen our website, with Terry saying he was innocent. Then you saw me, and you knew then I wasn't going to go away, I was going to keep digging for my friend. So you gave me the hotel card. You wanted me to think it all had something to do with the boys being pressured to help the Rebbe, and the families leaving, when it didn't. And you couldn't resist coming back again, after Toyve Walther came in your shop, upset, discussing his plans to make a fuss at the tish. So you found me and told me I should go, because you knew what I'd see. You knew what you could make me think. You did the same to me over the last few days as well. You didn't come to my house the night before last because you needed me. You came to check whether I believed Yitzie was guilty. But you made a mistake. You stayed the night, because – you were being honest with me then – you genuinely couldn't face being alone. And when you were upset, and frightened, and your guard was down – that was when you told me about Micah running away.'

She shook her head. 'So why are you coming with me to Paris?' she said quietly.

'Come off it, Rescha. There isn't any Paris,' he said angrily. 'When Yitzie changed his plea, you realised you had to come back and try something else to make sure I didn't twig, so you came up with Paris. You haven't got a distant cousin there, have you? You mentioned Paris because you knew I knew the place, and you trusted that if you acted all innocent and bewildered, I'd probably take the bait and come with you. Well, you were right.'

They drove on in silence for a minute or two. The cityscape became emptier, and the houses shrank against the ever-expanding sky, which seemed to reflect the marshy greyness of the nearby river Lea. They were nearing Outrage territory.

'I was telling the truth about the trains being cancelled,' she said. 'And whenever you told me the truth, that's when I doubted you. I couldn't stop thinking about Yitzie at the tish, pulling Toyve Walther out of the way. I didn't know why that image kept coming back to me, until you came round and talked about Micah. Because it didn't make sense. The Walthers left the sect. So why didn't Yitzie try to murder them? He not only didn't try to murder them, he was friendly to Toyve Walther. Also, there was no way he could have put poison in those biscuits because he was allergic to just about everything in them. He didn't make them. You did. You killed those children.'

'Stop it,' she hissed at him, her eyes filming with tears. 'Stop it! Stop it!'

He stopped. He was angry with her, he realised, and less because of what she'd done, more because of the way she'd played him. He had to calm down, though. He had to get her to explain everything. 'Why?' he said, more gently. 'Why did you do it all, Rescha?' Deftly, her driving seemingly unaffected, she swung right onto Tottenham High Road. A street of old tops and new bottoms, Rex always thought. Old sash windows and crumbling gables on top of SuperDrug and CashInADash. A village teetering on a city.

'Have you ever come across anyone called Cohen, Rex? Or Levin? Or Levinsky, or some name like that?'

'A few,' he said, not sure where this was leading.

'They're called those names because they have kept the same... I suppose you'd say they are religious titles... and they've kept them, in their families, since our people lived in the deserts. Cohens and Levites. So you see, around here, you could have a man called Cohen or Levy sitting in that McDonald's with his computer, but he can never escape that his past is a priest, in the desert. If you are one of us, you never escape your past. It's like... a birthmark, or... a coat you can't take off.'

'You never seem to take yours off.'

'So. Maybe that's why,' she said, as the yellow signs pointed them onto Monument Way. It was like a motorway cutting through the middle of Tottenham: wide, empty, huge hedges obscuring whatever ugliness lay either side. 'Kovacs was writing his book. He needed some help with learning Yiddish and he met Yitzie. At the clinic. Yitzie said some things to him, about me, about the shop, that interested him because at the time, because of his book, he was looking for Rosa Brandt. So then he was really interested. He started to come to the shop. To ask questions about my family. Father. Grandfather. Great grandfather. Where we'd come from in the Old Country. What I knew. I didn't know that much. My grandfather and my father didn't explain any of it to me, and it's not like we'd got it written down or anything. I got tired of all his questions. In the end, I made Yitzie serve the first few customers every day, so I could avoid him. Kovacs started being friendly with Yitzie instead. Then I went to help on the allotments, to get out of the shop. He followed me there. Always there. Then one day, in the autumn, he phoned. Said he had something important to tell me. Asked me to come to his house. So I went.'

'Wasn't that a bit of a reckless thing to do? I mean – for a woman in your community?'

'So I went to Sheyner Sheytel and I hired a wig. And in a charity shop I got a scarf, and a leather jacket. Anyway, Yitzie thought Dr Kovacs was away on one of his trips. I didn't want to go. But I wanted to know why. You know? Why had he started to follow me everywhere? Why all the questions? So I went. And he took me down into that cellar of his, with all his books and his papers, and he showed me. We are family.' She corrected herself. 'We were.'

The emptiness became a snarl-up of roundabouts and traffic lights and converging arteries. Then, just as suddenly, they were in the almost rural calm of Chesnut Road, with its cottage-like houses and its wooden fences. This was where the first Outrage had taken place. Almost incredibly, it had once been a vista of belching chimneys and furnace fires. He had a feeling Rescha had brought them here deliberately. But she didn't stop.

'He showed me everything in his books. The terrorists who were here, down this place, they had an accomplice. His name was Kuznetz. His role was to stop them, pretend he was a hero, then take the money back to Latvia. But he didn't. He kept it. He took it to Liverpool, and he changed his name to Kovacs, and he became a rich man. George had found it out, because in his family there was a diary, an old diary, in Latvian, and nobody knew what it said, but he'd taught himself to read it. That was what started it. He hadn't really been interested in the robbery – he just wanted to solve a family mystery when he retired. So he started, and then he found out who he really was.'

'So how do you fit in?'

'Kuznetz had a family back in Latvia. Well, not a family. A girl-friend. She was called Rosa – Rosa Brandt – and she belonged to a very important family. The rabbis back then, they were like… aris-tocrats. Lots of money, land, servants. All marrying their sons and daughters to each other to make sure they got even more powerful. But Rosa ran away with Kuznetz the anarchist. A wilful girl!' Rescha smiled sadly, as if she would have liked someone to describe her that way. 'She fell in with the terrorists and got pregnant by Kuznetz. But then he vanished. And she had no choice but to go back to her fam-ily. They treated her bad, because she had a baby, and she'd brought shame on them. They married her off as quietly as they could. To a mamzer, called Feigenbaum. Maybe gave him the money to come over here and buy the shop as well, I don't know. They didn't have any more children. Just that one – the child who was really the child of Kuznetz. And that was my great-grandfather. Kovacs found it all out.'

With a little help from Tim, alias GoldVlad, Rex remembered. That must have been why Kovacs had seemed to lose interest in Tim's research. Because he'd already found out where Rosa Brandt's descendants had ended up.

'So then when your grandfather used to say they'd been ruined by a cripple, who…?'

'He meant Kuznetz. He had some problem because of polio. My grandfather's mother was almost obsessed with it, how her husband's family had been brought down. Kuznetz was her father-in-law – well, her husband's real father anyway. She must have been very bitter.'

'But by the time your father was a boy, all that would have been half a century ago. They had a business, a house, they were safe in London... what did your grandfather have to be so bitter about?'

She laughed as she turned onto Park View Road, the grim municipal flatlands fenced off behind peeling railings. Hadn't the robbers come up here, too, on a stolen milk cart?

'You people tell your children stories about Donald Duck, or rabbits called Peter. We tell them real stories, stories about how we suffered, but kept on going. In our houses, Haman is real, Hitler is real – like Moses and Rabbi Mendel of Kotzk. Our memories aren't long, they're forever. And just like we keep triumphs alive, we keep all the losses, too, and the bitternesses and the sufferings. All of them. List them. Grow them... It's... it's just part of who we are, part of being the people with the long memory. When I was a girl I used to dream about being suffocated, you know, by all these big, heavy, musty-smelling black velvet coats and hats.'

Rex swallowed. He felt chilled. 'So... You hated Kovacs because of the fate his great-grandfather had inadvertently dealt out to your great-grandfather?'

She flashed him a contemptuous look. 'Are you so stupid?

They were near the tip. The seagulls were everywhere. And there was a gypsy family, delightedly pushing a shopping trolley away, stuffed with electrical goods and part of a bed.

'Rescha. Can we stop?'

She didn't seem to have heard him. 'Kovacs thought it was all very funny. He thought there was something funny about it – that he'd ended up like he was, free-wheeling, he called it, plenty of money, nice life, just down the road from me. Who was the opposite. The magical roulette wheel of history, he said.'

Rex could imagine that conversation taking place. And he could imagine how it would make anyone's blood boil. Even if they didn't know what a roulette wheel was.

'So you decided to poison him?'

'No. I didn't. He said he'd changed, from the sort of man he used to be, because of his heart attacks. He wanted to make amends. He called it *tikkun olam*. It means –'

'– repairing the world.'

'He was sarcastic about a lot of things. But I believed he was serious about that, about doing something, to mend things, make some good. And he had plenty of money. We had none. And Yitzie was too ill at that time even to help in the shop, and our old van was breaking down all the time. I said – okay. Do your healing. So he bought us this van.'

Rex nodded. It made sense. Kovacs' wife had mentioned his fits of generosity. The spiffy van, so smart and cool and utterly out of place outside Rescha's shop.

'I should have stopped there, but then the council put up the business rates, and I asked him for a loan and he said it was okay, it was a gift. Then we needed some rewiring done in the shop, and he was happy to help. I don't know why. It just… the best I can say is that it really seemed to amuse him. Perhaps it was the power. I didn't like it, but I needed the money. Then in December, just before Hanukah, we got a shock. A terrible shock. See, we took out a mortgage on the house and the business, years ago, an endowment mortgage. It came to an end and they said we owed them eighteen thousand pounds. I didn't understand how that could happen – for years we'd made all the payments on time. But Kovacs explained it. He said he would help. But this time, I had to give something back.'

'What could you give?' he asked. Her look told him just how stupid his question was. This wasn't anything to do with history, but something far, far older. Lust.

'He said it would be just once. But you know what he did? He waited until I had… done it for him.' She shuddered. 'And when I came downstairs, and I was dressed again, he had an envelope waiting on his desk. It was half. Half the money. He said he had enjoyed it so much he wanted to make sure there'd be a next time. I went back upstairs to be sick. That's where I got the idea.'

'Of killing him?'

'Poisoning him. I made myself once, with the cassava, not preparing it properly. Dordoff showed me how to do it right. He told me: be careful, people can die if you get it wrong.'

They'd turned onto Watermead Way now, skirting the marshes before crossing them. He heard a siren in the distance and felt reassured. He hoped they were being pursued eastwards, like the robbers had been.

'But I didn't try that way first off. I didn't believe it would work.'

'So what did you try?'

She sighed. 'Years ago, I had a miscarriage. A baby was all I wanted. You see goyishe girls with them all the time, two, three babies and they don't even want them. But it turned out I couldn't even have that. I took some poison from Yitzie, this kind of white powder he used for cleaning gold. He stopped me. I promised him I'd never do it again and I gave it back to him. But I didn't. I mean, I kept some. I was sure I'd want to do it again, and I'd read it was very quick.'

'Cyanide?'

She nodded. 'But he'd found out where I put it. I put it in that hole – behind our bed. And he took that, too. I don't know when. Might have been years ago. All I know is, when I went to get it, to do something about Kovacs, it wasn't there.'

'Because Yitzie was protecting you, wasn't he? He was always protecting you.'

She carried on, ignoring him. 'I remembered about cassavas instead. And I went to the library, and looked it up on the computer and I saw that Dordoff had told me the truth. There was poison in them, right there, if you didn't know what do with them.'

'Or if you did.'

She nodded. 'And Kovacs was such a fussy man. He always came in first – first customer of the day. And I watched him – he always took the same bag of *rugelach*... cookies, they are, from the same place in the pile.'

'Weren't you worried that it would be traced straight back to your cookies?'

'The symptoms are just like a heart attack. And he'd already had three.'

'So almost everything Yitzie told the police was true, wasn't it? He didn't make the biscuits, but he was serving in the shop before his appointment at the hospital...'

'I didn't mean for it to happen like it did. But those... bastards at the mortgage company phoned. And while I was on the telephone at the back, a customer came in and Yitzie served them. I thought it was Kovacs, that it had all gone to plan but then Kovacs came in, and I saw the cookies had gone.'

'So you realised the Bettelheim kids had taken the poisoned bag?'

'Yitzie told me they'd been in. I tried to run after them, but they'd disappeared.'

'And Kovacs understood?'

'He saw the way I behaved. And he'd seen the Bettelheim children coming out of the shop. Later, he called me.'

'Because he'd seen what had happened at the park...' Rex remembered the way Kovacs had visibly paled, and run away. Perhaps he'd guessed that this had been an attempt on his own life.

'He was calm on the phone. Said we needed to talk.'

'I remember the phone call. You didn't come back in the shop.'

'I got my... outfit, and I went straight round there. He was in his basement. He said he'd decided to terminate our... arrangement.

He was going to tell the police. I begged him and begged him. I promised that he could do whatever he wanted to me, anything he liked, if he didn't tell. He let me believe it. I mean – he said he would think about it, just to get me to leave and then, at the door, he said he'd changed his mind. He shut the door on me. I went out the main door, and I saw... a kind of kitchen knife just in the soil under the bushes. It seemed to be there just for me. It was the answer. The only answer. So I picked it up and I went back inside but he'd gone back up into his flat. So I tapped. Tapped sort of softly on his door, so maybe he would think it was somebody else now – like your neighbour. And when he answered, I stuck it into him. I left him alive, though,' she added. 'I ran to the bus station and I called 999, and I said I'd seen something... A disturbance. I tried to change my voice, and I said I lived in the road, but afterwards... I was sure they would know it was me. I thought they would pick me up straight away.'

'But you went back the next day. I saw you. Why did you do that?'

'I couldn't find the scarf I'd worn the day before. It was such a hot day, so I'd taken it off and put it in the jacket pocket. I thought it might have fallen out in the basement, or worse still, inside his flat. So I had to go back. I knew you could get into the basement through the window on the garden side. And I found it. I was so relieved I found it, I put it on and then – that black man came in, same as me, through the window. He was raving at me, calling me a thief and... he pushed me into that hook. If I'd had the leather jacket on I'd have been all right, but it was so stiff – I left it on the floor to get through the window. And I cut my back badly. It was bleeding a lot. I managed to climb back out, then I grabbed the jacket and just ran. But he came after me, that man.'

'And the reason the police believed Yitzie is because he told them more or less the truth. Except, it was you, not him.'

'He worked out most of it. When I came back from... seeing Kovacs, the shop was closed. He said he'd gone to see the Rebbe about something. But later, he told me he'd tried to follow me. Tried to follow me, but couldn't keep up, because of his heart. He'd seen the way I ran after the Bettelheim children, and that had started him wondering what was going on.'

'So he confronted you?'

'Not at first. He went to bed. He stayed in his bed for most of that week, except to talk to the police when they came. Then he went to the tish. And on the Sunday, after you'd gone, then he sat at the table and he asked me what I'd done. So I told him.'

'And he hit you?'

'He said nothing. Did nothing. He just turned away. Barely spoke to me again until the police came on Purim. And then he looked at me before he opened the door, and he said, 'I did it, Rescha. Not you. I did it.'

Rex's mind was racing. 'Why did he change his plea then?'

'Because he wanted to be a hero, but he couldn't. He realised he was going to die in that place, and he was terrified. When I visited, he pleaded with me to tell the truth.'

'What did you say?'

She looked at him blankly. 'I said no. That killed him, I think. But something was going to kill Yitzie soon, anyway.'

He stared at the road ahead. He realised that he hadn't known even a corner of the woman next to him. He had thought of Rescha as a victim. Perhaps she was. But she made victims of everyone around her, too.

'Yitzie loved you, didn't he?' he said, almost to himself.

They were nearing the Angel Road roundabout. The vast, Lego-like block of the IKEA store hove into view, navy blue and yellow against a grey sky laced with pylons but otherwise as empty as the marshes. The traffic was thick and fast here. Where had the sirens gone?

Rescha wasn't paying attention to the traffic. She just gave Rex an inscrutable look and said, 'I expect he believed he did.' Then she floored the accelerator. A lorry horn blared, and as the massive vehicle clattered close past them, Rex realised she was jerking the steering wheel towards it. And the car was out of control, careering onto a furious roundabout, towards its barren centre, and destruction.

She didn't fight him. She'd just given up, surrendered to death. In his last conscious moments, he was aware of pulling her slender body out of the way, and grabbing the steering wheel, stabbing, with his one good foot, down into the gloom of the footwell and trying to push her unyielding limbs out of the way of the pedals. He heard more horns and shattering glass, there was spinning, and a name suddenly popping into his head like a letter through a flap. Kuznetz. The Kaliker. The cripple. This one, long-ago extinguished soul that had changed so many lives. Ended them, too. But who was he? He only knew his name. He wondered if Terry would find out more. There was no time for him, Rex, to discover anything else. Because this was his end.

* * *

Liverpool. City of malt and salt-breezes. Cries of gulls and the strange, phlegm-hawking talk of the natives. To an old sailor it felt like home, but I wasn't going to let that happen. Every day the newspapers had more of it: synagogues burned, lodging houses ransacked, police raiding factories and workshops in the wake of the mess they'd dubbed the Outrage.

Starting to creep up the country, too, the madness. In Manchester, a mob angry about foreigners taking their jobs went and smashed up a soup kitchen for unemployed Jews. Not much logic to that, when you think about it.

Meanwhile, one of my two fine dung-headed colleagues lay dead, the other dying, and no one to say Kaddish for them. I tried not to be seen reading the reports too much.

Leah and I booked ourselves into a smelly little hotel just off the Dock Road, run by a pair of sweaty Austrian brothers, twins. Like Cain and Abel, they are, only in German. *Say that again I'll strangle you in your bed you fat fairy... You couldn't get a decent hold on your own cock you suet pudding.* Fight so much they don't even notice who stays. Some only come for an hour. Always in twos.

I decided I would be George Kovacs while I stayed here, which would not be for long – just until the next boat to New York. In the worst sort of tavern at the worst end of the docks, they showed me to a Laskar who, in return for ten shillings, knocked me up some papers in that name, not good, but good enough to buy time, if needed. I like the name. Hungarian for Kuznetz. I spent the morning at the Cunard Offices, asking about tickets. One ticket. One-way. If I could give the massed forces of his Imperial Majesty's Okhrana the slip, I reckoned, then I could get rid of one girl. Somehow. Though the precise means kept eluding me.

Man behind a hatchway told me, in the snot-clogged way of the place, nothing free this week – *nutn freee dis wiicchh serr* – third class or second. Come back next. The longer I waited, the more risk of someone finding out something, or the girl letting it out. Or else this whole strange isle of ham-limbed drunkards being advised by their newspapers to seek out and slaughter every foreigner in the land. They'd have to start with their own Royal Family, of course.

Went back to our little room – it smelt of smoke, burning paper. Leah was full of excitement. 'I've been out myself,' she said – said it like a challenge because I told her not to, not without me. 'To the Lutheran Seamen's Chapel. I told the pastor, my fiancé's a Hungarian and we want to marry. What do we need to do? He said you can do it this afternoon, no questions asked, half a crown for the certificate, ten bob and a bottle for himself.'

I sat on the bed. 'Who's this Hungarian gentile you're marrying then?'

'Now George Kovacs, I believe you're teasing me.'

I took a deep breath. Better to tell her how it stood.

'I'm a Jew, I stays a Jew, and I'm sailing to America as soon as I can get a berth. You're not coming with me.'

Watched her face. Waiting for the trembling lip. Nothing came. Then: 'Sailing on those Hungarian papers of yours, would it be, George?' she asked, sweetly. 'Only I accidentally dropped them into the fire just a while ago.'

I looked at the girl. Slap her or murder her. Couldn't decide.

'You see, I've been thinking a lot, George. And how I see it is this. I killed Mr Parks. But there's only you the witness to that, and only me the witness to what you've been up to. So that kind of binds us together, doesn't it? Now. I think this is a very fair city. And we've got a nice pile of money, haven't we? More than enough to settle down and open a nice business and keep a fine little house. And we can't do that without being married, can we, George?'

Like an April tide. Gentle and inviting one minute. A bitch that'll see you drowned the next. Elephant and Torch might have been dung-heads, but they had some wisdom about them.

I went back to the tavern. The Laskar wasn't there. The landlord recognised me though – asked too many questions so I moved off swift. I had to get new papers, but where to go?

In the meantime, same day Elephant died in the hospital, I had to marry the girl in a sort of molten fury. Pastor hardly knows where to look. Afterwards I stalked off, up, up the big hill, until I couldn't walk anymore from the pains down my back and legs, then into a pub full of coloured glass and light, like one of their churches, a temple to their Higson's Bitter. Poured glass after glass into me, glasses of that watery, sour stuff they love so much, until the anger was doused.

A mere squall, I told myself. A delay in port. Play along for a few weeks, then just find a way out. Married man now – certificate to prove it. One Janos Kovacs, lately of Buda, now of Bootle Docks. Not watertight, but better than it was standing there on Scotland

Road with Missus Cutter's house burning down and a manhunt working its way across the marshes. Better than it is for Elephant and Torch.

A married man.

Slid into a hansom cab for the way back to the docks – or as far as the snivelling coward of a cabbie would dare take me. Started thinking of the duties of a married man. And the rights. I had some bad thoughts, I will own to that.

Thought – if she wanted to be a wife, Mrs Kovacs could give me some of what I'd longed for, before this mess, and probably – no, for certain – what got me into it.

Picture it on the ride home. Frilled linens coming down, ribbons unthreading to lay bare soft, white limbs. Pinkness. Heat and scents and hair and fullness. Some compensations, in life, there have to be. She is a beautiful shiksa, I think, and now she is mine, and I think I hate her, and I've a mind to go back and crash out all that hate that's in me right between her fat milky thighs and let's hear her squeal with it.

Right. In. Braces down. Breeches off. At that point, even a good Bible-schooled girl like Leah can see what her new husband has in mind. She's out the other side like a Daugava eel on the mud-flats, got a boot in her hand to throw.

'The only way you'll be doing that is by force, George Kovacs, and if it harms the baby then you'll have another death on your conscience!'

She might as well have thrown the boot at my head. 'What baby?' says I, stupidly, sitting on the bed, feeling it wither.

'Mr Parks put that… that thing of his in me two months ago and I haven't bled since. It's his. I don't mind a baby but no one's ever doing that to me again.'

Gizzard-hearted black-tongued bitch's bastard's Turk's whore. I cursed her and God and my own sorry fate as I grabbed up my things. Couldn't find the bag, just rolled them up in a shirt, before

I'd even got my own breeches back on. Ship, I thought. Get on a ship. Any one. I'll even take the Isle of fucking Man.

'Steady on, George. You won't get far without your money.'

I stopped. 'You burnt that too?'

She laughed. 'Don't be silly. I put it nice and safe in a savings account this afternoon while you were out drinking.'

Shema Yisroel. Hear O Israel. The Lord, Our God, the Lord is one. One He might be, but there's a greater and a worser power than He.

Epilogue

After the funeral, Susan and Terry went to the pub for a drink. It had to be a quick one, because there were busy times ahead. While the van containing Rescha Schild and Rex Tracey was ploughing across the Angel Road roundabout, Susan had been in a final meeting with the directors of a large, well-respected, left-leaning daily national newspaper.

The upshot was that, starting in a month's time, northeast London would have a new weekly paper: half focussed on the local, as before, but half looking beyond to the global. This would come out on a Friday, encouraging readers to invest in the heftier weekend edition of the national paper. It would be pretty much everything Susan had ever dreamed of doing in the first place – running a quality, politically and socially engaged local paper – though admittedly with less editorial control. In spite of the sombre occasion, she was happy, which was why she'd ordered champagne, to the astonishment of the landlord, whose patrons generally celebrated with vodka and Red Bull, in the rare event of them having anything to celebrate at all.

'I could never have swung it without your undercover mosque stuff,' she said to Terry at the bar. 'I'd been telling them we had national-quality staff, and they looked pretty stupid when they finally realised I was telling them the truth.'

'Glad to get back to my Christian ways though,' said Terry, taking a deep swig of his champagne. Then he looked around him, at the empty, yeasty-smelling room, and his face fell.

'Doesn't feel right, though, does it? Doing this without him. We shouldn't be celebrating.'

'Listen, Terry, believe me, Rex will be celebrating.'

'You reckon?'

'Well, maybe not right now. But when he gets out, he'll have a great deal to be happy about. He'll be back on the nationals – more or less. With, thanks to your researches, a major story to write about the two Outrages. Plus, he's in line for some sort of medal for steering that van to safety and averting God knows how many deaths.'

'Not to mention solving the murders and clearing a dead man's name.'

'Who'd have thought Rex Tracey would know how to switch on the voice recorder on his phone?'

They drank in silence for a while.

'Christ,' Terry said finally. 'The little bastard's going to be unbearable, isn't he?'

'Insufferable,' agreed Susan. 'Let's hope they keep him in for a while.'